"Wh... ...at havel—what ...have you done to me... ...what have you do..."

Before M... ...traced the ...inside. Sh...

She kn... ...ow you should step away—this was Sebastian, for heaven's sake!—but she simply couldn't make herself leave the circle of his strong arms.

"Robert is masculine," she breathed.

"Most men are," he answered, dancing heated kisses down the side of her neck.

"He's handsome," she forced out, hoping he couldn't hear the trembling in her voice.

"Hmm." His hand on her hip drifted upward along the side of her body, lightly tracing across her ribs. "We're brothers. We look alike."

"He's exciting...a risk-taker..." Her voice was a breathless hum. "He's thrilling."

"Lots of men are thrilling." He smiled wickedly against her neck at the reaction his clever fingers elicited from her. "I'm thrilling."

"*You?*" She gave a throaty laugh of surprise. "Sebastian, you're the most reserved, restrained man I—"

In one fluid motion, he whirled her in his arms and pushed her back against the wall, his mouth swooping down to capture hers and swallow her words as he kissed her into silence...

"In this thoroughly entertaining story, seduction and adventure take center stage. Nathaniel is far more honorable than he will admit, and Emily far braver than she ever imagined. Together, they form a formidable pair that readers are certain to love."
—BookPage

"Harrington has created a richly woven novel, complete with romance, a touch of mystery, and wounded, believable characters." **—Publishers Weekly**

"A fast-paced, high-action thrill ride punctuated by hot and sexy games." **—FreshFiction.com**

DUKES ARE FOREVER

"A touching and tempestuous romance, with all the ingredients Regency fans adore."
—Gaelen Foley, *New York Times* bestselling author

"Harrington's emotionally gripping Regency-era debut, which launches the Secret Life of Scoundrels series, is ripe with drama and sizzling romance...The complex relationship between Edward and Katherine is intense and skillfully written, complete with plenty of romantic angst that propels the novel swiftly forward. This new author is definitely one to watch."
—Publishers Weekly (starred review)

"As steamy as it is sweet as it is luscious. My favorite kind of historical!"
—Grace Burrowes, *New York Times* bestselling author

"Pits strong-willed characters against one another, and as the sparks ignite, passion is sure to follow. There is a depth of emotion that will leave readers breathless. The pages fly." —*RT Book Reviews*

IF THE DUKE
DEMANDS

ANNA
HARRINGTON

FOREVER

NEW YORK BOSTON

Copyright © 2017 by Anna Harrington
Excerpt from *When the Scoundrel Sins* copyright © 2017 by Anna Harrington
Cover design by Elizabeth Turner
Cover illustration by Chris Cocozza
Cover copyright © 2017 by Hachette Book Group, Inc.

Forever
Hachette Book Group
1290 Avenue of the Americas, New York, NY 10104
forever-romance.com
twitter.com/foreverromance

First Edition: February 2017

Forever is an imprint of Grand Central Publishing. The Forever name and logo are trademarks of Hachette Book Group, Inc.

The publisher is not responsible for websites (or their content) that are not owned by the publisher.

The Hachette Speakers Bureau provides a wide range of authors for speaking events. To find out more, go to www.hachettespeakersbureau.com or call (866) 376-6591.

ISBN: 978-1-4555-9725-3 (mass market), 978-1-4555-9724-6 (ebook)

Printed in the United States of America

OPM

10 9 8 7 6 5 4 3 2 1

Dedicated to Sarah Younger,
who convinced me to write
about the Carlisle brothers,
and to Kayla Haley,
whose love for Milton is even
greater than mine

A very special thank-you
to the world's best editor,
Michele Bidelspach,
for her patience and insight,
to Jessie Pierce,
for putting up with
all of my odd requests and
technical helplessness,
and to Professor Robin Jarvis,
for help in
researching nineteenth-century
adventurers and their books

PROLOGUE

Mayfair, London
May 1820

*S*ebastian Carlisle strode up the front steps of Park Place just as the first pinks of dawn began to lighten the sky.

Damnation, he'd been out later than he'd intended. *Far* later. But his parents disapproved of the women whose company he favored, so he'd had no choice but to spend time covering his tracks. After all, that talk with Father last year when he'd gotten caught with Lady Bancroft provided enough of an object lesson to last a lifetime. Good God, he still felt the embarrassment of that evening. He didn't know which was worse—being threatened to a duel by Lord Bancroft or seeing the disappointment on Father's face.

So he'd promised to put the reputation of the family and its legacy before all else. Including his own pleasures.

But he was a Carlisle, for heaven's sake! Did Father truly expect him to give up all his wild ways? Certainly, he'd reined himself in and was decidedly more careful now, including staying away from the married ladies of the *ton*. But he also had a rogue's reputation to uphold, and truly, what good was there in living like a monk? As fine as he felt as he let himself inside the house, with the lavender scent of the actress who'd spent the night entertaining him still lingering on his skin, he knew he'd made the right decision last night. What Mother and Father didn't know wouldn't hurt them. And he did so love the theater.

Apparently, he considered with a grin as he remembered the woman's eagerness, the theater also loved him.

Careful not to wake the still-sleeping household, he strode into the front foyer. And froze.

His youngest brother, Quinton, sat on the floor at the bottom of the stairs, his elbows resting on his knees and his head hanging in his hands.

An icy foreboding slithered down Sebastian's spine. His brother shouldn't have been here. He and Robert should still have been out wreaking havoc on St James's Street until long past dawn.

"Quinn?" he called out gently, suddenly afraid to break the stillness of the house.

Quinton lifted his head and stared blankly at him, as if he didn't recognize him. His face white, his eyes red-rimmed, all of him shaking violently…The rasping words tore from him—"Father's dead."

No. Sebastian's body flashed numb as he stared at Quinn and tried to comprehend the words as they swirled inside his head. No, he couldn't have heard correctly. *Impossible!* Father couldn't be…"Dead," he breathed out, no sound on his lips.

Quinn leaned his head against the banister and squeezed his eyes shut as anguished grief twisted his face.

Oh God…"Mother!"

Worry for her consumed him. He ran up the stairs without feeling his feet on the marble steps, without being aware of anything except the deafening rush of blood pounding in his ears and the fierce thumping of his heart, so brutally hard that each beat pierced a stab of pain through his chest and ripped his breath away.

He reached the second floor landing, stopped, stared down the hall toward the family's bedrooms— The world plunged away beneath him.

His sister, Josephine, sat crumpled in the hallway outside the door of their parents' bedroom, weeping inconsolably in the arms of her husband, so hard as if she would break into pieces. Leaning against the wall, Robert stared blankly at his hands. Scarlet red...covering his fingers, staining his clothes. Blood. *Father's blood.* A blinding pain shot through him, and Sebastian grabbed for the banister to keep from falling.

He gathered himself with a deep breath and walked stiffly past them into the room. Strong...he *had* to be strong for them. He was the oldest, the heir. It was his responsibility to protect his family. Father would have expected it of him. What he wanted to do was scream.

Inside the dimly lit room, Richard Carlisle lay in his bed. Sebastian's heart stopped. Father wasn't dead, surely. Not with his eyes closed so lightly like that, his face calm. He was sleeping, that was all, except that he lay fully dressed on top the coverlet, even in his boots. A red-stained towel lay beneath his head. So unnaturally still...Sebastian stared at his chest, waiting for it to rise and fall, holding his own breath as he waited for proof that the others were all wrong, that Father wasn't...But no breath came, and when Sebastian could no longer hold his own, the air rushed from him in a choking sob.

Mother...*oh, dear God, Mother*. She sat on the edge of the bed, holding her husband's hand tightly in hers. So pale, so weak and frail, her face so blank—only her eyes revealed any sign of life still left inside her, glistening bright in the dim light of the lamp.

Sebastian knelt beside her and placed his hand on her knee, the grief inside him now a burning pain. When she didn't look at him, he whispered, "Mother?"

"Yes?" But she didn't look away from his father, her hollow gaze fixed to his face.

"Mother," he repeated and reached up to gently pull her hand away from his father's, to hold it in his. So cold, like ice, her fingers gripped his as if he were the only anchor now holding her to this world.

She looked down at him, and the grief he saw in her ripped him apart. "Sebastian," she murmured as recognition pierced her grief, "there's been an accident…"

His eyes blurred with stinging tears, and he nodded, his voice choking in his throat.

"Where were you?" She reached a trembling hand to cup his cheek. "We couldn't find you."

Guilt poured through him with a self-loathing that burned so hot that it scalded his soul. "I'm sorry," he choked out.

She whispered, "He asked for you."

The weight of the world crashed down upon him, suffocating, crushing. Its weight was unbearable. With every inch of his body and soul aching with a guilt he feared he'd never be able to absolve, he buried his face in shame against her knee. "I'm sorry…I'm so sorry…"

CHAPTER ONE

Islingham, Lincolnshire
January 1822

*M*iranda Hodgkins peeked out cautiously from behind the morning room door. The hallway was empty.
Thank goodness. Drawing a deep breath of resolve, she
hurried toward the rear stairs and reached a hand up to
her face to make certain that her mask was still firmly in
place.

The grand masquerade ball that had been held in celebration of Elizabeth Carlisle's birthday had ended, and now the
guests were dispersing...those who had come only for the
evening's ball into a long line of carriages, those few remaining for the last night of the house party into their rooms in
the east wing. And the family would eventually make their
way to their rooms in the west wing. *Exactly* where Miranda
was headed.

She scurried up the dark stairs, knowing the way by heart
from years of playing at Chestnut Hill with the Carlisles
when they were all children. She knew which steps squeaked
and how to move over them without making a sound, just as

she'd attended enough parties here to know that the servants would be busy in the lower rooms of the house and that the family would take several minutes to say good night to all their guests.

If this had been any other night, she wouldn't have been sneaking around like this. She would have gone home with her auntie and uncle and stayed there, instead of changing into her second costume of the evening and sneaking back to Chestnut Hill. And she would have entered right through the front door instead of through the cellar, with no one thinking twice about seeing her in the house that bordered her auntie and uncle's farm and that felt like a second home to her.

But this wasn't just any other night. Tonight, she planned on declaring her love for Robert Carlisle. The man she wanted to marry and spend the rest of her days making happy.

And the man she planned to surrender her innocence to tonight.

She reached the landing and felt carefully in the darkness for the latch to release the door. She'd known Robert since she was five, when her parents died and she came to live with Aunt Rebecca and Uncle Hamish, when she'd met the entire Carlisle family and been welcomed warmly into their embrace as if she were a long-lost relative instead of the orphan niece of one of their tenants. Seldom a day went by that she hadn't been at Chestnut Hill, playing in their nursery or gardens. But a stolen kiss from Robert when she was fourteen changed everything. For the first time, she had evidence that Robert thought of her as more than a friend, even if he'd never attempted to repeat it. She hadn't stopped dreaming of him in the intervening years, and during the past two years, since his father passed away and he returned to live at Chestnut Hill, she'd dared to dream of more.

Oh, he was simply wonderful! He'd always been dashing, with that golden hair and sapphire blue eyes that all the brothers shared, along with the tall height and broad shoulders, that same Carlisle wildness and charm. The three men were so much alike physically that they even sounded the same when they spoke. But their personalities were completely different, and so was the way they'd treated her. Sebastian had already been sent to Eton by the time she arrived in Islingham and so was too busy to pay her much mind, and Quinton had been...well, *Quinton*. But Robert had paid the most attention to her, had always been kind and supportive, even when he'd teased her mercilessly, just as he had his sister, Josephine. Since he'd returned to Islingham to help Sebastian with the dukedom, though, he'd also matured. Bets placed in the book at White's had *never* thought that possible. But Miranda had always known how special he was, how dedicated to his family and especially to his mother. And tonight, she planned on showing him how she felt about him.

Her hands shook as she silently closed the door behind her and paused to let her eyes adjust to the dim light in the hallway. Heavens, how nervous she was! Her heart pounded so hard with anxious excitement over what she'd planned for tonight that each beat reverberated in her chest like cannon fire. She'd never attempted to seduce a man before, had never even considered such a thing, and her entire knowledge of how to please a man came from the barmaid she'd paid to tell her everything the woman knew about men. Which had proven to be a great deal, indeed.

Yet Miranda had no choice but to carry out her plan

tonight. Time was running out. She could no longer afford to wait for Robert to tire of temporary encounters with the string of women he was rumored to have been involved with since university and crave something deeper and more lasting. Or wait for him to realize that *she* could be the woman to give him that. He would be in London soon for the season, and once there, he'd court Diana Morgan, the general's lovely daughter he'd talked about since last fall. And the woman he'd spent the house party chatting with in quiet conversation, taking for turns about the gardens, waltzing with tonight...If Miranda didn't take this chance now, she would lose him forever. And how could she ever live with herself then, knowing she'd never dared to reveal her true feelings?

She knew tonight could go horribly wrong, that he might not return the feelings she had for him...But she also knew it could go perfectly right. That he might finally see her as the woman she'd become and the seductress she could be rather than as nothing more than the friend who had always been there, like a comfortable piece of furniture. How would she have lived with her cowardly self if she didn't at least *try*?

Drawing a deep breath, she pushed herself away from the door and hurried down the hall, counting the rooms as she went...two, three—*four*! This was it, the one the footman had told her was Robert's.

She slipped inside the dark room, then closed the door and leaned back against it, to catch her breath and somehow calm her racing heart. There was no turning back now. In a few minutes, Robert would walk into his room and find a masked woman draped across his bed. By the time her mask came off and he realized that the woman was her, he would be too enthralled to see her as simply plain

Miranda Hodgkins any longer. She would show him that the same woman who was his friend could also be his lover and wife.

And finally, he would be hers.

Her eyes adjusted to the dark room, lit only by the dim light of the small fire his valet had already banked for the night. A new nervousness swelled inside her that had nothing to do with her planned seduction. Heavens, she was in Robert's room. In his *room*! His most private space. But instead of feeling like an intruder, she felt at home here amid the large pieces of heavy furniture and masculine furnishings. As she moved away from the door and circled the room, her curiosity getting the better of her, she passed his dresser and lightly ran her hand over his things…his brushes, a pipe that she was certain had belonged to his father— Her fingers touched something cold and metal.

She picked it up and turned it over in her palm, then smiled. A toy soldier from the set Richard Carlisle had given to the boys over two decades ago for Christmas and long before she'd come to Chestnut Hill. Her throat tightened with emotion. The set had always been the boys' most prized possession, and several of the soldiers had been secreted away in Sebastian's trunks when he left for school, much to Robert and Quinn's consternation. That Robert would be so sentimental as to keep such a memento of his father…just another reason why she loved him.

Lifting the soldier to the faint smile at her lips, she circled the room to take in as much of this private side of him as possible. A typical bachelor gentleman's room, she supposed. Then she laughed with happy surprise when she saw the stack of books on the bedside table. Of course, he was well-educated; Elizabeth and Richard Carlisle had made certain of that for all their children. But Shakespeare, Milton...*poetry*? A warmth blossomed in her chest. She loved poetry, too, and discovering this romantic side to Robert only made her certain that they belonged together.

A noise sounded in the hall. With her heartbeat thundering in her ears, she raced to the bed, kicked off her slippers, and draped herself seductively across the coverlet. That is, as seductively as possible, because her hands shook as they pulled at her costume to spread it delicately over her legs and to check once again to make certain that her mask was still in place.

The door opened, and her heart stopped.

Miranda stared at the masked man silhouetted in the doorway and swallowed. Hard. The only conclusion to this night would be her utter and complete ruination.

Exactly what she hoped for.

Praying he couldn't see how her fingers trembled, she reached a hand toward the draping neckline of her costume to draw his attention to her breasts...er, rather to what there was of them.

Robert's sapphire blue eyes flickered behind the panther mask. The shocked surprise in their depths faded into rakish amusement, and his sensuous mouth curled into a slow, predatory smile.

Her belly pinched. *Oh my.*

Without shifting his eyes away from her, he closed the door behind him.

Oh. My. Goodness.

He stalked slowly toward the bed, reminding her of the graceful panther his papier-mâché mask proclaimed him to be. He stopped at the foot of the giant four-poster bed, and his gaze heated as he stared down at her through the soft shadows.

"Well, then," he drawled in a voice so low that it was almost a whisper and one as deep as the darkness surrounding them. "What have we here?"

She drew a breath for courage. "I saw you at the masquerade tonight." Her nervousness made her own voice far huskier than she intended. *Thank God.* She had to carry off this seduction tonight. She simply *had* to! "And I wanted time with you." She paused for emphasis. "Alone."

He smiled at that. "You weren't at my mother's party." With a slow shrug of his broad shoulders, he slipped off his black evening jacket and tossed it over the chair in front of the fireplace. "I would have remembered you."

Miranda nearly scoffed at that. He would have remembered her? From among the two hundred other females of all ages crammed into Chestnut Hill's ballroom for the Duchess of Trent's birthday? Hardly!

From behind his mask, his eyes drifted over the dress, and heat prickled across her skin.

Well . . . *maybe* he would have remembered *if* she'd been wearing the same flimsy crêpe dress currently draped over her rather than the costume in which she'd arrived. A clinging, sleeveless rose-colored gauze creation with matching mask, this dress had cost her a small fortune from months of saved-up pin money and her salary from the orphanage. It had also required several secret trips to Helmsworth to visit the dressmaker there, whom she'd hired so that no one in Islingham would suspect what she was up to. But all the subterfuge was worth it, because the whole effect turned her body into a long-stemmed rose. Instead of this, though, she'd been announced to the party at the beginning of the evening wearing the pumpkin costume that her auntie had made for her, complete with a stem sticking out of her hat, and Robert hadn't given her a second glance all evening.

But he certainly noticed her now as she reclined across his bed, her back propped up by a pile of pillows and the hem of her skirt scandalously revealing her legs from the knees down. *Bare* legs, too, because she couldn't afford to purchase the lace stockings that matched the dress.

"Perhaps you didn't notice me because I was dancing with other men," she offered coyly. Tonight, her mask made her bold and free to say flirtatious things she never would have had the courage to utter otherwise. "But I'd much rather have been dancing with you."

She saw his hand freeze for just a heartbeat as he reached for his cravat. "Then the loss was definitely mine." His eyes trailed from her low neckline down her body, across the curves of her hips, and over her legs. "And your name, my lady?"

Her heart jumped into her throat. Oh no, she couldn't tell him *that*—not yet! She'd worn the mask and costume purposefully so that he would see this other side of her before he dismissed her outright. So that he would have an opportunity to see her through new eyes, to look upon her as a woman instead of the girl he'd always known. If she revealed her identity so soon, he'd never see her as anything more than a friend.

So she whispered, "Rose."

He untied his black cravat and tossed it away. "Lady Rose," he murmured. Knowing amusement touched his sensuous mouth at her completely fabricated answer. "Is that why you're in my room, then?" His sapphire eyes stirred heat beneath her skin everywhere he looked. And dear heavens, he was looking everywhere! "Because you want to dance with me?"

Dance. The word shivered down her spine as she watched him slip free each button of his black waistcoat. They both knew he didn't mean waltzing.

Electric tingles of excitement raced through her. This was it. The moment that would bring her the man she'd loved. The moment when her life would change forever...

She drew a shaky breath. "Yes." The word came out as a husky rasp. "Very much."

His full lips tugged into a seductive smile, and he slipped off his waistcoat, then dropped it to the floor. The muscles of his arms and shoulders rippled beneath his black shirt as he reached up to unfasten the half dozen buttons at his neck, the firelight playing across his golden blond hair and his handsome face still hidden behind the mask. Her heart thudded painfully against her ribs when he tugged his shirttail free from his black breeches to let it hang loose around his waist.

He was undressing. And not for sleep. For a moment, she forgot to breathe.

When she remembered again, her breath came in a soft sigh. Which caused his blue eyes to darken with quick arousal as he took the sound as an invitation to...to—

She swallowed again. *Very* hard.

Well, that *was* why she was lying on his bed, for goodness' sake. To be ravished. But heavens, she was nervous! Trying to hide the trembling in her hands and be the seductress he would want, she ran her palms up and down her thighs, each stroke upward pulling the crêpe material with it until her legs were bare to her thighs. His eyes keenly followed every caress she gave herself. Because of the mask, she couldn't see whatever other emotions might be flickering across his face, but she could see his eyes and mouth, and those both struck her as intense. Predatory. Aroused.

Goodness.

He reached up to remove his mask—

"No!" she gasped.

He froze at her outburst. Then curiously tilted his head as if he'd misconstrued her meaning.

But he'd understood perfectly. She couldn't let him remove his mask. If he did, then he'd expect her to remove hers—oh, she wasn't ready for that! Not until she was certain that she'd made him want her as much as she wanted him, and somehow not just for tonight but always.

"The masquerade was so much fun," she explained quickly, silently praying that he'd believe her, "that I should hate for it to end so soon."

"It won't." He stole a wandering glance down her body. A heated promise lingered in that sultry look.

"Please don't remove your mask, not yet." Then she added as enticingly as possible, "My Lord Panther."

He inclined his head toward her in a gentlemanly nod.

A thrill raced through her. Robert had never shown her such deference before. Of course, though, he didn't know that it was her in this costume, she thought with a twinge of chagrin. But he would soon, and then everything between them would change.

"As you wish, Lady Rose." Another heated smile, this time as he stepped forward to lean his shoulder against the bedpost and stare unapologetically at her body. "Your costume is quite beautiful."

"Do you like it?" She raised her hand to her neckline again, drawing his attention back to her breasts as she arched her back in an attempt to make them appear as full as possible.

"Very much," he murmured appreciatively.

"Good." Her trembling fingers trailed up to her shoulder

and to the satin bow holding the bodice in place. "Because I wore it just for you."

He parted his lips as if to say something, but she pulled loose the ribbon in a seductive move she'd practiced all afternoon. The shoulder of her dress fell down, nearly baring her right breast. He fixed a hungry stare on her, whatever he was about to say lost forever.

With a sound that was half groan, half growl, he grabbed his shirt and yanked it off over his head, then started forward, crawling up the bed toward her on hands and knees. Very much a panther stalking forward to claim its prey.

Her eyes widened, and she slowly sank down onto her back as he crawled up the length of her, trapping her between his hands and knees. She certainly hadn't expected *this*! Or the way he lowered his head to lick his tongue across her bare shoulder, as if he were tasting her before deciding whether to toy with her a while longer or devour her whole.

"Mmm," he purred against her flesh as his mouth moved to her neck, where she was certain he could feel her pulse pounding beneath his lips. "Perhaps it's good that I didn't notice you at the party after all."

"Why is that?" She shivered as his teeth nipped at her throat, unprepared for the pulse of heat that shot straight down to her toes. This was nothing like the kiss he'd given her all those years ago.

"I would have embarrassed myself in the middle of the ballroom trying to get to you." He traced his fingertip over her bare shoulder, drawing invisible patterns across her skin and down toward the swell of her breast. "We would have danced, I'd have made certain of it."

His finger dipped under the edge of her dress and, finding no stays nor shift to impede him, grazed seductively over her nipple still hidden beneath. She gasped, and he smiled delightedly at her response. Apparently he had decided to toy with her after all.

Then he slipped his hand completely beneath the gauzy bodice to cup her bare breast. "So we'll dance now," he murmured.

Heat radiated into her from his large hand as he gently massaged her, and she wiggled beneath his touch, suddenly unable to lie still as she bit back a moan of happiness. She'd dreamt for years about having his hands on her like this, touching her, caressing her...but she'd never once imagined it would feel so warm and wonderful. So soft yet urgent.

"Lovely dress." Shifting his weight back onto his knees, he reached his free hand toward her other shoulder and deftly untied the bow. With a tug, her bodice fell away and revealed both breasts to the firelight. And to his eyes, now dark with desire as he gazed hungrily down at her. "So very lovely."

Despite the goose bumps that sprang up across her skin everywhere he looked, she resisted the nervous urge to cover herself. This was Robert, and he, of all people, had the right to see her. Because she'd known him since she was five. Because she loved him. Because she wanted no one else but him to ever see her like this, tonight and for the rest of her life.

She shyly bit her bottom lip. "You don't find me... plain?"

He gave a laugh, and the deep sound rumbled through her, swirling down to land between her legs. He lowered his head toward her. "Hardly."

Her breath strangled. For a moment, she thought he was lowering his mouth to kiss her...*there*, on her bare breasts. Instead, his fingers gently lifted her chin, and his lips met hers in a kiss so tender that it left her shaking. His mouth was warm, surprisingly soft, and oh-so-wonderfully skilled as he languidly explored and tasted hers, with none of the boyish eagerness she remembered from before, none of that sloppy, inexperienced kissing. This was a man who was confident in himself and knew what he wanted.

And what he wanted—she shivered—was *her*.

"You're trembling." He touched the tip of his tongue to the corner of her lips.

She shook so hard that she had to grasp the coverlet beneath her to hold herself still. "I-I'm n-not."

"Now you're lying," he scolded, smiling against her mouth.

He caught her bottom lip between his teeth, and as he bit down gently, he lowered himself over her.

No, she thought as his hard body sank onto hers, definitely nothing boyish about him any longer.

"What else can I do to make you tremble, hmm?" His hand reached down for her skirt and pulled it slowly up her thighs. The promised shivers trailed in its wake.

Miranda rolled back her head and gave herself over to him. She'd wanted this moment for so long, and now that it was finally happening—oh, dear Lord, *it was happening*! She could hardly believe it wasn't still only a dream. Robert in her arms, his lips on hers, his hands caressing her seductively. Her heart pounded so hard she could hear the rush of blood in her ears, so rapidly she was certain he could feel it, because when she placed her palm on his bare chest, his heart raced beneath her fingertips.

He nipped his way down her throat, then farther down to lick his tongue into the valley between her breasts. When she shuddered and wrapped her arms around his neck to bring him closer, his lips closed around her peaked nipple and sucked.

She moaned, her back arching off the mattress. "Robert…"

He froze, his mouth stilling on her. Then slowly, he released her breast and lifted his head. His blue eyes pinned hers. "*What* did you say?"

"I didn't say anything. I just—"

"Christ!" He pushed off the panther mask and revealed his face.

Oh God.

The air ripped from her lungs. "Sebastian."

Oh God oh God oh God oh God!

"Who are you?" Sebastian Carlisle grabbed her mask and yanked it down. His eyes widened in stunned surprise. "Miranda?"

He stared at her as if he couldn't believe— Oh, he was *looking* at her! Red heat flushed her face, and she slapped hard at his bare chest. "Get off me! Get *off*—"

His hand clamped down over her mouth. "Shush!" Anger furrowed his brow. "Someone will hear you."

"I don't care!" she mumbled against his palm.

"You will if they find us together"—another sweep of his gaze down her body—"like this."

With a mortified groan, she rolled her eyes. She wanted to die!

He crooked a brow in warning to keep her voice down, then withdrew his hand and rolled off the bed, muttering angrily beneath his breath as he snatched up his shirt from the floor and yanked it on.

Miranda scrambled to cover herself, but her fingers shook so hard that she could barely retie the bows at her shoulders. One knotted pathetically.

He wheeled on her. "What are you doing here, Miranda?"

"Me?" she squeaked, her hand jerking and creating another knot. "What are *you* doing in Robert's room? You'd better dress and leave before he—"

"This is my room." He pointed possessively at the floor.

"Your— *No*," she protested firmly even as she took a frantic glance around, although she wouldn't have known the difference between any of the brothers' bedrooms at Chestnut Hill. But this was Robert's, she was certain of it, along with the toy soldiers and poetry books. "I asked the footman. He told me *this* room."

His eyes narrowed. "You asked a footman which bedroom belonged to Robert?"

"I was discreet." She sniffed at his insinuation that she'd been reckless enough to confide her plan for seduction to a footman. If a woman planned to drape herself across a would-be-lover's bed, she certainly wouldn't announce it to the household staff. Even she knew that much. "And I wore a mask."

He placed his palms on the mattress and leaned toward her, bringing his face level with hers. "Exactly how does a masked lady go about asking a footman which bedroom belongs to a bachelor gentleman?"

Ugh, he was so frustrating! She pushed at his shoulders to shove him away, but of course he didn't budge. The man was a veritable mountain of muscle and aggravation.

With a huff, she folded her arms across her chest and raised her chin. "Wearing *her* mask, she goes to a footman at the party, slips him a coin, and points to the gentleman in *his* mask, then asks in complete anonymity which room is—"

He held up a hand, stopping her. "If the gentleman

was wearing a mask, how did you know which man you pointed to?"

"Because I bribed Robert's valet yesterday to find out what mask he'd..." The blood drained from her face as she realized her mistake. "Oh no."

"Oh yes." With a grimace, he tossed the panther mask onto the bed at her feet. "We switched masks before the party. The man you pointed to tonight, Miranda, was me."

Her stomach plummeted. "Sebastian, I had no idea."

"Obviously." He drew up to his full six-foot height and looked down at her with that authoritative look that all the Carlisle brothers—and *especially* Sebastian—thought they could level on her simply because they'd all grown up together. "Now, we've determined *how* you ended up here." He folded his arms across his chest, the intimidating pose one she knew well. "Tell me why."

But she had absolutely no intention of telling him *that*. Wasn't she already humiliated enough? "It doesn't matter. I—I need to leave."

She scooted to the edge of the bed, her hands tugging at her skirt with each wiggle of her hips to keep her legs covered, although she didn't know why she bothered, considering he'd just had his mouth on her breast.

Her face burned. Oh God—Sebastian's mouth had been on her *breast*!

"Now—" Her voice choked with panic and mortification. "I need to go *now*."

"Stay," he commanded with that regal air all three brothers had inherited in varying degrees from their father and which Sebastian as the current Duke of Trent owned in spades.

She stilled at the edge of the bed, silent in her humiliation.

"You expected Robert to come to his room and find you lying in his bed, dressed like that." His blue eyes flashed with incredulity. "Are you and he…" At least he had the decency to look away as he stumbled over the accusation. "Intimate?"

"No!" She blinked back the stinging tears. Her humiliation had reached new heights now, never mind the fact that intimacy with Robert was exactly what she'd hoped for tonight.

"Then why were you waiting in bed for him?" he pressed.

With a groan, she hung her head in her hands. All she'd wanted was a simple seduction, but her dream had become a nightmare. "Oh, what does it matter?"

He arched a brow. "Because he's my brother, and I care about him." His voice softened. "And about you."

Ha! She didn't believe that for a second. The oldest of the three Carlisle brothers, Sebastian was the one she knew the least well yet the one who had annoyed her the most, probably because he was a decade older than she was and impatient with the games she and his siblings had played. He'd been fifteen when she arrived at Islingham, already enrolled at Eton and so away most of the time. Even on those rare visits home on holiday, he'd been too interested in spending time with his father and learning about the estate to be anything more than distantly friendly to her. By the time he'd reached university, he was more concerned with chasing women and having a good time with his brothers carrying out whatever wild scheme they could concoct than whatever was happening in Islingham. And the wilder, the better.

Until Richard Carlisle became a duke. Then the rowdy, unmanageable brothers became more serious, especially Sebastian, who as the heir had always felt the weight of the responsibilities he would someday bear. He'd paid her scant attention before; now that he was the duke, he barely noticed that she existed at all.

"Miranda," he sighed patiently, "I can't think of any good reason why you'd be in Robert's bed."

She grimaced. "No, of course not—I mean— Oh, blast it!"

She didn't care that she'd cursed in front of him, especially since the Carlisle brothers were the ones who taught her to swear when she was a child. Especially since Sebastian would never have seen her as a demure, polite society lady in the first place. And especially since she knew he wouldn't care that she'd made such a muddle of things tonight.

But she also knew that he fiercely protected his family and that he wouldn't let her leave until she explained what she'd planned for his brother.

So she grimaced in defeat and admitted softly, "Robert's going to offer for her, I know it."

"Who?" he puzzled.

"Diana Morgan." Her eyes blurred with a hot mix of anger and humiliation, and her shoulders sagged beneath the weight of it. "General Morgan's daughter. He invited her to the house party, and he's going to court her this season in London."

"What does that have to do with— Oh."

"Yes." She rolled her eyes. "*Oh.* Tonight was my last chance to be noticed by him as someone other than a friend. So I wore this costume." She gave a hopeless wave of her hand to indicate the dress that now crumpled with wrinkles from him lying on top of her. Good heavens, how could something cost so much when there was so little to it? "And the only person who saw me in it was you. No one important."

His mouth twisted dourly. "Thank you."

"Oh, you know what I mean!" Her hand darted up to swipe at her eyes. "But I thought that if Robert could see me like this then maybe...just *maybe* he'd..." She shrugged a shoulder, feeling utterly pathetic. "Notice me."

"But...*Robert*?"

With a cringe of humiliation, she shoved him away to scramble off the bed. She barely remembered to snatch up her mask before rushing past him toward the door.

A sob strangled in her throat. What a horrible, horrible night! All she wanted to do now was flee and never again show her face at Chestnut Hill, or in Islingham Village, or anywhere in England for that matter, so she wouldn't accidentally run into Sebastian. Or Robert, because Sebastian was certain to tell his brother about this. Oh, what a hearty laugh the two of them would—

"Wait." He grabbed her arm and tugged her back toward him.

Set off-balance, she stepped backward, and her legs tangled in the gauzy skirt. She fell against him, and his arms went around her to steady her.

Fresh mortification heated her cheeks. She'd tripped in front of him like some graceless dolt, then fell right into his arms. So pathetically. Her eyes blurred. Tonight was proving to be nothing but one humiliation after another.

"Let me go," she pleaded.

His arms stayed firmly around her. "Miranda, I am sorry." His apologetic voice was surprisingly kind. "I had no idea that you..."

Raising her gaze to his, she steeled herself against the pity she knew she'd see on his face.

What she saw instead was incredulous curiosity. "I'm just surprised," he explained gently.

Her throat tightened. Surely he hadn't meant that as an insult, but when heaped on top of the other humiliations she'd experienced tonight, his words hurt. "Surprised to find me in your room?" She stuck her nose into the air with a peeved sniff. "Or surprised that I might possibly have feelings for your brother?"

"Yes," he answered honestly, "to both."

With an angry groan, she pushed against his chest to shove herself away.

He took her shoulders and held firm, his solid body not budging an inch. "And, frankly, that you would want Robert in the first place instead of some nice man from the village."

She bit her lip to keep from screaming. Was that how all the Carlisle men saw her? As a silly country gel destined to marry a boring vicar or farmer and spend her life polishing church pews or chasing pigs on a farm? Was that the best they thought she could do with her life? Oh, she wanted so much more than that! She wanted adventure and excitement, a large family of her own to love, and a home right here in Islingham, surrounded by the people she loved and would do anything for. She wasn't daft enough to think that she could marry someone of rank, like a landowning gentleman or a peer.

But the *brother* of a peer...

Yet if Robert thought no more of her than Sebastian did, then he would never notice her as a woman with whom he could spend the rest of his life, and everything she'd gone through tonight was a thoroughly humiliating, horrible waste of time. And money. She might as well have been placed on the shelf tonight and marked *Do Not Touch*, because her life as she wanted it to be was irrevocably over.

She turned her face away, blinking hard. She wanted to laugh! And cry bitterly.

"For what I did earlier," Sebastian apologized as he sucked in a deep breath, "I am truly sorry."

Yes, she supposed he was, now that he knew it was her and not some temptress he thought had wantonly sneaked into his room for a night of bed sport with the duke. After all, he hadn't appeared particularly apologetic when he'd been pulling up her skirt.

He squeezed her shoulders in a gesture of friendly affection. The same hands that moments before had been caressing her naked breasts and had her liking it, that even now sent tingles through her—

"Oh God, no!" She pressed her fingers to her lips with horror at her sudden outburst—and even more horror at herself for liking the way he'd touched her. *Sebastian* of all men!

"Pardon?" He frowned, bewildered at her behavior.

"I mean, no apology is necessary. It was nothing." She stepped back, and this time he let her go. "A mistake, that was all. And I would greatly appreciate"—another step away, because if she kept putting steps between them she could reach the door and flee into the hallway before the tears overtook her—"if you would kindly keep what happened here tonight a secret."

"Of course," he agreed solemnly.

Embarrassment burned her cheeks. "I mean it, Sebastian. If you tell anyone, especially Robert or Quinton, I'll… I'll…"

"You'll do what?" he challenged at her weak attempt at a threat and lowered his head to bring his eyes level with hers. Drat the man for being so tall! And so…duke-like.

She boldly stuck up her chin as inspiration struck and

blurted out, "I'll tell your mother what really happened to that Chinese vase your father gave her for Christmas!"

For a moment he stared at her blankly, simply unable to fathom her. Then his eyes narrowed, as if he were sizing up an opponent in Parliament instead of the annoying gel from next door, and he drew himself up to his full height...So *very* tall. Odd, how she'd never noticed that about him before. Or how much more solid that very tall body was than Robert's, or how his golden hair fell rakishly across his forehead and made her want to brush it away.

It was amazing, the details a woman noticed about a half-dressed man after he'd had his mouth on her.

"Do we have an agreement, then?" she pressed.

A lopsided threat at best—her reputation for a vase that had met its shameful demise years ago during a secret spread that the brothers had thrown while their parents had been away in London. But his mother had loved that vase, and Miranda wasn't afraid to use it to her advantage.

"Agreed," he said.

Thank God! She turned toward the door, taking a deep breath to run—

He reached over her head and pressed his hand against the door to keep her from flinging it open. "Wait."

Wait? Her heart skipped, then thudded so hard in her chest that she winced. The infuriating man was also terribly cruel...*Wait?*

When she looked over her shoulder at him, she thought she saw his gaze dart up from her breasts. But that was impossible. Sebastian wouldn't be looking down her dress like that, not now. Now when he knew who she was... would he?

But when he reached back for the jacket he'd tossed over

the chair and held it out to her, she rolled her eyes, feeling like an absolute cake. Oh, he'd been looking at her breasts all right... and pondering a good way to hide them.

"Best not to be seen sneaking out of my room, Lady Rose," he cautioned. "In that dress."

She slipped on the jacket, and knots tightened low in her belly when she breathed in the scent of him wafting up from the superfine material. She bit back a defeated groan. *Of course* he would have to smell good.

Then he gestured for her mask, and she handed it over. He lifted it into place and tied it behind her head. When he rested one hand on her shoulder while the other slowly cracked open the door, the heat of his fingers seeped into her skin, all the way down her front to her breasts. Beneath the gauzy costume, her nipples tightened traitorously at the memory of his hands on them.

At that, her stomach plummeted, her humiliation complete. Even her own body was conspiring against her tonight by fraternizing with the enemy.

He peeked past her into the hallway, then lowered his mouth to her ear. "Go down the back stairs to the ground floor. The downstairs hall will be empty and dark by now. Go out through the terrace door in my study, and stay close to the garden wall where the shadows are darkest until you get past the stables. And *don't* let anyone see you." His deep voice tickled across her cheek, and she shivered. "Especially my mother."

"How do you know so much about sneaking out?" she asked in a whisper, surprised by the detail of his instructions.

He answered with a sultry chuckle that rumbled through her. "Because I'm a Carlisle brother."

When she turned her head to look at him over her shoulder, his hand slapped against her bottom. She jumped.

"Go!"

She stepped into the hall and fled from Chestnut Hill as fast as her feet could take her. Her *bare* feet. Groaning at her own foolishness, she rolled her eyes because she'd left her slippers behind in his room. And there was no going back for them.

Ever.

CHAPTER TWO

Lady Rose.

Sebastian frowned. What had Miranda been thinking last night?

But that had always been the problem with her, he decided as he stared out the window of his study across the sweeping front lawn as the last of the house party guests set off in their carriages to return home. She rarely thought before leaping, and last night, she'd nearly leapt herself right into the fire. He frowned irritably. Into *his* fire.

What the *hell* had she been thinking?

He blew out a harsh breath and ran his hand through his hair. Christ, what had *he* been thinking?

She'd surprised him to the core when he'd walked into his room and found her there, draped so delectably across his bed in that silky crêpe and lace confection that barely covered anything and so reminded him of a frosted cake that he found himself salivating to lick the icing from her. He should have known he wasn't fortunate enough to have such an alluring beauty offer herself up so freely like that on the night of his mother's birthday party, but *good God*—after a suffocating sennight of being forced to be the perfect peer, quashing every impulse and urge to be as unrestrained as his brothers and actually enjoy himself for once, he'd yearned to taste just a bit of the wildness he used to have.

At that moment, with a night of freedom being offered to him so temptingly, he simply hadn't cared how she'd gotten there. Or for that matter her true identity beneath the mask. All that mattered was once again being able to enjoy himself. To peel her dress away until she was naked, then cover her body with his and—

"Sebastian!" A half-eaten breakfast roll hit him square in the back.

He wheeled around, a sharp curse on his lips for his youngest brother, Quinton, who balanced on his lap a plate half-filled with his third helping of breakfast and held a second roll in his hand, ready to fire off at any moment.

But next to his brother sat his mother, and the concerned look she gave him silenced him immediately. "You were lost in concentration," she said gently, worry lacing her voice. "Didn't you hear me calling to you, dear, when we came into the room?"

Sweet Lucifer, he hadn't. "No," he admitted grudgingly. Running a hand through his hair, he drew a deep, patient breath. Lady Rose had managed to distract him from his own family, which no woman had done since the night his father died. But then, no other woman in his bed had ever been Miranda Hodgkins.

The gel was an absolute menace.

Forcing a relaxed smile, he walked back to his desk. "My apologies for being distracted."

Quinn and his mother sat in two chairs on the other side of the massive piece of mahogany-inlaid furniture where his late father had managed their estate of Chestnut Hill, then in more recent years where he'd also overseen the newly awarded dukedom whose lands had once belonged to their former neighbor, the Earl Royston, along with the manor house of Blackwood Hall and its holdings. And all of it now fell to Sebastian to manage.

His brows drew together as he pushed all thoughts of masquerades and the sweet scent of rosewater from his mind to concentrate on the reasons his family had been summoned together in his study. "I was watching to make certain that the last of the party guests set off without any problems," he explained.

Not exactly a lie. Technically, Miranda had been a party guest, although she lived on one of the estate's tenant farms with her aunt and uncle. And she'd been sent off last night with many, many problems in her wake.

"Shall we start, then?" Elizabeth Carlisle smiled patiently.

Sebastian couldn't help but return her smile. With her golden blond hair and luminescent skin, even after a late night at her own birthday celebration, his mother was beautiful in the slant of sunlight that fell through the window onto her lavender morning dress. His heart tugged for her, and a familiar knot of grief tightened in his throat. Nearly two years had passed since his father's unexpected death, and although she was officially out of mourning, she still preferred to wear lavender in the mornings. A part of her would always grieve for his father, just as he knew she would never remarry. Theirs had been a true love match, and Elizabeth Carlisle would never take another man into her heart the way she had his father.

He cleared his throat and nodded at the empty chair beside her. "Should we wait for Robert?"

The middle Carlisle brother was most likely still outside saying his good-byes to Diana Morgan and her parents. General Morgan had been invited to the house party because he was an old friend of Richard Carlisle's from their army days, yet the attention Robert had paid to the man's daughter had surprised the entire Carlisle family. Especially his mother, whom Sebastian knew was torn between encouraging the match and convincing the poor girl to flee for her life.

Mother shook her head. "He'll be here as soon as he can." She smiled, her eyes sparkling. "No need for him to be rude to the Morgans by hurrying them along."

Sebastian crooked a brow. So his mother had come down on the side of the match after all. Poor girl, indeed.

"Then let's begin." He sat behind the desk and settled in for the meeting. "We need to discuss the family's plans for the upcoming season."

Normally, family business wasn't conducted so formally. All of them preferred instead to discuss their plans casually during dinner or over coffees in the drawing room afterward, then be content to let Sebastian take care of all the details. But this season's difference filled the air with a crackling electricity, and he wanted to make certain everything went smoothly in London for them. For once.

He owed it to his mother as well as to the title—and especially to his father's memory—that this season the Carlisle brothers didn't behave like...well, the Carlisles.

They'd terrorized the Lincolnshire countryside since they'd first learned to walk, then moved on to plague Eton and Oxford in turn. So it had only been a matter of time until the three of them focused their attention on London, where the whiskey was stronger, the card games played for higher stakes, and the women were decidedly more sophisticated. Until four years ago, what they'd done in the city hadn't mattered much, with their family having almost no social standing among the quality despite their father's barony, leaving them free to gamble, brawl, and chase women to their hearts' content.

Then everything changed. His family was granted the former Earl Royston's estate when the earl committed treason. At first, their family received only the land, not the title, but when the Regent was petitioned by Edward Westover, Duke of Strathmore, and Lord Bathurst, Secretary of State for War and the Colonies, both men made clear exactly how much the Carlisle family had participated in exposing Royston's treason and in preventing the slaughter of the War Office's best agents overseas. Prinny relented and bestowed a new dukedom.

Overnight, the Carlisle land holdings more than quadrupled in size, and their modest wealth became a fortune. No one could overlook the three brothers' antics now, and whatever anonymity they'd had as sons of a baron disappeared as sons of a newly minted duke. Sebastian knew even then what the others had yet to realize.

What Prinny had granted wasn't an award but a punishment.

Then the worst came. His father was tossed from his horse, struck his head, and died. The loss had been devastating to all of them, and their grief had been debilitating for months. But Sebastian didn't have time to flounder. All the responsibility for the estates and the family had landed directly on him, and he worked his way through his grief by working his way through the estate books.

Nearly two years had passed, and not one day had yet

dawned when the family didn't feel Richard Carlisle's absence. So the house party they'd held during the past sennight—the first soiree of any kind since Father's death—signified more than his mother's birthday. It was also a marker of all the changes their family had endured during the past few years and survived. And privately, Sebastian hoped they could once again focus their attention on the future and on protecting the reputation of the family. Especially from themselves.

He leaned back in the leather chair. "For once, we're all going to London and remaining there for the entire season." He paused meaningfully. "Together," he emphasized, letting the gravity of that settle over them. "So I think it's vital that we discuss our plans." He narrowed his eyes at Quinn, knowing the trouble his brother could cause. "*All* our plans. So we can avoid any problems which might arise."

In the past, the Carlisle family had never all been in London at the same time. His father had sat for every Parliament session, taking his position as baron seriously although he'd never acquired much political power in the Lords. Mother and Josephine went only to purchase a few dresses, *if* Josie went at all because his sister preferred to remain at Chestnut Hill to help with the children at the Good Hope Home. And all three brothers came and went as they pleased, sometimes not seeing one another for weeks even while residing within the same London town house.

But this year, circumstances brought them all together for the season. Josie now lived in London with her husband, Thomas Matteson, Marquess of Chesney, and their children. Sebastian was required to attend Parliament, having more power within its committees than his father could ever have imagined, and while he sat in the Lords, Elizabeth Carlisle would visit with Josie and her family. Robert would undoubtedly spend his time courting Diana Morgan. As for Quinton, *he* was going only so Sebastian could keep an eye on him.

"I'll be residing with Josephine and Chesney at Audley House," his mother volunteered to start the conversation, "leaving you and your brothers at Park Place." Her shoulders heaved with a long sigh borne of years of suffering her sons' wild antics, and she slid a sideways glance of warning at her youngest son. "Please don't burn the place to the ground."

"Well, there go my May Day plans," Quinn muttered, only half-sarcastically.

Sebastian's eyes narrowed. Oh yes, Quinton was certainly coming to London, where he wouldn't let his brother out of his sight until June. Of next year.

"No May Day?" Robert sauntered into the room, interrupting what had been a promising start to the conversation and now throwing it into chaos.

Quinn gave his brother a deflated look as Robert crossed to the coffee service on the side table and reached for the urn. "No bonfire."

Robert paused mid-pour, aghast. "Where's the fun in May Day without bonfires?"

"I know." Quinn grimaced. "So much for our Maypole."

"Did she cancel the donkey rides, too?"

Elizabeth Carlisle rolled her eyes in weary exasperation, and Sebastian couldn't help but smile. His younger brothers had plagued their poor mother with one wild scheme after another all their lives. Even now, as grown men responsible for helping with the dukedom, the two couldn't help but antagonize Mother every chance they could.

Looking at his brothers now and hearing the relaxed

rhythm of their banter, it would have been easy to believe that they were the same as they'd always been, that their father's death hadn't changed them. But Sebastian knew better. It had changed all of them to their cores.

In the dark months following Father's passing, both of his brothers had matured quickly and stepped up to assume large responsibilities for the dukedom. In that, they'd proven themselves well—Quinton as a successful estate agent, assuming supervision for the day-to-day operations of the workers and tenants, and Robert as a sharp business mind, taking on the bank accounts and business investments where a large portion of the family's wealth was kept. Sebastian had been grateful for their help, knowing neither brother had to work given the ten thousand pounds each had inherited. Quinton had stashed his away, with dreams of buying his own land as soon as Sebastian found an agent to replace him here, while Robert had invested his in business ventures and nearly doubled it already, earning himself a fine reputation as a businessman in the process.

But when the two of them were together like this, they fell back into old habits, giving a glimpse of the rascals they'd been only a few short years ago.

Some things never changed. Sebastian only hoped that *this* season no donkeys were painted green in the process. Or set on fire.

"Are the Morgans off, then?" he asked as Robert splashed a generous amount of whiskey into his coffee, then fixed a second cup when Quinn gestured for one.

"Just." Robert handed the coffee to his brother and sat down heavily onto the empty chair, kicking out his long legs. "I promised to call on them as soon as we arrive in London."

Sebastian's chest tightened as he remembered Miranda's heartbroken words about his brother. "Does this mean you intend to court Miss Morgan?"

Robert smiled. "Yes, I do."

He frowned. No one in the Carlisle family anticipated a marriage, yet Robert's intentions appeared serious enough to draw Miranda's attention and set her off on her madcap adventure last night to stop him. She could be flighty as a songbird at times, too boisterous and lively for her own good. Yet in her concerns about Robert and Miss Morgan, Sebastian didn't doubt her intuition. Apparently she'd noticed something the rest of them hadn't. "Do you plan to offer for her, then?"

Robert raised the cup to his lips and dodged, "If it comes to that. I do like her a great deal."

His gut tightened in sympathetic dread. News of an engagement would devastate Miranda, who truly seemed to love his brother. Although looking at Robert now, gulping down whiskey-drenched coffee to combat a hangover, God only knew why.

"There's no hurry to propose, you know." Sebastian couldn't stop the inevitable, but perhaps he could delay it. And truthfully, although he liked Miss Morgan, he wasn't certain that she was the best choice in wife for his brother. Too demure, too genteel...too unsuspecting. "Best to wait until mid-season at least. Just long enough to give the girl time to realize what she's getting herself into."

Quinn grinned. "And flee."

And just long enough to give Miranda's heart a chance to heal. Sebastian nodded, for once agreeing with his youngest brother.

"Perhaps you're right," Robert agreed, taking a swallow of coffee. "There's no hurry, I suppose."

Relief swept through Sebastian. Miranda could bother him to no end with her uncontrolled exuberance, but she didn't deserve to be wounded.

"Besides," Robert chided, "you're the one who should be getting married, Seb, not me." He gazed with mock innocence at Sebastian over the rim of his coffee cup, an expression that did nothing to hide the flickering gleam in his eyes indicating that he wanted to cause trouble. "You're getting old."

"I am not old," Sebastian grumbled. "I'm only thirty, for heaven's sake."

"And crotchety." Quinn popped a bite of sweet roll into his mouth, oblivious to the glare Sebastian shot him.

Robert continued, "Isn't it time for you to find a wife of your own and produce an heir—"

"Or six?" Quinn finished.

Sebastian glanced between his two brothers, pausing as he considered sharing with them the decision he'd made at dawn after a sleepless night of tossing and turning in rosewater-scented sheets, thanks to Lady Rose.

He'd been contemplating the idea of marriage for months now, ever since he'd inherited, if truth be told, when he'd come to realize how much of a help a wife could be. He hadn't been prepared for the emotional burden of becoming a duke, or the loneliness of it. He had no one to confide in, not even his own family. His brothers had never felt the same duty for the title that he had and so wouldn't be able to understand that he felt imprisoned by it, that he chafed from it so much that sometimes he thought he would go mad, or how deep his jealousy ran that they could choose their own life paths while his had been thrust upon him. For Christ's sake, he couldn't even get foxed anymore or spend the night with a woman for fear of what it might do to the title's reputation. The night his father died had driven home that lesson. And as for his mother...how could he expect her to listen to his complaints when what had given him this burden in the first place was her husband's death?

Last night had made him come to a decision about his future and the ongoing absence of a woman in his bed, one who truly belonged there instead of those women he'd known before, who had given him little more than physical release and a night's distraction from his responsibilities. The exact same thing he'd wanted to take from Lady Rose when he'd first walked into the room and found her draped so invitingly across his bed.

What he needed was a wife, one who would be a proper duchess and a guiding hand at his side, one in whom he could confide his troubles and take solace. One who was a reflection of what was important to him. A true partner, as his mother had been to his father. Maybe then he wouldn't feel like a prisoner in his own skin.

"Yes, it is time," Sebastian agreed soberly, stepping to the edge of the cliff. Then he drew a deep breath and jumped. "That's exactly what I plan on doing this season."

The room froze around him, with Robert's coffee cup raised halfway to his lips and Quinn stopping mid-chew. The only movement was a sudden widening of his mother's eyes in stunned surprise. Not even the sound of breathing disrupted the shocked stillness.

Then his mother blinked. "That's..." She blinked again, not quite able to clear the shocked expression from her face. "That's..." She tilted her head as if she couldn't possibly have heard him correctly. "*Marriage?*"

His brothers continued to stare as if he'd just sprung a second head.

With a grimace, he rolled his eyes. *Good Lord.* From their collective reactions, he might as well have just admitted to attempting to kill the king. He'd expected them to be surprised. Not shocked speechless. Despite his protests, at thirty he wasn't young anymore, and although it pained him to admit that Robert and Quinton were right, he did need to produce an heir. Or six.

"I've been contemplating the matter for some time now," he clarified, drumming his fingertips with agitation on the desktop, "and have decided that a marriage is in the best interests of the dukedom."

"Oh," Quinn said quietly around the last bite of sweet roll in his mouth, a stunned expression still on his face.

Damnation. Wouldn't the three of them stop staring at him like that?

Finally, Elizabeth Carlisle smiled gently through her bewilderment. "If that's what you want…It's wonderful, Sebastian, truly."

A niggling suspicion in his gut told him that his mother had just lied to him.

But given that she had her hands full coming to terms with Robert's sudden courtship of Diana Morgan and preventing Quinn from ever courting anyone, he didn't blame her for her surprised reaction to his sudden announcement. He'd certainly been surprised enough himself in the past twelve hours.

"The timing is right. The most eligible ladies will be gathered in London for the season," he continued, reciting the speech he'd practiced in his head while his valet had been dressing him this morning. Barlow had bemoaned the entire time that he hadn't helped Sebastian undress last night after the party. And a good thing he hadn't, given the unexpected appearance of Lady Rose in his bedchamber. "All their extended families will be in residence, which will give me a good opportunity to examine their pedigrees. I need a respectable duchess, a highborn wife befitting the title and its holdings."

Quinn laughed. "It sounds as if you're choosing a horse!"

"Oh no, not at all," Robert disagreed with a teasing wink at Quinn. "Seb wants more spirit in his horse than in his wife."

Sebastian ignored both of them and concentrated on his mother's growing frown, more troubled by that than he wanted to admit, as he finished with the coup de grâce to his brothers' joking—"Someone who can give me an heir."

That sobered both brothers immediately.

All four of them knew how important it was that Sebastian father a son. If he didn't, the titles, the estate, and all the responsibilities would fall to his brothers. No one wanted that to happen. Least of all both of them. Oh, they would help him whenever he asked, yet they also wanted the freedom to live their lives however they chose and pursue their own paths of success, along which they were already rapidly excelling. But assume all the responsibilities completely? *Never.*

His mother's troubled frown melted into one of concern—and *that* bothered him even more than the frown. "An heir is an important duty, of course." Motherly love and worry filled her voice. "Yet there are other considerations."

He nodded. "She must also understand the necessity of privacy and sobriety." A woman not at all like Miranda, he thought, once again piqued at last night's events. What on earth had she been thinking? She could have rained scandal down on both their families if anyone had seen her sneaking in or out of his bedroom. "Having us together in

London will allow for all of you to give approval before I make an offer."

"But, Sebastian, dear," his mother said gently, "that is not our decision to make."

"Your opinions are very important to me." The title was as much theirs as it was his, and the decision of taking a wife could prove a momentous one for the future of the entire family. "We'll use the season to conduct a logical, well-reasoned search for a duchess."

Robert and Quinn looked at each other, then hooted with laughter.

Sebastian scowled at them. They could at least take the matter seriously, and if not seriously, then at least hold their peace. And stay out of his way.

He leveled his gaze on Quinn, the cold expression making his brother choke on his laughter. "And what, exactly, do *you* plan on doing this season while the rest of us are productively engaged?"

Quinn grinned. "Conducting a logical, well-reasoned search to find as many women as possible."

"Hear, hear!" Robert raised his coffee cup in a toast. "To sweethearts and wives—"

"May they never meet!" Quinn finished, clinking his cup against his brother's.

Sebastian shook his head. How was it possible that all three of them shared the same set of parents?

Having learned years ago that it was better to ignore her sons' antics than to risk encouraging them by giving them attention, his mother sat forward in her chair and turned her cornflower-blue eyes on Sebastian. Her love and concern for him shone in their depths. "I think it's a wonderful idea that you are serious about starting a family. But I hope you choose a wife for the right reasons."

"I will," he assured her.

She reached across the desk and placed her hand over his. "And that you have a marriage as loving and wonderful as the one I had with your father."

"I will," he repeated, although with much less conviction. He squeezed her hand as a knot of emotion tightened in his throat, then pulled away. As a duke, love was a luxury he couldn't afford. After all, he wasn't searching for a loving wife but a perfect duchess. One to make his father proud. And to be fortunate enough to find both in one woman... well, fate had never been that kind to him.

He cleared his throat and leveled his gaze on Robert. "And the family's investments? Anything to report?"

Robert nodded, and suddenly, with the turn of conversation, he wasn't the same man who had just joked with Quinton about May Day and marriage. He was mature, responsible, confident. The change was palpable. "I've moved capital from our accounts into the funds with the Bank of England. A low-risk investment just as you requested. The yields will sustain the principal and incur modest growth, enough to roll over into new land purchases in a few years, if you still want to expand the family's agricultural holdings."

Sebastian studied his brother, not letting the pride he felt for him show. Anyone looking at Robert now would never have suspected the wild scapegrace he'd been just two years ago or how he'd successfully taken over the Carlisle family's financial investments in the intervening years. Or how much Father's death had rocked Robert to his core. "You advise against property purchases? Wealth lies in land."

Robert shook his head, his face as serious as Sebastian's. "We have enough land to support the estate twice over. What we need are capital investments not tied to real estate. The wars are over, and the empire's changing. New trade opportunities are springing up every day, and we'd be wise to invest a share of our profits in factories, trade, and goods."

Quinn elbowed him in the ribs with a wink. "The ladies love it when you talk like that."

Robert said nothing but hid his grin behind the rim of his cup of whiskey-coffee as he raised it for a sip.

"And you?" Sebastian turned his gaze onto Quinton. "Is the estate ready for spring?"

"The repairs to the dairy barn are set to start as soon as the cold weather breaks, and we've managed to mend the stone wall on the east pasture, as well as deepen the irrigation ditch ahead of schedule. I've decided to make allowances to the tenants this spring for losses in last year's drought. We're not obligated to, but..." He shrugged casually, as if that project alone hadn't taken weeks to bring to fruition. Quinton had found a hidden skill in dealing with the estate's daily operations, and all his charm had certainly helped relations with the tenants. "Trent has offered to supply free seeds for this year's plantings."

Sebastian arched a brow, not because he was upset at his brother for making promises on his behalf but because he was proud of the way Quinton had risen to the challenge of overseeing the estate. "Trent is, is he?"

Quinn grinned at Sebastian's expense. "And quite happily, too. I've also got an estate agent lined up to oversee everything while we're in London." A hopeful tone crept into his voice. Quinn was chomping at the bit to find his replacement. As soon as he did, he could leave Islingham and carve out an independent life for himself on his own property. "If he does well, you should consider keeping him on."

"We'll see." Quinton might be ready to charge out into the world on his own, but Sebastian wasn't ready to give him up just yet. As he glanced between his brothers, he knew how lost he would have been these past two years without their help. "Any other business to discuss?"

"I have plans for London, too," Mother spoke up.

"Of course." Sebastian's eyes softened on her, knowing how beneficial this season would be for her. He'd been worried about her this winter and knew that London would reenergize her spirit. "You want to spend as much time as possible with Josie and the children."

"No, dear." Her lips curled into a pleased smile, and her eyes gleamed, reminding him of the joyful woman she'd been before his father died. "Miranda Hodgkins."

His heart stopped.

And when it started again, the lurch ripped his breath away. He cleared his throat to keep down the panic that his mother had somehow discovered what had happened last night. *Almost* happened. "What about her?"

"She's done a remarkable job with the orphanage these past few years."

That was what she wanted to say? He smiled with relief. "Yes, she has. A wonderful job by all accounts."

Her smile turned beaming. "So I've decided that we will sponsor her for the London season."

Dread surged through him, numbing him in a flash. "Pardon?" He prayed that he'd heard incorrectly, that his mother had confused Miranda with someone else, that there was another young woman who needed a sponsor for the season.

"I want Miranda to come to London with us this season, so we can express our gratitude for all she's done for the orphans and the village. And for our own family as well."

Oblivious to his distress, she continued enthusiastically, "She has no one except Rebecca and Hamish, and they're not in a position to give her the season she deserves. We are. And we should."

"To what end?" His chest tightened. Young ladies made London debuts in order to snag husbands. Was his mother seriously considering an attempt to marry off Miranda to some London dandy?

As if reading his mind, she answered, "Only for the experience of it, I assure you. Every young lady should be able to enjoy the excitement of a London season at least once." She added, almost in afterthought, "Although I wouldn't chase away any gentlemen who might spark an interest in her."

Wordlessly, he slid his gaze to Robert. Did his mother have any idea of where Miranda's true interest lay?

No, of course she didn't. His mother wasn't cruel. If she did know, she wouldn't place Miranda in a position to see Robert wooing anyone else.

When he didn't agree, her smile dissolved. "It was your idea, Sebastian."

His idea? Impossible. Yet a fuzzy memory formed painfully at the back of his mind of a passing conversation in the carriage returning from Christmas morning service, a conversation he'd dismissed at the time as unimportant. A London season, introductions, a new wardrobe...all things better left to the ladies, especially when his attention was focused on the estate as he watched it roll past the carriage windows, of repairs that needed to be made to the stables and a new bridge built over the creek between the south meadows, a new roof installed on Blackwood Hall, the walls reinforced around the western pastures... *Wouldn't it be nice, Mother, if you gave Miranda a London season?*

Good God. He *had* mentioned it.

"We owe it to her," Elizabeth Carlisle continued, her eyes glistening. "She was a great help to me after your father's death when Josie had to return to London. I don't know what I would have done without her. It would be lovely if we could repay her kindness."

He conceded that point. Miranda *had* provided important support for his mother during that dark time. She'd stopped by Chestnut Hill every day on her way home from the village to check in on them, often came with her aunt and uncle for Sunday dinners, and cajoled his mother into shopping trips to the village or delivering baskets to the tenants, which Sebastian had come to suspect were nothing but excuses for her to take his mother out of the house and away from her grief.

They *did* owe her a great deal for her kindness. He only wished there was some other way to repay her than with a London season.

"It would break Miranda's heart if she didn't have this opportunity," she insisted.

Sebastian grimaced. It would break her heart to watch Robert court Miss Morgan.

But Mother was right. With only Rebecca and Hamish to care for her, no connections in society except for their family, and not enough money to buy the gowns, accessories, and everything else she would need for a proper debut, Miranda had no chance at a real season without the Carlisles' help.

And yet, the last person he wanted to deal with in London was Miranda, especially when he was hunting a wife and she was hunting Robert. He couldn't imagine a more potentially disastrous situation for all of them.

"Perhaps we should wait a year," he countered gently,

doing his best to maneuver himself out of the sticky situation in which he had unwittingly placed both Miranda and himself. Up to their necks. "With this being the first season for the family out of mourning—"

"Certainly not." His mother straightened her spine in that way she did when she prepared to do battle with her sons, in the past over everything from snakes in laundry baskets to racing cows down High Street. "Besides, I'm looking forward to it myself." Her face softened at the slightly selfish admission, and a lightness and happiness came over her that Sebastian hadn't seen nearly often enough since Father died. "Josephine never had a proper debut, and since none of you three have yet to secure wives and grandchildren for me to spoil—"

All three men glanced guiltily away from her, to cast their gazes onto the floor, the wall, out the window—*anywhere* but on their mother.

"Then I'll have Miranda to dote on." She beamed happily at the idea. "And sponsoring her will give me the opportunity to finally assist with a young lady's London season."

Sebastian shook his head, knowing the headaches of a season. "Invitations to court and vouchers to Almack's, all that pomp to suffer, all the social hoops to jump through—"

"Shopping trips to Bond Street and visits to the dressmaker for beautiful ball gowns." Her eyes shined at all the possibilities of the season. "Carriage rides through the park, grand balls, art exhibitions, musicales, nights at the theater..."

As she continued to tick off a long list on her fingers, Sebastian knew he'd lost. After last night, he wanted to keep Miranda as far away from him as possible, but he would also do anything to make his mother happy.

And yet, not wanting to be accused of not trying to stop

this goose egg of a plan in four weeks when all hell broke loose, he warned solemnly, "The girl causes nothing but trouble."

She smiled patiently at him. "In case you haven't noticed, Miranda is no longer a girl."

Oh, he'd certainly noticed *that*, all right. Which was the biggest trouble of all.

"She simply needs supervision and a proper place to channel her exuberance," she assured him. "I'll take care of her and all the arrangements, and since we'll be staying with Josephine and Chesney, you'll hardly see her. You'll barely know she's in London at all."

His mother's assurances did nothing to alleviate the uneasiness clawing at his gut, but he had no choice. He wouldn't do anything to take away the first signs of excitement in Mother since Father died. If it took giving Miranda a proper London season to make his mother happy again, then he'd do it.

Even if it killed him.

"Very well," he grudgingly acquiesced. "We'll give her a season."

His mother beamed happily, and Sebastian's chest lightened. Whatever problems Miranda did manage to create in Mayfair, seeing that happiness again on his mother's face would be worth it.

He hoped.

"Good. It's all settled then. If you'll excuse me." She rose from her chair, and all three of her sons scrambled to their feet. "I have a house to see to, to make certain all is put back to order." She headed toward the door, then paused to glance back, a knowing gleam in her eyes. "Including the cupid statue from the rose garden fountain that somehow found its way into Lord Batten's bed."

Robert and Quinn exchanged guilty glances, then dropped their gazes to the floor, saying nothing to incriminate themselves.

With a long-suffering sigh and shake of her head, she glided from the room, a perfection of matronly force.

Robert and Quinn flopped back down into their chairs. Sebastian crossed from behind his desk to the coffee tray, not bothering with the pretense of coffee as he poured himself a cup of straight whiskey.

He shot Quinn a glance. "Were you really planning on setting a May Day bonfire?"

"Seb." His youngest brother feigned injury at the accusation. "You know we'd never do anything like that."

"Not for May Day," Robert piped up in his brother's defense. "But Guy Fawkes—"

"An imperative," Quinn interjected resolutely. Then he grimaced with disappointment. "But the donkey rides *were* true."

"Not anymore." Sebastian took a gasping swallow of whiskey. "I don't want any trouble this season. It's going to be hard enough for Mother to be in London for the first time since Father's death. I don't want any of us to make it harder for her than it needs to be."

Quinn nodded, suddenly serious. "Then it's a good thing she's bringing Miranda. Truly, Seb. We all know you don't like her, but—"

"I like her," he interrupted, far more defensively than he'd intended. He *did* like her. She was sweet and endearing in her own way, when she wasn't causing trouble. But while he was searching for a duchess, he simply preferred to like her from two hundred miles away.

"But she *is* good for Mother," Robert concluded seriously in that peculiar way all three brothers had of finishing each other's thoughts.

Quinn nodded. "Miranda will keep her busy."

"And keep her mind off Father," Robert finished soberly.

Sebastian sighed in grudging agreement. "Just keep Miranda from causing problems for *me*, will you?"

"Sorry." Quinn shook his head with a wide grin. "I'll be too busy looking for my own women to keep close."

"*Looking* but not finding," Robert goaded with a laugh.

"Oh, I'll catch them all right." Quinn kicked his feet up onto the corner of the desk and laced his hands behind his head as he leaned confidently back in the chair. "As easy as salmon fishing in Scotland. They'll be taking the bait and begging me to—"

"Throw them all back once they've seen the size of your lure?" Robert finished.

Quinn laughed. Then, realizing that the barb was at his expense, he snapped his mouth shut and glared at his brother.

"No one will be throwing anyone anywhere." Sebastian smacked at Quinn's feet for him to take his boots off the desk. "So keep your drunkenness to places where no one knows you, and don't gamble where they don't. And if you must go whoring—"

"Salmon in Scotland," Quinn reminded him pointedly.

Robert shook his head. "The size of the lure—"

"Be careful," Sebastian finished somberly. "I don't want anything bad to happen to either of you. Or to Mother."

Both brothers stared at him quietly for a moment, understanding the grimness behind that warning, then nodded their compliance. Relieved that he'd managed to corral his brothers' antics, if only temporarily, Sebastian blew out a long breath and took another sip of whiskey.

Robert slapped Quinn on the shoulder. "Maybe Chesney can get us into Boodle's."

"Or White's," Quinn added.

"What's the use of having a marquess in the family—"

"If he can't get us into the book at White's—"

"Or under a skirt at Boodle's?"

The two brothers grinned at each other.

"No," Sebastian said firmly, the start of a headache throbbing behind his eyes. The two of them could try Job's patience.

Instead of dampening their enthusiasm, his admonition only drew a laugh from Robert. "That's because you're afraid we'll take all the pretty women before you get to them."

He scowled. He loved his brothers and would do anything for them...if he didn't kill them first himself. "That is not—"

"Sowing wild oats before you shackle yourself to some lord's prim daughter is all very fine and good," Quinn advised Sebastian with mock solemnity, as if he were an Oxford don delivering a lecture.

Robert joined in. "But best not to get caught doing anything that could turn you into a pariah for the well-bred ladies."

"Don't drink where anyone knows you—"

"Don't gamble where they don't—"

"And if you must whore, be careful," the two brothers finished together. Then they glanced sideways at each other and grinned.

Sebastian shook his head. *Good God.* The two of them together was exhausting.

He rubbed at his forehead to ease the headache that they put there, but he also took their teasing warning to heart. He couldn't risk even a hint of scandal this season given his need to find a bride and his desire to make his mother happy, but he knew it wouldn't be his brothers who would cause problems. They might be wild and careless, but they also knew how important this season was. That alone was enough to keep them well-behaved until at least the end of June, May Day bonfires and donkey rides aside.

No, the risk to his season came in the form of a petite country gel with unruly strawberry-blond hair, a pert nose dotted with freckles, and a penchant for stirring up trouble.

Tossing back the rest of the whiskey, he welcomed the burn down his throat. He knew what he had to do about Miranda.

It was time the two of them came to an understanding about her behavior.

CHAPTER THREE

~

"Arrrh! Arrrrrrrh!" Miranda raised her wooden sword high above her black-felt hat with its white-stitched skull and crossbones and gave her best imitation of a pirate. "Make 'im walk the plank! That's the punishment for a landlubber—to the plank wi' 'im!"

"To the plank!" All the children around her yelled and raised their own little sticks like swords. Then they took a loosely tied Mr. Grundy, the man hired to do maintenance around the orphanage, and led him toward a short board lying flat on the grass between the sheets and blankets tied to the clotheslines stretching across the rear of the garden. So loosely tied, in fact, that when he reached up to scratch his nose, the rope coils fell down around his ankles, and he had to yank them back up into place. All around them, the sheets billowed on the afternoon wind like a ship's sails.

Miranda laughed, a bubble of happiness swelling inside her. Such a good time they were having! And she was so glad for it. Both she and the orphans needed a break this afternoon during one of winter's rare warm days, with the children having spent all morning inside at their studies and she at taking inventory in the basement storage rooms. A long list of tasks still awaited her, but she couldn't resist stealing away for an hour of play with them.

"Any last words 'fore ye join Davy Jones in 'is locker, ye scurvy dog?" She circled the wooden sword toward Mr. Grundy. He'd had the happy misfortune this afternoon of taking his lunch at the same time as the children and so had gotten caught up in their play, although the unabashed grin on the older man's face told her he enjoyed the fun as much as she did.

"To be or not to be," he recited, his hand held dramatically over his heart, "that is the question."

"And none of that soliloquy-in'," she warned. "You lousy Dane!"

"Plank! Plank!" the children sent up a chant.

Miranda laughed, nearly doubling over and losing all hope at playing a convincing pirate captain now. Oh, how she loved these children!

Since Josephine Carlisle married her marquess and left for London, Miranda had taken responsibility for managing the Good Hope Home. In the three years since she'd been caring for the home and its two dozen orphans, she'd grown to love it more than she'd ever thought possible. The responsibility challenged her, the orphans adored her, and her life finally had a sense of purpose beyond caring for her auntie and uncle.

The best part, though, were the children—always so energetic, so full of life and hope. Being around them made her feel good about herself and the possibilities in the world.

Even now as they flocked around her as their pirate captain and forced poor Mr. Grundy to walk the plank, she had a precious glimpse of what it must have been like to grow up with brothers and sisters. Oh, Rebecca and Hamish had been very good to her, loving her and raising her as if she were their own, but they were childless. They didn't always understand her and the boundless energy that sometimes swelled inside her until she thought she would burst if it didn't get out. And *that* usually caused more trouble for her than she wanted to admit, as most of the villagers and farmers could attest.

What must it have been like to be part of a large family, one full of noise and confusion and all the wonderful pandemonium of a well-lived household? That was why she was drawn to the Carlisles, she supposed. Chestnut Hill had always been so happy and energetic, so full of loving disorder, and there was always some scheme of one kind or another that Josie and her three brothers had planned in which she could join. Certainly, her home with Auntie and Uncle was very nice, but it was always too silent, too still. Too serious for comfort.

The joy of organized chaos—she laughed as the children forced Mr. Grundy to jump from the plank onto the pretend ocean of grass. Well, she'd certainly found it!

"And so they go to it," she announced with a dramatic flourish of her wooden sword. "Rosencrantz and Guildenstern are dead!"

As the children sent up a loud cheer, and even a supposedly drowned Mr. Grundy joined in with the hurrahs, she made a daring leap off the makeshift ship.

Her sword caught the edge of a billowing sheet. It tangled in the material and jerked her off balance. She tumbled into the sheet and fell to the ground, rolled across the grass as the sheet wrapped around her, and landed directly at the toes of a pair of highly polished boots.

Lying on her back, she raised her eyes slowly with embarrassment, squinted against the bright sun, and met the scowling gaze of...Sebastian Carlisle.

Oh no.

Suddenly shouts and panic broke through the group of children. Instead of helping her up, they scattered into the rows of sheets, through the garden, and away. All of them fled like rats on a sinking ship, along with Mr. Grundy, who gave her a polite doff of his cap before disappearing around the side of the building.

Cowards. Miranda groaned, wrapped up like a pirate mummy, now completely defenseless. With *him* of all people. Oh, the humiliation of it! She'd much rather have walked the plank herself.

The concerned frown darkening his face deepened as he leaned over and offered her his hand. "Are you all right?"

She sighed and tossed away her wooden sword before she decided to use it on him. "I'm fine."

With no other choice unless she wanted to flop on the ground like a fish to free herself from the sheet, she took his hand, and he helped her to her feet. His reproving expression as he reached up to remove her pirate hat told her as clearly as if he'd shouted it from the village green that the duke didn't approve of their roughhousing.

Well, so what if he didn't? The children were hers to oversee, and they deserved time to play and to simply behave like children. The adult world would grind away their enthusiasm and innocence soon enough. The way it had apparently done to him.

"What were you doing out here?" He darted a questioning glance at the ship's deck that the children had fashioned roughly from old boards, small barrels, and boxes. "Why weren't the children at their studies?"

"They *were* at their studies." She yanked her hat away from him. If he thought she'd let him cow her simply because he saw her in that flimsy dress last night, he had another think coming. Although, she considered with an inward grimace, he'd seen a lot more of her than that *out* of that dress. Still, she would not be intimidated by him. Lord Panther or not. "They're studying Shakespeare."

He blinked as if he hadn't heard her correctly and glanced down at the skull and crossbones she'd sewn onto her hat. "Shakespeare?"

"They're acting out the pirate scene from *Hamlet*."

His brow lifted patronizingly. "There is no pirate scene in *Hamlet*."

"Well, there should have been," she countered and bent down to pick up her sword. It was all she could do not to let out an irritated *humph* of annoyance. "Shakespeare mentions pirates in act five but never shows them, so the children wrote their own pirate scene."

"I see." His lips twitched, although she couldn't have said whether from irritation or amusement. "So you're teaching them to rewrite Shakespeare." He paused, barely a heartbeat, but there was a world of disapproval in that beat of silence. "I'd hate to see what you'd do with Milton."

Miranda bit back the urge to tell him that the children had been working hard all morning and needed a break from being cooped up indoors. That she'd spent all morning herself in the dusty, cramped, dark basement while the children had been diligently doing their maths. That he of all people should understand how draining it was to do nothing but toil, given all his responsibilities and how he spent nearly all of his time with his nose buried in the account books and in lists of everything that needed to be done for the estate and Parliament.

But after the embarrassment of last night, she wasn't certain that she needed to justify any of her behavior. Certainly not to *him*. Lord Panther, indeed.

So she folded her arms across her chest, the end of the wooden sword pointing at him, and asked, "What brings you to the orphanage?"

"Actually," he murmured, "I came looking for you."

Her eyes widened. "Pardon?"

He was—she gulped—*looking for her*? His words curled heatedly through her as unbidden memories rushed over her from last night of that same low voice purring in her ear, telling her how lovely she looked, how much he wanted to dance with her…

And what a goose she was! Because he certainly didn't mean that he'd come *looking* for her, just as he hadn't meant all those things he'd said last night when he thought she was someone else. So why would he be—

"We need to talk." He grimaced as he pushed the end of the sword away from him and lowered his voice. "About last night."

Panic instantly tied her stomach into knots. Had someone found out what she'd done? What *they'd* almost done? She crushed the felt hat in her hands as she forced herself to keep breathing and not faint.

He reached beneath his redingote and withdrew her red slipper from where he'd tucked it into his waistband at his back, then dangled it in front of her by its long ribbon. "You left your slippers behind last night, Cinderella, and I don't want you trying to sneak back into my room to retrieve them." His eyes gleamed teasingly at her. "You might accidentally end up in the wrong room again and frighten Quinton to death."

Fresh humiliation flooded through her. Glancing around

the little garden to make certain that they were hidden from sight behind the rows of billowing sheets, she made a quick grab for her slipper. Her fingers just missed as he lifted it up easily out of her reach.

Drat the man for being so tall! And broad. And muscular.

"Give it to me, please," she said in that same no-nonsense tone she used with the orphans and held out her hand.

But he kept it out of reach, just beyond her grasping fingers. "Not until we talk."

Knowing she wouldn't receive her shoe until he decided to give it to her, she gave up and placed her hands on her hips in frustrated aggravation at him for toying with her like this. And the blasted man was most likely enjoying it, too. "I told you. Last night was a mistake." She looked down at the ground to cover her embarrassment, although she couldn't have said which embarrassed her more—that he'd bared her to his mouth and hands, or that she'd liked it. "I would hope that you understand how—"

"Mother and I have decided to sponsor a season for you. In London."

Her eyes flew up to search his face. A season...oh, it couldn't be! "Truly?" she breathed, her heart pounding with too much hopeful excitement to let her speak any louder.

With a slow smile, he nodded.

A London season! She'd dreamt of this since she was a little girl, only to give up on the fantasy at her last birthday, when she came into her majority and realized it would never happen, that she was too old. But now, for him to offer—oh, it was simply grand! She couldn't imagine anything more special, more magical...a debut sponsored by a duchess and a marchioness, escorted by a duke, complete with beautiful dresses and fancy bonnets, quadrilles and waltzes, all kinds of soirees, dinners, breakfasts, carriage rides—

"Oh, thank you!" She laughed with happiness and threw her arms around his neck as she hugged him. She simply couldn't believe it!

She stepped back to collect herself. Oh, she couldn't stop smiling! Or stop the ecstatic pounding of her heart. "Thank you so much for this opportunity," she somehow forced out past the knot of gratitude in her throat. "It's more generous than I can express, and I know how fortunate I am to have this last chance for a season."

"Last chance?" His gaze narrowed disbelievingly as it swept over her, as if noticing her for the first time. "How old are you?"

Her chest squeezed with irritation. Didn't he remember the birthday party Auntie and Uncle hosted for her last November, which he and the rest of the Carlisles attended? He was terribly busy overseeing the dukedom, but still... She sighed out, "One and twenty."

A dark flicker passed through his eyes, and he looked at her again, long and hard, from the top of her head to the tips of her half-boots. She shifted uncomfortably beneath his gaze, although she suspected that he was seeing her, finally, for the woman she'd become instead of the girl he'd always known. And to think that all it took for him to realize that was finding her in his bed.

The irony was biting that she'd hoped for just that. Except from the *other* Carlisle brother.

But when his lips tugged into a faint grin as his gloved hand reached up to tuck a stray curl behind her ear, her heart sank. She knew she was wrong, that he'd never see her as anything other than the girl next door. Even after Lady Rose's unfortunate unmasking last night beneath those very clever hands of his.

Although why it should matter at all to her how Sebastian

Carlisle saw her she had no idea. Except that it now did. Last night had changed a great deal between them.

"You deserve this season," he told her, surprising her. Then he astonished her when he added quietly, "And you've earned it, with the work you've done for the orphanage and for the kindness you've shown my family. It's the least we can do for you."

She stared at him, speechless. She had no idea what to say to *that*.

"It will do Mother good as well." His voice softened with concern. "Make certain she enjoys herself, will you? She hasn't had an easy time since Father passed."

At the worry in his eyes, her shoulders sagged. Drat him that she couldn't even stay angry at him. Sebastian was sometimes arrogant and always frustratingly proper, but the man truly cared for his mother.

"I'll do my best," she assured him. And meant it.

He nodded, pleased by her acquiescence, although she was certain he didn't realize that she only agreed with him because of the duchess. Certainly not because of him.

"But what does this have to do with last night?" She made a slow reach for her slipper, only for him to pull it away. Again. She rolled her eyes.

"Robert will be there. And you were right." His gaze turned dark as midnight with silent sympathy as it held hers. "He plans on courting Diana Morgan."

Her eyes stung, and she gave a jerking nod, unable to find her voice. She knew this was coming—had known since last fall, in fact. Someone as beautiful as Diana Morgan... *of course* Robert would fall for her. And her for him. How could she not, as perfect as Robert was? But knowing it was coming didn't do anything to lessen the pain. Miranda simply hadn't expected this moment to feel so... empty. And dreadful. She pressed her clenched hand against her chest, as if she could physically fight back the gnawing ache.

"You'll have to see them together," he said gently, "attend the same events, sit next to them at dinners...Can you do that?"

Another jerking nod. Suddenly, her season didn't seem so wonderful anymore.

"I'm sorry, Miranda. I know you care for him."

And always would.

Nodding, she looked away and blinked to clear the blurring tears from her eyes. At that moment, she didn't know what hurt worse—that Robert had chosen Miss Morgan, or that she'd never had the chance to make him notice her. When she'd finally gathered the courage to tell him how she felt and the resolve to show him the woman she'd become, it had all been wasted. On the wrong brother. She would have laughed if she didn't hurt so much.

Then Sebastian said, almost carefully, "I'm going to London as well."

She held out her hand again in hopes that he would be a gentleman and simply hand over the slipper. Then she could go back inside the orphanage, hide in her office, and cry without anyone seeing. "Of course you're going. You have to attend the Lords and escort your mother."

"And find a wife," he added quietly.

Her gaze darted up to his. In stunned disbelief, she searched his face for any hint that he was teasing, but found nothing in his expression but somber sincerity.

A wife? *Sebastian?* She'd never known him to care anything for courting or the marriage market or...well, for that matter, to show matrimonial interest in any woman. Even before he inherited, he'd never seriously courted anyone, preferring the sort of trysts and assignations that were the fodder for gossipy old hens across England. But he had always drawn female attention wherever he went and unknowingly left a string of broken hearts in his wake. He *was* a Carlisle, after all. But a wife...

Her hand fell limp to her side. She didn't know how she should feel about that. Or what to say...except, "Well, you are getting older, I suppose."

With an exasperated grimace, he lowered the slipper. The time for games was apparently over.

"I need to find a duchess and produce an heir." His eyes never left hers, but their brightness dulled. She knew how dedicated he was to the dukedom, but her chest tightened with unexpected sympathy that he should find marriage to be just another expectation to be fulfilled. Simply one more responsibility resting on his shoulders. "This season presents the perfect opportunity. I can be married by August."

August. Standing there in the pale January sunlight, the heat of summer seemed so far away. Until she looked into his eyes, when it suddenly felt as close as next week. Why was she so struck by his decision? It was to be expected, after all. He was a duke, and he would need a son to inherit and carry on in his footsteps.

But Sebastian with a wife...Miranda simply couldn't fathom it.

Of all the questions swirling through her confused mind, the first one that popped out before she could stop it—"But what if you don't find one by August?"

He chuckled, the deep sound rumbling across the small distance between them and seeping into her chest, where it pulsed warm all the way out to the ends of her fingers and toes. Ruefully, she remembered once again the heat of his mouth on her body and of his soft compliments falling through her, and her heart thumped hard against her ribs.

"Don't worry, I'll find one," he assured her. Then his laughter died away, and he muttered with a self-deprecating grin, "It's amazing what inheriting a dukedom can do for a man's popularity."

Which should have made him happy to know that his pursuit of a wife would be easier, she considered sadly, but obviously it didn't. He'd been so much more relaxed when he was younger, more spontaneous and convivial...more free. *Alive.* But that handsome young man she remembered who always had a charming smile for everyone and so easily laughed his way through the day had disappeared. And in his place now stood a duke.

For a moment, she forgot her embarrassment over last night and her frustration with him, and her heart ached for him.

He smiled at her, but the forced expression never reached his eyes. "I'll have to beat them away with a stick."

She held out the wooden sword. "Then you can borrow mine."

He laughed as he took it from her and made a show of examining it, his eyes crinkling. And she couldn't help but smile back.

"I wish you luck, Sebastian," she offered awkwardly, "if marriage is what you truly want."

"It is."

But his smile faded, the momentary lightness she'd seen in him gone. Immediately, she missed it. How much happier would he be if he would simply let himself be the carefree young man he once was? If he let himself laugh more often? If he could let himself forget for a few hours each day that he was the Duke of Trent and could simply be Sebastian again?

But just as with his marriage, she simply couldn't imagine that either.

He jabbed the tip of the sword into the ground, leaving it jutting up into the air at his side. "If you truly wish me well, then I ask you to behave yourself when we're in London."

Instantly, all her frustration flooded back. She crossed her arms indignantly. "I'm not a child in leading strings who needs a nanny. I'm a grown woman, in case you haven't noticed."

"Oh, I noticed." The heated look he gave her sent electric tingles pulsing through her, and she couldn't stop the flutter of her silly heart. Or the confusion that swirled through her immediately in its wake. "But you have to admit that trouble has a way of finding you."

She stared at him, stunned both at his quiet accusation and at her reaction to him. "I don't know what you mean."

He arched a brow. "Did you not set fire to the mercantile last year?"

She was aghast! "That was an accident. A lamp was left burning on the floor where anyone could have kicked—"

"Set loose all of Mr. Latimer's chickens, let the sheep into the barley field, ruined Mrs. Cooper's prize pie?"

"Those were all unintentional, and you know it." She couldn't believe that he was attempting to use such innocent accidents against her, especially when she'd only been trying to help everyone.

He pinned her with a stern look. "Rerouted the creek?"

At that one, she hesitated, a hot blush of embarrassment creeping up from the back of her neck. Well, maybe that *one* was intentional. But she'd done it only to help the farmers whose fields were too far from the creek to water their crops during the drought. She'd had only the best interests of the village at heart. "That was an honest mistake."

"I'm still picking rocks out of the south pasture."

She winced. Good Lord, the man could carry a grudge! Was it her fault if problems seemed to pop up in her wake? Problems she had nothing—well, *almost* nothing—to do with? Certainly, she would agree that when she was younger she was a bit of a handful, always getting into trouble. Or rather, trouble somehow always finding her. But that had all stopped since she assumed oversight for the orphanage and found her path in life, finally having somewhere to channel all her energy. With his head always in the estate books, Sebastian simply hadn't realized that yet.

And what was the alternative, to ignore the difficulties of the villagers and the neighbors she loved? She'd been too young to help her parents when they caught fever and died, and as long as she had the energy to help others—and it seemed she *always* had plenty of energy to spare—she would however she could. Oh, how could she *not* help someone who needed her?

But perhaps not again with irrigation.

She took a deep breath of patience. "Those all happened years ago."

"The mercantile fire," he reminded.

"*Most* happened years ago," she corrected. "Besides, no serious damage was done." When he silently arched a dubious brow at that rationalization, clearly remembering the destroyed bolts of cloth that had been the fire's only victims when the lamp she'd accidentally kicked spilled oil over them, she added, "I won't do anything to cause problems for you in London, Sebastian. In fact, I doubt we'll see each other very much at all when we're there. So you'll be free to attend Parliament and court all the ladies you want, while I'm with your mother and—"

She stopped in mid-sentence as a thought popped into her

head. A perfectly wonderful, amazingly brilliant idea. Her lips parted as she considered...Oh, it would be *perfect*!

Sebastian's eyes flickered in a combined expression of trepidation and alarm at her enthused expression. When her smile widened as she contemplated what she was about to do, his alarmed trepidation only deepened.

She tilted her head thoughtfully. "Will Robert be staying with you in London?"

"Yes, at Park Place." His face darkened with full-out suspicion. "Why?"

She nearly laughed. Oh, a perfectly *amazing* idea! "Then I'll be on my best, perfectly proper behavior," she boldly agreed. Her toes tingled at how flawlessly her season was coming together when only a few moments ago she'd been certain it was ruined. And another chance with Robert right along with it. "In fact, I'll even help you with the ladies if you agree to—"

"How could you possibly help with that?" There was no heat behind the question, only open disbelief. And more apprehension.

She sent him a pitying look. "You have no idea of the true power plays which take place within women's retiring rooms, do you?"

Sebastian only stared at her, his lips parting slightly and his sapphire eyes widening, obviously having no idea how to respond.

"Bachelor," she chided with a shake of her head, softly clucking her tongue at his naïveté. "And you men think you run the country."

"We do," he replied and folded his arms across his broad chest. "Some of us more than others, in fact."

She brushed that off with a wave of her hand. "I will behave myself"—although she knew that was an unnecessary promise because she was certainly capable of avoiding trouble for six months, for goodness' sake—"and I will help you however I can in finding a wife."

A smile of relief tugged at his lips. "Thank you for—"

"*If* you agree to help me with Robert."

He froze, stunned by that. Then he sent her a dubious look, as if she were a bedlamite. Or foolishly in love with a man who had yet to notice her as a woman. "What kind of help, exactly?" he asked deliberately.

"Just to get noticed by him as someone other than me... Well, other than the person he thinks is me, anyway." She grimaced at herself and at the impossible task she was most likely setting for herself. But she had to try. She would never be able to forgive herself if she didn't try one last time to make Robert love her. "To give me a fair chance against Diana Morgan, that's all."

He blew out a weary sigh, his doubting thoughts about her crazy bargain evident in every inch of him. "Miranda—"

"You won't have to do much," she assured him, rapidly trying to persuade him into agreeing and to convince him that she wasn't mad. Or at least, not *very* mad. "The time I'll have together with him will be limited anyway." Especially since she would be staying with Josie and her family. "Just help me be *noticed*, that's all."

He leaned toward her and lowered his voice. "But I've seen how you try to get yourself noticed when it comes to Robert."

"That was a mistake," she whispered.

"Then you agree that you were wrong to sneak into—"

"Oh no," she corrected, blinking. He had it all completely wrong. "I *meant* that it was a mistake to trust the footman. Next time, I'll ask the butler."

He stared at her, his eyes narrowing, and she suspected he

wanted to throttle her right there in the rear garden. "This is madness."

A terrible thought struck her, and her stomach plummeted. "Because you don't think I'm good enough for your brother," she accused, her eyes stinging at the words. "You don't approve of me for him."

"*That* isn't it at all." His eyes softened sympathetically. "We're all fond of you, you know that. Including Robert. We only want the best for you." He paused. "*I* want the best for you."

Something about the way he said that made her heart skip. "The best isn't Robert?"

"I love my brother, and I trust him with my life. He's a wonderful man who would be fortunate to have you." He arched a brow. "I'm just not certain that he's the best man for *you*."

"He is." She said the words with all the conviction she could muster, yet they still sounded thin to her own ears. "You've met Diana Morgan, and you know me. Which one of us do you think is better suited for your brother?"

He stared at her hard for a long moment as he considered that. Then he shook his head. "You'll have to do exactly as I say. Are you willing to do that?"

Hopefulness surged inside her. "You'll help me, then?"

"I won't allow any kind of scandal to damage the family's reputation," he warned, "or to prevent me from finding a proper wife." His blue eyes trained on hers, leaving absolutely no room for misunderstanding on this point. "Not even if it costs you Robert."

"I would never do anything on purpose to harm your family," she told him, her voice filled with enough raw honesty that the doubt in his eyes vanished. "I love your family as much as I do my own, and I would never want to see them hurt. Especially by something I did."

He blew out a long breath. "All right," he agreed, succumbing to her negotiations. "I'll help you with Robert *if* you behave yourself."

Goodness, were they back to *this* again? She jabbed a finger into his chest. "If *you* behave *your*self—"

But the sudden harsh narrowing of his eyes cut her off in mid-sentence, and she slowly pulled her hand away. There were times when she knew she shouldn't push Sebastian, and this was one of those times. Especially since he'd just agreed to help her.

"I mean it, Miranda. I'll only help you with Robert if you don't cause any problems." He added meaningfully, "Like scandalously sneaking into gentlemen's bedrooms wearing masquerade costumes."

Oh, that. *Again.* "That wasn't scandalous." She waved it away. Surely he knew scandals only occurred when people found out what happened. After all, no one had yet found out that she'd also accidentally flooded the butcher's shop when she was thirteen, and she had no intention of telling him. "I made certain no one would know. It was just—"

"Surprising as hell," he admitted with a bewildered frown, "to find you of all women in my bed." He dropped his gaze down her front and murmured, "In that costume."

Everywhere his blue eyes lingered, heat prickled beneath her skin, the same way he'd warmed her body when he'd stared at her bare breasts last night in the firelight. Was he thinking about that, remembering...*Impossible.* Not Sebastian. He certainly wouldn't flirt with *her.* He'd made that perfectly clear last night. When he thought she was Lady Rose, he couldn't keep his hands off her. But when he found out that his enticing Rose was Miranda Hodgkins, he couldn't get away from her fast enough.

Men. Would she ever understand them?

"If I had known it was your room, I never would have gone there." She sniffed peevishly. "After all, you weren't the brother I was looking for."

His face darkened. Instead of being relieved at that, he seemed even more annoyed.

Which only worked to make her more annoyed at *him*. "You and I wouldn't suit at all, Sebastian." She folded her arms crossly over her chest. Reaching for the wooden sword was simply too tempting. "At least Robert knows how to have fun and enjoy himself."

His eyes flared, and a deep heat flickered in their depths. "Make no mistake." He took a single step toward her, suddenly reminding her of the predatory panther from last night as he closed the distance between them until he could whisper in her ear simply by lowering his head. "I most certainly do know how to enjoy myself." His husky voice poured through her like a warm summer rain as his hot breath tickled against her ear. "A few more masked minutes last night, and you would have discovered exactly how much."

She shivered, an unexpected tingle flaring low in her belly. Her breath hitched in her throat, and for a moment, she couldn't move. Didn't *want* to move. What she wanted was another one of those low, throaty whispers of his, another rush of liquid heat through her body landing right *there*, in that private place between her legs. He'd clearly meant his words as a warning, but her foolish body heard an aching promise. From Sebastian, of all men.

Oh Lord—she'd gone mad!

Her slipper still rested in his hand. She made a grab for it, wanting nothing more than to seize it and run, but he jerked it higher just as her fingertips brushed against it.

Propelled forward by the force of her lunge, she fell against him. Her body pressed only briefly against the front of his, but long enough to feel the hard muscles of his chest and thighs against her softness. Long enough that his free arm rose up to encircle her waist and catch her, holding her against him. Long enough for her to remember the warmth of his caressing hands on her hips and breasts, the delicious heat of his mouth on her body—

She shuddered at the electrifying contact and pushed herself away, retreating quickly to put several paces between them.

"I'll agree to the terms of our deal," she whispered, her eyes never leaving his despite the frantic pounding of her heart. Did he have this same effect on other women, this same unsettling pulse of confusion whenever they came too close? The same flash of fear that they might lose themselves in him? If so, then he needed her help in finding a wife more than he realized. Obviously, the man didn't know the first thing about how to behave around women.

Wordlessly, he held out the slipper.

Taking it from his hand, careful not to accidentally touch him, she hid it in her jacket pocket. "And its mate?"

"I'm holding it hostage."

Dread sank through her. "Hostage?"

He nodded, his blond hair shining golden in the sunlight beneath the brim of his beaver hat. "I'll use it to reveal your feelings for Robert if you don't hold up your end of our bargain."

"You wouldn't!" she gasped. Telling Robert how she felt about him had to be done at the right time, in the right way. Being shown proof that she'd been in his brother's bedroom, accidentally or not, was certainly *not* the right way.

He quirked up a brow in challenge, leaning toward her to bring his eyes level with hers. "Blackmail isn't just for Chinese vases."

Her mouth fell open at his audacity, her hands clenching into fists at her sides as her eyes darted toward the wooden sword, now hopelessly out of reach. "You are the most infuriating man who—"

"Who currently possesses your slipper, Lady Rose." At that, he moved back a single step, just far enough to be out of punching range. And rightly so, since he was the one who taught her fisticuffs when she was ten. "You'll get it back when I've found a bride and the marriage offer has been accepted. Not a moment before."

She arched a dubious brow. "And you won't renege on your promise to help me with Robert?"

"I'll help however I can." His eyes softened sympathetically. "But I cannot control his heart."

She glowered at him, knowing she had no choice but to agree. Not if she wanted Robert to fall in love with her. No wonder Sebastian excelled so brilliantly in Parliament if this was how he maneuvered his opponents.

"All right," she forced out grudgingly. "We're agreed, then?"

"We're agreed." He gave her a slow, confident smile.

Miranda stared at him, a riot of emotions bubbling inside her. She'd gotten exactly what she wanted—his help with Robert. So why did she feel as if she'd just struck a deal with the devil?

CHAPTER FOUR

Mayfair, London
One Wintry Month Later

$\mathcal{M}$iranda stared through the window at the grand town house that fronted the wide, tree-lined avenue and somehow kept her mouth from falling open in utter astonishment.

"We've arrived," Elizabeth Carlisle announced from the seat beside her in the carriage that had carried them for the past several days all the way from Lincolnshire. She leaned over to give Miranda a welcoming squeeze of her hand. "Park Place."

"Thank God," Robert muttered as he leaned forward on the bench across from them, where he had spent most of the trip slumped in sleep.

Miranda barely heard his grumbling, her attention rapt on the beautiful house. Four stories high and six bays wide, the house sat right upon the avenue, its red Georgian brick contrasting with its freshly painted white trim and tall portico. It was so much more inviting than those other houses they'd passed as they'd driven the last stretch of the trip by Hyde Park. Those houses, which sat back from the street behind wrought-iron fences, were grand, truly, but they held an air of arrogant inapproachability, while Park Place was inviting, bright...simply perfect.

So was London, every last filthy, congested, smelly inch of it. Oh, it was fabulous! They'd ridden for over two hours through the city, giving her wonderful views of the Thames and the dome of St Paul's, the imposing Tower and the narrow warren of streets and alleys in the City that gave way to the wider roads and avenues as they drove on west toward Mayfair with its tree-lined streets, beautiful open squares, and grand town houses. She'd never seen anything like it. It took her breath away.

She'd been to Lincoln when she was fourteen, on a trip with Uncle Hamish to settle a tax issue, but even that city with its great cathedral and castle was barely a village in comparison to London, with all its houses and large buildings, the crush of carriages and horses in the streets, the bustling pedestrians, and bobbing boats on the river. The city pulsed with excitement and energy, and she could hardly believe that she was finally here. *London!* Her heart sang with it all.

A glance at Robert's tired face as he waited on the edge of his seat for the footman to open the carriage door told her that he did not share her excitement.

But then, nothing during the trip from Lincolnshire had seemed to catch his imagination. He'd been more caught up in the drudgery of the travel than the excitement of it. So after a few attempts at conversation with him that led nowhere, and certainly not to any kind of intimate tête-à-tête that would indicate that he'd actually noticed her, she'd given up and spent her time staring out the window at the passing scenery.

Of course, he also had only his mother and her for

company, so she couldn't blame him too much for wanting to sleep away the hours. Sebastian and Quinton had gone down to London a week before, leaving Robert to accompany the ladies. Miranda suspected he wasn't happy about being trapped in a carriage for four days with the two women, although she was secretly thrilled to have so much time in his company. And more grateful to Sebastian than she wanted to admit for arranging this time with his brother.

The footman opened the door and moved aside with a shallow bow.

Blowing out a weary breath, Robert stepped to the ground and turned back to offer his hand. "Mother."

The duchess placed her hand into his, and he helped her from the carriage, across the footpath, and up the marble steps to the front portico.

Unable to tamp down her enthusiasm and wait for him to return for her, Miranda hurried to her feet and stuck her head out the open door to stare up at the house. Oh, it was grand! And so beautiful. Mesmerized by the splendor of the façade, her eyes trailing from tall window to window, she moved down onto the step—

And missed.

With a soft gasp of surprise, she tumbled forward off-balance toward the ground.

Strong arms swept around her and caught her, lifting her gracefully and placing her gently onto the footpath.

With her view blocked by her new bonnet, she couldn't see the hero behind her who had rescued her, but it must have been Robert. Oh, it simply *had* to be! Her heart raced with equal amounts happiness and embarrassment that she'd fallen into his arms, although . . . should she feign a faint just to remain there a while longer?

Then she saw Robert on the portico, still at his mother's

side, and her heart sank. So it wasn't Robert who had rushed to her rescue after all. It must have been the footman, then, who had been kind enough to save her, except that the man had already moved to the back of the coach to help with the luggage. Which meant...

Oh no.

"Already causing problems, Lady Rose?" a familiar voice whispered teasingly at her ear. "And with your first footstep in London, no less."

Sebastian.

Ignoring the odd flutter he stirred low in her belly, she rolled her eyes, mortified that he of all people should be the one who saw her stumble. She muttered, "At least now I know why they call them *slip*pers."

He laughed. The soft sound rumbled into her back and made her heart race just as fast as before, although this time with equal parts embarrassment and...well, something else that she didn't dare admit to.

As he carefully righted her and set her away from him, Miranda was suddenly very conscious of the duchess's eyes on them, watching them curiously. But Sebastian didn't seem to notice as he smiled and formally greeted her with an incline of his head. "Welcome to Park Place, Miss Hodgkins."

She curtsied with a smile, grateful for his kindness even though it came with a great deal of teasing. "Your Grace."

With a signal to the footmen hurrying from the house to attend to the carriage, he took her arm as if she were a true guest to the house rather than the country girl he was sponsoring for the season. He escorted her inside while his mother and Robert were suddenly caught up in giving directions about sorting the luggage, which pieces should be taken into the house, which left on the carriage.

"Did you have a good trip down?" he asked quietly as he led her through the front foyer with its white marble stairs that wrapped elegantly around the room as they curled toward the landings on the floors above.

"Yes, a lovely time." Miranda craned her neck. She wanted to stop and gawk openly at the gorgeous house unfolding around her, but she'd already embarrassed herself once by not paying attention to where she was going. If she tripped again in front of him— Oh, she'd simply die! "The countryside was beautiful."

At that, he gave her a grimacing smile. The two of them were momentarily alone inside the house as he guided her toward the drawing room, and he lowered his mouth close to her ear. "I meant, did you have the chance to speak to Robert alone as you'd hoped?"

Disappointment panged inside her chest. No, it wasn't at all what she'd hoped. Oh, Robert had been pleasant to her as always and thoroughly doted on the two women whenever they'd stopped at inns along the way. But he'd treated her like a sister under his care rather than a woman he might fall in love with. For heaven's sake, he even called her by that annoying nickname the boys had given her when she was six . . . *sprite*. She cringed at the thought of it.

Unwilling to admit to failure so soon, though, she deflected, "We talked a little in the carriage when he wasn't sleeping." Which was most of the time. But Sebastian didn't need to know that. After all, he'd gone out of his way to make the travel arrangements so that she would be with Robert, and she didn't want him to know how miserably she'd failed to catch his brother's attention.

They reached the drawing room. He let her proceed him into the pretty room, decorated in soft creams and blues, silks and brocades, with delicate gilt edging tall mirrors positioned along the walls beside the floor-to-ceiling windows and two large chandeliers floating overhead. It was the most splendid room she'd ever seen, one that left no question about the Duke of Trent's wealth and position. If she needed a reminder that in London Sebastian was far more than a country estate owner, this room declared it in spades.

"What did you talk about?" he pressed curiously, catching her attention away from the grand room and the plump cherubs chasing each other across the painted ceiling.

"Fishing." She smiled innocently, fluttering her eyelashes.

He drew up short, his eyes widening in surprise. "Fishing?"

"Of course not!" She laughed at him, and his mouth twitched as he realized she was goading him. "Don't worry. I was painfully proper. I kept the conversation on all the appropriate topics for a young lady." She shrugged and untied her bonnet, letting the long ribbons dangle over her shoulders. "The weather, fashions, upcoming season events—"

"With Robert?" he interrupted in an incredulous mutter. "You'd have been better off with fishing."

Well, *that* was rude.

Or perhaps, she reconsidered glumly, he was irritatingly dead-on.

Her shoulders slumped dejectedly. "But those are all acceptable, ordinary topics for conversation."

"There's your problem." His gaze took a deliberate roam over her, drinking her in from the lace-edged hem of her pale green dress and matching velvet pelisse all the way up to her cheeks, which warmed of their own accord. He murmured, "You're not an ordinary woman."

Her lips parted slightly at his soft words, and once again, she found herself not knowing how to take him. Was he insulting her or complimenting her? Should she thank him or slap him? Heavens, the conundrum that was Sebastian Carlisle!

Instead, she puzzled, "Why do you—"

"There you two are!"

He retreated away from her as the duchess swept into the room with a beaming smile for them. Robert followed slowly behind and stopped in the doorway to lean casually against the frame.

Miranda's heart sank as she glanced at him, with an entire grand parlor now stretching between them. At that moment, he felt further away than ever before. She'd lost another opportunity to make him see her in a new light. Truly see *her*.

She glanced thoughtfully between the two brothers. Was Sebastian right? Was she taking the wrong approach by being a proper lady to gain Robert's attention? It was exactly what Sebastian wanted, but Robert didn't seem to notice how hard she was trying. Nor care.

She sighed out a heavy breath. Apparently, she couldn't please either Carlisle brother.

"The bags are sorted, and the trunks are to come on wagons tomorrow. So Miranda and I shall travel on to Audley House now," his mother announced with a sigh. In the soft sound, Miranda heard her longing to be done with the long trip and to settle into the house that the Marquess of Chesney had purchased for his new family just last year and only a few streets away from Park Place, much to the duchess's delight.

The two of them would be staying with the marchioness. Although to Miranda she would always be just Josie, she thrilled with excitement to know that this summer she was going to be the guest of a marquess, even if Robert was living in a separate residence. She only hoped Sebastian stayed true to their agreement now that they were in London and could find a way to arrange more time for her with his brother.

"Would you like to stay for tea?" Sebastian offered. "I'll ring for Saunders."

"No thank you, Trent," the duchess declined with a tired but affectionate smile. "I'm anxious to see Josie and my grandchildren."

Miranda was struck by his mother's use of his title, and her eyes darted to the duke. At Chestnut Hill he was always just Sebastian. More proof that London was a far cry from the casual country life of Islingham Village.

As she looked at him now, tall and imperial and perfectly matching the impressive grandeur of the city around them, she couldn't help but wonder where he preferred to be. Where he most felt free to be himself, where he was happiest...the village where everyone had known him since he was a boy, or the city where he was recognized as being the respected peer he had become. And how did he ever reconcile the two?

His mother tugged at her travel gloves. "I will send you copies of our schedules and all the events you will need to attend as Miranda's escort. Most likely, we shall need two weeks to shop for all the necessary accessories and have her dresses made." Elizabeth smiled at her with all the affection of a mother doting on her daughter, and Miranda's chest tightened with affection at the duchess's kindness. "You cannot be officially presented at court, of course, but I will arrange for an informal invitation to a drawing room with Queen Charlotte, if you'd like."

Miranda caught her breath as unexpected joy shot through her. A drawing room with the queen? Oh, she'd never dared to hope for something as extraordinary as that!

Sensing her excitement, Sebastian shot her a quelling

glance. "Make certain you purchase the proper kind of shoes, Miss Hodgkins," he warned, subtly reminding her of their agreement in a private language his mother and brother didn't understand. "We wouldn't want you getting into trouble. Would we, Robert?"

"Miranda can handle herself," Robert answered with a wink at her that sent nervous butterflies flitting inside her belly.

She stared at him, stunned into silence and unable to do anything but stand there and blush.

"Besides, we taught the sprite how to box when she was ten, remember? I think I can still feel the bruise she gave my chin." Another teasing wink…but this time, the butterflies dropped away with a sinking disappointment. Even after all those days together in the carriage, Robert still thought of her as nothing more than the girl next door.

"Miranda's a grown woman now," Sebastian reminded him gently. "In case you hadn't noticed."

Her chest soared. Oh, she could have kissed Sebastian for that!

His eyes met hers, and she thought she saw a dark flicker in their sapphire depths, one that made her suddenly and inexplicably nervous— Well, maybe not *kiss* him…

"I know how old she is," Robert assured him. "I went to her last birthday party when she turned twenty-one. You were there, too. Don't you remember?"

Sebastian's mouth twisted at that.

So did Miranda's.

"Robert's right. I am capable of taking care of myself," she mumbled her reply even as her heart thumped with frustration. But she was still happy to finally be in London for her season, and not even this latest setback with Robert could ruin her excitement. "Don't worry," she threw back at

Sebastian with a confident smile. "I know what slippers I need... and exactly where to find them."

Sebastian's eyes narrowed briefly at that, although she couldn't have said whether in annoyance at her cheek or admiration at her resolve. Nor did she have time to ponder which as Elizabeth Carlisle placed a kiss on both of her sons' cheeks to say good-bye, then wrangled a firm promise from Robert not to burn down the house as she took Miranda's arm to lead her out to the waiting carriage.

As she slipped from the room, Miranda tossed a hopeful glance over her shoulder at Robert with the brightest smile she could manage. But he only nodded a good-bye in her general direction and finally entered the room to flop down across the settee.

Her belly tightened with defeat. Fate hated her, that was it. That was why she was able to talk so easily with Sebastian and on all kinds of levels—apparently even secret ones—when she couldn't manage a simple conversation about the weather with Robert. Sebastian Carlisle, of all men! The brother she couldn't care less about... but the one she desperately needed if she had any prayer at all of catching Robert's heart.

* * *

When the two women left, Sebastian sat back on one of the wide window ledges and crossed his arms over his chest, his legs kicked out in front of him. He contemplated his brother, lying all akimbo across the settee with one foot sticking over the arm and the other tossed over the back, resembling a half-dead, drunken sailor on shore leave.

He was unable to squelch his curiosity. "So, how was the trip down?"

"Torturous," Robert groaned. He opened one eye, as if too worn out to open both, and squinted across the room at him. "Four days of female chatter and roads rough enough to kill both my kidneys. I'm lucky I survived."

Sebastian's mouth curled in amusement. Under other circumstances, he most likely would have enjoyed the unintended retribution he'd inflicted upon his brother for previous trips to the city when he'd been forced to escort Mother and Josie while Robert and Quinn came separately with Father. But right then, he had other concerns. Strawberry-blond, freckled-nosed ones. "Miranda managed well, then?"

"As well as can be expected. Mother simply adores her, you know, for what she did for her after Father's death. The two of them kept up a running stream of conversation the whole way." The other eye opened, and as he leaned up on one elbow to make his point, he glared at his brother with an expression somewhere between hang-dog self-pity and exasperation. "Four days of chatter about the weather, Parisian dressmakers, and the poetry of John Milton."

"She likes Milton?" he mused, oddly struck by that.

Robert closed both eyes and flopped back onto the settee, his hand covering his face. "Does anyone?"

"I do," Sebastian mumbled with a faint shrug.

"Then next time you can ride all the way from Lincolnshire with the two of them, listening to them expounding on multiple layers of symbolism and debating whether individual or societal influences were more important to Milton." He paused, then repeated slowly for emphasis, "*Societal influences*...Miranda actually used those exact words and expected me to have an opinion."

"And did you?"

He cracked open an eye and stared at his brother as if he'd gone mad. "I had no idea what she was talking about."

Sebastian smiled with amusement. He enjoyed Milton, but he was surprised as hell that Miranda did, too. "Didn't you learn anything at Oxford?"

"Yes."

He raised a brow.

"How to pretend to sleep in a coach."

Something inside his chest tore for Miranda at his brother's answer, and his smile faded. "Please tell me you didn't. Not all four days."

"Self-preservation, Seb. If I had to endure one more conversation between her and Mother about the merits of Belgian lace, I would have gone mad."

No wonder Miranda had put on a brave face when they arrived. She must have been heartbroken that Robert hadn't paid her any attention. "Did she enjoy herself, at least?"

"I believe so." He closed his eye again. "Her nose was pressed to the window for the entire trip."

Sebastian smiled at the image of Miranda behaving like a child at a candy shop. But he supposed the analogy was the same. To a vivacious, curious woman like her, England was a tempting treat to be savored. She'd never been out of Lincolnshire in her life, and every mile must have brought new sights and delights she'd only dreamt about. He could well imagine the stories she'd have to tell the orphans when she returned.

Good thing they hadn't driven through the moors, or she'd be adding all kinds of new scenes to *King Lear*.

Sebastian fished for more answers as he pried smoothly, "Did you have any time alone with her?"

"Only at night."

His gut clenched so hard, so fast that he lost his breath. *At night?* Had he completely misread this whole conversation? Had Miranda and Robert...*Good God.* His mind conjured all kinds of images of nighttime antics between the two of them at posting inns across England.

He took a deep breath and asked as calmly as possible when what he inexplicably wanted to do was wring his brother's neck for touching her, "Pardon?"

"At dinner when we'd stopped for the night at the inns," Robert clarified with a careless shrug.

An unexpected rush of relief coursed through Sebastian. He slowly unclenched his fists and blew out a silent breath. "You were able to talk to her then, to get to know her better?"

Robert opened both eyes and looked at him as if he'd lost his mind. Then again, he'd agreed to help Miranda find her way into his brother's heart. Perhaps he *had* gone mad. "I already know her, Seb. We all grew up together— Well, not you. You were away at school." He closed his eyes and slumped back down. "Maybe you're the one who needs to get to know her better."

That was the last thing Sebastian needed to do. After the night of the masquerade, he couldn't come to know her any better without taking her innocence. "I already know her," he said, carefully keeping his voice even. "She's become a fine woman."

"With more energy than anyone should possess. Good Lord! She wore me out, and all we did was sit together in a carriage."

"She simply enjoys herself, that's all." Although why he felt compelled to defend her, Sebastian had no idea. But Robert's criticism of her enthusiasm for life annoyed him. Most likely because down deep he couldn't help but be jealous that she could be so free with her life when he was trapped in his. "She's actually quite bright, enjoys drama and Shakespeare—"

"Thank God she didn't bring *him* up," Robert muttered.

Sebastian said nothing as he watched his brother drop his legs to the floor and sit up. Four days together in a carriage, and Robert still knew nothing about the woman Miranda had become. Sebastian felt sorry for him.

But he felt even sorrier for Miranda. If she didn't make Robert see her in a completely different light, as someone new and exciting rather than the neighbor girl he'd always known, she didn't stand a chance with his brother.

Before this season was over, Sebastian predicted, her heart would be shattered, no matter how much he helped her. He only hoped she had the strength to pull herself together and move on to another man. One more suited for her. One more tolerant of her enthusiasm and zest for living. Perhaps some nice gentleman farmer or banker's son—

"You?"

Sebastian's eyes snapped up to his brother's. Dear God, had he muttered his thoughts aloud? "Pardon?"

"I asked, how are you? How's your hunt for a wife going?"

Oh. Thank God that was all. With a silent exhalation, he pushed himself away from the window. "Good so far. I've made a list of names of promising ladies."

"As long as Diana's name isn't on it. I don't need the competition among the petticoat set. And speaking of petticoats..." Robert grinned. "Where's Quinton?"

"At White's with Chesney and Strathmore." Sebastian crossed to the fireplace and helped himself to one of the American cigars he stored in the humidor box on the mantel. "He's angling for membership."

"Does he stand a chance?" A defeated note sounded in

his voice. Understandably. Because if Quinn got member-ship, then Robert could be listed as his guest, and both brothers could come and go from the club as they pleased without having to wait for Chesney or Sebastian to accom-pany them.

"Yes." He bit off the end of the cheroot and spat it into the fire. "Quite certain of it, in fact."

Robert blinked with incredulity at the underlying impli-cation of that comment. "You petitioned the other members on his behalf?"

He nodded. "So did Chesney and Strathmore."

"Damn, that was good of you, Seb."

Bending down to light the cigar on the flames, he shrugged away the compliment. "I'd do anything for Quin-ton, you know that."

At that comment, Robert eyed him suspiciously. "And if doing this favor for Quinn also means it's easier for you to keep an eye on him at the same club where you belong?"

"A delightful bonus." He arched a knowing brow. This was Quinton they were discussing, after all. God only knew the trouble he'd get himself into on St James's Street on his own. And Sebastian truly did love his brothers, enough to keep them from their own destruction.

Robert laughed. "You getting Quinn a membership at White's...Good to know the old Sebastian isn't completely dead after all."

He fixed his brother with a hard look, suddenly irritated. "What do you mean by that?" he demanded, rising to his full height.

"That lately you behave like you're older than Moses but only have half as much fun. What happened to the brother who used to lead us into debauchery and trouble? The one who used to know how to have a good time. Who let himself actually *have* a good time in the first place."

"He became a duke," he answered quietly.

Robert must have heard the weariness in his voice, because his eyes softened. "Enjoy yourself this season, Seb, will you? It's London, for God's sake...a playground for rakes, rogues, and newly minted peers. It would be a shame if you sliced into a wedding cake before you had the chance to sample the tarts."

Sebastian grimaced at his entendre.

Leaning forward, elbows on knees, Robert grew sober. "I'm serious. Enjoy yourself." Concern darkened his face. "You've been working hard since you inherited. Too hard. No one can say you haven't made the title and your family your first concern in everything. Or not done Father proud."

Sebastian looked down at his cigar, studying the red tip as he rolled it in his fingers, his jaw clenched tight and saying nothing. *Damnation.* He didn't need to be lectured on his life by his little brother, who had no idea of how heavy his burdens were, no idea of the depth of the promises he'd made to their father. Or the stranglehold those promises still had on his life.

"So let yourself have a little fun this season, all right? You've earned it." Robert pushed off the settee, then helped himself to a cigar, tucking it inside his breast pocket as he headed for the door. "I'm going out to find Quinn. Join up with us later, all right? It'll be just like old times. Except without the belly dancers." He grinned as he disappeared out the door. "Maybe."

Staring daggers after him, Sebastian clenched the cigar between his teeth. Robert was wrong. He wasn't behaving like a curmudgeon. He was behaving like a responsible peer, one with his family's reputation and new title to worry about. One who would never let them down again.

Robert didn't understand the pressure he was under—*no one* understood. He was a new duke whom most claimed was an upstart who didn't deserve to be granted the title in the first place, whom every member of the quality would be watching like a hawk this season to see if he had the mettle to be a leader in the Lords and the presence to be socially acceptable. He could never take a single step nor make any decision without considering the ramifications of its outcome on his family, the tenants, all the estate workers and villagers...and most importantly, on his father's legacy. He could no longer be carefree and blithely happy the way his brothers could.

No matter how much he longed to be.

CHAPTER FIVE

Two Busy Weeks Later

*D*on't you think the palace is simply grand?" Miranda couldn't help but beam an excited smile as she sat on the corner of the picnic blanket spread over the lawn in Hyde Park and tried to engage Robert in conversation as he lay stretched out across the blanket next to her. Sebastian lay in the same pose on the other end of the blanket, watching and listening, and inexplicably making her nervous, even when saying nothing at all. "So many colors and gold leaf, such a beautiful gallery filled with paintings and portraits— Oh! And luxurious silks and brocades everywhere."

"I'd love to have gone to the palace mews." Robert plucked a blade of grass and focused his attention on folding it between his fingers. "Did you have a chance to visit them? Rumors say King George has the finest four-in-hand team in England."

Miranda's chest sank with a dull thud. She'd hoped she could impress him with her visit to court, even just a little, and convince him that she was just as fine as Diana Morgan because of it. Apparently, she would have been better off by taking her tea in the royal stables.

"No," she mumbled, "I didn't see any horses."

"Miranda had other things to worry about," Sebastian reminded Robert quietly as he lay on the opposite side of the blanket, the two men resembling golden bookends. "It was her first time at court, remember."

"And my last," she sighed with a touch of bittersweet appreciation now that it was over. Yet her spirits weren't dampened at all by knowing that her only visit to court was for an unofficial presentation to the queen with a dozen other young ladies and their sponsors, because it would be a day she'd never forget. "But it was truly marvelous."

The whole affair was wonderfully special for her, and she couldn't stop smiling. She'd been introduced like a real lady—to the queen! Elizabeth Carlisle had been so very kind to her, and Miranda couldn't help but wonder if this was what it was like to have a mother. Someone to fuss over her and look at her with pride and affection. She liked it, a great deal.

None of the Carlisle men had accompanied the women yesterday, not even Sebastian, as no men were allowed into the queen's drawing room. So when this afternoon proved unusually mild for March, Elizabeth Carlisle had insisted on a family outing to the park to celebrate. On the wide lawn stretching between the tree plantations and the Serpentine, Josie played with her toddler son and her six-year-old adopted daughter, and Thomas Matteson hovered nearby, as always an attentive father and husband. Quinn and Elizabeth Carlisle strolled a turn about the park to stretch their legs after the family picnic, the remnants of which still lay scattered on china dishes across the blanket in front of them.

Sebastian returned her smile. "I'm glad you enjoyed yourself. *My* first visit to court was rather disastrous."

"Oh?" Her curiosity pricked, she leaned toward him, mindful of the skirt of her yellow afternoon dress spread around her. "What happened?"

"My father had been summoned to see the king, so Mother and I waited in one of the drawing rooms. I was just four at the time." His eyes crinkled at the memory. "Somehow, I managed to sneak away from the nanny and wandered off."

"We were always sneaking away from Nanny," Robert put in with an impish grin at his older brother. "Sebastian was the ringleader *and* the one who got us out of trouble whenever we got caught."

"Which was all the time," Sebastian admitted when Miranda laughed lightly at that perfect description of the young man he'd been, long before she came to know him. "But Robert and Quinton weren't born yet, so I was on my own to cause trouble that day."

Miranda had never heard this story before, and she found herself seeing a whole new side to him. And, surprisingly, liking it. "And did you?"

"Heaps worth." His eyes sparkled at her as he reached toward the fruit plate to pluck off a grape. "I made my way into the formal dining room, where I fell asleep beneath the table. By the time the footmen found me two hours later, the entire palace was in an uproar." He laughed at the memory. "I cried inconsolably because I thought they would rescind Father's barony because I'd misbehaved."

A soft smile played at her lips. Sebastian as a little boy...she could barely fathom it. Always before, whenever she thought of Sebastian as a small child, she'd imagined him the same. Only shorter.

During these past two weeks in London, though, she'd come to see a different side of him, and it wasn't so hard to imagine him as a little boy now. Or see how much the title and all its obligations weighed on him. Did that little boy—for that matter, the carefree young man he'd been only a few years before—have any idea of the staid, responsible man waiting for him? And would he like the man he'd become?

And then, there was Robert. The more time she spent together with the two men, the more she began to realize how very different they were. Oh, they looked alike, with the same golden hair and blue eyes, the same tall and broad build, and especially right now, with the two of them lying on the blanket like matching statues. But their personalities were completely different, especially since Sebastian had inherited. Robert had sobered since Richard Carlisle's death; so had Quinton, to a lesser extent. But not like Sebastian. Sebastian had changed completely beneath the burden of the title, and despite the frustration and annoyance he often stirred inside her, in this aspect of his life at least, her heart ached for him. She wanted him to be happy, and she wasn't certain he was.

"And you, Robert?" She initiated another attempt to engage him in conversation. She refused to wave the white flag of surrender just yet—she *wouldn't*. "Have you been to court?"

"A few times. Not often." He shrugged his shoulders. "The royals don't usually want my sort anywhere near them."

"Your sort?" She frowned.

He gave her a half grin and reached over to tickle her on the nose with the blade of grass. "A Carlisle."

Forcing a soft laugh, she rubbed the tip of her nose. He was teasing her, like always. She should be happy about that, yet her chest squeezed with doubt. Could she actually be losing ground with him? After all, in her heart she knew that he would never have tickled Miss Morgan on her nose. It simply didn't seem like the type of flirtation a man would make toward a woman he found alluring enough to court.

"How about Almack's, then?" Her fingers pulled nervously at her lace-edged skirt hem, but she kept her bright smile firmly in place. Trying to keep a conversation going with the man was proving to be nearly impossible. The cold truth nibbled at the backs of her knees that she'd never had to try so hard with him in the past, when they were only friends. But now that her pursuits were serious, oh heavens, was there anything she could do to make him notice her as a woman? "We're going there for the first time tomorrow evening."

"Whyever for?" Robert fixed her with an expression somewhere between shock and dismay.

Miranda stared back in surprise. She certainly hadn't expected *that* reaction, and she glanced quickly at Sebastian to figure out what she'd done wrong this time, only to find him frowning disapprovingly at his brother.

"Because I have to have my interview there," she explained, her smile faltering, "so I can have my debut and waltz in the assembly rooms. The duchess said...Doesn't everyone go to Almack's?"

"Only ladies desperate to snag a husband from among a flock of sheep." He threw away the blade of grass and sat up. "And that's not you, sprite."

He rested his elbows on his bent knees and arched a brow at her. Finally, she had his full attention on her. But instead of making her feel warm and special, she felt uncomfortable. And increasingly worried that he would never see her as anything but the girl next door. The *sprite* who apparently needed his protection from gentlemen in assembly rooms.

He continued, "I thought the goal of your season was to simply have a good time in London, not find a husband."

"I suppose," Miranda deflected quietly, unable to answer truthfully that she did want a husband—*him*. She focused her attention once more on her skirt, lowering her face so he wouldn't see any traces of the frustration and disappointment churning inside her. Or give away her true feelings for him, which at that moment were also a churning knot of frustration and disappointment. "I didn't realize about Almack's..."

She'd had her invitation to court, and that had been a fairy tale. Nothing short of a perfect dream come true. Tomorrow night at Almack's would be her second official outing, to get the patronesses' approval, and then she could enjoy her own debut at the Countess of St James's annual ball, accept callers, and most thrilling of all, to waltz! She couldn't think of anything more romantic than whirling around the dance floor in a man's arms. Elizabeth Carlisle and Josie had both assured her that this was all the proper, appropriate sequence for a debut.

But now... she wasn't so certain of anything.

"Almack's is perfectly fine," Sebastian told her, reaching over to give a reassuring tug at her half-boot, just sticking out from beneath her hem. He grinned at her, then slid a sideways glance at his brother. "Robert doesn't like the place because they refuse to serve liquor, and he can't waste away the evening there gambling or talking business."

That made her feel better—slightly—and a faint smile tugged at her lips. "Then I shouldn't be concerned about flocks of male sheep?"

"Certainly not." Despite the smile on Sebastian's face,

she easily saw the concern for her in his eyes. Was he beginning to doubt her and their pact? Or had he already come to believe what she was beginning to suspect, that she and Robert were destined to be nothing more than friends? "Besides, the plans have already been made. Strathmore's going to escort you, and the colonel will definitely keep all the sheep away from you." He paused, barely a heartbeat, but Miranda noticed. Lately, and annoyingly, it seemed she couldn't help but notice every move Sebastian made. "And I would hate for you to miss the experience."

Her eyes stung at his kindness, and she blinked. Drat him for being nice to her. She knew how to handle Sebastian when he was being bossy and duke-like; she even knew how to ignore him whenever he was set on aggravating her. Which was quite often. But when he was being charming and agreeable like this, he confused the daylights out of her.

"Thank you," she whispered.

He popped the grape into his mouth, saying nothing. But his eyes sparkled at her and once more sent up that nervous fluttering low in her belly.

She cleared her throat and tried again to engage Robert in a conversation. "I hear that the new French fashions—"

"Are you going to Tattersall's tomorrow?" Sebastian interrupted, so suddenly that he caught Miranda by surprise. When she parted her lips to continue with her original comment, he slid her a pointed look and continued, "Heard Nathaniel Reed has a hunter for sale that he trained himself. Rumors are that his horses are good enough to rival Jackson Shaw's."

"I've heard that," Robert answered with interest. "Shaw has better bloodlines, but Reed's horses are better trained."

Miranda stared between the two men in disbelief as they

fell easily into a conversation about horses. Horses! She was a woman, she wasn't supposed to talk about *horses*. Didn't they know—

Oh.

She held Sebastian's gaze as understanding fell through her. Robert liked horses, so he would undoubtedly like a woman who liked horses, which was why Sebastian had steered the conversation there...to help her. But her heart sank anew. The large beasts simply terrified her. She knew nothing about horses, but she did know about...

"Fishing," she announced loudly, barging back into the conversation with all the subtlety of a church bell at midnight.

Both sets of blue eyes swung to stare at her with surprise, as if she'd just declared herself Queen of England.

Now that she had their attention, she smiled and hurried on, "I've heard that the salmon fishing in England rivals that of Scotland."

Robert glanced past her at Sebastian with an amused look she didn't understand. "I certainly hope so. So does Quinn." Ignoring both Sebastian's irritated scowl at his comment and Miranda's bewilderment, Robert pushed himself to his feet and brushed off his trousers. Apparently, the conversation was over before it had even begun. "Diana Morgan is walking along the Serpentine with Lady Jane Sheridan. I should go say hello."

Miranda's heart tore again, just a little bit more. How much more could she take of watching Robert with Diana before it ripped completely in two?

Robert looked down at Sebastian. "Isn't Lady Jane one of the women on your list?"

"Yes," Sebastian answered, the finality of the single word indicating that he wished to share nothing more about Lady

Jane Sheridan, the daughter of the Earl of Bentham and the woman whom retiring room gossip claimed was in the running to be that season's Incomparable. And whom Miranda knew had sparked Sebastian's interest.

Miranda watched her across the park, walking so smoothly as to almost glide over the grass, her face carefully shielded from the sun by a large bonnet and lace parasol, while Miranda's own bonnet sat unused by her side. Unable to resist the warmth of the afternoon sun, she'd removed the stiff, stuffy thing, even though the sun would certainly dot more freckles across her nose. Miranda doubted that Lady Jane had ever suffered a freckle in her life.

She sniffed and looked away. "She's beautiful."

"Not as beautiful as Diana," Robert put in, and his unwitting words felt like a knife to her chest. "I'll put in a good word for you, Seb."

"Don't you dare," Sebastian warned.

Robert laughed away the threat and gave Miranda a nod as he departed.

She stared after him, utterly at a loss. How did women like Miss Morgan and Lady Jane so easily capture men's attentions, while she struggled to make them notice that she was even in the room? Were ladies like that born with skills of seduction, or did they learn them? And if they'd learned them, then Miranda dearly wished someone would take pity on her and tell her how.

She watched Robert saunter up to the two women, who held their parasols daintily over their shoulders like porcelain dolls—

Another tug at her foot stole back her attention.

She turned to find Sebastian's blue eyes studying her curiously.

"Salmon fishing?" he repeated gently. She was grateful

that he had the decency to interject surprise into his voice rather than pity.

Her shoulders dropped in defeat. "Well, I had to try something."

After two weeks in London, she was having a grand time, almost as if living in a fairy tale, and all of it was so much more thrilling and exciting than she'd ever imagined.

Except for Robert.

He still treated her as nothing more than a younger sister, and she had yet to capture his interest. Or his attention. Annoyingly, she froze up whenever she was around him or said such inane things that he must have thought she was a goose. *Salmon fishing*...Oh, what a nick-ninny she was!

"What's the matter, Miranda?" Bewildered curiosity laced his voice. "Why can't you manage a conversation with him?"

She turned away, disheartened, as unshed tears stung her eyes. He made it sound so simple. As if she could just open her lips and enrapture Robert with her charm and wit. The way Miss Morgan did. Sebastian had no idea how difficult that was for her.

Difficult? *Impossible.*

"Because I'm always too nervous," she admitted quietly. "I want him to believe that I'm...That is, I—I don't think...If I could just..." She tossed up her hands in frustration. She couldn't even talk *about* him without tongue-tying herself. How was she ever supposed to be able to talk directly *to* the man? "With Robert, there's too much pressure to be..." She shrugged as her voice drifted off.

"Be what?" he prompted.

Then she sighed heavily, confessing to her deficiencies with a sag of her shoulders. "Someone interesting."

"You are," he assured gently.

She rolled her eyes. He was lying, she was certain of it. Sebastian Carlisle found her to be a lot of things—annoying, pestering, far too boisterous for her own good—but she was certain that interesting was not one of them. Still, it was sweet of him to say so.

"But not to Robert." She grimaced at herself, the past three weeks proving how truly dismal she was when it came to engaging him in stimulating conversation. Or any conversation at all. "I just can't *talk* to him."

Sebastian reached for a grape from the fruit plate, his eyes lowering away from her. "You don't have that problem with me."

"That's because you don't signify."

"Thank you," he drawled sarcastically, popping the grape into his mouth.

"You know what I mean," she scolded. "There's nothing to be nervous about with you because I don't want to impress you."

"Thank you," he repeated in the same sarcastic drawl.

Then she laughed, both at the sardonic expression on his face and at her own silliness, and pressed her hand against her mouth as she shook with laughter.

"Apologies," she choked out as she fought back her giggles. "It's just that you—well, you're a duke, so I don't have to make a good impression on you."

He crooked a brow silently at that, letting her dig herself deeper. And at this rate, she'd be to China by nightfall.

"That's *not* what I meant! I meant that Robert is more important than you." Her hand flew up to her mouth in mortification as she realized what she'd just said. Apparently, she couldn't talk to any of the Carlisle men without sounding like a goose. "Oh, I didn't mean *that*!"

With a stoic expression, he plucked one of the grapes

from the plate and took a quick glance over her shoulder at the lawn and his family scattered along its length to make certain no one was paying them any attention. Then he sat up and held the grape to her lips. "Open," he ordered.

She hesitated, suspicious at his sudden graciousness. Then she opened her mouth as he'd asked, and he popped the grape inside.

"That's better," he murmured as she ate the grape, unable to say anything more and dig herself even deeper. When she saw the twinkle of amusement in his eyes, she burst out into a new fit of laughter, nearly choking on the grape.

He grinned at her, one of the old smiles she remembered from when he was younger and carefree, before he became so serious. It was nice. Quite nice.

She quickly chewed and swallowed as the last of the laughter eased from her. "Sebastian, I am sorry, truly. I didn't mean any of that the way it sounded."

"Apology accepted."

He reclined again, once more assuming a pose that only Sebastian could somehow make simultaneously casual and imperial. The perfect picture of a powerful gentleman at leisure.

"I suppose I should address you as Trent when we're in London," she considered, struck by how every inch of him declared him to be the duke he was, even while stretched across a picnic blanket.

His amusement faded. "Please don't."

"All right," she agreed quietly, but in that fleeting moment, she sensed the weight of the title on his shoulders and knew how much he must appreciate the rare moments when he didn't have to be a peer. Like now. When he could be just Sebastian. "But only when we're alone, or I fear your mother will make me memorize more passages from

Debrett's because she doesn't think I understand how peerages work."

He looked at her in disbelief. "Has she?"

Miranda sighed wearily as she nodded and reached for a sugared orange slice from the fruit plate. "She means well, I know. She thinks that knowing who everyone is will keep me from embarrassing myself by saying the wrong thing." Not meeting his gaze, she stared down at the orange, her fingertips idly brushing off the sugar as she commented softly, "I'm not, you know."

"What's that?" he asked gently.

"Trouble."

She didn't have to look at him to know that he'd stiffened. She could feel it, so aware had she become of him since their encounter the night of the masquerade. "So you don't have to worry that I'll do anything scandalous this season and cause embarrassment for you. At least not on purpose." She smiled faintly at the orange slice. "But trouble does seem to find me, doesn't it?"

When he didn't say anything, his silence confirming her suspicions, she lifted her eyes and met his as he looked at her solemnly.

"Perhaps I used to be like that," she confided, "before I took over running the orphanage, but I'm not anymore." Just as she was beginning to doubt that Robert might ever see her for who she was, she was also beginning to doubt the same in Sebastian, no matter that she'd now been in London for two weeks and had managed so far to avoid getting herself into any sticky spots. "But you know me from when I was just a child, so you know all the silly things I did before I grew up. I'm ten years younger than you, remember, five for Robert and four for Quinn... You were all so much older than me, and whenever I visited Chestnut Hill—"

"Which was all the time," he interrupted with the start of a smile.

She smiled back, she couldn't help it. "Yes, I suppose." She took a deep breath and turned her attention back to the orange slice. "By the time I grew up, you were gone—Eton, Oxford, London. But in your eyes, I never grew up, did I? To you, I'm still just the same awkward and annoying girl from next door that I've always been."

She glanced up to catch him watching her, and from the guiltily thoughtful expression on his face, she knew she was right.

"I just want to help Auntie and Uncle, the villagers, your family... all the people I love. And sometimes that puts me in over my head." Her fingers pulled idly at the orange slice, the same way Robert had worried at that blade of grass. "I couldn't help my parents, you know. I was too young when they fell ill with fever. The physician wouldn't even let me into the room to see them because he was afraid I'd catch it, too."

She didn't dare look at him now, afraid of what she might see on his face... disbelief, annoyance, pity. Oh, that would be the worst of all! Because she wasn't telling him this to garner his pity; she simply wanted him to understand her. After all, if she couldn't get Sebastian to see her as a competent, strong woman, how on earth would Robert?

"The housekeeper made me sit in a chair in the hallway outside their door, for hours and hours each day. Each day eventually became weeks... I couldn't stand it. To be forced to sit still like that was bad enough, but to hear my parents inside their room only a few feet away, unable to go to them no matter how much I cried—" Her throat choked around the words.

"I'm sorry, Miranda," he murmured gently. He reached

out and rested his hand on her foot, and the physical connection soothed her. "I had no idea."

"I've never told anyone before," she whispered. What good would it have done? What good would there have been in pity? "I suppose I've been trying to make up for that ever since, to help everyone in any way I can." She forced a smile despite the stinging in her eyes at the fuzzy memories she had of that terrible time. "Truly, I don't go looking for trouble. It just seems to find me on its own." She tore off an end of the orange slice and thoughtfully chewed it with a contemplative frown. "I think it follows me around, just waiting to pounce."

At that, he laughed softly. The warm sound rumbled over her like a soft summer rain. "It doesn't lie in wait to pounce on you," he assured her, amusement rich in his deep voice.

"Oh?" she challenged lightly, lifting a brow. "Unlike a *panther*, then?"

He froze, the laughter dying away. "Point taken," he admitted, then cleared his throat. "But no one sees you as a child, Miranda. We just don't know what to make of you."

His comment pricked at her. "What do you mean?"

"Well, for one, you never sit still. You wear a man out just watching you. You're excited about every new experience, seeing every day as a new adventure—"

"It is." She stared blankly at him, not comprehending his point. Life was meant to be lived, to be embraced. Her parents' deaths taught her that. No matter that *he* seemed to have forgotten that since he inherited. "What's wrong with that?"

"Nothing. Except that so few people have that, that no one knows what to do with you."

"Including you, apparently," she accused with a peeved sniff.

He quirked a brow. "*Especially* me."

No, he knew exactly what to do...blackmail her for her slippers in exchange for good behavior. Although, she would have to admit, her London season was going remarkably well, most likely due to his influence and supervision. And he'd honored their agreement, going out of his way to help her with Robert, even if all their attempts had so far come to nothing. She owed him that much credit, at least. But she'd certainly never admit it to him.

"You have a nice laugh," she acknowledged softly instead, giving up completely on the orange and setting it aside. She sucked the drops of juice from her fingers. "You should laugh more often."

"Thank you," he murmured huskily.

When she looked over at him, her fingertips still at her lips, she caught him watching her, his eyes glued to her mouth. A heat flashed over his face so intense that she shivered. That same tingling from the night of the masquerade began to stir faintly inside her, and her pounding heart leapt into her throat. When his eyes lifted slowly to hers and held her pinned beneath his gaze, the tingle blossomed into a full-out ache.

"You're welcome," she breathed, her eyes never leaving his. She simply didn't have the willpower to look away. And a very confused, increasingly warm and tingly part of her didn't want to. Did he feel that, too? Was he just as confused as she was? Gathering her courage, she asked in a whisper, "The night of the masquerade when I was in your room, did you want— That is, have you thought—"

"Are you enjoying London?" he asked abruptly, tearing his gaze away and sitting up.

She blinked, her question choking on her lips. He'd interrupted her before she could ask if he ever thought about that night, about what they did—about what they'd *nearly* done. Because she still did, almost every night since, wondering what would have happened if she'd not made that slip of her tongue and unwittingly revealed herself.

She had to pause a moment to digest both the sudden change in conversation and the sudden change in him. But then, it was simply Sebastian returning to his duke-like self, wasn't it? The surprise, she supposed, was having for a few moments the concerned, sympathetic man who had listened to her about her frustrations over Robert and who understood the ghosts in her past. And who for a moment felt free enough to laugh.

"Yes, very much," she answered, ignoring the peculiar pang of disappointment in her chest. "A marvelous time, in fact."

"Good to hear." But nothing in the tone of his voice concurred with his words.

"And you?" The devil inside her couldn't help but ask, "Have you found any women to marry?"

He grimaced. "Good lord, you make it sound like a harem."

She laughed, which only caused his frown to deepen and her laughter to grow at his expense. "It is—the English equivalent, anyway. It's the marriage market, and you're a duke." She shrugged. "Most likely, you *could* have a harem of women trailing after you if you let yourself."

"I am not letting myself," he countered with an indignant scowl.

Robert's parting words came back to her. "But you've made a list."

He gave a curt nod. "A list is always helpful in making important decisions."

"I'm certain," she agreed with mock solemnity, fighting back the twitch at her lips.

He shot her a sideways glare that choked away all the laughter. Apparently, his search for a wife was not a matter of amusement.

She cleared her throat. "I will help you however I can, of course." They'd kept to their agreement, with Sebastian assisting her as much as he could with Robert and Miranda telling him whatever insights she'd gained from retiring room gossip and other *on dit* at the events she'd attended. So far, it seemed that every eligible lady in London was all aflutter that the Duke of Trent was seeking a wife this season. Including Lady Jane Sheridan. "So Lady Jane is on your list."

"Yes." His gaze traveled across the park to find the earl's lovely daughter still standing with her delicate parasol beside the pond, smiling serenely and chatting with Robert and Miss Morgan. "She has all the right qualities for a duchess."

"I see." Miranda frowned as she studied the woman. All the right qualities...Odd that she'd never before considered that a duchess should possess *qualities*. She'd simply thought they only needed to be loved, the way his father had loved his mother.

"She's the daughter of an earl, of an old title and a well-respected family," he commented, as if justifying his choice. "She'll know her role, both in society and in our marriage."

She bit her lip. Yes, Lady Jane was certainly all that, and more. She would undoubtedly make a fine Duchess of Trent.

But Miranda wasn't certain she'd make a good wife for Sebastian.

"And she knows how to run a large household like that at Blackwood Hall," he continued.

"Chestnut Hill, you mean," she corrected in surprise, her gaze swinging to him.

"Once we're married, we'll reside at Blackwood Hall," he explained. "Chestnut Hill will become the dower house."

"Oh." *That* took her completely by surprise.

Blackwood Hall was the grand manor house given to the family when Richard Carlisle received the title. It was currently closed up, the family preferring their smaller home of Chestnut Hill, where they'd lived for over thirty years. But of course Sebastian would live in the larger house with his duchess. How had that realization never occurred to her before, that he would be moving away from Chestnut Hill? But it hadn't, and a stab of unexpected loss struck her. Now he would be with a newlywed bride he might not love, in another house that wasn't his home, in a place where Miranda couldn't picture him *ever* being happy.

Her chest tightened with a sudden, fierce urge to argue with him, to tell him how mistaken he was, that he had all his priorities hopelessly mixed up in his search for a wife. But it wasn't her place to question his choice, or insist that he put his own happiness first. They were only childhood friends—

He deserved so much better!

"Lady Jane is all wrong for you," she blurted out, the words spilling forth before she could stop them.

"Oh?" His gaze flicked curiously to her. "What kind of woman should I settle on, then?"

"The kind you won't tire of in six months," she answered, a bit too boldly. "One you love."

"A lack of boredom has nothing to do with my choice in duchess," he commented as he looked away again. "Or love."

"Perhaps not." She rose as gracefully to her feet as possible and brushed her hands down the front of her yellow skirt to smooth out any wrinkles. Most likely, Lady Jane had never experienced a wrinkle in her life. Like freckles, they were simply not allowed into her world. "Although I think you should reconsider."

"And why is that?" He pushed himself to his feet as she rose. Always the perfect gentleman, she thought with chagrin. Even when she didn't want him to be.

"Because I know you, Sebastian, and your life will never be as simple as you'd like it to be." As an afterthought, she reached down for her bonnet and gloves. "Why complicate it even more by choosing the wrong wife?"

She set her bonnet in place over her hair, although the afternoon's freckle damage had already been done. Still, putting on her bonnet seemed like something a lady of the quality would do when leaving her companion for a stroll around the park, and she wanted him to know, no matter how mix-matched the comparison, that she could be just as refined as Lady Jane Sheridan.

His lips tightened as his mother and Quinn finished their turn about the lawn and returned to their picnic. "My life is *not* what—"

"Who would you rather be, Sebastian?" she pressed quietly, just low enough that his family couldn't overhear as they reached the blanket, and right at the last moment so that he couldn't answer. "A duke with a duchess whom everyone respects...or happy?"

CHAPTER SIX

"Curtsy to anyone who's a peer," Elizabeth Carlisle instructed to a raptly listening Miranda as the carriage rolled through Mayfair. "Address them as your lordship or your ladyship, but only the first time when you're introduced. Too many 'your lordships' makes you sound like a servant."

Sebastian rolled his eyes. As the ladies' escort to the Countess of St James's annual ball, he'd been subjected by proximity to last-minute lessons on proper etiquette all the way from Audley House. He should have ridden with Josie and Chesney, he supposed, and forced Robert to ride with the ladies, to give Miranda more time with him since her pursuit of his brother so far had been fruitless.

His gaze once more drifted across the compartment to Miranda, once more noting how beautiful she looked tonight.

No. He was happy to be right here.

Confusion wrinkled her pretty forehead. "But I don't curtsy to you and Trent."

"Certainly not!" His mother looked affronted by the idea, then she softened, giving Miranda's hand an affectionate squeeze. "Except for tonight, of course, when you do."

"Oh." Her confusion deepened. "But if I'm supposed to curtsy to peers, how do I know if they're peers if no one addresses them as your lordship or ladyship?"

Sebastian bit his tongue to keep from laughing. Leave it to Miranda to point out the illogical pomposity that was the English aristocracy.

His mother blinked, completely unprepared for that earnest question. "Well…just curtsy to anyone who looks important."

Miranda nodded gravely at that sage bit of wisdom.

"Oh, and I must introduce you to the Duke of Wembley. A most interesting man. He's had four sons, three daughters, two wives—"

"And a partridge in a pear tree," Sebastian muttered edgily, reaching the end of his patience.

If he had to listen to one more lecture straight from Debrett's, he would go mad. Tonight was Miranda's official debut, and of course, he wanted everything to go well for her. But his mother's instructions only served to make her nervous, and having had firsthand experience with the wreckage that a nervous Miranda could unleash… Well, *no one* needed that. Certainly not the St James House floors if she became too nervous to hold her glass of punch.

Tonight was going to be a trial for all of them.

Elizabeth Carlisle sighed patiently. "She needs to be prepared to meet everyone."

"Not Wembley," he contradicted. "The man's as old as—" Good Lord, he almost said Moses, but stopped himself just as he remembered that Robert had called *him* exactly that. Wembley was over twenty years his senior.

Was that how his brothers and the rest of the *ton* saw him, as stodgy and ancient as all that? "He's too old for Miranda," he said instead. "She needs to meet gentlemen her own age."

"I don't need to meet *any* gentlemen. I have enough on my plate just remembering my dance steps." Miranda laughed lightly at the idea of suitors, and the lilting sound filled the small compartment like music. "Besides, however should I know to whom to give my attentions?" She gazed at him through lowered lashes in a goading look he knew was meant to appear innocent but unknowingly made her look surprisingly alluring. Her eyes sparkled mischievously. "I haven't yet made out my list."

His jaw clenched. An *absolute* trial.

"Just enjoy yourself tonight, my dear. You deserve a grand debut." Mother hugged her warmly, placing a reassuring kiss on her cheek that made Miranda practically glow. Then she glanced out the window. "Oh goodness—we've arrived!"

Before the carriage came to a complete stop and the waiting footman could come forward to assist them, Sebastian had already opened the door and bounded to the street. Chesney's carriage stopped behind theirs, and the rest of the Carlisle family disembarked. As Thomas Matteson led Josie toward the house, Robert hurried to take his mother's hand as Sebastian handed her off to his brother to escort inside.

Then he reached back for Miranda.

When her gloved fingers slipped into his, he felt her tremble, and his chest clenched in sympathy for her. Yet she was a vision of composed elegance as she emerged from the carriage in a gown of green silk that matched her eyes, flattered her curves, and highlighted the red tones of her hair, which had been twisted and pinned into a mass of glorious red-gold curls on top her head. A silk-lined ermine stole warmed her shoulders, but she would remove it as soon as she entered the house, giving the crush of guests inside a glimpse of creamy smooth shoulders revealed by the ribbon straps of the sleeveless gown and a teasing hint of her breasts above the form-fitted bodice. With every inch of her, she appeared refined and beautiful, as if she truly belonged there among the quality.

She gave him a smile, one so nervous yet so filled with excitement that it tugged straight through him. He was glad she had this chance for a season, despite everything. She'd been waiting for this moment for far too long. And tonight, she shined gloriously.

Slipping his arm lightly around her waist, he helped her to the ground. "Careful," he teased, leaning over to whisper into her ear. "Just because you're wearing slippers doesn't mean you have to slip."

"Stop it, Sebastian," she reprimanded, tapping him gently on the shoulder with her folded fan as he placed her hand on his arm and escorted her toward the door. "I'm nervous enough as it is."

He gave her a half grin, then leaned in close again. "You look lovely." He caught the faint scent of rosewater on her skin, and his grin faded with a tight knotting in his gut as memories of the masquerade came flooding back. "Beautiful, in fact."

"Stop it," she repeated, this time more softly, and instead of a smack of her fan, a blush pinked prettily at her cheeks.

He raised her hand to his lips and lightly kissed her fingers, finding it endearing that she could blush so easily over a compliment that every other woman at tonight's ball not only expected but saw as her birthright. "I wouldn't lie about that."

Then she nearly did trip on the front steps as she turned to stare at him in utter incredulity.

"Careful," he warned again, hiding the warmth in his chest at her reaction. If he could so easily fluster her with the smallest of compliments, then what would she do if he told her the absolute truth, that not one of the women here tonight could hold a candle to her vivacity? And that he'd begun to admire her for it. With a nod, he brought her attention back to the entrance of the house. "You've arrived at your ball, Cinderella."

Ablaze with glowing lamps, St James House sat full, the crush of people inside already spilling into the front foyer and drifting out into the lantern-lit side gardens, despite the winter chill in the air. The countess's ball was always the most anticipated event of the season, one Olivia Sinclair carefully planned for months in advance. One Sebastian hoped his wife could match when he married and the time came to throw grand parties of their own.

He slid a sideways glance at Miranda, whose green eyes never stopped moving in an attempt to experience everything around her.

She would have gentlemen suitors this season, he was certain of it. How could she not, looking as beautiful as she did tonight, as full of life and glowing happiness? When she became a wife, would she be able to pull off an affair as lavish as this? The same woman who played pirates with orphans?

But then, this life was not hers in the first place, he reminded himself, feeling a stab of disappointment for her. This season, she was merely a visitor to this world, and the merchant or gentleman farmer she eventually married would have no need of formal balls and society soirees. Yet Sebastian had no doubt that Miranda would have given it her all. And *that* was what he admired most about her.

She handed her stole to the footman inside the foyer. Then Sebastian led her up the sweeping stairs to the first floor and along the hall to the rear stairs that curved down into the crowded ballroom below.

"You're going to be wonderful tonight," he told her in a low voice. Good Lord, how she trembled! "Just relax, be yourself, and enjoy your night."

"Are *you* going to relax, be yourself, and enjoy the night?" she countered in a breathy whisper.

No. Those days were over. For him, tonight was about finding a duchess. The most he could do was enjoy the ball through her eyes. "I'm not a debutante," he deflected.

"Too bad." She looked straight ahead, but he saw the smile pulling at the corners of her mouth. "You'd look lovely in pink bows and lace."

He choked back a laugh. Only Miranda could make him enjoy arriving at a ball.

The Master of Ceremonies waited at the top of the marble stairs, to take the invitations as each guest presented them and to announce their arrival.

Miranda tensed on his arm. When Sebastian glanced at her, the blush in her cheeks was gone, replaced by a pallid hue of pure nervous terror. But her smile was glued firmly in place, exactly as his mother had instructed. Even now, when she was terrified to the bone to be making her entrance, she was doing everything she could to please others, and his heart tugged for her. He understood that same pressure to please. But how on earth did Miranda do it, pleasing others while still being true to herself, while still keeping her love for life? He wished he knew, then maybe he could do it himself.

Hoping she wouldn't faint before he could get her to the bottom of the stairs, he presented their invitations to the Master of Ceremonies. The garishly uniformed man, complete with white powdered wig and high heels, turned and stomped his long staff, then announced in a voice loud enough to cut through the noise of the crowd, "His Grace, Sebastian Carlisle, Duke of Trent…and Miss Miranda Hodgkins!"

He heard her gasp as the roomful of guests turned to stare at them as they stood poised at the top of the stairs before descending.

"Breathe," he reminded her with a smile and a squeeze of her hand as they started forward.

Whispers rose through the ballroom below as he led her down, all the guests craning their necks to catch a glimpse for themselves of the new duke and the woman he was introducing this season. The *beautiful* woman he was introducing, he thought with chagrin as the stares of the men in the crush turned interested.

"Salmon fishers," he muttered irritably beneath his breath.

"Pardon?" She glanced at him, the color returning to her face as the next couple was announced and the attention of the room diverted from them.

"I said…so many well-wishers," he lied.

He didn't know if she believed him, but she was too nervous to press. Thankfully. The last thing he wanted to do tonight was explain Quinton's skewed theory of skirt-chasing to her and make her even more wary about the quality of the quality.

By the time they reached the floor, she was breathing normally again, her body much more relaxed and her cheeks once more the vivacious pink he found so charming.

He led her to his mother where she waited at the side of the room and released her with a bow. "Miss Hodgkins."

She lowered into a graceful curtsy. "Your Grace."

He grimaced inwardly. For some reason he couldn't name, it grated whenever Miranda reminded him of his title. When he was with her, he wanted only to be Sebastian. "Enjoy yourself," he told her. "I'll be back for the first dance."

She nodded as new anxiousness flittered across her face. Tonight was her formal debut, and as a special favor from the Earl and Countess of St James, they would dance the opening set as one of only six couples, with the full attention of the room on them. But oddly enough, he was looking forward to it, and to being the man who partnered her for her first society dance.

He retreated with polite nods to his mother and sister, to make his way through the crush in search of his brothers.

He found them near the refreshments table with glasses of Madeira already in hand and with Quinn doing his charming best to convince one of the footmen to bring him a bottle of St James's private reserve cognac. Sebastian helped himself to Quinn's glass, knowing from the size of the crowd gathered around the table that it would take a quarter of an hour before he could secure one of his own.

"You're in for a busy evening," Quinn taunted, slapping Sebastian on the back. "With Miranda to nanny—"

"And all those ladies on your list to *not* nanny," Robert finished with a grin.

Sebastian raised the glass to take a large, welcomed swallow. "Tonight, I only need to secure dances, that's all." That would give him enough time with each lady to discover who piqued his interest enough for more serious pursuit.

Quinn laughed. "Where's the fun in that?"

"This isn't about fun," Robert corrected with exaggerated earnestness, laying his arm across Quinn's shoulders. "This is about Seb finding a wife."

"Exactly," Sebastian confirmed, wishing Quinn would have succeeded in getting the brandy. Tonight promised to be an excruciatingly long evening.

He glanced around the ballroom, and his eyes fell on Lady Jane Sheridan as she stood surrounded by a group of admirers. She looked decidedly regal in her gown of pastel pink satin and pearl-encrusted headband that held back her sable hair in a fashionable Grecian style. Her smile combined both a subdued pleasantry and a studied demureness that spoke to her good breeding.

Standing just behind Jane's group of admirers, but clearly apart from them, Miranda shook with happy laughter over some teasing remark made to her by Thomas Matteson. Sebastian's brow furrowed as he watched her sink into an exaggerated, giggling curtsy to the marquess. Decidedly *not* subdued, and not an inch of her demure.

"Ah, the lovely Lady Jane," Robert mumbled as he followed Sebastian's attention across the room.

Quinn craned his neck with open curiosity. "Is she to be your duchess, then?"

"I haven't decided," he answered, tearing his gaze away from Miranda and back to the earl's daughter. But Jane was definitely at the top of his list, and he needed to make his way to her side before all her dances were taken. With Jane, he wanted a waltz. If he intended to court her—and so far, she was not only this season's Incomparable but his own as well—then he wanted time alone with her before he made his intentions known. "But she has all the qualities I'm seeking in a wife. Good breeding, respected reputation, a family with political influence—"

Robert and Quinn broke into laughter. Sebastian shot them a cutting look that quelled their amusement. The last thing he needed tonight was interference from his brothers.

Or from Miranda. His gaze once more drifted to her, just as she flirtatiously flitted her fan at a young dandy who had requested a dance. His gut tightened with fresh irritation.

"It's a shame, really—" Robert began.

"That they don't auction off wives at Tattersall's," Quinn finished, choking back his laughter.

Sebastian said nothing, choosing to ignore his brothers' antics tonight, and took another swallow of wine. They could taunt him all they wanted, but the reality was that his choice in wife was not his but one he owed to the title and to the prestige of the family. And to his father, for being with an actress the night Father died instead of with his family, a woman so inappropriate for him that he had to deceive them in order to be with her.

What he wanted as a man didn't matter.

"The dancing will start soon." He finished the glass of wine. "Go make your requests to dance with Miranda and make certain she has enough partners for the evening to enjoy herself."

"That won't be a problem," Quinn commented with a nod of his head, drawing Sebastian's attention to the interested looks of the men in the crush who noticed her arrival and were now making their way toward her.

"Good for her," Robert murmured, letting his own gaze trail appreciatively over her figure.

A flash of annoyance pulsed hot through Sebastian. The last thing he needed to worry about tonight was Miranda and those gentlemen who were clamoring to meet her, falling all over themselves to request a dance from her, doing their best to draw her attention... And why the hell was Robert looking at her like that? He'd promised her to help make his brother notice her as a potential wife, not like... *that*.

"Request a dance, Robert," he ordered, beginning to dislike the agreement he'd struck with Miranda. "And make certain it's a waltz."

He handed his empty glass to Quinn and strode forward, weaving his way through the packed room to Lady Jane. It was time to find a wife.

He reached her side, and the group of women parted around her to give him room to bow. "Lady Jane, you look lovely this evening."

"Thank you, Your Grace." She smiled warmly at him, her eyes sparkling. "So good to see you again, Trent."

They had been formally introduced two weeks ago at the Duke and Duchess of Strathmore's breakfast, held to toast the start of Parliament. The breakfast had gone exceedingly well, and Lady Jane had moved to the top of his list. Looking at her now, he knew he'd made the right decision.

The dynamics exuding from the group of admirers flocking around her changed palpably at his arrival. The men narrowed their eyes on him in competition, and the women on her in jealousy. Good Lord, he'd be grateful when he'd settled on a wife and could go back to avoiding all this courting nonsense.

Ignoring them, he smiled at her. "I would like to request a dance, my lady, if you have any left."

"I would be honored."

"Dare I hope for a waltz?" he pressed.

A smile played knowingly at her lips. "Will the first one do, Your Grace?"

His lips twitched. She'd obviously been reserving that dance for him. So Lady Jane was not only accepting suitors this season but accepting him most of all. Instead of being relieved that he had no real competition for her hand, his chest tightened with consternation at the manipulation of the whole marriage charade the *ton* enacted every season. In which he had now been swept up.

He nodded his head to accept the waltz. "And so they go to it," he mumbled beneath his breath as *Hamlet* inexplicably popped into his head.

"Pardon?"

"Nothing." He smiled down at her. "Before the dancing begins, it would be my pleasure to escort you on a turn—"

He cut himself off. From the corner of his eye, he saw Diana Morgan enter the ball on the arm of her father, General Morgan, and heard the whispered hush that fell across the party at her arrival. In her white satin dress and with her blond hair swept high onto her head in a pile of golden curls, the woman looked simply angelic, and her presence captivated the attention of the entire room.

Including Miranda, who turned away toward the wall and raised her fan, but not before Sebastian saw the anguished expression on her face. His heart broke for her.

* * *

Miranda blinked hard behind her fan, flitting it rapidly in pretense of being warm in order to cover the pain squeezing her heart. Diana Morgan...looking like an angel. She knew the woman was attending the ball; she'd surreptitiously confirmed it with Elizabeth Carlisle two days ago. But knowing that hadn't prepared her for the full force of the woman's arrival.

Miss Morgan looked lovely in her white dress as she floated down to the ballroom with her hair shining like spun gold beneath the chandeliers, and everyone in the room paused to watch her. Including Robert, who left Quinn at the refreshment table to go immediately to her side to welcome her to the ball with a low bow and kiss of her hand. And, judging from the length of time it took him to speak with her and her father before he returned to Quinton, to also claim several dances with her.

But of course he did, and who could blame him? Apparently, the retiring room gossip Miranda had been passing along to Sebastian was wrong. Lady Jane wasn't this season's Incomparable. Miss Morgan was. And leave it to the Carlisle brothers that they would end up with the two most sought-after women of the season, while she...while she...

Nothing! It mattered nothing about her. Oh, how could she ever compare? Even tonight, in the finest gown she'd ever worn, with her hair perfectly coiffed by Josie's maid and wearing the emeralds that Elizabeth Carlisle had lent her, she couldn't capture Robert's attention.

"Excuse me," she mumbled and hurried away from the group of Carlisle family friends who had gathered around her with the duchess and marchioness. She needed to find the retiring room. Desperately. To gain a moment of peace and quiet where she could gather herself and breathe, fight back the unshed tears stinging at her eyes, and find a way to go on with the rest of her evening without anyone knowing—

"Miranda."

Sebastian. She rolled her tear-blurred eyes as he stepped in front of her and blocked her flight. Of all the people to see her like this!

"Your Grace." Forcing a smile, she flitted her fan furiously in front of her face to give herself air and blink back the hot tears.

But he frowned at her with concern, clearly seeing right through her façade to the anguish beneath.

"We're needed to begin the dancing," he said quietly, his

eyes solemn. He placed a hand against her lower back to steer her away from the others before they could see the pain on her face. "Shall we?"

She nodded, unable to find her voice around the tight knot in her throat, and let him lead her away. Thankfully, he was also taking her the long way around the room to give her time to recover before they became the center of attention with the opening dance. He was too much of a gentleman to comment on her distress, but he'd come to her rescue, and she was more grateful than she could express.

He escorted her through the crush toward Lord and Lady St James, who stood waiting by the Master of Ceremonies to officially open the ball. They would be the first couple in the first set, the same set Miranda would dance with Sebastian for her introduction.

"She's lovely," Miranda whispered, her face falling.

"Yes, she is."

She couldn't bring herself to look at him as her humiliation over the futility of the past few weeks rose inside her. Hot tears threatened at her lashes. "I didn't mean Lady St James."

"I know," he said softly, his voice kind. "Miranda, perhaps it's time you gave up on Robert."

She shook her head. He was right; her head knew that, but her heart couldn't yet face the ramifications of surrendering the dream she'd held since she was fourteen. "Not yet."

He nodded in sympathetic understanding. "Then allow me to request a second dance with you. What do you have left?"

Her shoulders sagged. As her escort and the man introducing her to society, Sebastian was already obligated to take the first dance with her. Now he was also taking pity on her. "You don't have to."

"I want to."

Well, *that* was a lie. Still, it was thoughtful of him to offer, and the kindness warmed her chest and lightened the lead knot lying within. "Both of my waltzes are still free."

"Both?" His eyes narrowed, and with a fresh stab of humiliation, she knew what he'd just realized. That Quinn had taken a quadrille, so had the Marquess of Chesney and the Duke of Strathmore, as well as several other men she'd never met before tonight who all wanted to dance with her. Except for Robert, who hadn't yet requested a dance at all. "I thought you wanted to waltz."

"I do." She lowered her eyes, pretending to fuss with her gloves. "I was saving them for Robert, so he could have his choice." Long after she'd tugged the gloves into place past her elbows, she kept her gaze lowered, unable to bear the look of pity she suspected she'd see on his face if she glanced up. "Although your mother assured me that he would give me a waltz since he's the second oldest brother and it's my debut."

"He should have. And he will," he said firmly, although Miranda doubted that even the duke could make his brother pay her any attention now that Miss Morgan had arrived and stolen it all away for herself.

She shook her head in defeat. "It doesn't matter. There are other gentlemen here who will waltz with me, I'm certain."

"So am I," he muttered beneath his breath. Then he looked down at her with concern. "Be careful tonight with the gentlemen, Miranda."

She blew out a sigh, bracing herself for the onslaught of warnings he'd been giving her since she arrived in London, those seemingly endless cautions about how to behave among society and navigate all their unwritten rules.

Only Sebastian Carlisle could ruin her fun by being...
well, *himself*.

"Enjoy yourself, but don't have too much fun. Don't
draw unwanted attention, and try not to drink too much
champagne." He rattled off the warnings in a smooth litany
that left her wondering how long he'd been practicing them.
Most likely since the moment he and his mother decided
to give her a season. "Stay in the ballroom unless Mother
or Josie is with you, and stay away from the terrace, the
gardens—"

"Line the walls with the companions and spinsters," she
mocked with a wave of her gloved hand in the same warning
tone, "settle on the shelf without complaint, become an old
maid with only a herd of cats for company... Better yet, join
a convent."

"Precisely." He arched a brow. "I'm glad we've come to
an understanding."

Her mouth dropped open, aghast. "We've done no such
thing!"

He flashed her a smile, with the relief that he'd successfully distracted her from Robert visible on his face. "And I'd
be honored to take your second waltz."

Closing her mouth, she stared at him, wide-eyed and
speechless. Yet immensely grateful. And the stinging in her
eyes turned into tears of gratitude. She had to admit that
Sebastian could be quite dashing. When he wasn't being a
duke.

"Thank you," she whispered.

Saying nothing, his gaze holding hers, he raised her hand
to his lips to kiss it. A soft tingle spread up her arm.

"Ladies and gentlemen, the Earl and Countess of St
James!" the Master of Ceremonies called out from the top
of the stairs with a flourish from the orchestra. An excited

murmur went up from the crowd, and everyone moved back from the dance floor to let pass the six couples who would dance the first figures and open the ball.

Inhaling a nervous breath as the attention of the room once more descended upon her, she walked with him onto the dance floor.

"Do not dance with the same man twice," Sebastian continued with his warnings as they took their position opposite each other at the end of the row and despite the frustrated rolling of her eyes. "He'll assume he means more to you than he does."

She arched a brow. "You're dancing with me twice. Will you assume you mean more to me than you do?"

He frowned at her silently, too wise to answer *that*. Ha! Her spirits lifted with that little victory.

"I saw you speaking with Lady Jane earlier," she pressed, now emboldened. She raised her chin as the music began and the opening bows and curtsies were made. "Did you offer the same warnings to her?"

His eyes flickered, although she couldn't have said whether in annoyance or amusement. The couples swept forward. "Of course not," he answered between steps as they circled each other. "Lady Jane already knows society's rules." As they moved apart, he added, "She's refined in them."

They moved back to their original places, then stepped forward again. "She's boring," Miranda corrected in a parting jab, before sliding sideways to circle the Duke of Chatham. After all the warnings Sebastian had given her tonight, he deserved to be taunted.

"She's urbane," Sebastian countered with an amused glint in his eyes when she returned to once again circle him.

The figures took them away from each other to dance

with the other five couples, but each time they circled back, they argued. And Miranda enjoyed it far more than she should have. There was something about getting beneath Sebastian's skin that delighted her to no end.

"Dull," she rejoined with a playful flounce of her skirt, then danced away.

When they came back together, he murmured in her ear, "Delightfully sophisticated."

She raised her nose in her best impersonation of Lady Jane just to irk him as she stepped back. "Definitely snobby."

He greeted her return to him a few moments later with a smile. "Beautiful...like you."

When he trailed his hand behind her back as he circled her, she caught her breath at the subtle flirtation. The possessiveness of the light touch startled her, so did the heat of his fingers seeping through her dress. And so did how much she enjoyed it.

Miranda missed a step, the toe of her slipper catching on the marble floor, and she tripped. Instantly, Sebastian's hand was beneath her left arm and his right hand against the small of her back as he caught her and moved her smoothly into the circle.

He lowered his mouth close to her ear, his voice surely far more husky in his amusement than he intended when he murmured, "Graceful."

Unable to answer to that without highlighting her own clumsiness, she glowered at him through narrowed eyes as she slipped away to circle with the Earl of St James, the first and last couples coming together for the final figures of the dance. Sebastian turned away in his own steps to lead the countess.

"Graceful?" he prompted when they came back to face each other in their original positions, obviously enjoying their sparring as much as she to goad her like that. Or at least, as much as she had been, until he'd unwittingly compared her to Lady Jane. And found her lacking. And that stung more than she wanted to admit.

With the last flourishes of the orchestra, the couples all made their final curtsies and bows to their partners.

"Spoiled," she managed to get in, although what she'd wanted to say... *Perfectly wrong for you.* But then, if someone like Lady Jane was wrong for him, who was right?

He crooked a brow, having no idea of her true thoughts. "Well-behaved."

Her mouth fell open at that barb as indignant irritation flared through her. Oh, that devil! Before she could think of a cutting reply, the dance ended. Sebastian had gotten the last word. And a stinging one at that.

With her chin raised in defiance, she lowered into a curtsy deep enough to make his mother proud, no matter how aggravating the woman's eldest son. Then she let him place her hand on his arm as he led her from the floor, to return her to the duchess.

"I suppose," she acknowledged, the admission coming at great cost to her pride, "that Lady Jane seems like a nice enough woman."

Clearly surprised by that, he slid a sideways glance at her reluctant approval of his suit. "Thank you—"

"Although madness runs in her family."

His stride hitched, the only outward sign that she'd surprised him. "Pardon?"

"Must do," she said with a haughty sniff, "to want a stuffy, old duke like you for a husband."

With a soft laugh, he grinned down at her. Not just any smile, either. But such a warm and amused smile that he sent her insides melting.

Her heart skipped. No, not the grin. Not *his* grin! Sebastian would never set her heart pounding. Because if he did, then that meant that— *No.* To be attracted to Sebastian, of all men...How ridiculous! It was the fun of the dance, that was all, because it couldn't be anything more. Certainly not with him. Pursuing Robert was difficult enough; Sebastian would be downright impossible.

"Are you planning on dancing with her tonight, then?" she pressed, desperate to focus her thoughts on Lady Jane and away from the duke.

"Yes. The first waltz." He glanced down at her, lifting his brow. "Are you going to try to talk me out of it?"

"Not at all," she answered innocently with just a touch of pique that he would be so distrusting of her.

He tightened his lips at her denial, clearly not believing her for a moment.

"In fact, I think it's wonderful that you were able to find a woman who agreed to dance with you."

"More than one, actually," he returned, allowing a touch of playful arrogance into his tone.

She stepped away from him as he returned her to his mother's side, unable to resist giving one last parting shot in a low voice, "Then the madness is spreading."

She heard him choke back a laugh. With a calmly composed façade, he gave his polite partings to his mother and Josie. "If you'll excuse me, ladies."

Then he bowed deeply and overly formally to Miranda, going so far as to refuse to release her hand until he'd raised it to his lips and kissed it, no matter how much she tugged to try to pull free or how red her cheeks grew from her hot blush of embarrassment. He was doing this just to annoy her, blast him. And right in front of his mother and sister, too.

His sparkling blue eyes danced with mischief. "I need to find my next partner." He gave her a wink as he walked away. "Before they commit her to Bedlam."

Her mouth fell open, incredulous at his audacity. Oh, the devil take the man!

CHAPTER SEVEN

$\mathcal{A}$n hour later, Sebastian had not only danced with several of the ladies on his list, he'd also mentally crossed off most of their names. Oh, they were certainly all lovely, all graceful, yet annoyingly each one lacked... *something*. Something indefinable that he couldn't quite put his finger on but knew from its absence.

Worse, because he'd danced more tonight than he had at any ball since he'd inherited—in fact, quite possibly at any ball ever—rumors were flowing through the crush as fast as the Thames through London that the Duke of Trent was hunting a wife, which put all the marriage-minded mamas and their daughters into a heated frenzy. Which made him feel as if he were being hunted.

And speaking of prey... *Miranda*.

Even as he'd danced, he couldn't help but notice all the attention being paid to her tonight by the gentlemen who flocked around her like sheep, vying for her attention. Or a dance. Or one of those delightful laughs that floated from her. Or a flirtatious flitter of her fan that irritated him each time he saw her give one to whatever gentleman had spoken to her.

It was damnably annoying. How was he supposed to concentrate on finding a wife when she was behaving so carelessly? So flirtatiously. So... *happily*. Didn't she realize the attention she was drawing?

Except from Robert.

Sebastian's eyes narrowed on his brother across the room. He had barely left Miss Morgan's side all night, and even now they were engaged in a private conversation near the open French doors that led out to the dark terrace. Robert had barely noticed Miranda all evening. His attention had been only on the general's stunning daughter. And presumably on an attempt to convince her to join him in the gardens for a few moments alone.

Knowing there was no point in interrupting Robert now to remind him of his duties to Miranda this evening, not unless he wanted the two of them to come to blows, Sebastian snatched a glass of punch from the tray of a passing footman and headed across the ballroom.

Miranda's back was to him as he stalked toward her, and the semicircle of men gathered around her scattered as he approached. *Smart men.* He was in no mood tonight to deal with a bunch of self-avowed Corinthians preying on an innocent country girl like Miranda. He knew exactly what they wanted from her, and it wasn't conversation about fishing.

Her back stiffened, as if she sensed his approach before she saw him. "Trent."

"Miss Hodgkins." Unable to prevent the slightly piqued tone to his voice, he drawled, "You've made several new friends tonight, I see."

Somehow, she managed to face him, roll her eyes, and haughtily flit her fan all at the same time in a gesture of orchestrated impudence that half the ladies of the *ton* had yet to master. At the sight of her, standing there in her fine gown, her green eyes shining in the light of the chandeliers and her freckle-dotted nose jutting just slightly into the air, he couldn't help but smile. Which only made her expression grow even more irked.

Just to spite him, she lowered into a deep curtsy.

"Jealousy doesn't become you, Your Grace," she chastised with a dismissive sniff as she rose.

Jealousy? The woman was daft. "I'm not jealous." He offered her the glass of punch and added pointedly, "I'm being careful."

From the way she arched a brow at the punch without taking it, he half expected her to ask if he'd poisoned it. Instead, she accepted. "Thank you."

"Are you enjoying yourself?" He honestly wanted to know.

A slow smile spread across her face, the same beaming smile he'd seen her give at least a dozen times in the past hour to the men seeking her attentions. But when she aimed that smile at him, he felt it pull all the way through him, right down to his curling toes in his Hessians. And he knew then exactly why so many of the men flocked around her tonight. For nothing more than the favor of one of her smiles.

"Very much," she said softly. Then she leaned in closer, as if sharing an intimate secret. "Oh, Sebastian, it's the most wonderful night of my life!"

His chest warmed at that, and the sparkle in her eyes captured his imagination. She was so full of life and energy, filled with happiness and joy...and all because of a ball like any of the dozen or so grand balls that would be held this season. For half the young ladies present, tonight's ball was just another boring evening in a long string of season soirees. But for Miranda, it was a fairy tale come true.

"I'm glad," he returned in the same secretive voice. "You deserve a special night." Then he paused, asking carefully, "And your first waltz? Has it been claimed?"

She nodded with a widening smile. "Robert offered for it."

"Good." He should have felt relieved that his brother had stepped up to do his duty. Instead, he worried that the excitement she felt would only make her nervous again, and he didn't think his brother could tolerate another conversation about John Milton or Belgian lace. Then he instructed, despite the strange tightening in his chest, "Don't be afraid to enjoy yourself with him."

"Enjoy myself?" she repeated with an exaggerated pretense of being offended. "I thought I had to be painfully proper tonight and avoid all potentially scandalous behavior with gentlemen. Not draw unwanted attention to myself, not go onto the terrace or into the gardens, not be alone with any gentleman." She teasingly threw his earlier warnings back at him with a mockingly innocent wave of her fan at each one. "Not do...anything."

His jaw tightened. *Impertinent chit.* "Robert doesn't count. He's a Carlisle." And unfortunately for Miranda, the next best thing to a nanny tonight, given how little his brother had seemed to notice her once Miss Morgan arrived. "We're your guardians this summer. *We* are allowed to spend time alone with you." When he saw her brow start to jut up in challenge at that unwritten rule of society propriety, he interjected, "Just be yourself with him."

A shadow fell across her lovely face. "That's the problem, though, isn't it? I'm always myself when I'm around him, which is never—"

Her eyes widened as an idea struck her.

Sebastian's heart skipped in warning. Whenever Miranda got that look on her face, trouble always followed.

"Perhaps I shouldn't be myself." Her body tightened visibly as she contemplated the thought, as if a coil of excitement curled inside her, getting ready to spring. "Perhaps I should be Lady Rose with him and—"

"No."

She stared at him, her eyes blinking hard at his outburst.

Good Lord. The unexpected force of the single word surprised even him.

"Enjoyment," he corrected, immediately composing himself and pushing down whatever madness had just seized him at her mention of Lady Rose. With Robert. "Not ruination."

Mercifully, the orchestra gave a flourish to signal the start of the first waltz, which gave him an excuse to leave before he said anything else that made him look like a jealous nodcock. Which he certainly wasn't. Not at all.

"Your first society waltz is starting, Miss Hodgkins." He glanced past her shoulder. He didn't catch a glimpse of Robert in the nearby crowd, but somewhere in the crush of bodies, his brother would be making his way to her for the dance. Just as he needed to make his way to Lady Jane. "Enjoy yourself." *But not too much.*

With the unspoken warning hanging on the air between them, he weaved through the crowd to find Jane, who stood surrounded by her group of admirers at the side of the ballroom. Her eyes searched for him over her open fan as she whispered something to her sister.

But as the orchestra transitioned into the opening notes of the dance, he glanced over his shoulder to find Miranda still standing right where he'd left her, with Robert nowhere in the room and leaving her completely without a partner.

Sebastian cursed beneath his breath.

"Quinton." He grabbed his brother's arm and pulled him away from the small group of landowners who were discussing wheat prices. "I need you to take this waltz with Lady Jane and give her my apologies."

"Why?" Quinn glanced at Jane, who smiled demurely at Sebastian as she waited patiently in expectation of her waltz.

"Because Robert will be dead by midnight," he muttered, "and I'll be in Newgate for murder."

Quinton grinned. With a nod, clearly not caring about the real reason he had to dance with Lady Jane as long as Robert took the brunt of Sebastian's ire, he sauntered over to her. Sebastian watched just long enough to see Quinn make a bow to Jane before he spun on his heels and marched back to Miranda.

She wore a fixed smile on her face, the brave brightness of which belied the hurt he knew lingered beneath at being stood up for her waltz. Not just any waltz, too, but her first one in society. As she saw him approach, her smile faltered. Anyone else would have missed the flash of distress in her eyes, but he saw it, and it pained him more than he wanted to admit.

He took her hand and placed it on her arm, refusing to let her pull away. "Your waltz is beginning."

She blinked in confusion. "But Robert's supposed to—"

"Robert isn't coming," he told her firmly, his jaw clenched tight in anger at his brother.

She hesitated, then nodded wordlessly as understanding fell through her.

As he led her toward the dance floor, her smile faded into a sober expression that suddenly made her appear years older, suddenly far too world-weary. *Unhappy.* And he didn't like it. At that moment, he would have done anything to put a beaming smile back on her face.

"You don't have to do this, Sebastian," she said in a low voice only he could hear over the music and noise of the ball around them. "I'm not your charity."

"No, you're not." He bowed as she curtsied stiffly, then pulled her into position. "But we have an agreement. We promised to help each other this season." He looked down into her bright green eyes, finding a startling mix of misery and gratitude in their stormy depths that stole his breath away. A prickle of admiration coursed through him that she was able to handle his brother's thoughtlessness with such grace and aplomb. "And I always keep my promises."

Before she could retort, he stepped her into the waltz. They whirled together across the floor, the skirts of her dress flowing about his legs with each smooth glide and turn, and he was careful to hold her at the proper distance as they worked through the turns. She was more graceful than he'd anticipated, each of her steps matching his to perfection.

"Robert's in the garden, isn't he?" She lowered her face as they danced toward the opposite end of the floor. "With Miss Morgan."

He stiffened, knowing exactly what she meant. The two had probably sneaked away, to be alone and out of sight of the party, not giving the waltz with Miranda a second thought. Robert liked Miranda, of that he was certain, and would never intentionally hurt her. But Sebastian was also quickly coming to believe that his brother would never see

Miranda as anything more than the girl in braids he'd grown up with. "Most likely," he answered gently.

"It doesn't matter," she insisted, her gaze fixed to his cravat pin. But her voice lacked conviction, as if she hadn't yet convinced herself and needed to say it aloud to believe it. "Someone else would have come along to ask me to waltz, I think."

As he saw the interested looks sent her way from the men in the crowd as they glided past, he knew so. She'd caused quite a stir this evening, and for the next fortnight, the drawing room gossip among the ladies and the St James's Street gossip among the men would be nothing but talk of her. All of them wondering about her. The woman who was introduced by a duke, a woman of no fortune whom none of them had ever heard of before. And one with a figure and face that most men would find tantalizing enough to risk taking a closer look.

"Be careful with whom you dance tonight," he warned, turning his gaze back to her just in time to see her roll her eyes in aggravation at yet another one of his warnings. "I'm serious, Miranda. And don't flirt with any of them."

She laughed at that, the soft sound tingling through him like a fresh summer breeze. "You have nothing to worry about in that regard, since I don't know how."

"Oh yes, you do." His fingers squeezed hers as he held them lightly in his hand. "When you were Lady Rose, you flirted with me."

"But you don't—"

"Signify," he finished for her with a grimace, eliciting another soft laugh from her that almost took away the sting of the unintentional insult. "Yes, I know." He pulled her into a tight circle. "You thought I was Robert, and you flirted just fine with me—with him—then."

"Because I wasn't being me. I was being Lady Rose and all...seductive."

Oh yes, she had certainly been that, and his body heated at the memory of just how much. "You're the same person."

Her full mouth pulled down into a slight frown even as she continued to move light as a feather in his arms, her feet gracefully sweeping across the floor in synchronicity with his. "Lady Rose wore a mask, and you had no idea who I was. It's easy to flirt when a man doesn't know who you are."

He gazed down into her green eyes, noticing the flecks of gold that caught the light from the chandelier. How had he never noticed before how beautiful her eyes were, how large and expressive? "But that defeats the purpose of flirting," he murmured, "if the man doesn't know the woman's identity."

Her brow wrinkled in a puzzled frown. "What's the purpose, then?"

"Seduction," he answered, his voice a throaty hum he hadn't intended.

But then, it seemed he was always doing or saying things around Miranda that he never intended. *Seduction?* Good Lord...but he couldn't help himself. Especially when her lips parted in delicate surprise at the boldness of his answer. He stared at her sensuous mouth, remembering how sweet she tasted the night of the masquerade. How smooth her skin. How the scent of roses wafted up from her body and perfumed his bed with the floral scent of her for the rest of his sleepless night. And not just her physical allure but the pure energy of her. The sense of excitement that radiated from her. The wit and laughter that lightened his chest the way nothing else in his life had been able to do recently. That it was Miranda Hodgkins of all women—astonishing.

"Practice with me now," he cajoled, knowingly drifting toward dangerous waters but unable to resist the unexpected siren song of her.

She hesitated with a lingering look over her shoulder at the terrace doors. That glance clawed at his gut because he knew she was still searching for Robert. But Robert would not be coming for her. And Sebastian was selfishly glad that he wasn't.

"Come on, Rose," he teased. "Pretend I'm not some stuffy, old duke." He grinned at her despite the self-deprecating jab. "Pretend I matter."

"You do," she assured him, "just not like that."

His lips tightened, feeling a sting at her words. "*That* is not the way to start a flirtation."

She laughed easily, and her hesitancy melted into a bright smile. Which was the exact right way to start.

"That's better," he murmured appreciatively. "You have a pretty smile. You should use it to your advantage."

She scoffed. "You make flirtation sound like war tactics!"

"It is." He crooked up an experienced brow. "And just as deadly for the man caught unawares in a female's trap."

Another laugh, and another comfortable warmth blossomed in his chest at the sound. This time when he stepped her through the circle in the corner and started back across the floor, she moved deeper into his arms, and he let her. Not enough that anyone watching would have noticed. But *he* did.

"So," he continued shamelessly in his instruction, "you've also got the flirtatious laughter down." When she swatted him playfully on the shoulder with her fan in mock ire, she drew a grin from him. "And the fan work."

Another low laugh purred from her, falling through him in a simmering heat that inexplicably had him longing to follow Robert and Miss Morgan out into the dark garden with her. Good heavens, she was lovely tonight. Simply enchanting.

Except when she thought of Robert. So best to keep her attention away from his soon-to-be-dead ex-brother.

"We'll practice flattery next," he instructed.

"But you've already told me that I have a pretty smile," she reminded him, giving him another one.

He was quickly learning to appreciate her smiles. "Not of you. Me."

She blinked, surprised. "You?"

"If you want a man to know you're interested in him without showing up in his bedroom at midnight—"

"*That* was a mistake," she interjected with an irritated huff.

"Then you need to let him know in more subtle ways." He repeated for emphasis, "*Subtle* ways, Rose."

"All right," she agreed suspiciously. "Such as?"

"A small compliment that makes a man feel masculine and handsome. Confident." He led her through a gliding turn. "Most men like hearing that sort of thing, even if they know it's rubbish."

Her eyes narrowed as she took in that bit of dubious advice and contemplated what he asked of her, with a curious look of deep study and concentration. For a moment, her expression was damnably disconcerting as she tried to think up a compliment to give him, as if she had never truly noticed him before as a man. Which inexplicably irked him to no end. How could she have not noticed him before as someone other than the Duke of Trent, other than just a friend?

"What you're asking of me is impossible." She shook her head with a soft sigh of defeat. "Every man in this room knows the rank you hold, the power and influence you're gaining in Parliament. As for the ladies, you should have seen the way they all watched you when you crossed the room to ask me to dance." She shrugged. "What could I possibly add to what everyone has already told you about how wonderful you are?"

He stared at her, momentarily stunned speechless. What she'd just said was *exactly* the kind of compliment a man wanted to hear from a beautiful woman...

And he didn't believe a word of it. When he saw her lips twitch with amusement, his eyes narrowed. "You are incorrigible."

She laughed happily. "Perhaps." Her eyes shined, and for a brief moment, she shifted closer, somehow rising up on tiptoes as she danced to bring her mouth close to his ear. "But it *is* all true, you know."

Then she pulled back into her original position and looked at him shyly through lowered lashes even as the tip of her tongue darted out to wet her lips. The paradoxical effect of innocent seduction was mesmerizing, and for a moment, he forgot they were dancing in the middle of a crowded ballroom. For a moment, there was only Miranda. And the pull of her was undeniable.

"You are a wonderful duke, Sebastian, and you make your family so proud," she admitted, suddenly serious. Her soft voice was barely audible over the music swirling around them, yet every word reverberated inside him with an aching throb. "As for the ladies, I think they're all jealous of me for stealing you away for two dances tonight." She smiled at him with a small squeeze of her fingers around his, completely unaware of how that small touch pulsed straight through him to his core. "Thank you for waltzing with me. You came to my rescue when I needed you."

His mouth went dry, unprepared for the completely guileless, unpracticed allure of her as it spun through him and made him feel like a hero. Oh yes, she certainly knew how to flirt, even if *she* didn't realize it. "You're welcome," he rasped out, his voice surprisingly husky.

She shifted her gaze to their hands, where he held hers securely in his. "I'm sorry that you had to give up your waltz with Lady Jane."

"No harm done," he answered, bewildered at himself that he hadn't thought about Jane since their dance began. And a great deal confused that Miranda could so easily tie him in knots with only a smile but couldn't capture Robert's attention no matter what she did.

"The ladies in the retiring room will certainly be in a state for the rest of the evening," she commented. "Do you want me to put in a good word for you, or leave you to your own schemes?"

He blinked. The only scheme he cared at all about right then was figuring out how to bring her even closer in his arms. "Pardon?"

"Our agreement," she reminded with a soft smile. "You tried to make Robert notice me tonight, and it wasn't your fault that he didn't. But I can still be of assistance to you, if you'd like."

As he stared down at her, his mind blanked. He had no idea what to say to her about that. At that moment, the only woman in his thoughts was her.

The waltz ended, and he twirled her through the final circle with a lively flourish, one that had her laughing and sparkling as brilliantly as the crystal chandelier shining overhead. He bowed as she dropped into a curtsy, then led her from the floor to return her to his mother. The heat of her hand lingered on his fingers long after he released her and walked away.

Circling once around the ballroom, he hunted through the crowd with a single-minded focus, his anger increasing with each step. Not finding Robert inside, and knowing Miranda was right in her suspicions of what his brother had been up to instead of waltzing with her, he stalked through the open French doors and out onto the dimly lit terrace.

Robert stood alone on the far end in the shadows, leaning back casually against the side of the house. Obviously, he had been outside with Miss Morgan and was now giving her time to find her way back inside without creating the gossip of being caught returning together.

"Hey, Seb." Robert grinned as Sebastian approached. "How goes the wife-hunt—"

"You left Miranda without a partner for her first waltz." Clenching his hands at his sides, he demanded, "Why?"

Guilt darkened his brother's face, and his eyes widened as he realized what he'd done. "Oh Lord," he admitted in a low voice, "I completely forgot. I'd talked Diana into spending a few minutes out here on the terrace and..." He blew out a harsh breath and rubbed his hand at the nape of his neck. "Is the sprite furious at me?"

"She's not a *sprite*, Robert," Sebastian bit out, unleashing the anger that Miranda was too kind to show toward his brother. "She's a grown woman. And you didn't make her furious. You hurt her, both her pride and her heart."

At least Robert had the decency to look ashamed. "I lost track of time. I didn't—"

"What the *hell* were you thinking, to sneak off with another woman when you were supposed to be attending to Miranda this evening?"

Robert stared at him, stunned into silence. Sebastian's anger was out of character for him, but his younger brother also knew not to argue back, having lost too many fights to him while they were growing up. And tonight, Sebastian knew, Robert wouldn't stand a chance. Something about this damnable evening had him on edge, wound tight as a coiled spring, and just one wrong word from Robert, just one more unkindness to Miranda—

"If you *ever* embarrass her like that again," he threatened, "you'll answer to me. Understand?"

Robert nodded slowly, bewilderment on his face at Sebastian's behavior. "My apologies," he said soberly. "Won't happen again."

He unclenched his fists. "Make certain you claim her second waltz."

Robert's brows drew together, puzzled. "But it's already taken."

"Then take it away from the man!" he growled, spinning on his heel to storm back inside. Good Lord, he needed a drink, and none of that watery Madeira, either. He'd take an ax and chop into St James's private liquor cabinet himself if he had to—

"It's you, Seb," Robert called out after him. "She told me when I asked her for a dance. You're the man who offered for her second waltz."

He halted in mid-stride. For a single heartbeat, he hesitated, torn between the irrational desire for a second waltz with Miranda and the prudence of knowing better. *Damnation*, how much he wanted another dance with her. Another chance to hold her in his arms and laugh with her, another few minutes of precious reprieve from the stiff propriety of being a duke when he could simply be himself.

But Miranda wanted Robert. And he'd promised to help her.

"Take it," he snapped out and stormed away.

* * *

Miranda moved across the dance floor with Robert for her second—and last—waltz of the evening.

Knowing Sebastian had already claimed the dance from her, she'd expected him to come for her again, and truly, she'd been looking forward to another dance with him. She'd enjoyed the first waltz, far more than she'd thought possible. And the flirting lesson. That it was *Sebastian* of all men who had encouraged her to flirt with him—oh, she nearly laughed in astonishment at that! Since the season began, Sebastian had proven to be one surprise after another.

Instead, it was Robert who came for her while Sebastian claimed the waltz with Lady Jane that he had been denied earlier. For a heartbeat, she felt an unfathomable pang of disappointment that Robert wasn't Sebastian.

"I'm sorry, Miranda," Robert apologized with a squeeze of her fingers in his as he twirled her around the floor. "Your first waltz should have been with me, and I regret missing it with you."

Her belly tightened. Robert was apologizing, truly *apologizing*, and she should have been ecstatic that he'd cared enough about her feelings to regret the slight. Instead, though, all she felt was vaguely peeved at herself that she'd made such a small impression on him tonight that he'd so easily forget about her. Was Sebastian right—was it time that she considered giving up her hopes for Robert?

"There's nothing to apologize for," she whispered, because he expected it, and turned her face away to gaze out across the room.

Dancing with Robert was nothing like she'd imagined. Oh, it was a lovely waltz, and Robert was skilled in his steps, guiding her competently around the floor. But he simply wasn't as naturally graceful as Sebastian had been, as if they had moved together as one rather than the two separate dancers she and Robert were. There was also none of the casual teasing she'd experienced with Sebastian, nothing to put her at ease.

And certainly none of the flirting.

She didn't even attempt it with Robert. Because for all the tutoring that Sebastian gave her about how to catch a man's attention, he'd left unspoken what she knew to be the most important part—that a woman could only successfully flirt with a man who welcomed her flirtations. And during the past few weeks Robert had proven himself most unwelcoming to seeing her as a woman with whom he might flirt.

Miranda's heart sank. Even as she followed his lead, she blinked back the sting of the unshed tears and kept her smile firmly in place—the same one Sebastian had assured her was so pretty. Her heart was breaking, but she wouldn't let anyone see, including Robert. And *especially* not Sebastian.

Even now as Robert danced with her, his eyes strayed across the room to Diana Morgan, who kept looking back at him without trying to seem as if she were. Which was laughable, because on the other side of the dance floor Lady Jane kept looking at Sebastian, who kept watching Miranda and Robert instead of Lady Jane.

And Miranda simply didn't know where to look.

CHAPTER EIGHT

Two Frustrating Days Later

Sebastian frowned, unable to concentrate on the opera. Even the opening night performance of *The Magic Flute* couldn't hold his attention.

Tonight, his distraction was decidedly female. He'd been fortunate enough to secure a private box for the season, located right at the heart of the opera house and only two down from the Earl of Bentham's box on the right, where Lady Jane sat in the front row. While to his immediate left sat Miranda Hodgkins.

Both women wore the low-cut, tight-bodice gowns that were all the rage for evenings at the opera, but there all similarities ended. Lady Jane looked coolly regal in her sapphire-blue satin that accentuated the paleness of her skin and the dark chestnut of her hair, while Miranda in her emerald-green velvet and loosely pinned strawberry-blond tresses looked utterly soft and warm.

He frowned. Tonight, she was simply lovely.

Yet she was oblivious to the whispers and stares she drew

from the crowd around them, who had come to the opera less for the Mozart and more for the gossip...all of them wondering who she was, what she was like, if she was as lovely in person as she looked from a distance. Certainly a good deal of the *on-dit* flowing through the house tonight concerned him as well, curious if he were more to her than the man who sponsored her introduction. Of course, the whole situation was made worse by the enraptured way she watched the singers on the stage, each emotionally expressive aria mirrored on her face, when no one who was part of the quality actually came to the opera to *watch* the opera. Just another distinction between her and the other ladies in attendance. And as far as he was concerned, one in her favor.

Since she'd arrived in London, Miranda had blossomed. Sebastian couldn't deny that. And thankfully, with much relief, she also hadn't done anything to cause undue gossip, despite how her exuberance continued to draw attention, especially from the staid and dull matrons of the *ton* who wrongly saw her as competition for their own female relatives. But he could have easily laid to rest any assumptions that he wanted her for himself. Oh, she was lovely in her new city finery, and surprisingly clever and witty. Yet beneath the fancy gowns and intelligence still lurked the country gel who had set fire to the mercantile.

Which was why he'd put her right next to him, front and center in the box, so he could keep an eye on her, while simultaneously keeping an eye on Lady Jane.

Behind them sat Josie and his mother, who was thrilled by all the marriage-focused activity surrounding the family this season. Although he wasn't certain she believed his intent to wed by August, he couldn't be more resolved to the matter. During the past few weeks, he had continued to narrow down his list of potential wives, and still Lady Jane seemed the most promising. And clearly receptive to the idea, based on what Miranda had told him she'd overhead at various soirees. He wasn't officially courting her yet, but he'd been focusing his attention on her, making certain to speak with her privately whenever they met. But he'd yet to formally call on her, holding back from officially declaring himself. After all, there was no hurry to make a decision, and he wanted to be certain that no one else would prove a better choice for his duchess.

Less resolved to imminent marriage but openly courting Miss Morgan, Robert continued to insist to his brothers that he had no intention of offering for her anytime soon. His mother, though, certainly hoped differently.

Then there was Miranda.

Despite her protests that she wasn't seeking suitors, she'd been pursued since her arrival in London by several young gentlemen who had met her at one of her various outings and become smitten, deeply enough that they'd begun to call on her at Audley House. A few brave ones had actually possessed the spine to speak with him at Park Place about courting her, until he chased them away. *Good riddance.* None of them were right for her. And Miranda certainly wouldn't have given them any consideration anyway, if only because they weren't Robert.

His mother thought differently, however. It seemed that every time he turned around his mother was calling a man's attention to Miranda. Mother had gone so far in encouraging her to be courted, in fact, that she'd asked Sebastian to give Miranda a dowry should any young man decide to offer and should Miranda surprise all of them by accepting.

But Robert still had no idea that she loved him.

And then, there was Charles Downing, who sat at Miranda's left. The young man had met her at an art exhibition, and when Downing came to Park Place to ask permission to escort her to the opera, Sebastian had no good reason to refuse. A respected bank officer from a solidly middle-class family, Downing was conservative and staid, pleasant, and intelligent enough, with high moral values and a steady temperament—overall, perfectly harmless.

Yet something about the man irritated Sebastian, especially after Miranda agreed to allow Downing to escort her for the evening. Certainly, she'd agreed in order to please his mother, who was now encouraging her to change her mind about her season and accept suitors. But Sebastian also wondered if her feelings for Robert were softening, because she'd been trying less hard to capture his brother's attention since the ball.

So he decided that a night at the opera would be a fine idea for Miranda and Downing...and that the entire family would go *en masse* with them.

A burst of exuberant applause from beside him drew his attention back to her, just in time to see her wondrous expression at the Queen of the Night's first aria. Miranda Hodgkins may have been trouble personified, but he was grateful that he was here to experience her first opera with her. Seeing it through her eyes...*magical.*

She turned toward him with joy dancing on her face. His gut pinched at the sight. Dear God...she was beautiful. How had he never noticed before this season how truly alluring she was?

"Are you enjoying the music?" He leaned casually toward her to be heard above the applause, and because he wanted to be close to her tonight.

"It's wonderful," she answered with that beaming smile he'd come to know so well. That she liked Mozart as much as he did pleased him a great deal.

"Sadly, though," he teased as he lowered his mouth close to her ear, "no pirate scenes."

She slapped him gently on the shoulder with her fan. "Never underestimate the advantages of a good pirate scene," she chided.

He fought to keep from laughing, his lips twitching as he agreed with mock solemnity, "Certainly not."

"*Hamlet* would have been so much better with a pirate scene." She gave a long-suffering sigh. "It would have saved the entire play."

Then he did laugh, unable to hold back any longer. Glancing sideways at him, she gave him a smile that tugged mischievously at the corners of her pink lips. *Imp.* Only Miranda could make him laugh in the middle of Mozart.

But the laughter choked in his throat when he glanced past her and caught Charles Downing watching them both curiously. Then the man frowned at him.

Sebastian felt damnably uncomfortable. Clearing his throat and shifting away from Miranda, he glanced away in the opposite direction—

And directly at Lady Jane as she stared at him thoughtfully from her family's private box. Stiffly, he nodded a greeting to her, and she returned his acknowledgment with a demure flit of her fan.

Good Lord. Was no one but Miranda actually watching the opera tonight?

Unaware that they were under the attention of at least two sets of eyes, Miranda leaned closer to him and whispered, "Are all operas as much fun as this one?"

In the dim light, he drank in the way she looked with the soft shadows falling gently across her delicate face, the dark green velvet of her gown accentuating her softness and warmth, the single emerald pendant drawing attention to the graceful length of her throat. The low lamplight burnished red highlights in her hair that had been lifted into a soft pile on her crown with loose tendrils tickling at the sides of her face. But most of all, there was her enraptured expression as she hung on each note, entranced by the spectacle onstage.

"No," he answered quietly. *Only because you're here...* "But this is one of the very best. My favorite, in fact."

She sighed. "Mine, too."

"It's your only opera," he corrected, unable to help the amused smile playing at his lips.

"That's what makes it my favorite," she confided.

He chuckled softly as he continued to watch her watch the opera, entertained as much by the show of emotions playing across her face as by the show onstage. Coming from any other woman, he would have taken the comment as some offhanded remark from an uneducated gel who didn't possess the maturity to hold the attention of a man like him. Or a hollow attempt at blatant flattery. But from Miranda, the earnest comment was seductive in its simplicity.

Shakespeare. Milton. Now Mozart. He was beginning to see all the many, complicated facets of her even if he couldn't yet completely fathom the woman beneath. But he knew now that she wasn't the flighty chit he'd always assumed her to be. Miranda wasn't capricious or immature. She simply loved life and all the new experiences it offered, which the rest of them had grown too jaded to appreciate.

And he, more than anyone, knew exactly how mature she was.

When she leaned over to whisper to him, the side of her breast accidentally brushed his arm. He stiffened, feeling that innocent touch rush through him with the force of an electric jolt.

"Why isn't anyone else paying attention?" Her voice was little more than a breath, yet it made him tremble. She had no idea of the way she tied him into knots with only the soft tickle of her warm whispers in his ear. "Don't they realize how wonderful the opera is?"

"They don't have the same refined tastes as stodgy, old dukes and orphanage manageresses," he replied wryly with an exaggerated shake of his head. "No appreciation of the finer arts. Or of pirates."

She gave a throaty laugh at his teasing, one that fell through him like warm rain.

His gut tightened with quick arousal. She hadn't meant the laugh as a flirtation, but that was exactly how it had come out. And he liked it. Immensely.

Recklessly, he sought more. He leaned toward her, close enough to catch the delicious scent of roses lingering on her skin, and whispered, "Some of the people here haven't come to hear the music."

She puzzled. "Then why are they here?"

"To be seen in their finery and to see others in theirs, to gossip and catch up on the latest rumors..." He watched her expression as he added, unable to help himself, "For secret trysts."

"Secret trysts?" she repeated, her breath hitching.

He smiled at her innocence, a trait he'd so rarely found in the women who pursued him this season in their hopes to catch a duke. "Haven't you wondered why so many of the private boxes now have their curtains drawn?"

With a bewildered frown, she glanced at the opera house around her. "No. Why would they..." Her words trailed off into a soft, comprehending gasp.

Her eyes widened as if seeing for the first time the building that had surrounded them for the past two hours, realizing exactly what must have been going on at that very moment in the darkness behind those pulled curtains. Her pink lips formed a round O, although no sound came beyond a soft breath.

A devilishly wicked urge to smile gripped him. As he watched her with amusement, he wondered if the dim shadows of their box hid from him a hot blush on her soft cheeks. And grateful that they did, because he found himself enjoying this inappropriate conversation far more than he should. If he had proof that she found it arousing as well, he might be tempted to give her yet another lesson on flirting. One far more erotic and scandalous than before.

"But the king's box is also... *Oh.*"

He bit his inner cheek to keep from laughing.

She didn't dare look at him then, her eyes focused straight ahead. But the corners of her mouth curled into the start of a bewitching, wanton smile. Her eyes shining knowingly, she whispered, "Who knew opera could be so... inspiring?"

Then he did laugh and drew scowls from the people seated around them. But he didn't care. Talking with her like this was too liberating to stop. For a few moments here in the shadows, exchanging whispers with her, he could again be the mischievous rogue he'd once been, and he'd missed being that man. Greatly. Tonight with Miranda made him realize exactly how much.

"I don't understand these people," she whispered, a touch of bewilderment lacing her voice. "I mean, they can be *inspired* anywhere, but they're behind curtains, missing the most wonderful music."

He bit back the urge to tell her that many of the couples being inspired by each other tonight were not otherwise together except behind those closed curtains, because the curious woman would then want to know how he knew that. And Sebastian wasn't prepared to share with her how many nights he'd spent behind those very same drawn curtains himself, missing the opera.

"It's because of the singers," he pressed on, although he knew he should stop. This conversation was for courtesans and demimondaines, not for innocents like Miranda. But he simply couldn't help himself. The reaction she created inside him was too titillating to eschew. "Hearing all those high notes," he boldly whispered into her ear, "stirs a man's blood."

She froze for a moment, not visibly reacting to that blatant and wholly improper flirtation. For a heartbeat, he wondered if he'd gone too far and pushed the limits of their newfound friendship too hard—

Then she breathed out, "It's all that passion, isn't it?" She spoke so softly he barely heard her, but each word seeped into him like liquid heat. "Watching it onstage, hearing it swirl around you, becoming swept up in it until you're part of it…"

"Exactly," he murmured, then thrilled when she exhaled a shaky sigh in the first signs of quiet arousal.

"And if you're hidden in the shadows, in the darkness, where no one can see nor ever know…I suppose it would be tempting for a woman, too."

Shamelessly wanting to see more of how his words affected her, he asked, "Tempting how?"

"For a woman to be able to ask for what she wants." Her breathing grew shallow and rapid. "If she wants the man she's with to kiss her, or touch her…or something else."

The scent of rosewater filled his senses. "Would you, Miranda?" Intoxicated by her nearness, he pressed wickedly, "Ask for that?"

Even the shadows couldn't hide the blush that now darkened her cheeks or the way she trembled. "I—I might."

His heart skipped. Inexplicably, he wanted nothing more at that moment than to be alone with her in one of those boxes with its curtains pulled, hearing her ask for what she wanted from him, with nothing else in the world to worry about but pleasing her.

But that was what he wanted as a man. As a duke, he could never have it. His days of finding physical pleasures in theater boxes were over. They'd died right along with his father. Knowing that only sharpened his frustration.

"And you?" she asked in a breathy whisper, completely unaware of the turmoil she churned inside him. She didn't dare to turn her head to look at him. "Does the opera stir your blood?"

He stared at her profile in the shadows, his gut tightening at the raw pull of her, and confessed, "*You* stir my blood, Miranda."

She froze, except for her lips, which parted with a silent gasp of surprise. Then she slowly turned her head to meet his gaze, her eyes wide. Her breath came in soft, shallow little pants. "Sebastian—"

Suddenly, the audience burst into applause, destroying the illusion of privacy created by the shadows around them. He snapped his attention back to the stage as the curtain dropped for intermission and an army of attendants swarmed through the opera house to raise all the lamps. The theater became a flurry of activity as everyone rose from their seats to seek out refreshments in the lobby, gain a closer look at the other operagoers, and trade bits of gossip.

So did all the people inside his box. Except Miranda, who continued to stare at him in stunned confusion. He didn't blame her. He was damned confused himself at his own behavior, certain the Mozart had driven him mad.

He glanced past her at Downing, who rose to his feet with a puppy-dog smile for her. The man was completely oblivious to the scandalous whispers Sebastian had shared with Miranda only a few feet away. He should have felt guilty, he supposed, given both the man's close proximity and that Downing was here to capture Miranda's attention for himself, not to have it snatched away.

But guilt was the last thing he felt. He'd enjoyed that conversation too much to regret it.

"Do you like the opera, dear?" Elizabeth Carlisle stepped to her side and affectionately squeezed her hand.

"It's amazing," she confided, beaming. The improper conversation from just moments ago was now forgotten by her, even if *he* would be thinking about it for the rest of the night. "I want to go backstage and see all the costumes, the musicians, the stage sets...Do you think they'd mind if—"

"No," Sebastian refused firmly. "Proper ladies don't associate with opera singers and actors." Nor did dukes, he reminded himself with a pang of contrition. "They enjoy the performance from their seats."

But the determined look on her face raised the hairs on the back of his neck in warning. Oh, he knew that look. It was the same one he'd seen in the green eyes behind the masquerade mask the night she'd sneaked into his bedchamber.

When his mother and Josie moved toward the door to head into the hall with the rest of the crowd, Miranda slid away after them.

Oh no. That little force of nature was going nowhere.

Sebastian slipped between her and the door, just as his mother and Josie stepped out into the hall. They disappeared into the crush of bodies shuffling toward the retiring rooms and lobby.

"I think you would enjoy remaining in the box during intermission," Sebastian told her, his polite words belying the firm order in the tone of his voice. He knew perfectly well that the curious woman would find her way backstage and straight into trouble if he let her out of his sight for one moment. He slid a sideways glance to her right and smiled coldly at the banker, who hadn't left her side since he arrived at Audley House to escort her. "With Mr. Downing to keep you company."

Oblivious to the true meaning of the exchange between them, Downing's smile widened. "What a grand idea."

"But I want a glass of punch," Miranda insisted, irritation sounding in her voice at having her backstage plans thwarted.

Downing eagerly offered, "I'll fetch one for you."

"What a fine idea." Sebastian grinned at her. He might come to like the man after all.

Her eyes narrowed, her hands drawing into clenched fists at her sides as she glared at him. "And leave me alone in an opera box with a man, unchaperoned?" She arched a brow in challenge. "What if the music *inspires* us?"

Sebastian forced back the laugh rising inside him, both at her consternation and at her insinuation about Downing. The man was perfectly harmless.

He arched a brow. "Then that would be a magic flute, indeed."

A strangled sound of half fury, half mortification tore from her. And *heavens*, that was a neat trick! How her face turned so scarlet so quickly.

"Besides," he reminded her as he moved toward the door, "if you need anything, I'll be right outside."

As he stepped into the hall, the last glimpse Sebastian caught over his shoulder was of Downing smiling fondly at her while she stared daggers after him. He smothered down his laughter but not the smile that he couldn't prevent. After all, he felt freer to be himself tonight than he had in years. Who would have ever believed it would be because of Miranda Hodgkins?

Astonishing.

* * *

The second act began, but Miranda couldn't concentrate on what was happening onstage.

They had all shifted seats inside the box, thanks to Josie's suggestion that they rotate two chairs to give everyone a different view of the stage. That put Miranda in back next to Charles Downing and put Sebastian at the end of the front row farthest away from her.

Charles tried to lean closer and engage her in conversation, but while he was a sweet man and very attentive, he simply wasn't able to hold her attention the way the opera did as it unfolded on the stage below them. Or the way Sebastian had with that sordid conversation he'd lured her into, the one that made her pulse race with all the scandalous images he'd put into her head of what went on in private boxes behind pulled curtains.

And especially when he'd said that she stirred his blood.

She frowned as she stared at the back of his head, his attention focused on the stage below. Of all men to pull her into such an improper conversation... *Sebastian.* And she'd gone willingly, titillated by the brush of his hot lips at her ear and the faint ache his warm breath tingled between her thighs. The same way he'd made her feel the night of the masquerade with his talk of dancing when what he'd truly meant was ravishment. More, in fact—because it wasn't only a physical allure that drew her to him tonight, but also an intellectual connection. One she was beginning to suspect she'd never have with Robert.

Confusion swirled through her. She wanted to laugh at fate's cruel sense of humor, that the brother she wanted had yet to notice her as an alluring woman while the other engaged her in flirtations that made her head spin. But none of that mattered in the end. Because Robert wanted Diana Morgan, and Sebastian wanted a duchess. And the only person who seemed to want her...

She turned her head and caught Mr. Downing smiling at her.

Forcing a demure smile back at him, she turned away. *Heavens.* Nothing about courting and love was as easy as it appeared from the outside.

She needed air and a few minutes reprieve to collect herself before the opera finished and she'd have to plaster on a smiling face for the carriage ride back to Audley House, when she would have to pretend that nothing was wrong and confusion wasn't bubbling inside her. So she leaned forward and tapped Josie on the shoulder.

"I'm going to the retiring room," she whispered.

With sisterly concern, Josie nodded. "I'll come with you."

"Stay and enjoy the opera," she insisted, not wanting Josie to miss any of the production. "I'll only be gone a moment."

With an apologetic smile for the others, she rose from her chair and slipped from the box.

Except for attendants positioned outside the doors and one couple moving tardily back to their box, the hall was empty, and she hurried away, making her way quickly through the theater to the retiring room. She took a few minutes' privacy there to splash cool water on her face and calm her bewildered heart. Alone in the room, sitting at the dressing table in front of the mirror, she stared grimly at herself. To think that she'd promised to inform Sebastian of all the retiring room gossip in return for his help with Robert—what a sad state their pact was now in.

By the time her breathing had returned to normal, she'd convinced herself that Sebastian hadn't meant what he'd said about stirring her blood. That he'd only been caught up in the passion of the opera, exactly as she had been. Certainly it couldn't have been anything else.

But when she emerged from the retiring room, the last place she wanted to go was back to the box. Not when the only thing waiting for her there was more confusion. And Mr. Downing. So she asked directions to the back of the stage from an attendant in the lobby, then hurried away.

The opera house was like a maze, but she was determined to see backstage, to watch the singers up close and marvel over the sets and costumes. Most definitely not the province of respectable ladies, but oh, she simply didn't care! This was most likely her only chance to be backstage at an opera, and she refused to let the opportunity pass her by.

She was only fleetingly surprised that no one guarded the stage door nor tried to stop her when she slipped into the dark shadows of the wing. But then, who else would be sneaking back here but her? Taking hesitant steps, her pulse pounding like a drum in her ears, she carefully approached along the rear wall, creeping up as close to the lighted stage as she dared. The dark shadows and heavy set pieces from the first act that had been pushed aside into the wing hid her from all view. Not even the musicians playing in the pit nor the backstage hands busy with the technical elements of running the production could see her there.

It was simply amazing! In the darkness, she was free to watch the singers from only a few feet away, their voices so strong and vibrant that her chest reverberated with each note they sang. The effect was mesmerizing, and even though she knew she had only a precious few minutes' escape from the box, she couldn't bring herself to leave. The lamplight dazzled and the shadows thrilled, and her chest rose and fell with each musical phrase that poured from the two women on the stage. She barely remembered to breathe.

A hand touched her elbow from behind. She jumped, turning in surprise and ready to scream—

"Shh," Sebastian warned as he stepped up behind her, touching his fingers to her lips to keep her quiet. Then he nodded toward the stage, silently giving his permission to keep watching.

With a smile of gratitude, she turned back toward the stage. Excited happiness surged through her that he'd granted her this small concession and didn't demand she return immediately to the box. But neither did he move away, remaining close behind her. So close that she could feel the heat of his body radiating against her back.

Then he shifted even closer, and her heart pounded furiously. When he lowered his mouth to her ear as his hands lightly held her upper arms, the silly thing leapt right into her throat!

"I knew I'd find you here." The warmth of his breath tickled across her cheek and sent tingles coursing through her.

"I couldn't resist," she returned in the same soft murmur. He stood so close...could he feel the way he made her heart race with just a whisper, or know how the masculine scent of him made her ache? "Haven't you ever wanted something so much that you were helpless to resist?"

His fingers tightened almost imperceptibly on her arms. But Miranda noticed. At that moment, with her senses heightened by the music swirling around them and the interplay of the lamplight and dark shadows, she noticed everything about him, every subtle shift of his body, every deep breath he drew. His nearness confused her...yet also pleased her more than she wanted to admit.

"Yes," he murmured against her ear. That single word sent heat cascading through her and spun the confusion inside her until it churned into a tight knot in her belly.

Yet she kept her gaze locked on the singers, not daring to turn her head to look at him. If she did, he would see the unbidden effect he had on her, and she would never be able to live down the embarrassment. Especially when he'd most likely only followed her here to summon her back to the box like a chaperone. "Then you understand why I had to come backstage."

His lips curled against her ear in a teasing smile. "And abandon poor Downing?"

Oh, that smile! It twined around her spine and made her long to feel those lips against hers. "He seems capable of withstanding my abandonment," she countered in a breathless whisper.

His hands drifted slowly down her bare arms, fanning goose bumps in their wake. "You don't enjoy his company?"

"I couldn't—" Her breath hitched when his hands reached her wrists, and instead of letting her go, they slipped beneath her arms to rest on her hips. Well, *that* was definitely not the touch of a chaperone. Swallowing hard to clear the nervous tightening of her throat, she began again, confessing with a twinge of embarrassment, "I couldn't have the same kind of conversation with him that I had with you."

"I certainly hope not." He slipped one hand around to her front and splayed his fingers wide across her belly. "You'd have had the poor man in a lather."

She trembled, not knowing what to do or say. Sebastian was holding her in his arms, his hard chest brushing against her back, and his hand...Heavens, his hand! Good Lord, did he realize how scandalously he was holding her? Even if he meant only to keep her still so no one would see her move in the darkness and catch them watching from the wings, where he held her—

Suddenly *very* nervous, she gave a soft laugh, one that emerged far more sultry than she'd intended. Blast it! Even her laughs were against her. "Charles Downing? I think not."

"You don't like him?" he pressed, his lips brushing tantalizingly against her ear.

She squeezed her eyes closed against the shiver his hot mouth sent racing through her. "He's nice, but..."

"But he isn't Robert," he finished, a strange timbre dulling his voice.

Her heart skipped. That couldn't be jealousy she heard. Impossible! Certainly not from Sebastian. Still, though, she liked the sound of it, and she knew that now was not the time to admit to suspecting that Robert might never be hers, not if she wanted to hear it again. Which she did. *Very* much.

"No," she whispered, softly baiting him, "he's not."

He shocked her by nuzzling his mouth against her ear, and she gasped. That, oh, *that* was clearly not an accidental brush of whispering lips! He'd meant to caress her, and the warm longing it sent spiraling through her for another touch like that nearly undid her. Drawing a deep breath as she threw all caution and sense to the wind, she tilted her head to give him access to her neck and shoulder, unable to deny the temptation of having his mouth on her.

With a pleased smile against her ear, he took her silent invitation and nibbled at her earlobe. "What is it about my brother," he murmured, "that draws you so?"

Before she could answer, the tip of his tongue traced the outer curl of her ear, swirled down, and plunged inside. She shuddered at the delicious sensation, and his hand pressed tighter against her belly to keep her still in his arms.

The confusion inside her gave way to a tingling warmth that ached low in her belly. With one little lick, Sebastian had set her blood humming, making her body shiver and her thighs clench the way he had that night in his bedroom when she thought he was Robert. She knew who was kissing her this time, yet knowing he was the wrong Carlisle brother made no difference to the heat rising through her traitorous body. She should step away—this was *Sebastian*, for heaven's sake, and the most wrong man in the world for her, save for the king himself—but she simply couldn't make herself leave the circle of his strong arms.

"Robert is masculine," she breathed, her words barely audible above the aria swirling around them and fanning the longing inside her to be touched, in all the most wicked places.

"Most men are," he answered, dancing heated kisses down the side of her neck.

When he placed his mouth against that patch of bare skin where her neck curved into her shoulder, a hot throbbing sprang up between her thighs. She bit her lip to keep back a soft whimper. She shouldn't like having his hands on her this much, shouldn't let them wander over her so freely like this... certainly she shouldn't want to be touched even more intimately. But she did, and she could barely stand still in his arms.

"He's handsome," she forced out, hoping he couldn't hear the nervous trembling that crept into her voice or sense the confusion still simmering inside her.

"Hmm." His hand on her hip drifted upward along the side of her body, lightly tracing across her ribs. She trembled achingly when his fingers grazed the side swell of her breast, and she instinctively arched her back into his chest. "We're brothers. We look alike."

Oh, that was *definitely* jealousy! But her kiss-fogged brain couldn't sort through the confusion he sent swirling inside her to discern why he'd be jealous of Robert. Especially when his teeth nipped gently at her bare shoulder and his hand caressed once more along the side of her breast.

"Not so much alike," she countered, although she'd always thought Sebastian would be more handsome if he wasn't always so serious and brooding, with that perpetual frown of disapproval hanging over his brow. If he did more spontaneous and unexpected things . . . like licking a woman on her nape at an opera. *Oh my.* She shivered at the audacity of his mouth and at the heat it sent slithering down her spine.

"Very nearly identical," he mumbled, his mouth returning to her shoulder as his hand roamed up to trace his fingers along the neckline of her gown. Completely unexpected yet wantonly thrilling, the caress sent her heart somersaulting just inches from his fingertips.

"He's exciting . . . a risk-taker . . . " Her voice was a breathless hum despite knowing that in his rivalry with his brother he didn't want to touch her as much as he wanted to touch her before Robert did. At that moment, though, with his fingertips lightly brushing over the top swells of her breasts, she simply didn't care. At least not enough to make him stop. "He's thrilling."

He slipped his fingers into the valley between her breasts. When his fingertips traced slow circles against the inner curves of her breasts, she was powerless against the soft whimper that fell from her lips.

"Lots of men are thrilling." He smiled wickedly against her neck at the reaction his seeking fingers elicited from her. "I'm thrilling."

"*You?*" She gave a throaty laugh of surprise. "Sebastian, you're the most reserved, restrained man I—"

In one fluid motion, he turned her in his arms and pushed her back against the set wall, his mouth swooping down to capture hers and swallow her words as he kissed her into silence. Her hands clenched into the hard muscles of his shoulders as his body pressed against hers, and she stiffened beneath the startling onslaught of his lips, of his hips pushing into hers, all of him demanding possession of the kiss. And of her.

Aching heat flashed through her, shooting out through the tips of her fingers and toes. With a moan of need, she melted into the embrace. Her hands no longer clenched at him to hold him away but to pull him closer.

Stroking up and down her sides to encourage her to eagerly return the kiss, he mumbled something against her lips she couldn't quite make out...

"Open," he cajoled against her kiss. "Open for me."

Then he pulled back. A soft whimper of protest fell from her at the loss of him, until she felt his thumb caress over her chin, pull down with a gentle tug, and part her lips.

His mouth returned to hers, and this time when he kissed her, his tongue slipped gently between her parted lips to plunder the moist depths of her mouth and coax her into returning the new intimacy between them. One that left her trembling, hot, and bewilderingly wanting more.

Tentatively, she touched the tip of her tongue to his, and he groaned in response. Her pulse raced at the masculine sound. He liked it...Good heavens, he *liked* what she was doing to him! Seized by a wanton urge brought on by the scandalous way they were behaving and by the electric pulse of the opera unfolding next to them, she boldly caressed her tongue over his as she slid her hands across his broad shoulders to run her fingers through the silky hair at his nape.

Her body shivered and flamed in turns, craving his kiss and his touch even as she knew she should run away. This was Sebastian. *The duke.* The man who had never paid her any mind before this season except to chastise her for causing trouble. An old friend she'd known practically all her life. She shouldn't be feeling these kinds of sensations with him, these kinds of wicked pleasures...and oh, such pleasures! When his hand swept up to cup her breast, his fingers teasing at her nipple through her dress, she stopped thinking and simply let herself feel.

"Sebastian," she whispered as the aria's high notes vibrated into her. She arched her back to bring his hand tighter against her and increase the devilish pressure on that aching, hard point he squeezed between his thumb and forefinger.

"I told you that you stirred my blood, Miranda," he murmured heatedly as his lips once more found hers, this time to alternate between nipping sharply at her bottom lip with his teeth and soothingly stroking over it with his tongue. "Did you think I was lying?"

"Yes," she whispered honestly.

He laughed, and the deep sound tickled at her lips. "There's something about you that draws me...the way you pulse full of life, the way you make me laugh—"

"The way I keep letting you kiss me," she said with a stab of self-recrimination.

He grinned appreciatively at her. "That, too." He kissed her again, long and deep and possessive, to demonstrate to her exactly how much he liked it. "You are very inspiring, Rose, in every way."

She shivered at the loss of his heat as his hand left her breast and wandered down her body. "Am I?"

"Surprisingly so." His hand caressed languid circles across her belly, with each turn stroking achingly lower. "So much so"—he moved his mouth away from hers to kiss along her jaw and back to that sensitive spot just behind her ear that made her tremble—"that if we had a box all to ourselves"—his hand slid down her belly, as if seeking out the heat aching at her core—"I would be sorely tempted to show you exactly how much."

She moaned at his wicked words. The heat of his hand soaked through the thin velvet of her gown as if it wasn't there at all and seeped into her lower belly, blossoming the ache between her thighs just beyond the ends of his fingertips. Her existence became nothing more than his hard, strong body holding her against the wall, the masculine scents of brandy and tobacco filling her senses with each breath of him she inhaled, and the heat of his fingers caressing tender tracings of silent promises against her belly.

She buried her face helplessly against his shoulder as she trembled, all the blood inside her seeming to pool and pulse right there between her legs. Right where she ached for his hand to touch, to caress just a few inches lower—

"Rose," he whispered huskily, his body now shaking as hard as hers. His lips teased into a smile against her temple as he alluded to her words from their earlier conversation, "Let yourself be tempted... Tell me what you want from me."

"I—I don't..." Fresh confusion swirled through her, mixing with the sweet arousal he flamed inside her. "I don't know."

"Do you want me to kiss you?"

"Yes," she sighed out. *Oh, very much.*

His mouth captured hers again in an intense kiss that so thoroughly plundered her mouth that her toes curled inside her slippers. She clung to him, breathless and weak-kneed.

He murmured against her lips. "Do you want me to touch you?"

"Oh yes," she answered in a breathy whisper that turned into a moan when he did just that, when his hand slid lower and pressed into the valley between her legs as she'd longed for him to do.

He cupped her through her skirt, but the velvet might not have been there at all given the heat that seeped into her. For a moment, neither of them moved, and there was only the sound of their breathing and the rush of blood through her ears with each pounding beat of her heart. Then he gently rubbed against her, slowly increasing the pressure until he ground the heel of his hand hard against her. A wonderful and wicked shudder swept through her, and she gave over to the urge to step her legs apart, to give him greater access to that aching place between her thighs. A pleased growl sounded from the back of his throat.

"Tell me what else you want, Rose, how else I can please you." Not ceasing in his caresses, which were somehow both a torment and a pleasure, he trailed his mouth back to her ear and whispered hotly, "Do you want... something else?"

The words crashed over her with the final notes of the

aria, and she snapped out of the fogged reverie he had cast over her.

Something else... She knew exactly what he meant, what temptation he was dangling in front of her now. Just as she knew that tonight he'd been caught up in the passion of the opera and his jealousy, that he wasn't thinking as a duke who had set himself on finding the perfect duchess but as a man who wanted to flee himself, if only for the evening. The irony was biting. Unlike Robert, Sebastian now saw her as a physically desirable woman rather than as the pesky girl in braids who had grown up next door. But he still wasn't seeing *her*.

What he saw when he gazed at her was escape.

Applause filled the opera house and reverberated inside her. She stepped back from the circle of his arms as disappointment swept over her. "No, I don't want that."

He stared down at her, his expression a mix of heady arousal and utter bewilderment, as if he simply couldn't fathom her. An expression that ripped through her chest.

The softness of his voice couldn't hide the bitterness lacing through his words as he latched on to the only explanation he could find. "Because of Robert?"

"No," she breathed, and his handsome face blurred behind the hot tears welling in her eyes. "Because of you."

CHAPTER NINE

~~

Two More Frustrating (and Utterly Confusing) Days Later

*M*iranda leaned over the railing and laughed joyfully at the jugglers performing on the alley in front of their box at Vauxhall Gardens.

"Don't you dare ask if you can learn to juggle," Sebastian warned in that same grumpy voice he'd used with her all evening. For the past two days, in fact. Since he kissed her backstage at the opera and she rejected him, apparently wounding his male pride.

And tonight was proving no different.

She gave an insulted sniff, irritated at him herself for kissing her so wonderfully when he knew nothing could come of it. Kissing? Oh, the aggravating devil had dared to do so much more! "I would never ask such a thing." Then, because she couldn't help tormenting him the way he'd tormented her for the past two days, she added, "But knife throwing! Now *there's* a skill I'd lov—"

He shot her a murderous glare that silenced her in mid-word.

She swallowed, thinking better of finishing that sentence after all.

The man was incomprehensible. At one moment warning her not to do anything that would cause a scandal, and at the next kissing her in such a way as to ruin her reputation if anyone caught them. At one moment, treating her as if she were a child, then touching her until she moaned with the passion of a woman. First agreeing to help her with Robert, then behaving as if he were jealous. Jealous? *Ha!* Not when he had the lovely Lady Jane at his side tonight as his personal guest. Yet instead of paying attention to Jane and engaging her in the same rakish conversation he'd held with Miranda at the opera, he'd spent his evening grumping and growling over every move she made.

Good heavens. The conundrum that was Sebastian Carlisle could drive a woman mad.

With a heavy sigh, she rose from her chair. He grabbed her arm, stopping her. "Where are you going?" he demanded.

She arched a brow, daring him to challenge her, here amid all their family and friends. "I want a glass of punch."

He released her arm. "Do not leave this box."

"Your talents are being wasted as a duke." As she slid past him, she lowered her head as close as possible to his ear without drawing attention. "You should have been a gaoler."

He turned in his chair as if to make a second attempt to stop her, but she was already gone, slipping around the dining table where they'd taken supper as guests of the Earl of St James.

The countess had sent invitations to Audley House and Park Place for all of them to join the couple in a private box at Vauxhall for the season opening of the pleasure gardens. So the entire Carlisle family and their guests—minus Josie and Chesney, who preferred to enjoy a quiet evening at home—had piled into several carriages and made their way through the city and across the Thames to the gardens.

Oh, the place was simply magical! The gardens were awash in colored lanterns, cascading fountains, and illuminated transparencies and filled with people wearing all manner of costumes and dress. Performers paraded down the alley at the heart of the gardens, while acrobats performed on ropes and wires strung between the galleries where private supper parties were held by those lucky enough to rent boxes. Farther away, Chinese lanterns lit the way to the pagoda at the park's center where a band was finishing its concert. Behind the pagoda lay a dark maze of narrow, winding paths through the trees where Sebastian forbade her to go the moment they'd arrived at the entrance gate.

Despite Sebastian's grumpiness, Miranda was enjoying herself. In fact, she'd hoped to convince Quinn to take her up in the hot-air balloon, but he was having too much fun with his friends from Boodle's and wouldn't be pulled away. And then there was Robert, who sat in the back of the box and had no time for anyone but Diana Morgan, who sat next to him.

Tonight, Miranda wasn't happy with any of the Carlisle men.

She smiled gratefully at the box attendant as the man handed her a glass of arrack punch from the tray, then grudgingly returned to her seat beside Sebastian. With all of them crowded into the box, the chair beside his was the only one available, unless she wanted to remain standing beside the attendant. Which was a surprisingly tempting idea.

Especially when Sebastian warned, "And don't even *think* about tightrope walking."

Men. She was beginning to think they were of no worth whatsoever except for reaching for items high on tall shelves and changing carriage wheels.

"If you must insist on being in a foul mood all evening," she countered, reaching the limit of her patience, "then I wish you would find someone else to torment. I am not deserving of it."

When she was answered only by his silence, she glanced sideways and caught him staring at her, an inscrutable expression on his face. His dark eyes studied her closely, contemplating her long enough that she fidgeted beneath his blue gaze.

But she wasn't naïve enough to believe he felt either remorse or guilt for the way he'd been treating her. Oh no—not the man who used her slippers for blackmail.

Then he stood. "If you'll excuse me. I'll be gone only a moment."

Miranda bit back the urge to tell him that there was no need to hurry back and returned her attention to the performers.

A new group had moved into the alley. A man dressed all in black and a woman in a red feather-covered gown stood atop a small wagon pulled by a team of donkeys. With them on the wagon was a large wooden box and a small table.

Catching the audience's attention, the man performed a variety of magic tricks at the table with the assistance of the woman in red, including making a gold sovereign magically appear inside an unpeeled orange and pulling a dove from a hat that he released to fly over the crowd and disappear into the night. With each increasingly difficult trick, the audience cheered, and Miranda applauded right along with them. She knew the tricks were nothing but illusion and sleight of hand, yet she watched enthralled. Perhaps the night might still prove magical after all.

Mesmerized by the final trick, she sat at the edge of her seat and leaned forward against the railing to watch as the man prepared to place the woman inside the box and make her vanish.

"Stay away from magicians," a deep voice warned at her ear. Which could only have been Sebastian, so she scowled, refusing to take her gaze away from the illusionist. He'd returned far faster than she'd hoped. "They should be avoided at all costs."

"Why?" She rolled her eyes and braced herself for another one of his orders to behave herself.

"Because they're the worst kind of scoundrels and cads," he murmured gently.

Surprised by that, she turned to look at him. He reached up toward her hair, the strawberry-blond strands pulled into a simple knot tonight, and tugged gently at one of the loose tendrils curling down to frame her face. When he lowered his hand, a small paper rose dropped magically into his fingers.

Her lips parted, speechless, at his magic trick.

"You are right, Miranda. I had no business ruining your evening tonight or your night at the opera." His blue eyes held hers in private communication as he presented the rose to her. "I fear that I behaved no better than a magician. My sincerest apologies."

Her heart tugged as she looked down at the red papier-mâché flower cupped in his palm. She might never understand this man, but she couldn't stay angry at him, either, not when he apologized like this. Her fingers trembled as she accepted the flower.

"Thank you," she whispered.

His eyes stared softly into hers. "You're welcome." After a short pause, he added, as if unable to help himself, "But do stay away from the tightropes, will you?"

She laughed and pressed the flower against her chest, her eyes tearing up at his apology. "I will, I promise."

Of all the things for him to do tonight, she certainly hadn't expected this! A flower as a peace offering. And most of all, an apology. Her chest lightened with relief. Now, they could be friends again, as they were meant to be, and he wouldn't give what happened between them at the opera a second thought.

As if to prove her correct, Sebastian turned his attention immediately back to Lady Jane, who had tapped his shoulder to inquire about one of the other members of Parliament in attendance tonight. Jane smiled at him, that demure expression that came so easily for her. So urbane and beautiful. Even just sitting there, in her pale gray gown and white ermine stole, with strings of pearls woven through her dark hair, she was quietly graceful and refined. Exactly the sort of woman Sebastian wanted for his wife.

Miranda slumped back in her chair, her shoulders sagging. Which only made her feel even worse given how ramrod-straight Lady Jane sat on the other side of him. So she stiffened her spine, pulled back her shoulders, and once again missed the loose-fitting dresses she wore in the country.

"The more daring ladies wear them behind their ears," Robert piped up as he leaned over her shoulder and saw the flower resting on her palm. Only a few weeks ago, she would have been all aflutter to have him speak into her ear like this.

But now, oddly enough, she felt not a single butterfly rise in her belly.

But she didn't let herself contemplate what that meant as she slipped the flower behind her ear. "Like this?"

"Beautiful." He gave her a smile, then jerked his thumb toward the pagoda. "Diana and I are going for ices. Want to come along?"

What he meant was that they needed a chaperone. Her heart sank. A chaperone for another couple in love was the very last thing she wanted to be tonight.

But a glance at Sebastian told her that she couldn't bear to stay behind with him and Lady Jane either.

She forced a smile. "Yes, I'll come."

As Robert and Diana slipped from the box, Miranda rose from her chair and caught Sebastian readying to give her one more warning. But she raised her brow in silent challenge and walked out the door.

Bustling with excitement and activity, the gardens were a wonderland of sights and sounds as she wandered into the busy alley after Robert and Diana. Within a matter of minutes, she'd lost sight of them in the crowd, but she wasn't the least bit upset by that. Not when she had all of the pleasure gardens to explore, all the wonders to experience for herself now that she was freed from Sebastian's leash. Besides, Diana and Robert were going for ices, which meant she'd eventually find them at the refreshments booths near the pagoda, at that point where the well-lit alleys gave way to the dark, close paths in the wooded acres away from the galleries and stages.

Around her, finely dressed men and women strolled past, along with more daring persons wearing fancy dress and covering their faces with masks. Harlequins danced by. So did a troupe of puppeteers, working life-size puppets in their hands. Two acrobats, holding on to each other's ankles, rolled past like a human hoop. A juggler tossed flaming batons high into the air, and two men on stilts chased each other down the alley. Everywhere around her came strains of music, all being played by different quartets and bands. There would be fireworks later, but as far as she was concerned, the colorful crowd was enough fireworks for her.

As she approached the pagoda, she glimpsed Robert and Diana walking down one of the narrow paths leading into the dark trees. And decidedly *not* interested in fetching lemon ices. With a sigh, she hurried after them. If she was to be their chaperone, then she needed to stay with them whether they wanted her there or not. The last thing she needed was to give Sebastian any more ammunition to use against her.

The path grew narrower and darker as she went. Although lanterns had been strung from the trees, someone had extinguished them, leaving the path mostly in darkness, and she picked her way carefully, knowing Robert and Diana couldn't be too far in front. Up ahead where the path curved, she saw their two dark figures step into the bushes toward a small folly made to look like the tumbled ruins of a Greek temple. She followed. As she rounded the end of the ruined wall, she started to call out—

Then Robert pulled Diana against him and kissed her. Not with the desperate urgency that Sebastian had kissed Miranda at the opera, but with such tenderness, such gentleness that her heart broke.

Rather, it should have broken. After all, Robert was the man she'd wanted for years. So why wasn't she bothered as much as she should have been to see him kissing another woman? Was it possible that she didn't love him anymore? Or that she'd never truly loved him at all?

Oh, it hurt, she couldn't deny that. Letting go of a dream she'd chased for so many years was painful, but not the blinding pain she should have felt, the raging jealousy, the sorrow so fierce it should have buckled her knees and sent her to the ground. Wasn't that what all the poets claimed a broken heart felt like? Utter desolation?

Instead, all she felt was grief at losing her dream, and a sense of finality. As if she'd known all along that this was how her pursuit of him would end.

And an odd blossoming of relief.

Needing time and space to think, she ducked behind the wall before they could see her. She paused, leaning against the cold stone to breathe deep and force down her utter shock at not being...well, utterly shocked.

Then she heard them, at first just low whispers as her ears took a moment to adjust to the quiet, sort through the sounds, and realize what they were talking about...*Her.*

"She fancies Trent," Diana said, her quiet words making Miranda's heart skip.

"Miranda?" Surprise rang through Robert's voice, and for a moment, he forgot to speak quietly. "Impossible."

"I just think, the way she looks at him sometimes..."

"Miranda's like a little sister. All of us think of her that way. Especially Seb."

Squeezing her eyes shut, Miranda pressed her hand against her chest. Surprisingly, that did hurt. A great deal.

"Anyway, he's set on Lady Jane," Robert continued. "He needs a duchess. Miranda can never be that for him."

And *that* was simply agonizing, even though she knew it was true.

"Trent doesn't love Lady Jane," Diana said softly.

"There's nothing in his eyes when he looks at her, and she can't keep his attention. But when he looks at Miranda, there's all kinds of fire."

"Because he wants to throttle her," Robert teased.

"No," Diana chastised, one woman defending another, and a guilty pang struck Miranda that she had been resentful of Diana for stealing Robert's attention. She'd never given the woman a chance, and now she regretted it. "He cares for her. He gave her that flower tonight."

A faint smile tugged at her lips as Miranda reached up to touch the paper rose still tucked behind her ear. Yes, he had given her that rose, and the way he'd given it to her made it even more special. Oh, she wasn't foolish enough to believe that Sebastian cared about her, not the way Diana meant. But he did care enough to apologize.

"Means nothing," Robert assured her. "They're a ha'penny each from the beggar woman who sells them behind the galleries as souvenirs."

With her heart tearing, Miranda slowly pulled down the flower and stared at it. In the dim shadows, the red paper petals showed black. She didn't care that it was only a cheap souvenir; it was the thought that was important, and Sebastian had made a special trip out of the box to buy it for her.

"That doesn't matter," Diana protested softly. "He still gave it to her. It was romantic."

"That wasn't romance," Robert corrected. "That was bribery because he needs her to behave around Lady Jane."

A painful stab sliced through her. Bribery...not an apology after all. The realization burned as if her heart had been ripped from her chest, replaced by a hollow of hot humiliation and anger. All she could do was lean against the stone to keep her knees from giving out beneath her and remember to breathe.

Oh God, how it hurt! She pressed her hand hard against her chest to fight back the rising anguish flooding through her, but it was no use. Her entire season had been nothing but one mistake after another, and the biggest mistake of all...

Miranda stared down at the dark flower. A drop of water fell onto one of the petals, soaking into the paper and running the dye. Only then did she realize that she was crying.

"Robert, I'm serious. I truly think your brother is attracted to her."

"Miranda Hodgkins is nothing more than a family friend. She's the last person my brother would want."

Her hand folded around the paper rose, crushing it against her palm. She shoved the unwanted flower into her pocket as she turned and walked away.

* * *

Sebastian frowned as he glanced down the alley toward the pagoda. He hadn't realized that fetching ices could take so long.

After being gone nearly half an hour, the others hadn't yet returned, and he was beginning to worry. Although Miranda was with Robert and Miss Morgan, he knew Miranda well enough to know that she could find trouble locked up alone in an empty room. Letting her run loose at Vauxhall was deadly. Pandora's curiosity got her into less trouble than what Miranda could be capable of committing here.

At least he'd made good use of their absence to speak

with Lady Jane. But frustratingly, the conversation with Jane was not nearly as interesting as the ones he'd shared with Miranda. When he'd attempted a decidedly flirtatious one, Jane didn't notice any of the entendres and sexual undercurrents. Or if she had, she hadn't dared seize on any of them.

A new worry blossomed inside him that he didn't find Lady Jane alluring. Sophisticated, yes. Beautiful and refined, certainly. But *inspiring*...not at all. And doubly unfortunate, he realized as he exhaled a long breath, neither inspiring sexually nor intellectually. He doubted that she would ever offer an unguarded opinion or argue with him about anything, especially Milton or Shakespeare.

Perhaps, though, his lack of interest was because they hadn't had the chance to be alone. Surely, if *he* were conscious of the eyes watching the two of them, then so was she, and as a well-mannered society daughter, she knew to conduct herself with reserve when in the public eye.

The answer was simple. He needed time with her in private.

"Would you care to join me for a stroll through the garden?" He extended his hand as he stood. "Perhaps we'll find the others."

"A lovely idea, Trent." With a pleased smile, she put her hand into his and rose gracefully to her feet. *Everything* Jane did was graceful. And proper. Which was why she motioned for the woman who'd accompanied her this evening to serve as chaperone. The dour woman, dressed in brown worsted wool, rose from her chair in the corner of the box and followed them out into the night.

The woman was certainly a good ladies' companion, Sebastian noted, because less than ten minutes later and just as they were reaching the close paths in the woods, she was gone from sight, separated from them in the crowd. So good, in fact, that he knew she would be gone as long as they were, only to be waiting near the box door when they returned.

A very convenient separation, and one Jane must have arranged with the woman prior to setting out for the evening in hopes of time alone with him. Exactly what he wanted as well, and relief warmed inside him at the similarity of their thoughts. More—being willing to be alone with him also meant she was amenable to marriage.

Jane didn't protest as he guided her into the wilderness of the close paths, where the lanterns had been extinguished— if ever lit in the first place. The darkness gave privacy for the pleasures that had earned Vauxhall's woods its sordid reputation.

"You're distracted this evening, Trent," she commented softly.

Sebastian bit back the fierce urge to disagree, offering instead, "My apologies." Because the truth was that he *was* distracted this evening.

This evening? He almost laughed. He'd been distracted since the night of his mother's birthday party at Chestnut Hill. And that distraction took the form of a petite strawberry blonde who always seemed to pop up in places she shouldn't, arousing him to madness. In the two days since Miranda made her operatic debut, the attention she'd garnered had only intensified. Men of all social ranks were calling on her. She'd become the talk of the season. He couldn't walk into White's without someone asking about her, and invitations from the ladies of the *ton* were arriving in a stream for her. So were the gentlemen callers.

While his mother assured him that the sudden attention

was harmless, the truth was that Sebastian didn't like it. Not at all.

But what could he do except follow his mother's wishes and allow gentlemen to call on her? He had no claim to her, nor ever would. That fit of madness that had him nearly seducing Miranda backstage at the opera was only that—madness to think that he could be with a woman because of the way she made him feel about himself. Because she made him laugh and challenged him intellectually. Because when he was with her he forgot about all the pressures of the dukedom resting on his shoulders and could simply be himself.

But being himself *was* being the duke, at every moment. The sooner he resigned himself to that fate, the better. And he'd never again be bothered with the madness of wanting to be someone he could no longer be.

"It's been a bit of a trying season," he explained, although downright frustrating was more accurate. In everything, he tried to remember the promise he made to his father to always put the dukedom first, especially with the women he associated with. But Miranda had completely turned his world on end. When he wasn't longing to spend time with her, he was riddled with guilt about the way he behaved whenever he was with her. What would Father have thought of him that every time they were alone together he nearly ruined her? *That* certainly wasn't the duke his father expected him to be.

"I'm certain it has been difficult for you," she agreed. Then, after a pause, "Miss Hodgkins is the talk of the *ton*. I can understand how she could be distracting."

"Oh?" He shot her a sideways glance. What the hell did Jane mean by that? Was she insulting Miranda?

But she smiled at him with patient understanding for

his situation, not a drop of animosity visible in her. "You're so busy this season—Parliament, your duties to your mother and sister, trying to keep your brothers in line...and now Miss Hodgkins. It's a wonder you've got time for me at all." She touched his arm in a sympathetic gesture. "So I certainly don't fault you for being distracted with all that you have to manage, and I hope you don't think that I do."

The tension eased from his shoulders. Thank God Jane understood all his responsibilities. Another reason that she was a good choice to be his duchess. "Thank you."

She pulled at her long gloves. Every inch of her was fashion plate perfection, right down to the bows on her satin shoes. "Yet she's become the favorite subject of this season's *on dit*. It seems that her...*exuberance* is all anyone wants to talk about."

He bristled in Miranda's defense. "She's simply enjoying herself, that's all. Her parents both died when she was a little girl, and her aunt and uncle who raised her had no children of their own." So they'd had no idea what to do with her, between overly strict tutors and letting her run wild with the Carlisles, and neither extreme was good for her. But during this season, so far she'd managed herself quite well. "She's just trying to find her way."

"I hope for your sake that she finds it soon."

Something about her tone struck him as icy. So did her lack of sympathetic comment on Miranda's past. "She will," he assured her, attributing her tone to not yet knowing Miranda well. "And I'm grateful you haven't let the gossip chase you away."

She smiled up at him. "I would never let another woman decide my suitors for me."

Her suitor. He wanted to be just that, so why didn't he

feel especially thrilled when she said it? In fact, after spending the evening at her side, he felt nothing for Jane beyond pleasant companionship. And that had to change if he was going to make her his wife.

When they reached a spot along the path where a vine-covered bower sat secluded amid the shadows, he led her beneath its arch.

"Will this do?" he asked.

She was sharp when it came to the sexual politics of the *ton*. There was no point in dissembling with her over why he'd led her here, just far enough down the path to give them seclusion yet not so far as to put her reputation in jeopardy. There would certainly be no seduction tonight, but enough intimacies could be shared to put to rest the unease in his mind about whether he and Jane suited. They had to. Not only did he need an heir, but he had no plans to ever go outside his marriage. The woman he married had to be everything to him…companion, counselor, lover. He would settle for nothing less.

"Perfectly," she murmured. Lifting her arms to encircle his neck, she gave that same demure smile she'd worn all night.

Suddenly, he was struck by an urge to put another expression on her face, one of passion and arousal. That same foggy-confused look of pleasure and need that came over Miranda's features whenever he kissed her. He cupped Jane's face between his hands and lowered his mouth to kiss her. He hoped to taste on her lips that vanilla-sweet flavor he'd recently come to crave, to tease the same eager response from her that flamed from Miranda every time he touched her.

With a sigh, she softened her mouth and returned the kiss, her lips meeting his with a well-practiced technique that told him she'd kissed many men in dark gardens before him. But as he kissed her, waiting for the passion to spark between them, he felt nothing. That same pulsing desire he experienced whenever he caught a whiff of rosewater, that familiar tightening low in his gut...all that was missing. He'd felt it with Miranda, for God's sake, so surely he should feel it with Jane.

But nothing. No passion, no fire. No desperate, nearly overwhelming desire to lose himself, body and soul, inside her.

Nothing.

Oh, her kiss was nice. She had a soft, kissable mouth, and she made no move to stop him as he coaxed apart her lips with his tongue and slipped inside, attempting to draw from her a moan of pleasure or a whimper of need. Any kind of reaction that showed she enjoyed being in his arms or that would heighten his arousal for her the way Miranda's soft mewlings sent his blood boiling. Although she returned the kiss, her mouth tasted nothing of the greedy hunger he wanted from her, her body not melting into his. The experience was not unpleasant, just...empty.

He pulled back and looked down at her. Except for her kiss-reddened mouth, her face appeared just as serene as before he'd begun to kiss her. He saw no signs at all of whether she'd enjoyed it, whether she wanted him to keep kissing her or to do more and dare to touch her the way he had Miranda, who'd made no attempt to hide what she felt. Even alone with him in the darkness, Jane was refined enough to not give over to unrestrained passions.

But she was what he needed, wasn't she? A respected and proper woman to be his duchess. One his father would have approved of, no matter that his heart wanted fire and passion.

Her eyes fluttered open, and she gave him that same damnable smile as before. The only difference was that this time, she ran her gloved fingers through the hair at his nape.

"That was nice," she whispered.

Nice? He bit back a laugh. *Nice* was the last thing he wanted.

She said softly, "I think we should return to the box now before anyone notices we're missing." As if sensing the emotions warring inside him, she rested her hand possessively on his arm. "Please understand. I have to guard my virtue, especially with you, Trent."

"Especially with me?" What the hell did she mean by that?

"You and your brothers have a certain reputation, you know."

Her eyes shined, as if she liked the idea of capturing one of the Carlisles, as if believing that silly bit of nonsense that reformed rakes made for the best husbands. They didn't. They simply made for reformed rakes.

The best husbands were men like his father. Those common, unassuming men with solid characters and generous souls, who provided well for their families and kept them safe, who were kind to those around them and demanding of themselves, who simply loved—

Sebastian drew a deep, pain-filled breath...Who simply loved their wives.

Her hand trailed over his chest to play flirtatiously with the buttons on his waistcoat, but his body didn't react, not even a quickening of his heartbeat. Being alone with her tonight hadn't aroused him one bit. It had only frustrated the hell out of him. "I'll go on ahead, while you wait fifteen minutes before trailing after. We'll say we were separated in the crowd."

"Of course." Apparently, she had planned out quite a good deal in anticipation of being alone with him. He gave her a final parting kiss, hoping he'd missed something from the earlier embrace, but his reaction to her was just as lackluster as before.

Then she was gone, slipping out from beneath the bower and heading back toward the alley, where her companion would be waiting for her behind the gallery with some ready excuse for how they'd all gotten separated.

Biting out a frustrated curse, he paced the tiny space beneath the bower. He'd never considered passion to be a priority when deciding upon a wife. Of course, he'd always assumed that the woman he selected would be just as amenable to bed sport as he was. But now, with his cold reaction to Jane, he began to doubt if the woman he married would share even that. He'd have to teach her how to take pleasure in intimacy, he supposed, how to enjoy herself, so he could enjoy himself with her.

Lord knew he certainly didn't have to teach that to Miranda.

He scowled. What on earth was wrong with him? Good God, *why* was he thinking of Miranda, of all women? When all she did was make him feel like a damn fool, a woman he should *never* want doing just that and leaving him frustrated and angry—

A commotion sounded from nearby in the dark gardens. Sebastian ducked out from beneath the cover of the ivy-laden bower and watched down the narrow path at the heavy shadows where the lanterns had been extinguished. A man's and woman's voices, heated in argument, grew nearer. He smiled with grim satisfaction. Well, it was good to know that some other gentleman was having just as rotten a time as he was this evening. Most likely, the two fought because one of them had caught the other in the bushes with someone else. A nightly occurrence at Vauxhall.

They drew nearer, nothing more than dark, bodiless arguing in the shadows. Then the woman's voice came through clearly—

"Just go away!"

Miranda.

She stormed out of the black shadows, her pace so fast that she was nearly running. And beside her, easily matching her strides, walked Burton Williams, Viscount Houghton's youngest son.

"Please," she pleaded, "leave me be. I don't need an escort to..." The rest of the sentence was lost as the two reached the start of the stone wall that cut through the bushes and added a layer of privacy to those wishing to hide among the shadows.

Sebastian started forward, anger rising inside him.

Williams said something to her, but she shook her head forcefully and kept walking. Without warning, the man grabbed her arm and yanked her against him. She pushed against him to break free as his mouth came down on hers.

Her hand cracked across his cheek.

Williams pulled back only far enough to snarl at her, "Like it rough, do you?" Then he shoved her back against the wall.

Sebastian grabbed him by the shoulder and pivoted him around as his clenched fist plowed into the man's jaw. The force of the surprise blow dropped Williams to the ground.

"Apologize," Sebastian demanded through gritted teeth as he towered over Williams at his feet, forcing out each word in a barely contained growl as red fury flashed through him.

Williams shot out, "The hell I will!"

"It's all right," Miranda assured him as she placed her hand on Sebastian's right arm to keep him from punching the bastard a second time. "It was only a misunderstanding."

He didn't believe that for a moment. And tonight, he was feeling just keyed up enough to engage in a full-out brawl to burn off the frustration and swirling energy inside him that he couldn't put to rest. The same frustration that had burned inside him since the masquerade.

"Apologize," he repeated.

Williams touched the trickle of blood seeping from his cut lip and bit out, "My apologies."

"Accepted," Miranda quickly answered and tugged on Sebastian's hand to lead him away. But he wasn't about to move before he was ready.

"Don't *ever* touch her again," he threatened as Williams climbed unsteadily to his feet. "And not one ill word about her to anyone unless you want a duel."

Williams laughed at that and sent a scathing look of contempt at her. "That poplolly isn't worth the waste of a bullet."

With Miranda still clinging to his right arm, Sebastian swung with his left. He caught Williams hard in the other jaw. This time when the man crumpled to the ground, he knew enough to remain down.

Anger coursed wildly through him, pulsing with each pounding beat of his heart as he grabbed her by the wrist and pulled her behind him down the path. He refused to let her go even as she called for him to stop, not looking back and forcing her to practically run to keep up with his long strides. No one in the crowd around them paid the slightest bit of attention. A woman being hauled physically from the gardens by an angry man was also a nightly occurrence.

"We're leaving!" he shouted at Quinn as he passed their box, his brother sitting on the front railing, surrounded by his friends. Thankfully, Lady Jane and his mother were nowhere in sight. "I'm taking Miranda home."

"Why?" Quinn yelled back through the noise as the first fireworks streamed into the air and burst overhead in a shower of brilliant reds and blues. Around them the crowd cheered.

"Headache," Sebastian snarled.

Quinn frowned with concern. "Miranda has a headache?"

"No," he muttered beneath his breath, "I do."

CHAPTER TEN

⁓

udley House!" Sebastian ordered the coachman as he yanked open the carriage door and set her inside on the bench. As he swung inside and slammed the door closed, he pounded his fist against the roof, and the carriage set off with a lurch.

Miranda's heart pounded furiously. He was angry, far angrier than she had ever seen him. He leaned forward, elbows on knees as he glared at her through the shadows of the dark compartment.

"What in the hell happened between you two?" His voice seethed with such white-hot anger that it shook.

She lifted her chin, preparing for battle. She refused—simply *refused*!—to show any weakness in front of him by looking away. Instead, she boldly glared back, silently daring him to keep pushing . . . because after the night she'd had, she'd gladly push back.

"I did nothing wrong," she defended herself. "I left Robert and Miss Morgan by the folly, and I was walking back to the box when Burton Williams met me on the path and remembered me from the St James ball. He insisted that he escort me back, to protect me." She nearly laughed at the irony of *that*. "I declined. But apparently, he isn't used to being refused by women."

His jaw clenched so hard that even in the dark shadows she could see the muscles in his neck working as he ground his teeth. "Did he hurt you?"

"Just my arm." She winced as she rubbed her forearm where Williams had grabbed her. Surely there would be a bruise in the morning.

"Before I arrived," he clarified slowly. He clenched and unclenched his fists in a cold, restrained fury that made her shiver. His eyes were black. "Did that bastard force himself on you?"

Understanding fell through her like ice water, dousing her own anger. Sebastian wasn't upset at her; he was furious at Burton Williams. So furious that if she uttered the wrong word she knew he would turn the carriage around, charge back to Vauxhall, and murder the man for daring to touch her.

"No," she breathed, her eyes never leaving his. "He did not."

Heaving out a harsh breath, he leaned back against the squabs and scrubbed a hand over his face. "I have to serve with Williams's father in the Lords. Houghton and I fill the same committees." He bit out a curse beneath his breath as he shook his head. "What would my father say about this?"

She whispered, "That he would be proud of you for coming to a woman's defense."

"The same woman I nearly ruined myself at the opera?" he challenged quietly.

Her chest tightened in sympathy for him, that he should doubt himself so severely in his father's eyes. "You and Williams are *nothing* alike. You're a gentleman who would never force his attentions on a woman." She couldn't read the emotions on his face through the dark shadows, but his shoulders remained stiff, his dark silhouette rigid in the swaying carriage. He didn't believe her. "If you're not a gentleman, then why did you give me that paper rose tonight?"

"Because I was anything but a gentleman to you." His voice matched the same low rumble of the carriage wheels over the streets. "I had no right to speak to you the way I did."

A smile pulled at her lips. All his silly warnings… "See? Williams would never have—"

"And absolutely no right to do what I did at the opera. I forgot myself." He held her gaze across the dark compartment. "It was a mistake."

Her heart skipped painfully. Hoping she'd heard him incorrectly, or that she'd simply misunderstood what he meant, she repeated in a stunned whisper, "A mistake?"

He answered soberly, "Yes."

The single word tore through her, ripping into her chest and squeezing so hard at her heart she thought it might pop. She blinked back the stinging that burned in her eyes.

"Which?" she somehow forced out despite the way her heart lodged into her throat. "Kissing me, touching me…or implying that you wanted me?"

"All of it." Shadows covered his face, making it impossible for her to read the emotions in him, but an underlying frustration scratched his voice. "I should never have kissed you like that or said those things to you. I didn't mean them."

"Then why did you?" She forced a steadiness into her voice she certainly didn't feel.

"I lost my head that evening. I was swept up by the music. That was all." He paused, then added quietly, "And I'm grateful that you came to your senses and put a stop to it."

She stared at him through the darkness, even as hot tears welled in her eyes and blurred his darkened face. It shouldn't matter what she meant to him, what he thought of her, or even if he thought of her at all—Sebastian Carlisle, Duke of Trent, was never meant for her. He was meant for women like Lady Jane. But somehow, his opinion of her had come to matter. Somewhere between all the fighting and all the plotting to find each other the people they thought they wanted, she'd come to care about him. More than she ever dreamt possible. And now, for him to say that what they'd shared was a mistake—

"Liar."

Her cutting accusation was little louder than a breath, but it tore through the compartment with the force of cannon fire. He flinched at its intensity.

"I know why you're saying this, why you're—" Her voice choked as a knot of emotion tightened in her throat. She forced out through her frustration, "Because you don't want to admit that you want me. Not the orphaned niece of your tenant. Not you, not a duke…someone who's supposed to want only fine ladies and society daughters." When she saw his eyes flare in the shadows, she knew she was right and charged on, remembering Diana's words at the ruins. "But you do."

He clenched his hands into fists. "I need someone who can be my duchess," he ground out, dodging her accusation.

"A perfect duchess who will never do anything improper, never stir up gossip nor cause any trouble? Yes, the duke in you does want that." Her heart raced with anger and something else just as dark, just as powerful. Something that had her wanting to stir the heated anger inside him until it boiled over. "But the man wants *me*," she dared to whisper.

"I don't," he bit out.

She shook her head, recognizing that for the lie it was. "I'm the girl from next door who will never fit the ideals of proper and well-bred, who's common and ordinary, with her freckled nose and garish hair. But who also makes you laugh and enjoy yourself. The woman who is completely wrong for the duke, but completely right for the man."

His eyes flickered in the shadows of the lamplight as he growled, "I do *not* want you."

"Yes, you do." Then she pushed him right over the cliff— "And you can't stand yourself for it."

With an angry, frustrated snarl, he grabbed her and yanked her across the compartment to him. She gave a soft cry of surprise as she landed sprawled across his lap.

He forced out through clenched teeth, his mouth only a hairsbreadth from hers, "I *can't* want you, goddammit!"

"But you do," she breathed, so softly that the sound was nearly lost in the shadows. All of her trembled. "And it isn't a mistake."

His gaze dropped to her lips, then his mouth came down hard and demanding against hers. Her mind swirled from the onslaught of anger and arousal burning through them both in equal measure. She opened her mouth beneath the hungry desire of his kiss and heard the low moan of need tear from her own throat.

When he plunged his tongue between her lips, she welcomed his rough assault, her tongue entwining around his and sucking him deeper into her mouth. Instead of being alarmed at his loss of control, she thrilled to it. She snaked her hand up to his nape and ran her fingers encouragingly through his silky hair as he continued to ravish her mouth in a kiss that was more hungry, more demanding and possessive than she could ever have imagined. One she wanted just as much as he did.

When she could no longer sustain the breathless kiss, she tore her mouth away to gasp for air. Her fingers tugged at his cravat and collar to bare his throat to her greedy mouth, and excitement surged through her to feel the tattoo of his pulse racing against her lips. He tasted delicious, of man and port and tobacco, and she couldn't get enough of him to satisfy her appetite. Couldn't torture him enough with her own kisses that fanned the angry burn inside him.

"I stir your blood," she mumbled against his throat, thrilling to know that it was true. "You told me so."

She licked her tongue over his Adam's apple and drank in each panting breath he took beneath her seeking lips. Her kisses tormented him, and she gleefully relished in it. She wanted to hear him confess that she was right, that kissing her and touching her wasn't a mistake, that he wanted her—

"I was wrong." He growled and once more seized her mouth beneath his. This time when his mouth covered hers, instead of kissing her, he traced the outline of her lips with the tip of his tongue in an inverted kiss that sizzled through her and left her aching for more.

Oh, a *lie*! But Sebastian was lying to himself as much as to her. Even now, heat sparked everywhere their bodies touched. She wasn't like Lady Jane or those other society ladies. Not proper, not demure, certainly not passive. But he wanted her just the same, and her heart leapt with joy over it.

She rose up to meet his mouth full-on and greedily devoured his kiss, letting her inexplicable ache for him sweep her away. As he kissed her breathless once more, she clung to him and met kiss for kiss, lick for lick, each bite for tantalizing bite. He couldn't hide the effect she had on him, and he was beginning to shake with the loss of his precious restraint. But she sensed a change in him, a reluctant capitulation rising up from deep inside him. One she knew cost him a great deal of his pride.

"I can't have you, Miranda." Belying his own words, he reached behind her back, and his clever fingers expertly unfastened the row of tiny hooks on her dress. "You'd be ruined, and I'd still be forced to marry someone else."

Her breath hitched as he pulled her bodice down to her waist and revealed the short stays beneath. A shiver of nervous excitement pulsed through her as his hand traced down the front laces. The heat of his touch seeped into her flesh through the stiff material, as if it wasn't there at all.

He brought his lips to her ear and confessed in a hot whisper, his fingers pulling the laces free from their eyelets, "But I still want you."

Then his mouth covered her ear, and his tongue plunged deep inside in the most erotic kiss she'd ever experienced, leaving her clinging to him to keep from falling away. Yet her heart soared. She could barely believe it—Sebastian Carlisle wanted *her*. The man who had once been nothing more to her than the aggravating neighbor next door had become her friend, and now had come to mean so much more.

When he pushed open her stays and tugged down her low-cut chemise to bare her breasts, she was unable to hold back the low moan that poured from her. The heat of his gaze burned across her bare flesh everywhere he looked. And he looked greedily, drinking her in with his dark eyes as she draped so wantonly across his lap. He smiled wickedly when her nipples pebbled in the cool air beneath the heat of his gaze.

"We're in a dark and private place," he murmured. His husky voice swirled around her, heating her from the inside out. "In the shadows where no one can see or ever know."

She shivered at the reminder of what she'd said to him the night of the opera, in that wholly scandalous, completely tantalizing conversation they'd shared in the shadows. One that had left her aching and all of her tense with longing. Then, as now, her breath grew shallow and rapid, and the tip of her tongue darted out to lick her suddenly dry lips. She whispered, "The kind of place where a woman might be tempted to tell a man what she wants?"

He slowly circled her left nipple with his fingertip, making it ache. "And a man might be tempted to give it."

"Yes," she sighed out. She arched her back against his touch, unable to lie still beneath the torturous tracing of his finger.

He laughed softly at her eager response, and the deep sound twined through her. Heavens, how she loved to hear him laugh! He was never more attractive than when he was happy, and her heart ached impossibly more for him.

"What do you want, Rose?" he murmured. "Tell me, and I'll give it."

She swallowed. Hard. She knew she should stop this, put an end to it before it got out of hand. But the temptation was simply too great, the way he made her feel too delicious.

With her heart pounding so hard she was certain he could feel it, she whispered, "Kiss me."

"As you wish." He leaned over and seized her nipple between his lips.

She gasped at his audacity. The sensation of his hot, moist

mouth against her cooled skin jolted her, and she shuddered violently, only to gasp a second time when his tongue licked over her, swirling around the nipple the same way his fingertip had done. This wasn't a kiss. This was so much more wicked, so much more delicious that her toes curled inside her slippers.

When he'd thoroughly laved her nipple into a hard pebble, leaving it hot and aching, the tip glistening wet in the dim lamplight, he moved to the other breast to begin the sweet torture anew.

She shifted restlessly on his lap, unable to lie still as he tongued her nipple. "Sebastian," she protested between fierce, little pants, "what are—"

"Shh," he whispered against her breast, his mouth not leaving her bare flesh even as he reached his hand up to caress across her upper chest, soothingly, as if calming a wild kitten. When she opened her eyes to watch him, something tugged deep inside her at the sight of his sensuous mouth at her breasts, something raw and purely feminine. Her thighs clenched against the hot ache that surged through her and stole her breath away.

Suddenly, he was through teasing. He took her breast deep into his mouth as he suckled greedily at her. So hard, so strong that his lips pulled the throbbing ache from between her thighs all the way through her like a rope, leaving her lungs panting for breath and her legs shaking as they draped open across his.

With one last tender kiss to her aroused nipple, he lifted his head and stared into her eyes. "What else do you want, sweet Rose?" he enticed, his voice hoarse.

"Touch me," she breathed, so softly that barely any sound fell from her lips.

As his dark eyes held hers for a moment, primal pleasure

flickered bright in their depths. Then he lowered his head and blew a cold stream of air across her wet nipple.

Jolted at the unexpected sensation, a cry tore from her. She bucked, but the hand that had been softly stroking her now held her down to keep her from squirming off his thighs. He blew against her other nipple, and she moaned at the sweet torture. Who knew the most tantalizing touch would be not touching her at all?

She whimpered, "Sebastian..." A dishonest attempt to halt his caresses, when the last thing she wanted was for him to stop. Instead, she somehow found enough clarity through her arousal-fogged brain to force out between panting breaths, "You aren't...doing what...I want."

"No. For once I'm doing what *I* want," he murmured, nuzzling his soft cheek against her breast. Then his mouth moved to the other breast, to suckle at her again, just as greedily as before.

She arched her back, thrusting her breast deeper into his mouth. "You're not...playing fair," she panted out.

He only laughed wickedly at her protest, as if he knew exactly what her body craved from him and how to torment her in the most wickedly wonderful ways. The deep sound tickled her nipple and rumbled down her spine.

He *wasn't* playing fair. She had breasts that he could easily expose, make peaked and aching, knead with his fingers and suckle with his mouth. *Men.* Even in intimacy they held all the advantages. It wasn't as if she could pull off his shirt and do the same to—

A thought struck her, an utterly delicious thought. She nearly laughed in impish delight at the devilishness of it. Oh, it would torment him in kind to what he was doing to her! But fair was fair, and if he could play by this new set of rules, then so could she.

Twisting on his lap to give herself room, she wriggled her hand down between their bodies, finding the buttons on the fall of his trousers and quickly slipping them free.

He tensed, his eyes darkening with intense arousal. "What are you doing?"

"Something else," she whispered her words from the opera. Letting herself be daring and wicked, ignoring the nervous tremble of her fingers, she slipped her hand inside his trousers before he could stop her.

He sucked in sharply through clenched teeth as his body instantly stiffened. With a throaty laugh, she boldly closed her hand around him and drew him free of his trousers, cupped against her palm beneath the folds of her skirt.

"Miranda," he warned in a hoarse rasp, but he didn't stop her.

She was too fascinated by his hard manhood beneath her fingers to heed any warning. So soft on the outside, so steely hard beneath, long and thick, surprisingly warm...She could have sworn she felt him pulse against her hand like a racing heartbeat, and when she traced her fingertips along his length and over his tip, she found a bead of wetness gathered at the tiny slit. She wrapped her fingers around his girth and squeezed.

He shuddered as a curse tore from his lips, and his hand darted down after hers.

Her lips parted in protest. How dare he pull her hand away when he'd submitted her to such delicious torture? That he would end this wonderful moment now—

"Like this," he instructed. His hand folded over hers and showed her how to rub the drop of moisture into his skin to make him slippery beneath her fingertips, how to squeeze and stroke over him...Up and down his shaft, from the engorged tip all the way to the base, hard and fast. He half growled, "Dear God, yes...just like that."

His eyes squeezed shut as he hung his head, drinking in the pleasure she gave him. There was no denying now how much he wanted her hands on him, and her chest soared with the newfound power she held over him.

He slid his hand away from hers and stroked up her body. His fingers tangled in her skirt and bunched it up around her knees, unable to raise it higher because of the way she lay across his thighs. But high enough to reveal the lace edges of her stockings, high enough that his hand easily slipped beneath to caress his fingers along the bare stretch of inner thigh. She whimpered as a wanton desire to be caressed between her legs engulfed her, to have his hand right there on the aching spot where she longed for it to be.

"I'm going to touch you now," he warned, his own breath coming in uneven pants as she continued to pump her hand over him. "If you want me to stop—"

"Don't stop!" The thought of his hands leaving her body was unbearable. "Please, Sebastian. I want this." His hand brushed up between her legs, and when his bare fingers teased lightly against her folds, she whimpered at how wicked it felt to be touched there, and how unbelievably good. "Oh yes...please."

He kissed her tenderly and groaned, "Rose."

His fingers began to more boldly caress her, sliding deeper against her with each stroke until he slipped inside. With a gasp of surprise, she quivered around him, then all those tiny muscles clenched down tight around his fingers as he languidly stroked inside her.

Moaning with need, she closed her eyes and spread her legs as far as her skirt allowed. She was behaving so scandalously, so wickedly—

And she simply didn't care.

His fingers felt too good as they both soothed the growing ache inside her and intimately explored her body, his lips too strong and hot-moist for logic to persuade her to stop. Her entire existence narrowed to the swirling plunges of his long fingers inside her, to the masculine scent of him that filled her senses, to the shaking of his hard, muscular thighs beneath her. She'd never imagined that surrender could feel so victorious. And judging from the soft, guttural grunts of pleasure that came from him as she continued to stroke him, neither did he.

"Sebastian," she panted, now begging for something more, something she couldn't name but knew he could give her. Her hips writhed over his thighs, her body silently pleading for release from the mounting ache he flamed inside her.

He twirled his thumb and touched the little nub nestled into the top of her folds. A jolt of pleasure shot through her so hard, so fast that she cried out beneath the breathtaking delight of it.

His mouth seized hers and muffled her cries, but her hand clenched hard around his erection, squeezing with a fierce stroke. She heard him groan against her lips, felt him jerk against her palm—a wet warmth spilled across her fingers.

For a moment, she couldn't move. She could do nothing more than lie there and let the shuddering waves of pleasure lap over her. Her body was simultaneously stunned by what had happened and instantly relaxed as she draped herself across his lap, her breasts bare to the shadows and her legs spread wide. She breathed deep and slow as she found her breath, enjoying the rapid flutter of her heart in her chest and the low heat that slowly diminished between her legs.

Only then did she open her eyes and realize he was staring down at her, an unreadable expression on his handsome face. Only then did she comprehend...She lifted her hand and saw her fingers glistening in the dim lamplight.

"Oh," she whispered, so soft the word was barely more than a breath. Then she realized what she'd done—good Lord, what *they'd* done together—and a hot blush flushed her cheeks. Mortified at her own brazenness, she tried to scramble off his lap. But she was still lying across his thighs, still off balance with her dress now all akimbo, and all she managed to do was catch him in the abdomen with her elbow. "Oh!"

Despite the rush of his exhaled breath, he didn't move to set her away and instead held her shoulder to keep her still. His other hand reached up to untie his cravat, and he stared at her uncertainly as he pulled the knots free and unraveled it from around his neck. He asked gently, "Are you all right?"

All right? No, she wasn't all right. She'd just—in a carriage! Oh Lord...She blinked back hot tears, praying he couldn't see them in the dark shadows. "I'm fine," she lied as he took her hand and gently wiped her fingers clean with his neck cloth.

Guilt crossed his face as he glanced away but assured her quietly, "Don't worry. You're still innocent."

A tear fell down her cheek. No, she wasn't. She was a long way from innocent in all this. That wasn't what he meant, of course, but the riot of emotions roiling inside her made it impossible to think straight.

He turned to toss the cloth out the window. "I didn't plan for— *Christ.*"

"What is it?" She scrambled to sit up and follow his gaze out the window. She gasped. "We're on Audley Street!"

He grimaced, yanking her skirt down around her legs. "Straighten your dress. *Now.*"

She slid off his lap to the bench across from him, her fingers shaking so badly she could barely lace up her stays while he buttoned his trousers. Mortification poured through her. Oh God, what had they done? Her first season, her first trip to London, and she would be completely ruined if anyone saw her like this, simply because of her foolish pride and anger. And because of her growing attraction for a man she had no business desiring.

"Let me help." He turned her in the seat to quickly fasten up her dress.

She slipped the last sleeve cap back into place as the carriage came to a stop. Seconds later, the tiger flung the door open wide.

She rushed from the carriage without waiting for Sebastian to escort her inside, moving so quickly that she nearly tripped on the front steps as she ran to the door. In her humiliated desperation to flee, she didn't care how ungraceful she looked, nor did she dare glance back to see if he had even gotten out of the carriage to watch her leave. Because she couldn't have borne it if he hadn't.

Thankfully, the butler was already at the front door and holding it open, and she hurried inside, then straight through the front foyer and up the stairs. She shook so badly that she wasn't certain how she was able to put one foot in front of the other, all of her in shocked confusion at her actions tonight. She needed to reach the safety of her room before she broke down in tears. Or in anger at herself. The confusion swirled through her so hard and fast that she didn't know which—

"Miranda?"

Oh no. The very *last* person she wanted to face at that

moment... She stopped at the sound of the soft voice behind her and bit back the urge to cry as she forced a smile onto her face and turned to face Sebastian's sister.

Josephine Carlisle Matteson, Marchioness of Chesney, leaned against the doorway of her sitting room in her dressing gown, with her dark hair already brushed out and hanging loose around her shoulders. A book rested in her hand, and a smile lit her face. She looked comfortable and completely at ease after spending the evening at home with her children.

"You've returned early." Puzzled, she glanced past Miranda at the stairs. "Did the others come with you?"

"They're still at Vauxhall," she answered, praying Josie couldn't see the slight tilt to her coiffure or the sagging in her bodice because she hadn't had time to lace up her stays as tightly as she should have. Or the red color of her kiss-bruised lips. Or the wrinkles in her skirt— Oh heavens, she wanted to die! "Sebastian escorted me home. I..." She forced out the lie, hating herself for lying to the woman who had always been like a sister to her, "I had a headache."

Josie frowned at her with concern. "Are you ill?" She reached for her hand in worry. "Should I call for Dr. Brandon?"

"Please don't." Her chest sank like lead, because now she could add the guilt of lying to her oldest friend to the guilt of tonight's carriage ride. She forced a smile. "I'm feeling better already."

"Good." Josie squeezed her hand and released it. "It's probably just all the noise and excitement of the gardens. It can be overwhelming."

That lesson she'd learned better than anyone. "Yes."

"Why don't you come in and have a cup of chocolate with me?"

Not letting her refuse, Josie linked her arm with Miranda's and led her into her sitting room. Miranda bit back a groan of exasperation. What a cake she was! She couldn't even flee like a coward to her room successfully.

"Higgins just brought up the tray, so it's still warm. Chocolate always helps me to fall asleep." Josie sat on the edge of the settee and poured two cups of hot chocolate from the porcelain pot, then held one up for Miranda. "Maybe it will help your headache."

"Thank you," she whispered, truly touched by Josie's kindness. And thoroughly mortified by what she'd done tonight with her brother. She'd gotten caught up in the moment, in the way he made her feel so beautiful and wanted and in her own confused feelings for him. She'd stopped all logical thought and simply let herself be swept away.

Josie motioned toward the chair across from her. As Miranda sank down onto it, fresh tears blurred her eyes at what she'd done tonight, and she blinked them away, grateful that she could blame them on her headache, if necessary. She accepted the cup of chocolate but fidgeted nervously with it, having no taste for it.

With concern creasing her brow, Josie settled back against the cushions and asked gently, "Something happened tonight in the gardens, didn't it? Something that caused your headache." She paused knowingly. "Or someone."

Miranda's eyes snapped up to hers even as her stomach fell away through the floor. "I don't—" She swallowed. Hard. But the knot of confused emotions stayed stuck in her throat. "I don't know what you mean."

"Your face is flushed, and your dress is mussed." Josie gave a gentle, understanding smile. "We're all alone tonight, so we can talk in private if you want to share what happened."

Fresh guilt stabbed through her that she had to dissemble with Josie when the marchioness was being so kind to her. She should have been thrilled that Josie wanted her to confide her secrets, just as they had as girls at Chestnut Hill. But she simply couldn't. Instead she said nothing and raised the cup to her lips to hide any traces of the confusion and remorse she felt over Sebastian.

Josie continued, "Thomas is at Strathmore House with the colonel and Kate, and Mother won't be back until after the fireworks. They're her favorite part of Vauxhall. So you can tell me..." Josie leaned forward, with eager expectation shining in her eyes as she asked secretively, "Was it that nice Mr. Downing?"

Miranda blinked, her mind blanking. "Mr. Downing?" Then she caught her breath. Oh, good heavens! She'd completely forgotten that Charles sent his regrets at the last minute. And how terrible was she that she hadn't missed the man at all? "I had a headache, truly," she insisted, still dissembling. Although, from the ache blossoming behind her eyes, it would soon prove true.

Josie's smile curled higher with disbelief. "If you don't deny it, I'm going to assume you got caught up in the romance of the gardens." Her eyes shined as she sipped at her cup. "It's been known to happen."

Miranda looked down solemnly into her chocolate. It wasn't romance that had caught her tonight but a stodgy, old duke. One who proved to be not so stodgy nor old after all.

Her heart sank. The worst part—oh, the very worst part!—was that she couldn't even blame her recklessness on simple lust, because it was being with Sebastian that had made it so wonderful. Being with an intelligent, witty, thoughtful man who for a few precious moments tonight had stopped being a duke and had simply been himself.

"So it *was* a romantic encounter, then." Caught up in the excitement of the secret, Josie set her chocolate aside. "And the man?" she pried without daring to name anyone, although Miranda could tell from the gleam in her eyes that she suspected Charles Downing. "Do you like him?"

"No," Miranda denied quickly. "I mean, yes—no!" Oh, she simply couldn't think straight! She groaned softly in frustrated confusion as she hung her head in her hand. "I don't know."

Josie sat forward on the edge of the settee and lowered her voice. "When you kissed him, did he make your toes curl?"

Oh, Sebastian did so much more than curl her toes! He'd set her entire body afire, in a way she was beginning to suspect no other man could have done. "Yes," she admitted. Then, she added hesitatingly in a whisper, "I think ... I might have curled his toes, too."

Josie beamed. "Ah, so he likes you!"

"No." Sadness flashed through her, adding to the confusion of emotions already swirling through her like a tempest. She wasn't naïve enough to believe that he did. Not the way Josie meant. Because even after all they did tonight in the carriage, even though Sebastian admitted that he wanted her, he'd also been very clear that he would never let himself have her. Not the proper duke in search of his perfect duchess. But for one impossible moment tonight, when she was coming apart in his arms, she wished he could have been just a man.

"I see," Josie murmured gently, a world of sisterly sympathy in those two words. She pressed gently, "Does he know how you feel about him?"

"Oh no!" She would be mortified if he found out! "I could never tell him." Especially when she wasn't certain herself exactly what she felt. And especially when she was certain that he would look on her with pity if she did.

"But how will he know if you don't tell him?" With her eyes sparkling at the prospect of playing matchmaker, Josie shrugged casually. "And what do you have to lose?"

"My pride." Miranda heaved out a deep sigh.

Josie smiled gently at her. "I don't think—" The sound of the front door opening downstairs reached them, interrupting their conversation, and her smile brightened. "Thomas is home."

Their private moment was over, and Josie rose gracefully to her feet, to be able to welcome her husband home. The look of love that flashed across her face at hearing her husband returning to her made Miranda's heart ache fiercely with jealousy. Would she ever know that kind of deep love and affection? The kind of love in which her husband not only loved her but completed her?

Miranda set down her cup and moved to the door, excusing herself for the night. She wanted nothing more than to pull the covers over her head and not crawl out of bed until August.

"Miranda?" Josie called out to her to give her one last piece of sisterly advice. "If you really like this man, then you need to tell him how you feel. I know that showing your heart to another can be scary, but you shouldn't pass up this opportunity. You need to ask yourself which you'd rather have—your pride or a chance at love?"

She thought of Sebastian and bit her lip. Which indeed?

CHAPTER ELEVEN

~

*W*ith a groan of frustration, Sebastian punched angrily at his pillow and rolled onto his back to stare up at the high canopy of his bed.

Miranda Hodgkins... *Christ.*

He'd gone mad. That was the only explanation for what had happened in the carriage. The woman had frustrated him to the point that he'd ceased all rational thought and restraint, pushing him right to the snapping point. And beyond.

Somehow, when he wasn't looking, Miranda had grown up and become a woman. A very ripe, delectable temptress who knew exactly how to drive him into a frenzy the way no other woman ever had. Yet what angered him the most, what still made his blood run hot thinking about the encounter even now hours later, was knowing how completely wrong for him she was but wanting her anyway. In every way. And not just physically.

That was the part that stirred the most frustration inside him. Oh, she was pretty, all right, especially when she gave him that expression of innocent seduction when she bit her lip as she looked at him. But he'd been with women far more beautiful than Miranda, and none of them affected him the way she had. No, with Miranda it was more than physical attraction. She possessed a vitality and spirit that drew him, most likely because he had so little of that himself these days. When he was with her—when it was just the two of them together laughing or discussing poetry, debating politics, or simply walking silently together through the park— then he wasn't the Duke of Trent. Then he was simply Sebastian. And he was happy.

He longed for that—to have all of her with him, in every way. Ways he simply couldn't have as a duke. Including in his bed. And not just for one night.

Madness!

He rested his forearm over his eyes. Whatever caused this insanity—that unruly hair that couldn't make up its mind whether to be red or blond, her laugh that always poured out of her at exactly the wrong moment, the way the stubborn gel stood up to him when most men had the good sense to be cowed, how she could infuriate him on the turn of a single word or make him laugh just as quickly—in the morning, he would put an end to it. They would come to an understanding. He would apologize; he would calmly explain that what happened between them could never happen again, that it had been a mistake—

A mistake? He laughed bitterly at himself. Wasn't that how he'd gotten into this situation in the first place? Heaven only knew what would happen if he told her that a second time.

Even now as he lay staring into the darkness, the guilt gnawed at his gut. He'd been a cad, nearly ruining her—

twice now, in fact—when he knew damned well that he could never marry her. He needed a suitable wife and duchess, one his father would have approved of. Certainly not the orphaned niece of a tenant farmer whom society would never accept. And that sent stabbing up inside him the worst guilt of all—because he knew his responsibility to his rank and to his family, knew that if he ruined her it would make it difficult for her to find a husband... yet selfishly he still wanted her and the happiness she could bring.

He was so tired of being Duke of Trent, so tired of the burdens he carried, so tired of wondering if he were living up to his father's expectations. But when he was with Miranda, he could be himself. Not a peer whom everyone depended upon and whom everyone looked to for respectability, leadership, perfection...

But he *was* Trent. Always would be. And there was no help for it.

With a frustrated groan, he again punched the pillow and gave up completely on sleep.

The click of the opening door disturbed the silence of the room, followed by the rustle of soft movement.

He blew out an aggravated sigh. His valet was a good man and dedicated to his service, but tonight Sebastian didn't want the fire banked or the drapes drawn. He wanted to be left alone to wallow in his misery. "What is it, Barlow?"

When the valet didn't answer, Sebastian bit back a curse and sat up, the coverlet falling down around his hips—and froze.

Miranda.

She stood by the door, ethereal like a ghost in the soft shadows, wearing a wide-brimmed hat and a driver's coat that covered her from neck to shoes. But he would have recognized that pert nose anywhere, along with the determined lift of her chin and the clenched hands at her sides. A fury in men's clothing.

His eyes narrowed in quick anger. So it wasn't enough to frustrate him in the carriage by giving him a taste of what he could never have. She'd now come to taunt him some more in his own home.

"What are you doing here?" he demanded. The damned woman was pushing him right to the edge of his patience.

"Swallowing my pride," she whispered, her enigmatic words as soft as the firelight playing its fading shadows across her face.

She reached up and removed the hat, and as she dropped it away, her hair tumbled down freely around her shoulders and back. His gut clenched as instant arousal pulsed through him.

Beneath the coverlet that hid the lower half of his naked body, his cock hardened at the memory of what they'd done in the carriage, so suddenly that he inhaled a pained breath through clenched teeth. He watched in sweet torment as she reached down to slip off her left shoe and let it drop away to the floor, then did the same with the other. With each piece of clothing she removed, desire coiled tighter inside him.

"You need to leave," he ordered, his voice far huskier than he'd intended. And far from convincing.

"After I had to try all the bedroom doors before I found you? No."

"If someone discovers you here—"

"I'm tired of your warnings, Sebastian." She boldly held his gaze across the room. "From now on, I'm doing whatever I want."

With trembling fingers, she unbuttoned the long coat. Each button she slid free revealed a stretch of flesh or thin gauzy material beneath, each one a punch to his gut. Unaware of how torturous it was for him to watch her undress, she pushed the coat off her shoulders and let it fall to the floor around her feet. Then she stood as still as a statue, as if daring him to look his fill of her, wearing the same dress she'd worn the night of his mother's party. His mouth went dry.

God help him. Lady Rose had returned.

Knowing he had to get her out of the room so he wouldn't repeat the mistake from the carriage, no matter how much he wanted to, he chastised, "You're making a habit of stumbling into my bedchamber by accident."

"No accident." She shrugged a nearly bare shoulder beneath the satin ribbons that held the loosely fitted bodice in place. "I found exactly the right room this time."

His cock ached for her, and his head swam with confusion. She was completely wrong...yet so perfectly right.

"What we did in the carriage," she told him softly, "it isn't over. You and I have unfinished business."

His tolerance snapped. Biting out a curse, he leapt from the bed and charged across the room like a bull. She gasped when she realized he was completely naked and averted her eyes, then she retreated until her back hit the wall beside the door.

But Sebastian closed in on her, frustration and aggravation boiling inside him. He planted his hands on the wall on either side of her shoulders, not caring what she thought of having a naked man standing so close to her that he was almost touching her. And not only a naked man but a fully aroused one, too. But at that moment, with the temptation she presented only flaming his frustration until it tightened inside him like a spring, he didn't give a damn.

"I won't marry you just because I touched you," he

ground out through clenched teeth. "So if that's why you're here—"

"I'm not here to trap you into marriage." Still not daring to look at him, she raised her chin in a flash of indignation.

He took her chin and forced her to look at him. Her eyes flared brightly in the dim shadows, mirroring the anger he was certain shone in his. "Then why are you here?"

"Because I like you," she breathed, the confession tearing from her so softly that her words were barely a sound at all, "so much more than I should."

His heart stuttered painfully as he stared at her, momentarily stunned. He didn't dare let himself believe he'd heard her correctly. He simply *couldn't* have. Because if he had... *Dear God.* To be this close to having a chance at happiness, only to know that it could never be his—

"Miranda," he rasped out, unable to say anything more as his voice caught in his throat. She had no idea of the temptation she presented for him, or the torture she was putting him through.

All of her trembled now as she whispered, "And I thought maybe..."

"What?" he pressed, lowering his head until their eyes were even and his mouth was so close to hers that he could feel the heat of her panting little breaths shivering over his lips.

"Oh, you infuriating man!" She shoved at his shoulder, but he refused to back away. "I want to do it again, damn you! What we did in the carriage—" Her voice cracked with frustration and embarrassment. "I came here because I hoped you might like me, too, enough to want to—"

He lunged forward and captured her mouth beneath his.

Unable any longer to resist her, he shoved his hand into her hair and grasped the silky strands between his fingers, to hold her head still beneath his kiss as his mouth ravished hers. He was ravenously hungry, both for the taste of her and for the vivaciousness radiating from her that drew him the way no other woman ever had, and he devoured her kiss in great, greedy mouthfuls.

A whimper of need escaped her. He drank in the sound, his blood surging hot with desire as he plunged his tongue between her lips to taste the sweetness inside, reveling in the electric thrill that cascaded through him. She was infuriating, challenging, aggravating to a fault... and wholly irresistible. She liked *him*, and not the title he'd inherited but the man he'd shaped himself to be. With nothing more than that whispered confession, she'd completely undone him.

A groan of surrender tore from the back of his throat, and he was lost in her. At that moment, with her softness pressing against his hard body, making herself vulnerable, he didn't give a damn about the dukedom or propriety; all he knew was that he needed her in order to escape the prison his life had become, if only for one night. *All* of her.

He tore his mouth away from hers and nipped at the tender column of her throat as his hands stroked up and down her body. Now that she was here with him, he didn't want to stop touching her, as if in some irrational fear that she truly was nothing but a ghost and would vanish in the night.

"I don't want to do what we did in the carriage," he rasped out, then licked at the hollow of her throat where he could feel her heartbeat racing. For him. The sensation left all of him aching.

Clinging to him, she gasped for breath as she panted out in confusion, "You don't? But I thought—"

"I want so much more than that," he breathed hotly against her lips, before kissing her languidly and reveling in her soft response. "I want all of you, understand?" He cupped her breast against his palm through the thin material, and she shuddered. "I want every breath and shiver, every laugh and smile..."

He lowered his head to take her nipple between his lips, teasing at it gently until it pebbled against his tongue even through the crêpe. When he lifted his head, a wet circle showed on her gown where he'd had his mouth on her, a possessive mark that revealed her dusky nipple behind the translucent material.

"Every secret in every inch of you," he promised against her lips, his mouth returning to hers.

Moaning softly, she arched her back against the wall to push her breasts harder against him. He throbbed at the delicious sight of her, her eyes closed as if his nearness was unbearable but her full lips parted with desire to be taken. A beautiful contradiction, just like the strong yet kind woman she was. So fierce yet so fragile. The woman who could never be his... who was now his for the night.

"If you want to leave, you need to go now," he warned, his voice little more than a rasp in his aching need for her. "If you stay, you'll be ruined. And I cannot marry you."

Her eyes fluttered open, and she stared up at him, her green depths a stormy sea of excitement and desire, arousal and nervousness. He traced his thumb across her bottom lip and elicited from her in a soft whisper, "I don't want to leave."

Cupping her face in his hands, he rested his forehead against hers, squeezing his eyes shut against the swell of emotions. Relief and affection warred in equal measure with the guilt churning inside him, yet he still wanted her, still needed her, even knowing that he could never offer her a future without betraying his father's faith in him. Something he would *never* do again with any woman. Even Miranda.

"I don't need any more warnings from you, Sebastian. I know what I want." She slid her mouth along his jaw to his ear and whispered, "I want to inspire you."

He exhaled a long breath in an attempt to slow his racing heart as it jumped into a furious beat. "You already do, Rose," he murmured. "More than you realize."

"Then show me."

He grinned wickedly at that, and his hand stroked slowly down her body and slipped beneath her skirt to tenderly caress between her thighs. "You mean like this?"

She moaned and rolled back her head. "That's a good start," she agreed in soft pants, her tongue darting out to wet her lips as her sex began to quiver with quick arousal against his fingers. "Oh yes...that's good...*very* good..."

With a low laugh, he reached over to the door and threw the lock.

* * *

Miranda bit back the moan on her lips as his fingers continued their gentle caresses between her legs. Oh, those clever fingers! Her body heated instantly, and the ache at his fingertips grew even more intense than it had been in the carriage now that she knew how good it felt to have his hands on her, stroking her, exploring her. She gasped as he grazed the sensitive nub buried in the top of her folds, and her arms clenched around his neck to keep from falling to the floor.

Then his hand slipped away. The sudden loss was unbearable, and she whimpered and wiggled her hips invitingly to coax him back.

"Shh," he murmured, his lips resting against her temple as his hands stroked soothingly down her arms to her hips. "We've got all night, sweet. No need to rush."

"But I want—"

"So do I." He lifted her off the floor to carry her across the room to his bed. He laid her on the mattress, then followed down on top of her. "Very." He kissed her lips. "Very." His mouth slid down her throat to kiss into the hollow between her breasts. "*Very* much."

"Sebastian," she moaned plaintively as fire flared inside her fluttering belly, her fingers combing through his silky hair as he continued to cover her cleavage with kisses. To have Sebastian's attentions on her was so much more wonderful than she could have imagined, this time alone with him far more precious.

"You wore the masquerade dress," he mumbled, then he placed a savoring kiss on the inside curve of her breast.

"Yes." She fought to breathe, not understanding how a simple kiss could steal her breath away. "You'd said you liked it."

"A great deal." His lips curved into a devilish smile at her thoughtfulness. "Lady Rose."

She couldn't resist running her fingertip over that smile, then laughing as he bit playfully at her finger. So unlike the Sebastian who had been so glum and reserved since his father's death, so unlike the duke who had been so stern and cross with her these past few weeks. Oh, she very much liked this version of him best. This was the man whose arms she wanted to be in tonight, whom she wanted to give herself to, knowing how tender and careful he would be with her.

He lifted onto his forearm beside her to flutter his hand along the side of her body. "You know what's even better than you in this dress?"

Heat rose everywhere he touched. "What?"

"You out of this dress," he murmured hotly.

Her breath hitched at the pulse of nervousness his words sent spiraling through her. He'd seen her uncovered from the waist up. But he'd never seen *all* of her.

He gently tugged at her skirt. "It's only fair." The heat in his eyes as he stared down at her set her on fire. "Since I'm not wearing anything."

Sweet heavens, he wasn't! Her belly knotted with trepidation. While she hadn't looked at him, not *there*, she had the feeling that he very much planned on looking at her everywhere. She worried her bottom lip between her teeth. "But what if…"

"Hmm?" Another caress of his hand up and down her body, this time pulling the skirt higher up her thighs.

She trembled as goose bumps covered her bared legs. "What if you don't like what you see?" she whispered aloud her fear, so soft her lips barely formed the words.

His eyes softened with understanding. "But I will like it," he assured her even as his hand inched up the skirt until the hem lay just beneath the juncture of her thighs. "I'm positively certain, in fact."

She trembled, all of her tensing in sudden apprehension. She didn't want him to stop, but…"But what if you don't? Can I—" She choked as he inched the hem even higher, exposing her triangle of feminine curls to the cool night air. Thankfully, his eyes never left hers. She didn't think she could have borne it if he'd looked down at her at that moment. "Can I put the dress back on?"

He chuckled, and the warm sound rumbled into her. "Yes, you can." The fabric slid across her hips to her belly. "But you won't want to."

As he untied the ribbons at her shoulders to release the bodice, then slid the dress over her head and off, she closed her eyes. She didn't want to see his expression when he saw her completely naked for the first time, if he compared her to those fine ladies he'd been with before and found her lacking—

"Dear God...you are so beautiful."

She smiled as a soft laugh of happiness and relief bubbled from her. Sebastian thought she was *beautiful*! Even wearing nothing at all. She was right—he would make tonight wonderful for her, the way no other man could.

She opened her eyes. Wildfire tore through her at the raw desire she saw on his face as he gazed down at her, and she shivered from the intensity of him. Everywhere his eyes lingered on her body flames prickled beneath her skin, the force of it nearly overwhelming.

"I'm sorry to tell you this." He rubbed his thumb across her bottom lip and said with teasing solemnity, "But the dress stays off all night, I'm afraid."

"Sebastian!" she scolded, her cheeks flushing with an instant blush.

Laughing, he lowered his head and nuzzled his cheek against hers, and his midnight beard scratched tantalizingly across her soft skin. So very masculine. And for this moment, all hers. Her heart soared with the joy of that.

"Have I ever told you how much I enjoy the way you blush?" He placed a kiss on her lips before she could answer. "How *inspiring* I find it?"

Which only caused the blush to deepen and left her speechless.

"It starts here." He brushed his lips across her cheekbone. "And lingers here." Then down her jawline to her neck. "And here." Down farther until his mouth was on her breast. "And ends right here."

When he took her nipple between his lips and sucked, she arched up off the mattress with a strangled gasp. Oh, his wicked mouth! He knew exactly how to torture and pleasure her at the same time, how to softly suck yet generate a fierce ache all the way down between her legs. How to make her whimper for more beneath the breathless onslaught of licks and sucks and nibbles.

"Such a beautiful blush," he mumbled against her breast. "Which makes me wonder..."

She bit her lip to hold back her curiosity as long as she could, even knowing he was baiting her— "Wonder what?" she asked, unable to help herself as her fingers ran wild over his shoulders and bare back, loving the feel of his muscles rippling beneath her seeking fingertips.

"If other places on your body also blush."

She tensed. Surely he didn't mean—

"Like here." He lowered himself to lick at her belly in slow, languid circles as his hand stroked along her inner thigh. "Or here."

Oh heavens, he *did* mean...And he couldn't—simply couldn't! Not *there* of all places.

With a push at the headboard, she slid herself down beneath him, until her eyes were level with his, her bare toes touching his calves. She wrapped her arms tightly around his shoulders to keep him right there.

"Do *you* blush?" she asked, as seductively as possible despite the nervous twitter in her voice as she turned their playful conversation onto him. "How about here?"

She placed a kiss in the middle of his chest, and he chuckled. But when she slid her mouth sideways and captured his flat male nipple between her lips and sucked at him the way he'd done to her, the laughter strangled in his throat.

Turnabout was fair play, after all. He shuddered as she took his nipple between her teeth and nibbled—oh, how very much she enjoyed their play!

"Or here?" she whispered, running her hands down his bare back to cup his hard buttocks against her palms.

When she squeezed, he inhaled sharply. Her name came as a soft warning on his lips. But he'd been warning her all week—all season, in fact—and she was tired of his warnings.

If he truly wanted to warn her, then she'd give him something to worry about. "*Here.*"

She slid her hand between them and folded her fingers around his erection, and a plaintive groan tore from him. She gave a devilish laugh and stroked along his length the way he'd shown her in the carriage.

"Sweet Lucifer," he murmured as he rose up onto his hands and knees over her to give her room to work her pleasures on him. His head bowed low, and his eyes squeezed shut.

He hung large and stiff in her hand, and with each stroke, he seemed to grow impossibly larger and harder. Like magic. She twisted her palm around him, teasing him with her fingers the way she wanted him to do to her again before the night was over. *All* night, he'd promised her. And she planned on savoring every precious moment of it.

Tentatively, yet urged on by the low growls of satisfaction coming from the back of his throat, she slipped her second hand down between his legs to cup his testicles against her palm. He shuddered at the contact, and she thrilled with it. A wantonness swelled inside her that she'd never known before, and as he rested heavy against her palm, with her other hand still stroking his shaft, she gently squeezed.

His hips bucked as a curse shot from his lips.

He grabbed her hands away and lifted her arms over her head. "Keep doing that," he cautioned in a husky voice, "and the night will be over sooner than we'd both like."

She laughed and rose up to lick her tongue across his collarbone. The delicious taste of him made her even more bold, even more confident in herself. Testing his resolve, she wiggled her hips. He let out a growl of warning and pinned her to the mattress with his hips.

"I'm sorry," he rasped hoarsely against her lips as his mouth found hers again, kissing her hard and urgently. All of him shivered hotly.

"For what?" She stilled instantly, and her heart pounded with a mix of nervousness and arousal. Had he changed his mind? Did he not want her after all?

"I can't wait any longer for you." He reached down and hooked her right leg around his waist, then the left, until his body hovered just above hers in the cradle of her thighs. "I wanted to savor you, but I need you too badly." His hand caressed between her legs, and she trembled at the delicious feel of his fingers against her, the wonderful caresses she so much enjoyed. Only Sebastian could make her feel this special. "You're so wet and warm already..." He sucked at her bottom lip and purred, "Good."

"Good?" She was mortified that he would mention *that*, and the blush flared up across her cheeks again.

He groaned. "Very much so."

When she felt his fingers parting the soft lips of her sex and the tip of his erection settling against her, she realized what he meant. "Sebastian," she whispered, and touched his cheek, trying to show him how much she cared about him, how special he had become to her. Without hesitation, knowing tonight was good and right only because of him, she begged for what she wanted most— "Please."

He lowered his hips and sank inside her, one unhurried inch at a time.

Holding her breath at the slow invasion, she tightened her

arms around his shoulders and buried her face against his neck as her body expanded to take him in. With each inch he sank deeper, the cradle of her hips widened around him, and she shifted uneasily to make herself more relaxed. Not painful, not exactly, but the growing pressure was decidedly uncomfortable. She forced down the sting of disappointment that this new intimacy wasn't nearly as pleasant as what he'd done with her in the carriage. Still, being close to Sebastian was wonderful, and she sought to drink in the quiet strength and delicious warmth of him.

Then he stopped moving and lay motionless above her, still raised up on his forearms.

She opened her eyes, expecting a smile from him, but hard-won restraint hardened his face, with his jaw clenched tight and his eyes screwed shut. Every inch of him was tense and taut, hard and smooth as marble. Her heart pounded with uncertainty.

"Sebastian?" she breathed, and the soft sound of his name fell through the silence between them, mixing with the joined pounding of their hearts.

He opened his eyes and gazed down at her, and the raw need in their blue depths ripped her breath away. Then he whispered her name and plunged his hips down against hers, thrusting fully inside her and tearing through the thin resistance of her maidenhead.

Miranda gasped at the sharp pain of being filled so completely so suddenly, at the weight of his hips fully seated against her spread thighs—but his mouth covered hers in the sweetest, gentlest kiss imaginable, and soothed away the cry on her lips. The contradiction of sensations sent her spinning.

Then he began to move, this time rocking his hips against hers to stroke slowly and smoothly inside her, and the pain dissolved into utter pleasure. Oh, it *was* wonderful! He was doing to her with his body what his fingers had done in the carriage, only so very much *more*...more filling, more silky smooth, more delicious weight pressing down on her. His entire body caressed hers with each plunge and retreat, as if making love to her with his entire being. Any doubts that still lingered about giving herself to him tonight and expressing with her body the feelings she didn't dare utter aloud vanished like fog beneath the morning sun.

She buried her face in his shoulder, breathing in deep the sweet smell of him that filled up her senses, taking a quick lick of his sweat-salty skin to taste him. *Delicious.* It was impossible that any other woman had ever felt as complete as she did with Sebastian inside her, impossible that any other man could be this much of a perfect fit with her, both with her body and with her heart. She nearly laughed as sheer joy bubbled inside her. Sebastian Carlisle, the most impossible man in the world for her, had proven to be the perfect man with whom to share this moment.

"You are so beautiful, Miranda," he whispered against her temple, and his sweet words made tears gather at her lashes.

"So are you," she choked out.

He laughed softly at her slip of the tongue and kissed her, so heatedly, so possessively that she shuddered at the intensity of it. How could she not care for this man when he made her feel this special? Did he even realize the effect he had on her? She slid her mouth away from his to caress her lips across his cheek so that he couldn't see the flash of emotion on her face, because she knew that she could never tell him.

He groaned, and his large hands grabbed her hips, guiding her in a shared, primal rhythm. Her body instinctively knew what it needed from him, arching off the bed to eagerly meet each thrust of his hips with her own until she nearly exhausted herself. Yet she still craved more, still yearning for the wondrous release he had given her earlier, the same release she was certain his body was capable of giving her now.

"Sebastian," she whimpered, shifting beneath him in an attempt to bring him impossibly closer to the throbbing spot inside her, helpless against the aching intensity spreading through her body and the warmth blossoming in her heart.

"Yes, sweet," he murmured, as if knowing exactly what she needed. He hooked his arms beneath her knees, lifting her legs and rolling her onto her upper back. "Whatever you wish."

He lifted his hips and thrust hard, grinding his pelvis against her and shooting a jarring shudder of pleasure through her. She gasped at the intensity of having him so far inside her at such a new angle, joining the two of them impossibly closer and stealing her breath away.

He pulled back until only the tip of him remained inside her, then he drove forward again. And this time, oh, sweet heavens, *this* time—

Dark spots flashed across her eyes. Sparks shot through her, flying out the ends of her fingers and toes. Her body convulsed violently around his, her intimate folds quivering as all the tiny muscles inside her bore down around him, then released with a shudder so intense that a cry of pleasure poured from her.

He kissed her and drank in her cries as he continued to stroke inside her, but she was unable to do anything more than simply lie there trembling as the undulating waves of release spread over her. Now his thrusts came fast and deep, soft little growls of his own need for release filling her senses, swirling inside her head and engulfing her.

One last, powerful thrust—then with a groan, he pulled quickly out of her. His arms clasped her tightly to him as he shuddered, and she felt a rush of liquid warmth against her inner thigh as he spilled himself onto the mattress beneath her. He collapsed on top of her, his heavy body pressing against hers and his forehead resting against her bare shoulder as he struggled to regain his breath.

Amazed by what had just happened between them, for a moment not believing that it hadn't been only a dream, Miranda lifted her hands to caress his back. Beads of perspiration wetted her fingertips. She smiled as she kissed his temple and tightened her arms around his trembling body. How could she have ever been wary of this wonderful, amazing man when she had the power to make him tremble so helplessly like this? How could she have been so blind to him for so many years?

Caught up in the exhilaration of being in his arms and of the astonishing pleasures he brought to her, she laughed a soft little giggle of pure happiness.

He lifted his head to smile down at her, his blue eyes bright with satisfaction and soft with affection. "What is it, sweet?"

"I was just thinking," she admitted as she brushed her fingertips at the sweat-dampened lock of blond hair that fell across his forehead, "that a love scene would have made *Hamlet* perfect."

He laughed and lowered his mouth to hers, to kiss her with a sultry languidness that tasted of happiness, pleasure, and...Was that possession? But she supposed he had a right to feel that way, since she'd given herself to him tonight in every possible way, all the way down to her soul. And she didn't regret a moment of it.

But when he shifted his weight away to lie beside her on

the bed, Miranda knew she had to be careful with her heart. Sebastian would never think of her as belonging to him beyond the physical passion they'd just shared. He'd been very clear about that. Oh, certainly he would be kind and caring as much as he could, but they could never have more than this. She knew that; she'd accepted that before she came here tonight. And yet, as his strong arms wrapped around her and drew her back against his chest, his lips nuzzling against her nape, she had to admit that belonging here with him was nice.

Very nice, in fact.

So nice that she could easily become used to being with him like this, the protective strength of his arms encircling her, the warmth of his breath tickling against her neck, his heartbeat pulsing quietly into her bare back. As if he didn't want to let go of her.

But she couldn't stay, and even now her eyes stung at the thought that this would be the most he could ever be to her. A friend, a lover…someone with whom to share laughter and affection but not a future. Sebastian might find joy with her, but the Duke of Trent had to find a life with someone else.

She blinked hard. "I should leave," she whispered into the dark shadows as the ache in her chest began to grow stronger.

"Stay." He reached down to draw the coverlet over her to keep her tucked into bed with him, then placed a delicate kiss on her bare shoulder. "We have all night, remember."

She latched on to the only excuse she could give without revealing her heart. "I need to return to Audley House before the servants wake and see me slipping in through the cellar door."

"I'll make certain you return home safely without any

problems." His arms tightened around her. "But for tonight I want to hold you right here."

Even as he said that, though, his words slurred from exhaustion, and his voice thickened with sleep. So she stayed, because she knew he would soon fall asleep and then she could slip away without disturbing him. And without him seeing the tears she was certain would fall. Not in regret—never. She would *never* regret a moment of tonight. But she knew she would mourn for what more they would never share.

Sebastian Carlisle...Whoever would have thought she would have surrendered her innocence to *him*? All these years her heart had been infatuated with Robert and never once considered that it might very well be Sebastian whom she wanted to kiss her instead, with whom she wanted to engage in scandalous conversations at operas and plays, whom she...

Loved.

Her heart skipped hard as the utter hopelessness of their situation washed painfully over her.

He was an impossible choice, yet she'd known when she came here that what she felt was so much more than simple physical attraction. Somehow, creeping upon her so slowly that she never saw it coming, she'd fallen in love with the other Carlisle brother.

And there was no hope for it.

CHAPTER TWELVE

~ ~

*T*hunder rumbled through the silence of his room, and Sebastian stirred from sleep. His eyes opened slowly to the gray darkness of a morning rainstorm striking at the windows, the coals in the fireplace now completely cold. But the bed was warm. He smiled as he languidly stretched. He'd awoken happier than he had in years, and his body ached pleasantly in places where it hadn't ached in far too long. All because of Miranda.

"Rose," he whispered blissfully as he rolled over, "are you—"

The bed was empty. He flung back the coverlet and bolted to his feet to search for her. She wasn't in the adjoining sitting room nor in the connecting bedchamber after that. The realization hit him like a bucket of ice water.

She was gone.

He scrambled into a pair of trousers and yanked a shirt over his head, then charged from his room to search the house for her. But the town house was quiet, and there was no sign that she'd been there at all last night, except for the small stain of blood on his sheet where he'd taken her innocence and the scent of rosewater, which still clung to his skin.

He charged downstairs. The frustrating woman had left him in the middle of the night, without a chance to say good-bye or explain to her the way things had to be between them going forward. She'd *left*, damn it! When she should have stayed all night, when she should have been emotional and clingy like any other woman would have been. Oh no, not her—she never did as expected, not even in intimacy. She'd sneaked out under the cover of darkness as if she'd never been there at all. As if last night meant nothing to her.

And *that* bothered him most of all.

He flung open the breakfast room door and caught a flash of movement from the corner of his eye. "Miranda!"

Quinn turned away from the buffet, his heaping plate in his hand, and popped a sweet roll into his mouth. "Why would Miranda be here?" he mumbled around the roll.

Why, indeed? Sebastian's shoulders sagged with more disappointment than he wanted to admit. He'd been looking forward to spending the morning with her, to prolonging their night together. He'd felt more relaxed and at peace last night with Miranda than he had in the company of any other woman in his entire life. And he felt more alive than he had in years. For a few hours, she'd lifted the weight from his shoulders, and he'd wanted that lightness and sense of freedom to last as long as possible before the burden settled back onto him. Even now he felt his back growing tighter.

But Quinton was still staring at him in bewilderment, still waiting for an answer.

He forced a casual shrug. "Mother mentioned something last night about Miranda bringing something over this morning sometime," he muttered as he slumped down into his chair. Well, *that* was certainly vague. But the answer seemed to satisfy Quinn, whose attention had already returned to the kippers piled on his plate. "I thought I heard the front door."

"Must have been Saunders fetching the post." Quinn sat at the table and snatched up the morning *Times*, which the butler had already ironed and left at Sebastian's place. Then he glanced up and frowned with concern. "You look like hell this morning."

"Thanks," he grumbled, stealing a slice of bacon from his brother's plate and taking a bite. He *felt* like hell this morning.

"So . . . you had a woman in your room last night."

Sebastian choked.

Quinn slapped him hard on the back with an appreciative grin. "Sowing wild oats before you're leg-shackled, then?"

He rolled his eyes. Leave it to Quinn to bring up his search for a wife, something he hadn't thought about since he parted from Lady Jane at Vauxhall. That moment now seemed like years ago rather than less than one day, and something that felt as if it had happened to someone other than him.

Quinton arched a brow, his eyes shining mischievously. "And how is Lady Jane this morning?"

"It wasn't Jane Sheridan," he corrected in a growl, despite knowing that Quinn was simply baiting him. Then he came as close as he could without openly lying— "It was a woman from Vauxhall." There was no point in denying he had company last night. He should have known he would never be able to keep Miranda quiet, not with all that eager passion bubbling inside her. Nor had he wanted to. One of the things he liked best about her was her exuberance. He poured himself a cup of coffee and took a long swallow of the black liquid, letting it burn down his throat. "Jane Sheridan isn't the kind of woman who has trysts in a gentleman's bedroom."

"Pity." Quinn sighed in exaggerated disappointment and returned his attention to the newspaper. He asked with mock solemnity, "Still set on marrying her anyway?"

Instead of laughing at his brother's teasing—or even scowling at him—Sebastian stared down into his coffee as fresh guilt rose inside him. What happened last night with Miranda was special and amazing, a wonderful gift he wasn't certain he deserved. Yet it didn't change the fact that he'd promised his father to find a proper duchess to represent the title and his family's legacy. Or that Miranda, with her pirate plays and boisterous laughter, was not that woman.

But the events of last night had proven one very important point to him with complete certainty—Lady Jane Sheridan would never be his wife.

"No," he said somberly, raking his fingers through his bed-mussed hair. "I'm not marrying Jane."

Quinn froze in mid-chew, his eyes darting to his brother. "Are you certain? She seems perfect."

"She is." Jane *was* perfect in every way—perfect for some other man.

He frowned, puzzled. "I thought she was at the top of your list."

"She was. But not any longer." He gulped down half a cup of coffee, wishing Quinton would talk about something other than his hunt for a wife. He couldn't even entertain the thought this morning of courting anyone, not when his skin still smelled of Miranda. Not when his chest continued to ache with disappointment that she wasn't here with him.

"But you're still planning on finding a wife this season, then?" Quinn pressed.

"Yes," he grumbled into his coffee cup. Although he had no idea how he'd manage to do it when the only woman occupying his mind was Miranda.

"And this woman from last night—"

"Is not the sort of woman Father had in mind to be Duchess of Trent," he interrupted firmly to put an end to the conversation before Quinton could question him further. The very last person he wanted to discuss with his brother was Miranda Hodgkins, especially when he had no idea how he felt about her himself. Except that she confused the hell out of him. The thunder rolling overhead and the rain beating at the windows only dampened his spirits more to realize how right she was for him when they were alone, how wrong in every other way.

And if he held a riot of emotions inside him at the memory of last night, then God only knew what confusion Miranda felt. Because while he'd never experienced a woman like her before, she'd never experienced any other man.

Quinn returned his attention to the paper and scanned the land listings as he did every morning, hunting for possible properties he could purchase and turn into an estate of his own. Sebastian knew that his brother had chafed under the limitations of the work he'd done for the dukedom during the past two years, despite being brilliantly successful at managing the estate's operations, and that he wanted to forge his own path away from the influence of the Carlisle family. Sebastian certainly understood that. He suspected that by the end of the season Quinn would have made up his mind where that path would take him, and that possibility both pleased Sebastian and spiraled hot jealousy through him.

"Just keep in mind that you can have a mistress once you're married," Quinn threw out helpfully as he simultaneously popped a strawberry into his mouth and traced a forefinger down the listings as he read them. "Most every peer does. It's nearly expected of a duke."

A mistress…He stared at his coffee as a dark, desperate thought surged through him of the only way he could have both his respectable duchess and his passionate lover. The lady he needed as a duke and the woman he wanted as a man. Perhaps Quinn was right for once. Perhaps he could make Miranda his mistress and—

No.

A wave of self-loathing surged through him. She deserved better than being his mistress, and he would never use her like that. Just as he knew that once he married, he would never go outside his marriage, for either pleasure or companionship. He wanted the same kind of marriage his parents had, one of friendship, support, and love. *A mistress?* Christ, what was he thinking?

He wasn't, that was the problem. When it came to Miranda, all rational thought ceased. Even now she bothered him to distraction, creating more questions than answers. She'd come to London in pursuit of Robert, but last night, she'd come to him. She knew he couldn't offer her a future, yet she'd surrendered her innocence anyway, asking for nothing in return. She'd admitted to having an affection for him, yet she'd vanished in the night without a word.

His male pride wanted explanations.

But his heart simply wanted to see her again.

He set the coffee aside and asked as casually as possible as a plan began to form in his mind, "What do the ladies have scheduled for this evening, do you know?"

"They're attending a museum lecture with Emily Grey." Quinn turned the page. "And Robert and I are planning on heading to St James's Street."

Sebastian bit back the urge to ask if that was wise, given how many nights his brothers had spent in the clubs recently. But he didn't have time to worry over them. Not when he had to deal with the oncoming storm that was Miranda.

"Robert and I will most likely be at Boodle's all night," Quinn said pointedly, then glanced up from the paper and sent Sebastian a crooked grin. A not-so-subtle signal that he'd have the house to himself if he wanted to invite back the woman from last night. "*All* night."

He grimaced into his coffee. He should have been glad that his brothers were willing to help cover his tracks, just as they'd done for one another all their lives, no matter what kind of trouble they'd gotten themselves into. But this time, it grated, reminding him of the very last time he'd secreted a woman away in order to be with her. He'd sworn to himself that he would never do that again, that he would never darken his father's memory by placing a woman before his family. But that was exactly what he'd done last night with Miranda; he'd been unable to deny himself a night of happiness with her, and this morning, he despised himself for it.

She deserved better from him. For Christ's sake, *he* deserved better from himself.

Yet it didn't stop him from wanting to be with her again.

"We'll probably be out until dawn," Quinn added, pretending he was still interested in the newspaper listings.

"Then I'll most likely join you," Sebastian answered dryly, wanting to put an end to any of his brother's suspicions.

"Of course you won't," Quinn replied with a knowing wink and raised the newspaper between them.

* * *

Miranda took a deep breath and tried to focus on the museum's evening speaker. She'd been looking forward all week to hearing Georgiana Bradford talk about her most recent African adventures and to meeting the famous adventuress in person, but now, she couldn't remember a word of what was being said. Something about crocodiles and rapids, pyramids and... Oh, concentrating was impossible!

Her eyes pressed closed in misery. She'd lost her innocence. To Sebastian Carlisle, of all men. It was all she could do to bite back the groan at her lips and not interrupt the lecture as she once more thought about last night.

She didn't regret being with him. How could she? The night was simply magical. He was tender and caring with her, even laughing with her to put her at ease, and in those precious few hours together, he'd been more relaxed than she'd seen him in years. If ever. Yet it wasn't only being intimate itself that was wonderful but also afterward when he held her in his arms, the deep rumble of his voice when he told her she was beautiful, and how happy she was to simply lie next to him. Being with him proved more special and thrilling than she could ever have imagined being with a man would be. Precisely because that man was Sebastian.

But it was Sebastian she cared about, not the Duke of Trent. It was as if she'd left Vauxhall in the carriage with one man, then left the arms of another three hours later. Two men, indeed—the Duke of Trent, who wanted a society lady with good breeding and sophisticated manners for his wife, and Sebastian, who wanted *her*, a woman who was the exact opposite of all that. The Duke of Trent, who frustrated her with his obsession with propriety and station, and Sebastian, who she loved. No matter that she wanted to spend the rest of her life with Sebastian, the Duke of Trent made that impossible.

Oh, she was a fool! Even though she knew she had no future with him, she couldn't help replaying in her mind all the wonderful moments they'd spent together, all the soft touches and affectionate kisses, all the happiness and laughter. She desperately wanted to be with him again, and not only for the scintillating pleasures of the night. She wanted the chance at a life with him, to create a home together in which there was love, comfort, laughter, children...oh, lots and lots of children!

She wanted nothing less than his love. But he would never let himself give it.

Dear God—what *was* she thinking? And this time she did hang her head in her hands and groan.

Sitting next her, Lady Emily Grey whispered with concern, "Are you all right?"

She nodded at Josie's sister-in-law, who had accompanied her to the lecture. Although Miranda had sneaked through the streets of Mayfair last night on her own, twice, she didn't dare venture out to a society event without a proper chaperone. So when the other ladies had begged off, Miranda had practically dragged Emily out with her tonight because she didn't want to miss the lecture...and because spending a quiet evening at home, surrounded by Sebastian's family, would have been pure torture.

So now she sat in a gallery at the British Museum, refused to let her eyes stray to Lady Jane Sheridan sitting in the front row with her mother and sister, and tried to concentrate on the lecture without hearing a single word.

Lady Emily frowned. "You look rather ill."

"Only a headache," she assured her. Sebastian was that, all right. Her own personal trouble-rousing, heartbreaking headache.

Emily squeezed her hand. "We can leave, if you'd like."

"No, I'd like to stay." She forced a smile. "I'm finding the lecture fascinating. Truly."

The look that Emily gave Miranda told her that she didn't believe her. But her friend knew not to press. "All right. But if your headache grows worse, we *will* leave." Emily was only a few years older than Miranda, but she had the demeanor of a well-seasoned mother and the regimented authority of a colonel's wife.

With a smile of genuine warmth at the woman's concern, Miranda nodded. "Agreed."

Emily released her hand and glanced past her down the row of chairs. "Oh—there's Olivia Sinclair. I promised to help her plan her upcoming garden party. Would you mind if I excused myself for a few minutes to speak with her?"

"Not at all." And Miranda might be able to use the time to actually hear what new knowledge Miss Bradford had to share about the ancient Egyptians. After all, that *was* the point of being here. Not to wallow in her own misery.

Emily rose and made her way to the Countess of St James. The two women were quickly ensconced in a private discussion, their heads bowed together to catch each other's low whispers.

Miranda turned her attention back to the young woman standing at the front of the room, holding a large crocodile skull in her hands. Georgiana Bradford was a wonder. One of the foremost adventurers of the day, with her exploits rivaling that of any man, she was brave enough to travel the world, face down natives in jungles and sandstorms in the deserts... while Miranda couldn't seem to survive a season in London. Or find a way to save her heart.

A prickle stirred at the back of her neck, sensing him before she saw him—

Sebastian.

She allowed herself one glance over her shoulder to be certain and instantly regretted it, unprepared for the shock of electricity that jolted through her upon seeing him. Standing just inside the gallery hall, he looked magnificent in his evening clothes of a maroon brocade waistcoat and a black jacket of superfine, with a sapphire cravat pin the same deep blue as his eyes that offset the golden highlights in his hair. He was dressed elegantly enough for an evening on the town... or one of slow seduction in his own bedchamber.

Turning away before he saw her and she melted completely into a puddle, she fixed her gaze on Miss Bradford even as her heart slid down to her knees. What on earth was *he* doing here? A museum lecture was certainly not the type of event that a Carlisle brother would attend, and the duke's unexpected appearance was stirring more interest throughout the curious audience than the lecture.

But Lady Jane was in attendance, Miranda realized, her heart sinking further. So were the rest of the ladies on his list. So of course he was here. Nothing about last night had changed his pursuit of a proper duchess, which only increased the jealousy Miranda already felt. And her heart slid right through the floor.

But Sebastian didn't head for Lady Jane. As whispers and hushed greetings rose in his wake, Miranda realized that he was walking in a different direction...toward *her*. Each step that brought him closer worked to tighten the knot of nervousness in her stomach. She sighed in relief when he turned down a different row from hers, only to feel a wave of dread sweep over her as he settled into the chair directly behind hers.

When the whispers at his arrival settled down and the room returned its attention to Miss Bradford, he leaned forward and spoke low at her ear. "You weren't at breakfast this morning."

Her belly fluttered achingly, and a low heat simmered inside her at the innuendo whispered in their private language, one that the women sitting around them would never have understood. Or even suspected. After all, everyone knew the Duchess of Trent was her sponsor for the season, just as everyone knew Sebastian was hunting a wife—in fact, multiple bets had already been placed in the book at White's for when he would make an engagement announcement and to whom, most of them waged by Robert and Quinton. So no one would have given a second thought that he sought her out, likely believing he was simply checking up on her tonight in his mother's absence before heading out to the clubs.

Carefully keeping her emotions from her face, she whispered over her shoulder, "I wasn't hungry."

"You were hungry enough last night."

Ignoring that innuendo, if not the cascade of heat it shivered down her spine at the memory of exactly how ravenous both of them had been for the other, she kept her gaze straight ahead. She didn't dare to look at him for fear of the blush that would color her cheeks and give them away. Or the regret she might see in his eyes.

"I was concerned," he pressed in the same low voice. "Are you not feeling well?"

There was no point in dissembling. She'd enjoyed herself a great deal, and he knew it, having felt her body's reaction to his, if still completely unaware of her affection for him. "I'm feeling very well, thank you," she returned in a voice far huskier than she'd intended.

From the corner of her eye, she saw a self-pleased grin pull at his lips, and then the telltale blush did heat at the back of her neck after all. Oh, the devil take him!

"So am I," he admitted in a sultry whisper that made her breath hitch.

"Shh!" The matron to Miranda's right turned in her chair to scold them for making noise, her narrowed eyes swinging between the two of them in a chastising glower.

Miranda couldn't see Sebastian's response, but the older woman stiffened suddenly, then smiled like a schoolgirl as a faint blush touched her cheeks. She fanned herself rapidly and turned back to the lecture.

Miranda rolled her eyes. Leave it to Sebastian to charm his way into the hearts of even the most overbearing matrons with just a smile. More proof that the man was a force of nature.

She frowned, turning in her chair to finally look at him. "Why are you here?"

"My brothers are at Boodle's for the night," he informed her.

Her heart skittered as a pang of longing pulsed through her. She knew what he meant—that they would have Park Place all to themselves for the night, and that he had come for her. All she had to do was whisper *yes*, and she'd spend another magical night with him. He probably had the carriage waiting out front for them right now and a ready excuse for Lady Emily so he could spirit her away.

Squeezing her eyes closed, she shook her head, at both his invitation and at her own foolish temptation to accept. What good could come of it? Another wonderful night of being in his arms, of feeling beautiful and special in that way only he could make her feel, simply to be reminded again at dawn that he could never be hers for more than a few fleeting hours secreted away during the night...and then not at all once he decided on a wife.

"Lady Jane Sheridan is also in attendance this evening," she informed him as evenly as possible, not wanting him to notice the unbearable jealousy swelling inside her and mock her for it, for daring to be jealous of a woman so far beyond her social rank that the two of them weren't even comparable. "I'm certain you'll want to pay your regards to her."

Cold silence answered her. As she held her breath, fearing his biting reply, she knew she hit the arrow home and that he was seething behind her. In the few weeks since they'd arrived in London, she'd come to know him so well that she could sense his moods even without seeing him.

The lecture ended. Everyone stood to applaud as Miss Bradford took her bows.

But when Miranda started to rise, he placed his hand on her shoulder and gently kept her in her chair as he murmured, "But roses are my favorite evening flower."

Her eyes stung that he could say such things yet still not want a future with her. That he could plan a night alone with her when the woman he wanted to marry sat at the front of the room. "A pity then," she muttered as she shrugged off his hand and rose to her feet, no longer caring if he thought her jealous, "that dukes prefer *prim*roses."

She moved to walk away, but he took her arm and stopped her.

"Please let go," she demanded gently, unable to jerk her arm away for all the pairs of eyes around them. Then she seized on a feeble excuse. "I want to meet Miss Bradford. Your mother generously gave me one of her books, and I wanted to tell her how much I enjoyed reading it."

His gaze flicked to the front of the hall and to the crowd already gathering to meet the daring adventuress. "It's your debut season," he reminded her pointedly, as if she needed a reminder of that! "Discussing a book in front of these people will make you look like a bluestocking."

"Good, because that's exactly what I am. And it's time everyone realized that." She choked out, unable to stop herself, "Especially you."

He arched a puzzled brow. "I know who you are, Miranda."

Oh, that was a lie! He only thought he knew because he'd seen her naked and exposed. But even then, when his hands and mouth had been on her, with the weight of his body pressing deliciously down on her, he saw the woman he wanted to see. Not the woman she truly was. One capable of being just as fine and proper as the society ladies standing around her. One who would make him as equally as good a wife—*better*, in fact. While these ladies saw only his title when they looked at him, Miranda saw the man beneath. While they wanted his title and fortune, Miranda only wanted to make him happy.

Suddenly aware of everyone around them, and desperate to flee before he saw her distress, she pleaded, "Please let—"

"Spend the night with me," he countered, briefly lowering his mouth as close to her ear as he dared. "We won't make love if you don't want to. We'll simply sit together and talk." His eyes softened on her. "I just want to be with you tonight, however I can."

She stared at him, her lips parting, so stunned at his unexpected words that her heart stuttered with anguish. She didn't know whether to laugh or cry.

God help her, even now with her heart breaking because she knew she could never truly be his, she still wanted him. She still wanted to yield to that velvet voice and the strength of his body, to the happiness and peace she felt when she was alone with him, to the laughter and joy he gave her.

She glanced toward the front of the room, where Lady Jane now stood watching them, patiently smiling at Sebastian as she waited for him to approach. As was her right. And of course, he would. After all, he belonged at Jane's side, not here in the back of the room with her.

She shook her head. "I don't think that's a good idea."

"I do. A remarkably fine one."

"Sebastian," she whispered, pleading for his mercy yet unable to help the pained longing in her voice. She wanted to be with him in the wonderful way he was offering, held safe and warm in his strong arms all night, talking and revealing themselves. But would one more night of happiness ever be enough recompense for the heartache she knew would follow?

Turning her face away so he couldn't see the raw emotion flashing over her, she choked out, "I cannot."

"Yes, you can," he insisted.

"No—I want to be with *you*, Sebastian." Sadness pained mercilessly inside her chest. "Not the duke."

"I *am* Trent," he bit out in frustration.

With a slow shake of her head, she lifted her gaze, and

a dark flicker of surprise crossed his face when he saw the glistening in her eyes. "When you're with me, when you're laughing and smiling and free...who are you then?" With every ounce of her being, she desperately willed back the hot tears blurring his handsome face. "Because that's the man I want to be with, the man I want to see happy, now and for the rest of his life. And the pity is that he doesn't want that enough for himself to claim it."

She pulled her arm away and shifted past him quickly enough that he couldn't make a second grab for her without causing a scene, right in the middle of the quality's most staid and respectable ladies.

She blinked rapidly, forcing back tears as she weaved through the chairs to put as much distance between them in the crowded gallery as she could. Even now as she made her way to the front of the room, she felt the heat of his gaze on her back, with the same burning intensity as if his hands were touching her. She shivered and squeezed her eyes shut.

She'd been such a fool! For antagonizing him last night in the carriage and then going to his room...for dressing up in the masquerade that started it all...for wanting him to accept her just as she was. And after last night, a not-so-tiny part of her had also idiotically hoped he would forget his plans to marry a society daughter and consider her instead. But nothing had changed, except that she was now hopelessly in love with a man who was impossible for her.

She glanced around the gallery at all the young ladies and their marriage-minded mamas who protected their virtues like bulldogs. Miranda wanted to laugh at them. She could have told them the real truth about sex, that its dangers lay not in falling to ruin but in falling in love.

She and Sebastian had to end all this foolishness in which they'd entangled themselves. There was no other choice. They would be as they were before, only friends and neighbors and nothing more. It would be difficult—sweet heavens, it would be heartrending!—but it had to be done. Starting right now.

But when she drew a deep breath and turned around, Sebastian was gone.

CHAPTER THIRTEEN

Sebastian strode into Park Place in the same foul mood in which he'd left it earlier. But now, he reeked of cigar smoke and whiskey from hours spent in search of distraction at Boodle's with Robert and Quinn, where he'd gone directly after leaving the museum. And after Miranda's rejection.

"Good evening, Your Grace." Saunders greeted him at the door with a stoic nod, the experienced butler knowing better than to comment on either his angry glower or the state of his appearance. "Shall I call for Barlow?"

Sebastian waved the man off. "I'll undress myself tonight. I don't want to be disturbed."

His fingers tore at his cravat as he bounded up the stairs toward his rooms— No, not *his* rooms. His father's rooms. He grimaced. Not even his father's, because Father had occupied Park Place for only two years. The *duke's* rooms, that's all they were, the man who used them as interchangeable as the sheets on the bed. And now Sebastian was simply the one shouldering the weight of it. A weight he'd never wanted less than tonight.

Damn Miranda and her cutting remarks about primroses! Didn't she realize the impossible situation he'd been placed into? That he had to put the dukedom first before everything, including his own wants and desires? What did the infuriating woman want from him, for God's sake, to marry him herself?

Miranda Hodgkins as Duchess of Trent. Good God, what would Father say to that?

And *that* was the problem. Because a part of him that he didn't dare acknowledge wanted exactly that. Even knowing how wrong Miranda was for him, she was also perfectly right. For those precious few hours when he was with her, he felt liberated from the rest of his life, and carrying on with the title's demands seemed bearable. When she smiled at him or made him laugh, he relaxed and could be himself, without fear of judgment or recrimination, in a way he could with no one else. She simply made him...happy. And knowing how fleeting that happiness was made him miserable.

He opened the door to his sitting room and stopped.

For a moment, so did his heart.

Miranda sat in his reading chair by the fire, wearing not the masquerade gown this time but a plain, cotton night rail covering her from wrist to neck and surely all the way down to her ankles if not for the cashmere throw draped across her legs as she sat with her bare feet tucked beneath her. Her long hair hung over her shoulder in a loose braid secured with a green ribbon, and she gazed at him through spectacles perched on her pert little nose, reading Miss Bradford's book on her lap. She couldn't have appeared more different from both a society lady and Lady

Rose if she'd tried. Yet she looked for all the world as if she belonged right there, as if she waited like that every night for him to come home.

His breath hitched at the sight of her, all comfortable and ready for bed. What a fool he was for spending those last hours tolerating his brothers' antics at Boodle's when he could have been right here, putting her to bed.

He closed the door and drawled with a half grin, "I didn't recognize you without your masquerade costume."

She smiled nervously, but the teasing shine in her eyes made his chest warm. "I can leave a calling card and come back in the morning if you'd like, to be properly announced."

Not a chance in the world. He wasn't letting her out of his sight tonight, not for one moment.

"How do you keep getting in here?" He stepped toward her and dropped his unwanted cravat to the floor. Although truly, he didn't care how she got here. He was simply damn glad that she was. "Should I have a talk with Saunders about security? After all, if a wisp of a woman can keep sneaking inside my bedchamber to torment me, how safe can I be from someone who really wishes to do me harm?"

Her smile brightened at his sardonic teasing, her nervousness vanishing. She gave a soft giggle, and his shoulders lightened with relief. Ah, that was better. That was the Miranda he knew and lov—

No. *Not* love.

He cared about her; he would admit to that, and even now the warmth of her presence invaded his chest and eased the tension from his shoulders. And certainly he'd felt a reckless desire to be with her tonight, even though he'd promised her that they would do nothing more than talk, if that was what she wanted, although he now prayed that she wanted far more than conversation. But that didn't mean love. It *couldn't*. Because loving Miranda would be torture when he had to pledge his life to another.

"I have a key to the terrace door," she answered. Unaware of the turmoil churning inside him, her emerald eyes shined in the firelight and only served to draw him even more strongly to her. "Josie thought it would be a good idea to keep a spare one at Audley House since the family is spread across two households for the season." Private amusement touched her voice as she added, "To make it easier for all of us to come and go as we please."

He nodded with mock solemnity, appreciating his sister's foresight more than he could ever tell her. "Wise woman, my sister."

"Very," she sighed deeply. The neck of the night rail slipped down her shoulder and revealed barely an inch more of creamy skin, but that was all it took for his cock to stir to life. Her head tilted curiously as she watched him shrug out of his jacket and toss it away after the cravat. "Do you always undress in your sitting room?"

"No." *The faster to ravish you tonight*... but he thought better of admitting that aloud, for fear of frightening her away. "I have a dressing room off my bedroom." He nodded toward the open pocket doors to the left and the room beyond, where he could just make out the outline of his bed in the shadows. And then, because something dark and punishing inside him couldn't help it, he motioned to a set of closed connecting doors on the opposite wall from his bedroom. "That will be the duchess's room through there, which also has a dressing room of its own." He was thrilled to the point of aching that she was here tonight, but best to remind her of the rules upfront. Before she expected what he could never give. "Which also happens to be bigger than mine."

"As well it should be," she agreed quietly. "After all, she'll be the duchess. You're only the duke."

He gave her his best arrogant grin. "I think you missed something when you read Debrett's. I'll outrank my duchess."

She shook her head at his naïveté. "Your father was a duke. Did he outrank your mother?"

He paused, the negative answer on the tip of his tongue. Then he admitted the truth with a lift of his brow. "Touché."

When he reached to unbutton his waistcoat, she sat up. The cashmere throw slipped to the floor at her feet. "Do you need Barlow to undress you? Should I wait in another room—"

"No." He held her gaze, then his shoulders slumped as the weight of the title, the fortune, and the family's reputation slid away and left him nothing more than a man beneath her soft eyes, if only for the night. At that moment, he knew exactly what she meant earlier at the lecture about wanting to be with only the man and not the duke. He answered gently, "I want you right here."

Slowly, she sat back and watched as he unbuttoned his waistcoat, her eyes following each movement of his fingers. His heart raced beneath her close scrutiny as his blood began to heat. Who knew simply letting a woman watch him undress could be as much fun as undressing her? But that was Miranda's doing, all right. The woman had inverted his world.

"I didn't expect to see you tonight," he admitted quietly as he slipped off the waistcoat.

"I didn't expect to be here, either. But I couldn't settle down and sleep. I kept thinking about you and what I said to you tonight at the lecture—I regret it."

"There's nothing to apologize for." He shouldn't have surprised her at the lecture like that. But he couldn't help himself. As long as there was a possibility that she would say yes to being with him tonight, he'd had to try.

And thankfully, he'd succeeded.

"I knew I wouldn't be able to sleep," she continued, "unless I spoke to you tonight to tell you that."

He fought down the smile of pleasure that threatened at his lips. "Have you been waiting here long?" He pulled loose the linen shirt tucked into his trousers. "Looking like that."

His gaze roamed over her, enjoying the deliciously comfortable and oddly arousing sight of her. He should have been angry to find her here wearing her nightgown. Had she been wearing a regular muslin dress, he could have managed some kind of excuse for her presence if they were found together. But in that—*scandalous*. Yet he grinned, finding a new appreciation for her sense of impropriety.

"Two hours," she answered.

Guilt tightened his gut as he pulled the shirt off over his head. "If I had known, I would have returned sooner." Hell, he never would have left.

"It's all right," she whispered, her eyes shamelessly drinking in his bare chest and the flat ridges of his stomach. "It gave me time to read." She pushed the glasses into place on her nose in order to see him better.

He laughed at her eagerness, his chest warming with affection.

He approached her then, carefully removed her spectacles

and set them on the fireplace mantel, placed both hands on the chair arms on either side of her, and leaned in for a soft kiss. Her lips parted beneath his with a welcoming sigh.

Home, he thought as contentment fell through him. She felt like home…

Pulling away, he sat on the floor at her feet and tugged off his boots, then leaned back against the chair, his shoulder resting against her leg, and closed his eyes. "That's better," he murmured when she reached down to brush her fingers through the hair at his temple.

"Which," she whispered when he rested his head back against the chair cushion, "being undressed or me combing your hair?"

"Yes." He turned his head and placed a kiss against her palm.

She laughed lightly, and the comfort of the soft sound soothed him. How had he managed these past two years without her? And dear God, what would he do without her once they returned to Islingham? Already the pain of separation ached in his bones. And his heart.

Leaning forward, she reached down to place her hands on his shoulders and massaged at the knots in his muscles. "Did you have a good time at Boodle's?"

"No." He hung his head forward to give her access to his shoulders, enjoying having her hands on him in even so innocent a touch. Her kneading fingers felt wonderful, and he knew he could easily grow used to such spoiling. "But Quinton and Robert had a marvelous time." They still were, in fact. Quinn hadn't lied. The way those two were carrying on tonight, they would be there until dawn. *Good.*

"That doesn't surprise me." She pressed her thumbs along the vertebrae in his neck and released the tension he carried there. "You're so different from them, you always have been." She lowered her head to bring her lips close to his ear, and a hot shiver of longing curled down his spine. "You were always the serious one, even as a boy. Even when I first met you, when you must have been fourteen or fifteen, you seemed so much older." Her hands stilled on his back as she asked, "Why are you so different from your brothers?"

"Because someone had to keep those two from killing themselves." He reached for her hand, drew it down over his shoulder, and kissed her fingertips.

When she didn't laugh at his teasing, he tilted his head back to look up at her. Concern darkened her pretty face, and it pained him that she should be so worried about him. He didn't dare let himself consider that her feelings for him might go beyond friendship. He couldn't. Not without hating himself for never being able to return those affections.

"Because I was the firstborn," he admitted, saying aloud to her what he'd never uttered to anyone else in his life, not even to his parents. Yet confiding in Miranda like this was easy, and with each word of his confession, his shoulders lightened. "Because I knew that I was the heir, that someday I would be responsible for the title, for Chestnut Hill and the estate, for my family's well-being." He reflected soberly, "If a man cares about his family and his reputation, the responsibility of all that changes him."

He knew plenty of peers who cared nothing for their families nor the estates they owned. They were spoiled and arrogant men who spent their days wasting time on one frivolous pursuit after another and their nights whoring, drinking, and gambling away not only their fortunes but the inheritance of their progeny. He would never allow himself to be one of them.

"Everything he does, every decision he makes, it all has

ramifications not just for himself but for those he loves. And the weight of that…" He shook his head, unable to articulate the heaviness that constantly plagued him and always would, the knot in his chest that never seemed to ease, the responsibility he felt not just for his family but every one of the villagers and tenant farmers on Trent land. Oddly enough, except when he was with Miranda. "It wears."

She placed a soft kiss at his temple, and he closed his eyes, drinking in the sympathy and solace she offered.

"I understand," she whispered. He was certain she did. Miranda had a way of understanding him better than anyone else. But when she slipped her arms around his neck to pull herself closer, guilt surged through him that even now she worried about him slipping away and leaving her. "But something tells me it's more than that which troubles you." She brushed her fingertips through his hair at his temple. "What is it? What's making you so unhappy?"

He sucked in a deep breath, suddenly shaken that she was able to see into his heart so easily. "I made a promise to my father when he was awarded the dukedom that I would do everything in my power to make myself worthy of the Carlisle legacy."

"You have," she told him softly. "Your father was always so proud of you. Oh, he loved Robert and Quinn, and Josie was always precious to him, but *you*, Sebastian…" She trailed her fingertips along the side of his face. "When he looked at you, his eyes would shine with pride, and his chest would swell. If he could see you now, he would be so proud of the respect you've brought to your family, all the good you've done for the estate tenants and the villagers, the responsibilities you're taking on in Parliament for England."

Instead of comforting him, her words only stirred a wretchedness inside him, one he'd been fighting to quell since his father died and his life ceased being his own. "You don't understand. He expected me to be selfless in every decision, to put the dukedom before everything else, including my own wants."

"He didn't mean before your happiness." She shook her head. "He certainly never thought that holding you to that promise would make you unhappy or—" Her voice broke, and she finished softly, "Marry a woman you don't love."

He took her hand and brought it down to his chest, pressing it over his heart, where he was certain she could feel its beat beneath her fingertips. And where he hoped she would ease his anguish as he admitted bitterly, "Perhaps not...but he certainly wanted respectability. At all costs."

Her fingers tensed in his, and he felt her draw a sharp breath.

"Right after he was awarded the dukedom, Mother fell ill, do you remember?" he asked gently.

"Yes." She squeezed his hand in empathy, and a rush of comfort seeped through him from that small gesture. But not nearly enough to compensate for the anguish of the memories he was sharing with her.

"When Father came to tell me, he found me with a woman. One he did not approve of, and one he thought was not worthy of our family."

"You were planning on marrying her?"

"No," he told her as gently as possible, knowing how much this might damn him in her eyes, "because she was already married."

Sebastian held his breath and waited for her response, but thankfully, she said nothing, although he deserved any disparaging remark she might have leveled on him. But of course, Miranda would never have done that. She was always kind, especially when he didn't deserve it.

He let out his breath in a long sigh. "Mother recovered, and Father and I had a long talk about my responsibility to the family and our legacy, to the title and its responsibilities. That was when I made my promise to him, but even then I didn't realize the full meaning behind it, or the effect it would come to have on my life. I was a Carlisle, after all. I wasn't going to listen to reason, not when it concerned the women with whom I was intimate. So I kept doing what I did before, only I was much more careful to hide my tracks." He folded his hand around hers and held tight as he murmured, "So careful, in fact, that the night my father fell from his horse and hit his head, no one could find me. I was hidden away for the evening, this time with an actress I'd met at Covent Garden. By the time I arrived back here at Park Place, Father was dead, and I never had the chance to say good-bye."

"Oh, Sebastian," she breathed, so grief-stricken for him that she couldn't find her voice. She wrapped both of her arms tightly around him and rested her cheek against his. He felt the wet of her tears on his cheek, but instead of increasing the guilt and anguish inside him, her tears were an absolution for the raw wounds he'd carried inside him for the past two years.

"His death changed everything." He paused, then repeated gravely, "Everything."

Her fingers stiffened in his, and he knew she understood his underlying meaning as she slowly sat back and swiped at her eyes with her free hand. "That's why you think you have to marry someone like Lady Jane," she breathed, so softly he could barely hear her, but each word ripped into his heart as painfully as if she'd sunk her fingernails into his chest. "Because of what happened that night."

"I owe it to my father to find a good duchess," he said quietly.

"You owe it to yourself to be happy, no matter whom you marry." She inhaled a deep, ragged breath and offered, as if trying to convince both of them, "Your father would want that."

"I'll be happy enough." His happiness was not a consideration. Robert could court and marry Diana Morgan simply because he fancied her, and Quinn could spend his life as a confirmed bachelor. But not him. Even before he decided to find a wife this season, he knew the choice in brides would not be his own. Happiness, and certainly not love, would never enter into his decision.

"You've settled on Jane Sheridan, then." Her whisper was not a question.

When she tried to slip her hand from his, his fingers tightened around hers, refusing to let her go. For tonight, at least, she was his. "No. I've decided not to pursue her."

Her lips parted with surprise. "You've given up looking for a wife?" Her voice held a timbre of hope, and that pierced him with more shame than anything she'd said before.

"No." Then, because he wanted no secrets between them, owing her at least that much respect, he added, "I still need to find a wife by season's end."

And then Miranda would be lost to him forever. He wouldn't make her his mistress, and once he took his vows, he would never go outside his marriage. He wanted the same kind of marriage his parents had, one of loyalty and fidelity, trust and comfort, and if he didn't love his wife when he married her, well, that would come in time. But he would have the marriage that the title needed.

So why did he feel as if he were about to lose everything?

When he saw the crestfallen expression flit across her face, he told her, "Enough—I don't want to talk about marriage anymore." He squeezed her hand. "Not tonight."

Gratefully, a soft happiness returned to her eyes as she gazed down at him. "What do you want to talk about, then?"

"Well, if we have to *talk*," he teased seductively as he turned toward her, "then I'd much rather talk about you."

"I'm not very interesting." Then she tried to chase away that self-deprecation by wryly commenting, "Perhaps we should discuss salmon fishing instead."

With a laugh, grateful for her teasing that chased away the somber turn that their conversation had taken, he rose up on his knees to bring his face even with hers and brushed his knuckles against her cheek.

Her eyes closed at the soft caress, as if it was too much to bear, and his heart panged. She was unbelievably sensitive to his touch... And those lips, full and pink, so sweet— When he took her chin and tilted her face up to his, they parted with a breathless sigh so inviting that he couldn't resist the urge to kiss her. Just a gentle touch of lips to lips, a caress so soft as to be barely a caress at all, but the innocence of it stole his breath away.

"Miranda," he admitted, his voice a hoarse rasp, "you are the most interesting woman I know."

Her eyes fluttered open, and she gazed dubiously up at him as she bit her lip, somehow shy and wanton at the same time. A delectable mix of contradiction, just like the woman behind the stare.

"For instance." He ran his fingers over the edge of her night rail's neckline. "You wore this to seduce a man."

"I didn't wear this to seduce you, silly." A smile played at her lips at the absurdity of that. "This is what I wear to sleep in every night, and I needed to see you so badly that I didn't stop to change." She shrugged a shoulder. "And anyway, I assumed that eventually I would end up in bed, so what was the point in changing only to have to change back again?"

He fought down a smile. Only Miranda could make that logic make sense. "Well, if you're tired, I won't stop you from taking one of the guestrooms," he answered, keeping his face carefully stoic as he tried to suss out her intentions for the rest of the night, "or going home in a carriage to your own bed."

A flash of grim knowing crossed her face, as if she'd expected that response. Closing her eyes, she nodded. "After everything you shared tonight, I understand if you—"

He leaned in to kiss her. "But not before I ravish you." Unadulterated heat poured through his voice despite his earnestness as he added, "Several times, in fact."

Her eyes darted up to his in a mix of wonder, excitement, and quick arousal. He heard the soft catch of her breath in surprise. "You still...want me?"

The vulnerability underlying her whisper nearly broke his heart. *Want* her? Good Lord, she had no idea what he felt for her. It went far beyond simple *want* to something he could barely fathom. Something that terrified him with its intensity.

"Yes," he admitted, cupping her face against his palm and brushing his lips across her cheek. "Very much. And I hate to correct you," he admitted as he shifted away just far enough to rake a lecherous gaze across her, stirring up a blush in his wake, "but I find you surprisingly seductive in this night rail." He trailed his finger down from her neck, between her breasts and down to her lower belly, making her squirm. "Because I know how beautiful you are beneath, inside and out."

Her eyes glistened in the firelight with telltale tears, and the sight clenched at his chest. "So I can stay?"

"If you'd like."

She smiled. "I'd like it very much."

So would he. But they had one more piece of unfinished business to settle tonight.

Ignoring the hot stab of jealousy in his gut when he thought of Robert and the feelings she held for his brother, he drew a deep breath and said quietly, "There's something I need to know." He lifted her hand to his lips to suck at her fingertips. She tasted like vanilla icing, sweet and addictive. "You love Robert, but you came to me. Why?"

"I don't love Robert," she confessed softly, in little more than a breath. "I thought I did, but it wasn't love. I know now that it was only infatuation and habit."

"And me?" When she hesitated in her answer, he touched the tip of his tongue to her palm, and she trembled.

Her answer was so brutally honest when it came that it sliced through him, leaving him raw and wounded. "I can't help myself."

"Neither can I," he whispered, then reached up to unfasten her hair.

*   *   *

Miranda's pulse fluttered at the heated look he gave her as he untied the ribbon and slowly unbraided her hair. She closed her eyes to revel in the wonderfully decadent sensation of his fingers sifting through her strands, loosing the waves until they lay in a thick curtain around her shoulders.

When he reached for the hem of her night rail and peeled it slowly up her body to reveal her to the firelight, she raised her arms above her head to help him remove it. She sat still and let him look his fill of her, bathed in the soft light. A proper society lady would have been embarrassed, she supposed, to display herself so audaciously. But she wasn't a society lady. She was simply Miranda. And she would never be embarrassed in front of him for this.

"You are beautiful," he whispered as his hands roamed languidly over her, up her body from her bare toes to her neck and slowly back down. He was touching her as if discovering her for the first time, and she trembled at the intensity of it. "How did I never notice that before this season?" he murmured, his fingertips lightly tracing down her arms, over the curve of her hips and along her thighs.

"You weren't looking," she whispered, heat rising beneath her skin.

"I'm certainly looking now," he assured her. Goose bumps sprang up on her skin wherever he touched, like magic. And when he lowered his mouth and placed his lips against her bare shoulder, all of her shivered with liquid heat. The sensation was pure heaven.

Releasing her, he slid down to kneel before her on the floor, his hands splayed wide as they slowly caressed down her thighs. When he gently nudged apart her knees, her hands shot out to grab his shoulders and stop him.

"What are you doing?" she gasped, sudden alarm knotting her belly.

"I'm going to kiss you," he explained gently, lowering his mouth to caress his lips across her knee.

Heavens, he wanted to kiss her *there*! She shook her head adamantly, her hands clenched into fists against his bare shoulders. Oh no, he simply couldn't! "I don't— I mean, I don't think that you want..." Embarrassment choked off her words.

"But I do," he assured her, taking another caress of his

lips against her leg, this time moving higher up her thigh. "Very much. You are lovely, Miranda, and I want to kiss you everywhere." When she shuddered with nervousness so intense that all of her stiffened, he rested his head on her lap to gaze up at her. "I won't if you don't want me to, but..." His blue eyes softened with understanding. "Why don't you want to, sweet?"

"It's different from what we've done before," she whispered. She was certain that every other woman he'd been with knew exactly how to please him, but she simply didn't know how. The frustration and jealousy of that mixed with her embarrassment and sent a hot blush into her cheeks. "What if I disappoint you?"

"You could never disappointment me," he answered, his voice strangely hoarse.

She gazed down into his eyes, wanting desperately to believe him. And yet..."I don't know what to do."

"Then I'll teach you."

"But you're—" *You're never going to spend another night with me like this.* But she couldn't bear to admit that aloud. The pain would be insufferable. "You're not very patient," she amended, not wanting to spoil the night by voicing truths better left unsaid. After all, dawn would come soon enough and expose them all.

"Trust me, sweet." He lowered his mouth to her thigh, continuing his path toward the ache throbbing at her center. "I am very—" He placed a kiss at the top of her inner thigh. "Very." The tip of his tongue traced along the crease where her thigh met her pelvis. "Patient."

His seeking lips found her, and her breath tore from her throat. A shiver of nervousness and excitement sped through her, making her gasp at this incredibly intimate kiss that electrified her to the ends of her hair and tips of her toes.

This scandalously wanton contact made all they'd done last night pale by comparison, and she couldn't help tensing in nervousness.

But when his lips continued to softly kiss her, all her doubts seeped away, and she relaxed beneath his mouth with a shuddering sigh. What he was doing to her was absolute heaven! And from the way he made soft sounds of appreciation against her, he also liked it. Very much.

"Sebastian," she whispered. Her hands, which had been pushing at his shoulders to hold him back, now dug into his muscles to encourage him. Never in all her fantasies of what men and women did together, how their bodies came together to give pleasure, had she ever imagined anything as decadent as this. This new type of kissing made her entire body shiver and shake, and she slumped boneless in the chair.

"You are delicious," he murmured against her between soft kisses, "and very delectable. Like icing on a cake."

Her arousal-fogged mind could barely understand... "Icing?"

He licked her, his tongue sinking deep into her cleft.

Her hips bucked beneath him. "Sebastian!"

But he only chuckled at her protest, refusing to relent in this sweet torture, and his large hands on her thighs held her legs open wide as he continued to take swirling licks. She closed her eyes, and all her existence faded until she was nothing more than the heat of his soft mouth against her, his tongue sweeping across her and delving deeper in slow, teasing circles.

"That feels... oh, that's nice," she panted out. "That's..." Rendered speechless, she moaned as his tongue plunged deep and sent the aching between her thighs flaring out to her toes and fingertips. Oh, it was simply wonderful!

The need for him flamed inside her, stoked even higher by all those wet noises his mouth made against her. She couldn't keep her own whimpers of need and moans of pleasure silent, not when her desire pulsed so hard that she couldn't breathe beyond rapid panting, not when she could no longer sit still in the chair and writhed herself against his mouth. Every inch of her pulsed, electric and alive.

His lips found the aching little nub buried in her folds, closed around it, sucked—

The soft sensation pounded through her. She gasped, losing what little breath she had left.

Then he sucked again, longer and harder, and the pleasure that shot through her was paralyzing. Her body tensed instantly, then released so hard that she cried out. Helpless, she crumpled in the chair, her body shuddering with each undulating pulse of pleasure that passed through her.

He rested his cheek against her thigh as she slowly regained her breath. She had the strength to do nothing more than lift a hand to touch his cheek in gratitude as the love she felt for him blossomed hot inside her and grew until it filled every inch of her, right down to her soul. If giving herself to him tonight was her last opportunity to show him how much he meant to her, how deep her feelings for him ran, then she would do it. She couldn't bear not to.

"Sebastian," she breathed softly as she blinked back the hot tears at her lashes, "make love to me."

"Whatever you want, sweet." He lifted her from the chair and lowered her melting body onto the floor with him.

He laid her on her back across the thick rug in front of the fire and moved away only long enough to strip off his trousers, then he covered her with his naked body and gently parted her legs. She tensed as he lowered himself into her, remembering the pain of last night, but his erection slid smoothly inside in one deep stroke. This time there was no pain. There was only the wonderful sensation of being filled by his warmth and strength as her body expanded knowingly to take him in. And this time, when he began to stroke inside her, she moaned in complete capitulation.

"Miranda," he groaned in her ear, careful to keep his weight from crushing her even as she wrapped her arms and legs around him to pull him closer. "You feel so good...you have no idea how much."

Oh, but she did know, because if she felt half as good to him as his body did to hers—*heaven*. And she never wanted to come back to earth.

"So warm and tight," he murmured. She wiggled beneath him, and he laughingly growled his pleasure. "So damnably eager."

She laughed with happiness, unable to stop herself. Sebastian was making love to her, and she wanted to impress on her mind every detail of this moment...the musky scent of their bodies uniting, the rippling of the hard muscles in his back beneath her fingertips, the masculine groans that he breathed into her ear each time he plunged deep inside her and made her folds quiver around his thick length.

But she wanted even more. She wanted to find some way to brand him onto herself so she could carry him with her beyond the dawn. "Teach me something new," she whispered, caressing her hand across his cheek. "Something special."

He stilled and gazed down at her, his blue eyes dark with pleasure as he searched her face in the firelight. "All right." He placed a kiss against her palm. "Something special."

Without pulling out of her warmth, he clasped his arms around her and rolled onto his back, bringing her up on top. Surprised at the quick movement, she straddled his waist as she perched on him, his manhood still inside her.

She stared down at him, and her lips parted in a stunned *O*.

As the realization slowly sank through her for why this was special, that in this new position they would be able to see the sheer happiness each brought to the other, her lips curled into a smile. With a gleeful laugh, she began to move, at first only in testing little swivels of her hips that elicited low pants of pleasure from him, then bolder thrusts that had his hands gripping at her hips to fight for restraint. Tucking her legs beneath her for leverage, she lifted up and down, raising and lowering herself along his hard length in a smooth slide that nearly brought him out of her, only to plunge down and bury him fully within her warmth again.

She tossed back her head with joy, her hands on his chest curling her fingers into the hard muscle. Oh, what a devilish position! The pounding of his heart beneath her fingertips, the pulsing of his manhood between her legs—she wanted to be wicked, wanton, and wonderful, and all for him. There was no hesitation now, only freedom to tease with her body and be teased in return, not satisfying the need for release but flaming it.

He leaned up on his forearms, raising his back from the floor until he kissed her. "Come now, sweet," he urged as his hips continued to roll and rock beneath her, his voice a hot whisper. He licked across her lips. "I want to see you find your pleasure."

His words cascaded through her, spilling into a thousand fingers of heat that swirled through her and lit her on fire. With a soft cry of desperate need, she began to ride furiously over him. Each thrust was sheer pleasure and greed, demanding and hungry, and she galloped hard, racing toward the oncoming release—

She shattered. Tossing back her head, she cried out his name as the wave of release took her, only to moan again as she felt him thrust up deep inside her and grind his hips against her to prolong the moment for her. Her folds quivered around his still-hard manhood as her body milked his to claim each pulse of shivering pleasure.

He thrust up beneath her in a plunge so forceful that he lifted her off the floor. She clung to him, desperate to join her soul with his, desperate for him to feel how much she loved him. A second release gripped her, a second cry of surrender tearing from her throat. Then he joined her, slipping from her warmth to shudder out his own release a heartbeat later.

He fell back onto the rug, and she collapsed onto his chest, utterly spent and completely satiated. For a moment, she couldn't breathe, not from exertion but from the overwhelming emotions swirling through her. Engulfing her, sending her spinning through space and somersaulting her heart beyond control…

When her breath returned and she opened her eyes, she was again on her back, with Sebastian once more lying over her, as if he, too, didn't want this moment to end. With his fingers entwined in hers, he held her arms out from her sides, pinning her there beneath him. He stared down at her. His eyes were bright in the shadows, and his lips were parted, as if he wanted to say something but couldn't find the words.

For a long moment, they remained like that, the only sound their heartbeats echoing into each other.

Then a sob tore from her.

"Oh God, Miranda," he whispered gently, rolling his weight off her and turning her in his arms to cup her face in his hands with concern as she cried softly. Self-recrimination darkened his face. "I've hurt you." He tenderly kissed her lips and her cheeks, as if trying to take all her pain onto himself. "I'm so sorry—"

"You didn't hurt me." She pressed her eyes closed but couldn't stop the tears, no longer able to hold back the torrent of emotions cascading through her. Her heart simply hadn't been prepared for him, for the rush of happiness being with him brought. And the terrible anguish. "You were wonderful."

He kissed away her tears, but his distress for her was still palpable. "Then what is it? Tell me."

She shook her head, fresh embarrassment surging through her and coloring her cheeks. "I'm just being a silly cake," she whispered. She buried her face against his shoulder to hide from him, afraid he would see the truth in her...that she loved him, despite knowing that he would never love her in return. "I wasn't prepared for that."

"Are you certain that's all?" Concern sounded thick in his voice as he encircled her with his arms and drew her protectively against him. "You're trembling."

"I'm cold," she lied, unable to bear telling him the truth. Even now, with the masculine scent of him imprinted on her body and the physical pleasure he brought to her still lingering inside her, she couldn't bring herself to say it.

"What can I do to help?" He caressed his warm lips against her forehead in a gesture so tender that new tears formed at her lashes.

She touched his cheek, trying to ignore the unbearable desolation clawing at her heart. "Put me to bed? I'll be warmer beneath the covers."

He gathered her into his arms and lifted her from the floor. "You're not leaving tonight," he told her gently but firmly as he carried her into his bedroom. "You're spending the entire night this time, understand?"

"I can't," she whispered regrettably, resting her cheek against his shoulder. "I have to return to Audley House before the household wakes and notices I'm gone."

"There will be plenty of time to take you home." He murmured possessively against her temple, "But I want to greet the dawn with you in my arms, Rose."

Rose. She warmed with love. For the first time, he'd used the nickname not mockingly, not in tempting seduction, but in affection, and her heart pounded so fiercely for him that her chest ached.

She nodded against his shoulder, not wanting to leave him. Not tonight, not tomorrow...

Pulling back the coverlet with one hand, he placed her onto the bed. He leaned over and kissed her, his lips nibbling at the corner of her mouth in promise of more pleasures yet to come before the night was over.

"Sebastian?" she whispered tentatively.

"Hmm?" He nuzzled the nape of her neck as he settled in behind her and tucked the coverlet over them, her back along his front, his large body enveloping hers in its warmth and strength.

"You should be happy."

"I am," he murmured, his hand stroking possessively over her hip. "Very happy."

"No, I mean..." She pulled in a deep breath and whispered, "I love you, and I want you to be happy."

She felt him tense against her, although his body never moved. His arms kept their same, secure hold around her, his lips still resting against her nape, but she sensed the change in him, so well did she know him.

"I don't expect you to feel the same," she whispered,

hoping that if she kept talking that her heart wouldn't break from the silence that came from him. "I know you don't, but—" Her voice choked.

Slowly, he rolled her onto her back so that he could look down at her. His expression was inscrutable in the shadows, but his bright eyes matched the glowing coals in the fireplace for intensity as they searched her face. For a painfully long moment, neither of them moved, and the only sound was the pounding of her heart and the rush of blood through her ears. She held her breath. Oh, she'd made a terrible mistake! So utterly foolish to tell him…

Then he lowered his head and kissed her so tenderly, with such affection and sweetness, that she trembled from the intensity of it. He'd never kissed her like this before, and her silly heart didn't know whether to leap for joy or shatter irreparably.

"No one has ever…not once…" he murmured against her mouth, and she could taste the surprise on his lips.

He lifted his mouth from hers just far enough to trace his fingertips affectionately over her lips, as if he didn't dare let himself believe that she'd uttered those words. Then he grinned at her, a boyish smile of pure delight, one that melted away her worry and replaced it with warmth. And hope.

He cupped her face against his palm and languidly brushed his mouth back and forth across hers. "*You* make me happy, my sweet Rose."

Her heart soared, this time because she knew she didn't have to worry any longer about coming in second to Lady Jane or any of the other society ladies from his list. She could love him now, freely and openly, and he would realize that she would make as fine a wife for him as any society daughter. More—because she truly loved *him*, the man beneath the title.

"You have no idea how special you are, do you?" His hands stroked lovingly down her body. "And you *are* special to me, Miranda, more than you realize."

As he continued to kiss and caress her, she closed her eyes against fresh tears. Her heart filled so completely with love for him that it burned, with a pleasure-pain that threatened to consume her.

"Then show me," she whispered.

As he murmured her name and lowered himself over her to make love to her, the world around them faded away, until only the two of them existed. The shared rhythms of their hearts heralded in her joy like the pounding tattoo of drums, and she clung to him, never wanting to let go.

CHAPTER FOURTEEN

~ ~

$\mathcal{S}$ebastian opened his eyes and smiled. Miranda was still in his bed.

The morning sunlight fell dimly muted into the room from behind the pulled drapes but brightly enough for him to enjoy the sight of her naked body beside him, her back to him as she slept on her side with her strawberry-blond hair covering the pillow like silk. The poor thing was exhausted, and he was responsible, because halfway through the night he'd aroused her again to repeat the special trick he'd taught her. This time, thank God, there had been no tears, only cries of passion. He didn't think he could have endured seeing her sob in his arms a second time.

He smiled against her temple. Last night had been one surprise after another, from the moment he'd walked into the room and found her waiting for him to the quiet way she'd admitted that she loved him.

She *loved* him... Good God. He still couldn't believe it. Not only had she dared to utter the words, but he could taste it in her kisses and feel it in the way she'd made herself so vulnerable to him. No woman had ever told him that before or made love to him like that, with so much affection behind the passion.

But then, no other woman was Miranda.

He had no idea what he was going to do about her or about his own growing feelings for her. Selfishly, he didn't want to think about the future. At that moment as she lay sleeping next to him, all warm and deliciously bed-rumpled, smelling intoxicatingly of roses and the sweet musk of sex, he was at peace. He was happy, happier than he'd ever been in his life. And he didn't want to acknowledge the world beyond his bedroom door.

She stirred in her sleep and shifted closer until her bottom rested snugly against his hips. Slipping his arms around her, he smiled against her hair as she awoke with a long, soft sigh.

"Sebastian," she whispered, rolling onto her back, her body still warm and pliant with sleep.

"Good morning, Rose," he murmured. Then he shifted over on top of her and was rewarded with the sight of her breasts displayed deliciously in the morning light. He lowered his head to place a kiss on her pink nipple.

"Yes," she breathed, "good morning." With her eyes still closed, awake but drifting on the edge of dreamlike sleep, she breathed out another deep sigh and arched her back toward him. "Oh...a *very* good morning..."

He chuckled softly. Unable to deny himself from taking even this small pleasure that she so freely offered, he took her nipple between his lips and suckled gently at her. He closed his eyes and let himself enjoy this quiet moment when she still belonged completely to him.

Her body wakened further until she was fully aroused and

panting softly. If the way her nipple hardened against his tongue was any indication, she was already craving him inside her again. *Good.* Because he planned on making love to her once more before he let her out of his bed.

Reluctantly releasing her from his lips, he raised his head and whispered her name. Her eyes fluttered open, and the happiness he saw in their green depths took his breath away.

Oh yes, she loved him. And if he wasn't careful, she'd have him loving her right back.

She reached up to trace her fingertips over his cheek. "Do you often wake up like this in the morning?"

"No." He touched his lips to hers and grinned against her mouth. "But with you, it's my favorite way."

"But you've never woken up with me before."

He teasingly repeated her words from the opera, "That's why it's my favorite."

A bubble of laughter escaped her, then she bit her lip with a hint of shy seduction that sent his heart skittering. "Mine, too."

Slipping her hand behind his neck to run her fingers through the hair at his nape, she turned her head to glance at the window.

"It's after dawn," she whispered. The happiness on her face faded, and he felt its absence like a blow to his gut. "I should have left hours ago."

He nibbled at her throat to distract her and immediately felt her pulse race beneath his lips. Sweet Lucifer, the woman was insatiable, but so was he when he was with her. "I'll take you home later." Although his mind was already whirling to come up with a way to keep her right there in his bed for the rest of the day.

She arched a dubious brow. "And what excuse will we

give for why I'm not at Audley House when your mother goes looking for me?"

He lowered his head to once more kiss at her breasts. "We'll tell her that her eldest son is a debauched philanderer"—he took her nipple into his mouth and worried it between his teeth until a scrumptious shiver of arousal raked through her—"who kept you chained naked to his bed all night and ravished you insatiably until you begged for mercy."

"Oh," she replied, deadpan. "So the truth, then."

He laughed, nuzzling his cheek against her breast and enjoying the scratch of his morning beard against her soft skin. He couldn't remember the last time he'd laughed so much while in bed with a woman, if ever. She was one surprise after—

The door flung open. Quinton bounded into the room.

"Thought I'd head to Tattersall's today and—" He halted and stared. "Dear God, apologies! Thought you'd be alone by now. I'll just . . ." He whirled for the door, then stopped. And glanced back. Bewilderment darkened his face. "Miranda?"

She gave a soft shriek of mortification and pulled the coverlet over her head.

"Get out," Sebastian ordered, cold fury speeding through him.

"But—but—" Quinn stammered, staring in stunned disbelief. "*Miranda?*"

"Get the hell out!"

The door shut with a bang, and Sebastian dragged in a deep breath for control. With concern for Miranda pulsing through him, he slowly pulled down the coverlet, only to find her hands firmly pressed over her face. All of her shook violently.

"It will be all right," he told her as gently and reassuringly as possible. "It's only Quinn. I'll take care of him."

"What will you do?" Her voice was a pained whisper from between her fingers, one that tore into his heart. In her humiliation, she was unable to open her eyes and look at him.

"I'll explain everything and swear him to secrecy." And when that didn't work, he'd toss his brother's murdered body into the Thames. "It's Quinn. He would never do anything to hurt you."

"It's Quinn!" she choked out in exasperation from knowing his brother as well as he did. "When has he ever been able to keep a secret?"

"Starting now," he said with conviction. "Stay here. I'll be right back."

He slipped out of bed and yanked on his trousers. When he looked back at her as he headed out the door, she'd once again pulled the coverlet over her head. Seeing her like that ripped into his chest, feeling the pain of her humiliation right along with her. And that only fueled his fury as he charged after his brother.

"Quinton!" he bellowed and raced down the steps.

He found his youngest brother in the entrance foyer, within steps of slipping out the front door and escaping. Grabbing his arm, he shoved him back against the wall. Anger seethed in every inch of him...anger at Quinton for barging into his room and finding them together, and anger at himself for being so caught up in Miranda that he'd recklessly left the door unlocked.

"You didn't see anything," Sebastian threatened through gritted teeth, his hand clenching at Quinn's cravat.

"But Seb...*Miranda*?" Quinn stared at him incredulously, blinking with visible confusion and surprise. "How long— I mean, when—" In his shock, he stumbled over his thoughts. "For God's sake! We all grew up together. She played in our nursery until she was twelve."

"She isn't twelve anymore," he bit out. Christ! Didn't any of his siblings realize she was a grown woman?

Quinn lifted a brow. "Obviously."

He tightened his hold on Quinn's collar. "It is none of your business, and she doesn't deserve to be ruined. If you say one word about this—if Mother or Josie finds out—so help me, Quinton, I will string you up between two trees in Hyde Park and—"

"I won't tell them," he promised, and Sebastian released his hold. "Good Lord, Seb, I would never say anything that could harm her. Or you. You know that." Quinn shook out his shoulders and pulled at his cravat, heaving out a long breath of irritation that Sebastian would think so little of him. "I like Miranda."

He blew out a hard breath, his shoulders sagging as the emotions he felt for her crashed over him. "So do I."

Quinton grinned. "Obviously."

With a growl, Sebastian shoved him back against the wall again. "She was never here, and you didn't see anything," he slowly forced out, each word a cold warning. "Understand?"

"She wasn't here," Quinn repeated solemnly, knowing not to bait Sebastian again if he valued his life. "And I didn't see anything."

He stepped back, taking a deep breath to steady himself and to figure out what to say to Miranda before he returned upstairs. Dear God, she must have been completely mortified. And now terrified that her reputation would be ruined. To be discovered like that—

Robert stepped out of the breakfast room and elbowed Quinn in the ribs. "What didn't you see?"

"That Seb's sleeping with Miranda," Quinn answered immediately.

Robert blinked in confusion. "Hodgkins?"

Sebastian's furious gaze swung between his brothers, not knowing which one of the two to kill first. "Not one word, do you understand?" he threatened, his anger barely controlled as he clenched and released his fists. "Both of you! Not one word about any of this to anyone."

"*Hodgkins?*" Robert repeated, stunned.

Sebastian rolled his eyes, at that moment wanting to be an only child more than he ever had in his life. "She is a good and kind woman who doesn't deserve to be hurt because of me. The only mistake she made was trusting me when I have the two of you for brothers." After all the times they'd covered for one another with women in the past, he prayed he could trust them to protect his privacy one last time. And hers. But just to be certain, he jabbed Quinn in the shoulder, and his brother wisely retreated back against the wall. "Not one word. To anyone. If she's hurt because of you—"

"I thought you were hunting a wife," Robert interrupted, still bewildered.

"I am." A swift stab of pain sliced into his chest as he uttered the words, the unbidden flash of betrayal toward Miranda unexpectedly piercing. "That hasn't changed."

Robert frowned. "So you're marrying Miranda?"

Quinn grinned. "Mother's going to faint when she hears this!"

"She isn't hearing a word of it, understand?" Sebastian scoured his hand over his face, as if he could physically fight down the churning emotions roiling inside him. Or the guilt that threatened to consume him. The weight of the dukedom came crashing back onto him, and his shoulders sagged beneath the crushing burden of it. Worse, because for a few precious hours last night, he'd tasted happiness, and now he knew how empty his life was going to be going forward without her.

Robert shook his head, concern for her visible on his face. "But Miranda—"

"I'm not marrying Miranda," he ground out, anger pulsing through him as the guilt gave way to desolate wretchedness and overwhelming frustration. Why wouldn't the two of them shut up about Miranda and marriage?

"Does Miranda know that?" Quinn pressed.

"It's none of your business," he growled, adding jealousy at Quinn's concern to the already growing knot of emotion choking the air from his lungs. "And you'll forget about this, both of you." He snapped a murderous glance between Robert and Quinn. "I am marrying the daughter of a peer, just as I've always intended. Miranda has absolutely nothing to do with that decision. She never has, and she never will, no matter what happened between us."

No matter that she made him happy. Or that she loved him, more deeply than any other woman ever had. Or that he knew he'd never have the same depth of peace and comfort again that he'd experienced in her arms.

She was the orphaned niece of one of his tenants. In truth, no better in social rank than a barmaid, shop girl, seamstress...His father would never have accepted her as duchess.

He said again for good measure, to convince himself more than his brothers, "Never."

Quinn repeated annoyingly, "Does Miranda know that?"

Robert answered grimly with a nod toward the stairs. "She does now."

Sebastian turned and gazed up to find Miranda standing

on the top landing, wearing the same driver's coat she'd worn to the house two nights ago, covering herself from neck to ankle. Only her hair, loose around her shoulders in a riot of strawberry-blond curls, gave any reminder of the way he'd found her when he'd awoken this morning, so sweet and loving. So happy.

His breath ripped from his chest at the raw pain that radiated from her. Even from two stories away, he could see her green eyes glistening with wounded tears as she stared down at them. The look of betrayal on her face devastated him.

"Miranda." His voice was a hoarse rasp of regret. "I didn't mean—"

She turned and fled down the hall.

His gut twisting with remorse, Sebastian rushed up the stairs after her and found her inside his sitting room, her hands shaking fiercely as she quickly pulled back her curls and tied them with the same green ribbon he'd removed from her hair last night. Tears fell down her cheeks even as she kept her face turned away from him in her anguish, and his heart shattered as he watched her collect herself so she could flee from the house. And from him.

"Miranda," he pleaded quietly, crossing the room to her and reaching for her shoulders. The sight of her pain ripped at his heart. "Please listen—"

She yanked herself away and put half the distance of the room between them. Instinctively, he knew not to follow.

"You said I was special," she whispered, unable to find a louder voice beneath her tears, although he knew he deserved to be cursed in screams. "I know it's not love, but—" She choked on a sob, and the soft sound sliced through him. "I never imagined this was what you meant."

He flinched at the recrimination in her voice. "I didn't."

She turned on him, her eyes flashing bright with furious tears as she accused, "The message or the delivery, Sebastian?"

His eyes met hers, guiltily returning the pain he saw in their stormy depths and hating himself for causing it. He ran a frustrated hand through his hair to keep from reaching for her again. "What do you want from me, Miranda?" His shoulders slumped in defeat beneath the unbearable weight of his life. And of her love. "Whatever it is, I can't give it."

Nothing had changed for him, no matter how much he enjoyed being with her. No matter how much peace he had found in her arms or happiness in one of her laughing smiles. He was still a duke, and he could never be free to marry whomever he wanted.

"I want *you*, Sebastian," she breathed in a heartbreaking whisper.

Her soft words fell through him with a pleasure-pain so intense that it ripped his breath away. At that moment, he recognized all the love and happiness that fate held dangling in front of him, all wrapped up inside a spirited woman with unruly strawberry-blond hair and a freckled nose—only to have it snatched away. The wretchedness of it was unbearable.

"I can't give it," he repeated, his voice choking.

"Even now?" she whispered, the pain in her voice heartbreaking. "Even after last night and all we shared?"

Damning himself to hell, he admitted quietly, "Even now."

She flinched as hard as if he'd hit her, ripping out what little was left of his heart. "But you're not marrying Lady Jane," she whispered, blinking rapidly to hold back her tears. "You told me last night that you..."

Her voice drifted away as the truth sank slowly through

her, and he watched as the fight ebbed from her, stealing away the energy and vivacity that he loved so much. She transformed before his eyes, from the beautiful woman set on seizing life for all it was worth to a dull shadow of herself. He'd never hated the dukedom or himself as much as he did at that moment.

"So it wasn't that you preferred Jane," she whispered, so softly he could barely hear her, but his heart felt every torturous word stab into his chest. "You simply never wanted *me*."

"That's not it," he bit out in his own pain and frustration, "and you know it."

Damnation! He'd been placed into an impossible situation, didn't she realize that? What did she want him to do—throw aside his obligation to his family by selfishly marrying the woman he wanted rather than one who would be best for the dukedom? Wasn't it enough that he had to carry inside him the guilt he felt over not being at his father's side when he died? Or did she want to haunt him, too, reminding him forever of the happiness and love he'd lost in her?

Once before, he'd chosen a woman over his family, and she had cost him the last opportunity to speak to his father. He would *never* put a woman before his family again. No matter how much he loved her.

"I would marry you if I could, Miranda." The soft confession tore from him with an anguish so intense that he winced. "I would give you a home and a family, and I would spend the rest of my days spoiling you. But I'm not free to marry you, you know that. Even before we left Islingham, you knew that I needed to find not just a wife but a duchess."

"But you need someone who makes you happy," she

whispered through the tears. "More than anything else I want—I just want to make you happy—" She choked, her words turning into a sob.

"My happiness is not your responsibility, Miranda. Neither is anyone else's." He kept his voice as gentle as possible, to compensate for the harshness of his words, but he had to make her understand how futile her feelings were for him, even with the best intentions behind them. "You want to help people, and that is selfless and wonderful. But you cannot save us all, just as you couldn't save your parents. Some of us are beyond your help, and you have to let us go." He paused, his gaze holding hers as the pain of the truth registered on her face. "You have to let *me* go."

She stared at him, as if clearly seeing him for the first time, and he watched the last tendrils of hope seep out of her. Then her watery gaze lowered to the floor, unable to bear holding his a moment longer, and her hand swiped at the tears sliding down her cheeks. The pain inside him was unbearable. *God's mercy*, how he hated seeing her cry! And with each tear, something tore deep inside him, until it shattered completely.

"You can't spend your life attempting to make up for your parents' deaths," he told her softly.

"Neither can you," she breathed out. Her soft words stabbed into his chest like a knife, wounding him more terribly than he'd ever imagined she could.

Then with a soft cry of frustrated anguish as she gave over to the torrent of tears, she snatched her spectacles from the fireplace mantel and shoved them into her pocket as she fled toward the door.

Unable to stop himself even now, he started after her. "Miranda, wait— Please!"

She glanced back at him, anger and wretchedness

marring her beautiful face. The ferocious look froze him in his steps.

"I know why I came here, why I gave myself to you. I wanted to be with *you*, Sebastian. Because I like being with you, and no other reason. And somewhere between the kisses and the teasing, amid all your warnings...I fell in love with you," she said quietly, her hands clenched at her sides. "You knew who I was. There was no masquerade mask this time. So you need to ask yourself—if I'm so wrong for you, why did *you* give yourself to *me*?"

Then she was gone.

He followed her into the hall, but the door to the back servants' stairs was wide open. There was no point in chasing after her. She would be gone before he could get to the ground floor to stop her, by now down the stairs and out through the back garden, running back to Audley House as fast as she could. And what would he have said to her anyway that could have softened the pain he'd caused her?

Muttering a string of curses at himself, at his brothers, at her—at everything that led them into this impossible situation—he stormed back into his rooms. He let the anger come, let it fill up the empty hole gaping in his chest where his heart had been, because he knew how to manage anger. What he didn't know how to handle was love.

He stopped and stared around him, struck by how different the room was now than it had been only minutes before, when they were still happy and she'd been safe in his arms. Her absence filled the space now, only reinforcing how silent and empty the house was without her in it. Worse, because nothing about the room showed she'd ever been here, that she'd ever admitted to loving him. Even her night rail was gone. The only remaining traces of her were the lingering scent of rosewater and her blasted book.

Snapping out a biting curse, he snatched up the book from the floor and tossed it onto the chair. It fell open, and a flattened piece of red paper slipped out from between the pages. His heart stopped as he recognized it. The papier-mâché rose he'd given her at Vauxhall.

He stared at it, unable to breathe beneath the icy pain that squeezed his chest like a fist and threatened to strangle away the tiny bit of life still buried deep inside him.

The aggravating, pestering, trouble-causing gel loved him and wanted to spend a lifetime making him happy, while he wanted nothing more than to let her.

And there wasn't a damned thing he could do about it.

* * *

"Where's Miranda?" Sebastian demanded as he stalked into the drawing room at Audley House that afternoon and found his sister, Josephine, standing at the window. There was nothing more to be said between Miranda and him, but he wanted to see her to make certain her reputation was still safe. At least that was the lie he told himself. The truth was that he missed her already and wanted to make certain she was all right, hating himself for the pain he'd caused her.

He placed a kiss on his sister's cheek as she turned away from the window and greeted him.

"That seems to be the question of the day," she mumbled, preoccupied.

"What do you mean?" His heart skipped with panic. It wasn't possible that news of what happened between them could have gotten here before him. Unless Miranda herself… *Good God.* His mind filled with all kinds of terrible possibilities. "Where is she?" He glanced around the room. "And where is Mother?"

"Mama is with Thomas in the carriage." She reached up to play nervously with the gold pendant hanging around her neck, soft worry creasing her brow. "They've gone after Miranda."

And then his heart stopped completely. "Gone after?" he repeated, his blood turning to ice with worry. "Where?"

She shook her head, and as if sensing his unease, she placed a reassuring hand on his arm. "Miranda wasn't in her room this morning when the maid went in to start the fire. Mama and I thought that perhaps she'd gotten up early and gone for a walk in the park."

He kept his face carefully stoic despite the hard worry twisting in his gut. No, she hadn't gone to the park. At dawn, she'd still been tucked into his bed.

But that didn't explain where she'd gone after she'd fled Park Place or where she was now. Fresh dread swept through him. "You said Chesney and Mother went after her."

Josie nodded with a concerned frown. "At some point, she came home, packed a bag, and left again. For Islingham." She picked up a note from the tea table and handed it to him. "She left this on her bed. She claims her season was a mistake and that she's needed back in the village."

He didn't have to read the note to feel the stab of guilt into his gut that he'd not only ruined her season and taken her innocence but, now, also driven her away. Already he felt the loss of her like a gaping wound he suspected might never heal.

"Mother insisted that she and Thomas go after her," Josie explained. "She hoped they might be able to catch the mail coach and bring her back."

"They won't catch her," he corrected grimly. As determined as she was when she fled Park Place, as distressed and angry in equal measure, they'd have to chase her all the way to Lincolnshire before they found her.

With a bewildered shake of her head, Josie bit her lip. "I don't understand. She was having such a lovely season. She even had suitors calling on her. Mr. Downing, especially."

Sebastian avoided his sister's eyes. No, not Downing. He'd made certain to chase the man away himself the morning after the opera when Downing arrived at Park Place to ask formal permission to court her with the intention of offering marriage. He'd behaved like a jealous nodcock, making certain the man begged off from their Vauxhall outing at the last minute. Had he known unconsciously even then that he wanted Miranda for himself?

"I thought they were becoming serious," Josie mumbled, her fingers once again worrying at her pendant. "I was certain that he would offer for her and that she would accept."

"What made you think that?" He feigned disinterest as he glanced at the note, hiding his growing concern for Miranda. She would be fine on the road by herself, he held no worries about that. In the past few weeks, he'd seen her change from the flighty girl who arrived in London and never looked before leaping to a woman who found the boldness to seize what she wanted, and he'd come to learn that she was far more than capable of taking care of herself. But he worried for her heart now. If he'd permanently extinguished the light in her, he'd never be able to forgive himself.

"Well, he kissed her," Josie answered, "and a bit more, apparently."

His eyes snapped up to hers. "*What* did you say?" Jealousy burned through him at the thought of Downing touching her. At *any* man touching her but him. "When?"

"The night you all went to Vauxhall." Not noticing the

way he suddenly tensed, Josie took the note from him and placed it back on the table. "She came home all flustered and mussed, and she admitted that he kissed her."

He grimaced painfully. "That wasn't Downing."

"Oh?" She looked up at him and blinked, slightly confused. "Then who?"

"That wasn't Downing," he repeated firmly instead, hoping the tone of his voice would discourage her from pressing.

She stared at him curiously for a moment, then she shook her head. "I suppose Mr. Downing doesn't matter now anyway. But I thought—" She caught her breath as a new thought struck her. "Perhaps she left because she was ill. She'd had those headaches…"

"They weren't serious," he assured her. Her only headache—and heartache—had been him. "Most likely she was homesick." And undoubtedly heartsick. Because of him.

Josie shook her head, not accepting that explanation. "Emily said that you stopped by the lecture and spoke with Miranda. Did she say anything to you about being unhappy and wanting to go home? You two have spent quite a bit of time together lately." Then her eyes narrowed accusingly on him, in the same disbelieving look she gave all her brothers whenever they tried to dissemble with her, ever since the day they'd strung up her dolls for archery practice. "*What* did you say to her at the lecture?"

"Flowers," he answered simply, offering nothing more. He loved his sister and hated keeping secrets from her, but he had no intention of sharing with Josie the subtext of that conversation. "We talked about flowers."

A dubious expression flashed across her face. "Well, you *must* know something about what upset her so," she pressed.

"After all, you two have been in each other's pockets since she…since she…"

Her eyes widened as the words died in her throat, and she stared at him in knowing disbelief. He could do nothing but soberly return her stare, with certain guilt written on every inch of him, and deserving of both her stunned silence and whatever accusation she would level at him as soon as she found her voice.

Her hand went to her mouth, and she stared at him, eyes wide. "My God, it was you," she whispered through her fingers. "With Miranda that night at Vauxhall…You're *him*— the man who curled her toes!"

With a roll of his eyes, he cursed beneath his breath. *Curled her toes?* He'd done a hell of a lot more to her than that. But he found it hard to regret those precious hours with her, even now, although he certainly regretted hurting her.

"You kissed Miranda?" Then her face broke into a thrilled smile, excited at the possibility that her brother and one of her oldest friends might have gotten swept up in the romance of the gardens. "Oh, Sebastian, I *never* would have—"

She froze, the words choking in her throat. He tensed with solemn dread, waiting for her to make the connection between Miranda not being in her bed this morning and him hunting her down here. For her to comprehend that he'd done more than simply kiss her. He knew the instant she realized it, when her hand fell limp to her side.

Josie stared at him, for a moment speechless. Then, as if pleading for him to prove her wrong, she whispered, "Sebastian?"

He looked at her grimly, remaining silent beneath her utterly bewildered stare. There was no point in denying his culpability in what she knew to be true, and no point in attempting to explain when he knew she wouldn't understand. He barely understood himself.

"Oh, Sebastian," she repeated with compassion and sympathy. He thanked God that he didn't see recrimination in her eyes. "You're why she left, aren't you?"

"Yes," he answered, his shoulders slumping under both the weight of his guilt and the desolation of the loss of her. She'd fled London because she couldn't bear being near him. And the truth of that was brutal.

"Then you have to go after her!" Urgency pulsed from her, and she reached for his arm to pull him toward the door. "If you ride your horse, you can easily catch up with her by evening and..."

But he didn't budge from where he stood. She let go of his arm and drew back to stare at him. In that look finally flashed the recrimination he'd been waiting for.

"You have no intention of marrying her," she accused softly.

"No," he confirmed, unable to say anything more. The earlier argument with Miranda over marriage had scraped him raw. He didn't think he could bear it a second time with his sister.

Her look of cutting reproach deepened, even as she reminded him, "But you have to." She lowered her voice as if she was afraid they'd be overheard, even as they stood alone in the room. "You've *ruined* her."

Her soft accusation tore through him. He answered quietly, his voice hoarse, "I cannot marry her, and you know it. So does she. She's known that all along."

He saw understanding fall over her, followed immediately by a grief-stricken expression of sympathy for him and concern for Miranda. To those in the *ton*, Miranda was no better than a barmaid, servant, or shop girl. But he knew better. He knew now how special she was, how fine and regal in her own way. Yet that made no difference in the distance between their stations or who he was expected to marry. No matter how much he cared about her, no matter how happy she made him, she could never be his duchess.

Her eyes softened, glistening with sadness. She rested her hand gently on his arm, still attempting to persuade him as she told him softly, "But if you care about each other—"

"I am a duke," he snapped out as he turned on her, the frustration and guilt inside him reaching a boiling point. "She is my tenant's niece and an orphanage manageress. Do you really think she's what Father had in mind for my wife? Do you?" The impossibility of having Miranda in his life and the loss of happiness he knew she would bring raged through him until he could no longer contain it, and he struck out in his anger. "I made a promise to Father that I would do everything in my power to serve the title well, including finding a proper wife. Can you stand there and honestly tell me that Miranda Hodgkins was the woman he had in mind to be Duchess of Trent?"

Josie gasped at the ferocity of his words and the palpable pain behind them. She slowly drew her hand away as the look of sympathy on her face turned hard, until she stared at him as if he were a stranger.

Immediately, he regretted lashing out at her. Drawing in a jagged breath of remorse, he explained ruefully, "I have no choice, you know that. I have to find a proper bride. Society expects it." His chest squeezed around his heart so hard that he winced. "And Father insisted on it. When I find the right woman, I'll marry her. I'll have a duchess by fall and, God willing, by next year an heir."

She straightened her spine, her eyes narrowing with

disdain. "Congratulations," she told him icily. "You've finally become a true peer. Just as arrogant and cold-hearted as the rest of them."

* * *

Miranda sat in the overloaded mail coach for Islingham, pressed up against the wall by the five other people crammed inside with her, and stared miserably out the window, with the small bag she'd packed in her hurry to flee resting on her lap. As the city drifted past outside, everything that had happened to her since the masquerade swirled through her mind and only added to the deep humiliation she felt at what Sebastian had told her, and to the utter anguish that pierced her at knowing she would never be good enough for him.

Well, she had been right. The night of the masquerade had certainly led to her ruination, all right, but not at all the way she'd intended.

The irony was heart-stoppingly agonizing. During the time since she stole into Sebastian's room by mistake, she'd lost her innocence and shattered her heart, she'd been accepted at court and humiliated in the home of the only family she'd ever known, and she'd fallen out of infatuation with Robert and into love with Sebastian.

Oh yes, she still loved him. She was certain of it. Because only love could make her feel this wretched.

She swiped a gloved hand at her eyes, the same pretty gloves that Katherine Westover, Duchess of Strathmore, had been kind enough to give her as a welcome gift when she arrived in London for what was to have been her dream season. Like the rest of her life, that, too, had been ripped inside-out. A London season was meant for a young lady to find a husband, not for her to lose her heart to a man who refused to marry her, even though he wanted to.

But Sebastian *would* marry, exactly as he'd planned all along. But not her. He would marry the daughter of a peer from an old and wealthy family, a darling of society who would be perfect on his arm at every event to which he escorted her. There would be a grand wedding, most likely at Chestnut Hill and at that beautiful time of year when August faded into September and the stately brick house always looked so beautiful. Of course, she would be expected to attend. To do otherwise would insult the entire Carlisle family, but how was she ever going to bear it? To have to sit there and watch Sebastian pledge his life to a woman he didn't love, one who stirred no passion in him, who would let him continue to live in that same, soul-killing way he'd been living since his father died...

A woman who wasn't her.

The tears came unbidden now, and she turned her head aside to keep the other passengers from seeing the anguish on her face and the pain that threatened to consume her. Her shoulders shook uncontrollably, and she pressed her hand to her chest. Dear God, it hurt so much that she could barely breathe! Being with him was supposed to have been pleasure. Now, though, she felt nothing but aching misery.

She'd told Sebastian that she wanted him, and she meant it. With every ounce of her soul and being. She loved him and wanted to spend the rest of her life with him, to make a loving home for him and bear him children. To make him laugh and smile. To simply make him happy.

But he could never be hers. She'd been a fool to ever wish for that.

She opened her eyes and gazed at the last bits of a tear-blurred London slipping away as the mail coach headed north past Hampstead Heath.

The city had held so much promise for her when she arrived, so much potential for fun and happiness this season. But now, how would she ever be able to think of the city again without thinking of Sebastian?

That was the problem with London, she decided as she closed her eyes again and took a deep breath in a futile attempt to choke back her tears. From the outside, the city appeared so inviting, so exciting and wonderful...just like the pleasures beneath the flickering Chinese lamps at Vauxhall Gardens.

But just like Vauxhall, when the lamps died and the dawn came, it proved to be nothing more than an ugly illusion. Like love, it was nothing more than a dream that would never be real.

CHAPTER FIFTEEN

Sebastian sat in the darkness of Chesney's study in Audley House and stared up at the portrait of his father hanging over the fireplace. It was a copy of the portrait that hung in Chestnut Hill that Mother had insisted Father sit for when he was awarded the dukedom, just as Josie had insisted that this copy be made and hung in her home after he died. She'd offered to have a second copy made, one Sebastian could hang in Park Place, but he'd refused her kindness. After all, he already had enough reminders there of his father.

But tonight, so much guilt swirled inside him that he needed to be here, because he could no longer tell where his guilt over his father ended and his guilt toward Miranda began.

Why did you give yourself to me? Her parting words reverberated inside his head, and he was unable to stop hearing them or seeing the tears that had streamed down her cheeks in anger, rejection, and frustration. Christ! He knew exactly *why*. Because she was beautiful and tempting, and he wanted her. It was that simple. Plain old lust. Couldn't have been anything else to make him so reckless as to—

A damned lie.

The truth was that he'd wanted to share the freedom and life in her, to experience that same exuberance for living that had died in him with his father. Because they were friends, and then they were more... and all of it had felt wonderful. So wonderful, in fact, that he hadn't stopped to question any of it until it was too late.

With a curse, he shoved himself out of the chair and stalked across the room to the shelf where Chesney kept his best cognac. He filled a glass overfull with the stuff, then swallowed down half of it in a desperate attempt to numb himself.

It wasn't working. Even as he wiped the back of his hand over his mouth, the image of her returned with fresh force— Miranda lying in his arms in his bed, admitting in a whisper so soft that he barely heard her... *I love you.* He squeezed his eyes shut as the next image came unbidden of her standing in his rooms in tears. What the hell did she want from him? He couldn't marry her, and she knew it. She'd known it from the very beginning.

But damnation, so had he. He knew he needed to marry the daughter of a peer, a lady with good breeding and fine standing in society. One whom Richard Carlisle would have been proud to call his daughter. *That* was what he needed in his duchess.

Although what he *wanted* in his wife... He bit back a groan of anger and frustration. What he owed to his father and to the family, to their legacy and reputation— Damnation! Wasn't he entitled to compensation in return for all the responsibility he shouldered? Didn't he have the right to claim some bit of happiness for himself in return? How long was he expected to be punished for one mistake?

"Sebastian?" His mother's voice reached him softly through the shadows.

He sucked in a deep breath at the intrusion. "Mother."

He turned to face her as she entered the room, closing the door after herself and shutting them together into the darkness. Even now, long after midnight, she was regal and dignified, carrying herself with confidence and grace. Every inch of her a duchess.

"I knew I'd find you here," she said quietly as she crossed the room to him. When she reached his side, she leaned up to place a kiss on his cheek. Her face darkened as she asked gently, her voice not a question, "There are too many ghosts at Park Place tonight, aren't there?"

More than she knew. He forced a smile and raised his glass to her. "Chesney has better cognac than I do."

He could tell by the way she paused that she knew he'd just lied to her. "Then pour me a taste, will you?" With a motherly squeeze of his arm, she walked toward the fireplace. "I think we both could use it tonight."

He arched a surprised brow at her odd request, yet did as she asked, splashing a swallow's worth into a glass and carrying it to her. He couldn't remember seeing his mother take a drink of the stuff in his life.

She took the brandy from him, and he frowned down at the cold fireplace. "Do you want me to ring for a footman to build a fire?"

She shook her head a bit wistfully. "You know, when I was young, we had to light our own fires."

With a twist of his mouth, Sebastian took that as his cue. He set his glass on the mantel and took up the poker to stir up the coals.

"There was always work to be done on the farm, so we all had to pitch in and do our share," she continued, a nostalgic smile pulling at her lips. "Including lighting the fires."

As the first fingers of flames snaked up from the stirred coals, he reached into the coal bucket and tossed a chunk onto the grate. "I'd forgotten about that, that you grew up on a farm."

"Not just any farm. Your grandfather was a tenant of the Earl of Spalding, your great uncle." The faint smile at her lips blossomed into one full of love as she looked up at her late husband's portrait. "That was how I met your father. Richard had come to the estate to pay his respects to the family for helping him with his army commission, and we met while he was riding up the lane. He was so handsome in his red uniform. I'd never seen another man like him in my life, so tall and imperial. Strong and powerful." Her smile faded with a touch of melancholy. "And the kindest man I would ever know."

He returned the poker to the rack and wiped off his hands. His chest tightened to know that he would never have that same connection to the woman he chose to be his wife that his father had with his mother. Already he felt the loss of it as palpably as if he'd lost a limb. "And it was love at first sight."

"Oh no! Not at all," she corrected with a faint laugh, surprising him. "There were lots of soldiers in those days, and all of them looked handsome in their uniforms. I was much too shrewd to settle for the first one who came riding along."

Raising the brandy to his lips, he hid his smile. "Of course."

"But your father was just as stubborn as I was, and over the next few months, he wore me down until eventually I agreed to marry him." The growing flames softly lit up the room around them, so that he could see the knowing smile on her face as she stared up at the portrait, still as much in love with her late husband as she'd been the day she married him. "I gave him all the trouble I could, too, in those first days of our courtship to make certain he would be willing to fight for me and stand by my side the way I thought a husband should."

"It worked," he commented quietly. His father had been completely devoted to his mother until the day he died.

She turned her head to look at him, and her face softened with concern. She said gently, "I hear there's a woman putting you through your own troubles."

He froze, the glass halfway to his lips. Anger flashed through him. "Josie told you," he muttered. "She had no right."

"You upset her."

He guiltily slumped his shoulders. These days it seemed he was upsetting every woman in his life. He blew out a hard breath. "I'll apologize to her in the morning."

"That would be gracious of you, but I don't think she wants an apology as much as to know that you are all right. She was worried about you." She paused sympathetically. "And about Miranda."

He stared down at his glass as he rolled it slowly between his palms, watching the way the cognac shined gold-red in the firelight. "There's nothing to be worried about."

"Hmm." She raised her own glass to her lips to take a tentative sip. "Seems to me there's a great deal."

He clenched his jaw, turning his anger onto himself. "It was my fault. I'll make certain Miranda's protected. I won't let her be punished for my mistake."

"And you, Sebastian?" She thoughtfully traced her fingertip around the rim of her glass as she slid a sideways glance at him. "Should *you* be punished for daring to care about that girl?"

He held her gaze for a heartbeat, then looked up at his father's portrait. "Yes."

He finished off the rest of his brandy in a gasping swallow, but there wasn't enough cognac in the world to dull the pain. Or ease the guilt.

"I must admit that I was surprised when your sister told me what had happened," she pressed gently. "Not only that you found Miranda attractive, but that you let yourself be intimate with her."

Embarrassment surged through him, and he shook his head. "This is *not* a conversation I should be having with my mother."

Her eyes sparkled with amusement at that. "My dear boy, where do you think you came from—a stork?"

"Yes," he agreed quickly with a very arched brow. Good Lord, he desperately needed more brandy. "Yes, I did. So did all my siblings." He paused to consider... "Except for Quinton, who was left by gypsies."

She smiled at that. Thankfully letting go of *that* aspect of the conversation, she turned her gaze back to the portrait.

Several moments of silence passed. Her smile faded as she commented thoughtfully, "She must mean a great deal to you if you're this troubled."

"She does," he answered quietly. There was no point in lying to his mother. She knew him too well.

"Hmm. Then what do you plan to do about it?"

What could he do? "Nothing."

"Because you're a duke," she said deliberately, "and she's the niece of our tenant farmer... who most likely lights her own fires."

He gritted his teeth at that subtle rebuke. "It isn't the same, and you know it. Father wasn't a peer when you married him. He was an army officer, free to marry whomever he pleased."

She set her glass away, apparently not having a taste for brandy after all. "Do you care about her, Sebastian?" she asked quietly but bluntly. "Or was she simply an evening's entertainment?"

He lowered his gaze to the fire, unable to bear looking at his father's picture as he admitted quietly, "I love her."

His mother's lips parted in surprise. She was too shocked by that to say anything.

"I know," he admitted, blowing out a hard breath. "Stuns the hell out of me, too."

Needing something to do, he set down his empty glass and took up the poker again, although the fire didn't need to be tended. After a few halfhearted jabs at the coals, he gave up, returned the poker, and began to pace.

"She's nothing like I thought she was," he admitted. "She's not at all flighty, just vivacious, although a bit beyond control when she gets swept up into the excitement of the moment." The memory of the opera came back to him in vivid detail, and he couldn't help but remember how excited she'd been that night. A faint smile tugged at his lips. "Do you know she reads Milton and rewrites Shakespeare?"

Mother blinked. "*Rewrites* Shakespeare?"

"There should have been a pirate scene in *Hamlet*," he explained, and truly, wasn't that obvious? Then the smile he'd been holding back fully blossomed into a grin of pride. "And you'd be so pleased with what she's done with the orphans."

"I am," she confirmed softly. "All the women who sit on the orphanage board think she's done a remarkable job."

"She isn't at all the annoying girl from next door any longer." And that was the problem. In the past few months, Miranda had grown into a woman in her own right.

"Does she make you happy?"

He stopped pacing and faced her, fighting back the urge to refill his glass. "More than I thought possible of any woman."

His mother hesitated, needing a moment to digest that bit of information, then asked softly, "Does she know how you feel about her?"

"She knows I cannot marry her."

"Cannot," she pressed, "or *will* not?"

In what his life had become, there was no difference. "I need a duchess, not only a wife." He shook his head. "A country bluestocking who knew nothing about society or its rules until this season…How can she ever become the duchess I need?"

Mother gazed at him sympathetically. "The same way *I* went from being a country girl to a duchess," she answered quietly. "One day at a time, with the love and help of my husband."

He shook his head. He desperately wanted to believe her. He wanted to hope that he could be happy in his choice of wife and the future they'd have together, but the situation wasn't as simple as she made it out to be. "She's the orphaned niece of our tenant farmer," he said. "She's no better in society's eyes than a shop girl, barmaid, or—"

"Actress?" she interjected gently.

He froze, his body flashing numb. The events of that terrible night of his father's death came crashing back, and he could barely breathe under the weight of it. She knew… Mother *knew*! But that—that was impossible. He'd covered his tracks too well, and he'd never seen the woman again after that night.

"That's where you were the night your father died. With an actress you'd met at the theater." Her eyes softened on him. "And you haven't forgiven yourself for it."

Her soft words pierced him like a knife, and he stared at her, searching her face for answers. How long had she known? Dear God, how much had he hurt her all these years, only for her to suffer his thoughtlessness in silence?

He squeezed his eyes shut against the memory, but it did little to stop the pain. "I should have been with my family, not with her."

She laid her hand gently on his shoulder. "How could you have known what would happen that night? Even if you'd been there, you couldn't have stopped the accident. No one could have."

The anguished words tore from him—"I could have been there to say good-bye."

"Oh, my poor boy." She cupped his face in her hands and tenderly kissed his temple. "That's the punishment you're still carrying inside you, isn't it?" she whispered, her voice strangled with tears. "The blame you still place on yourself...that if you hadn't been with that woman you would have been by his side. But we don't know that, either."

"I do." He opened his eyes to look at her, and her face blurred as the self-recrimination tore from him. "Because if I hadn't hidden her from all of you, hadn't lied about where I was, you would have known where to find me. You could have sent for me, and I would have—"

"Still arrived too late," she finished in a whisper, the truth too painful for her to find her voice. When his shoulders slumped beneath the weight of that, she reached up to lovingly brush a lock of hair away from his forehead. "You must stop punishing yourself for that night. You were a good son to your father, Sebastian. He was so proud of you."

"Proud?" He couldn't stop the bitter laugh that rose on his lips. "Of what, Mother? A string of dalliances with disreputable women, even after I'd promised him that I would put the title and our family before all else? Or lying to both of you because I knew he wouldn't have approved of the women I associated with?"

Her eyes softened with grief and compassion as she gazed silently at him.

"The night my father died, instead of being at his side to provide comfort to him and you, I was in the bed of an actress." The confession cut at him as he rasped out, "A woman I knew Father would never have approved of. I put my own selfish desires before the needs of the title and neglected my family."

"And you haven't let yourself have a moment's happiness since," she concluded gently. Then she added as she deduced, "Except with Miranda. And the guilt of that is eating at you, isn't it, my son? Because you think you were punished the night your father died."

"I know so," he admitted as he stepped away from her. He couldn't bear her concern a moment longer. "I knew I could never marry Miranda. I didn't put the dukedom first, or I would never have . . ." He ran a shaking hand through his hair. "I was only thinking of myself, not of the title."

"But, Sebastian," she reminded him gently, "*you* are the title now. How does being unhappy serve yourself well?"

His chest tightened so hard that he could barely breathe. His happiness . . . the same concern that Miranda had for him last night. Yet tonight, the answer was still unchanged. What he wanted as a man was of no concern. His wants and desires ended the night his father died, when he became Trent. "Father would never have approved of Miranda as my duchess."

"Oh yes, he would have."

He stared at her in disbelief. "She's not of the same station."

"No, she's not." She turned to gaze once more up at the portrait, with love glowing on her face. "And he would have only cared that she's a good woman who loves you for yourself and who makes you happy."

Uncertainty churned inside him. "But the actress—"

"*Her* he definitely would not have approved. But it would have had nothing to do with her profession." She turned to face him. "The reason I know about her and that night was because she came to Chestnut Hill a few weeks after your father died, looking for you. She'd learned that you'd inherited, and she planned to set herself up as the new duke's mistress. She didn't care about you or gaining society's respect—she only wanted your money." A self-pleased smile curled her lips. "I sent her packing so fast I think I frightened her."

"I had no idea," he murmured, surprised by his mother's fierce protection of her family during the darkest time of her life.

"At the time, there was no reason to tell you. You didn't need to carry that burden on top of the others you were already shouldering." She frowned, her face darkening with remorse. "But I now think I might have made a mistake in not telling you." She paused a long and thoughtful moment. "What did Miranda want from you?"

"She wanted me," he admitted quietly, still not quite able to believe it himself.

His mother tensed, her eyes narrowing at that. "She wanted to be duchess?"

"No," he corrected quietly, looking up at his father, "she wanted me to be happy, and she wanted me to love her. She didn't want the duke at all." He grimaced as the memory of her words fell through him like ice water. "She wanted *me*."

"It seems to me," she said as she smiled at him with love, "that she can still have you, if you allow it."

He didn't dare let loose the faint stirrings of hope that began to blossom in his chest. He knew better than anyone the obstacles still standing between them. Even with his heart pounding at the possibility, he shook his head, unwilling to believe it. "Society would cut her to pieces."

"My darling boy, you are a Carlisle. Your father was a soldier, your sister was a highwayman, and your two brothers are set on destroying St James's Street, one club at a time." With a knowing smile, she placed a kiss to his temple before she moved away toward the door. "When has anyone in this family ever truly cared about what society thinks?"

He stared down at the glass in his hands, his fingers trembling with the enormity of all that he'd learned tonight. For the first time in two years, hope warmed inside him that his life might be more than the burden of the title. That he might find happiness after all.

"She must hate me," he murmured, giving voice to his worst fears. "After all the pain I've caused her…How do I begin to make up for that?"

"Start by telling her that you love her." She paused to smile at him before she slipped out the door. "After all, that's what your father did with me."

* * *

"Oh, blast it!" Miranda looked down at the ruined column of figures in the orphanage's account book and nearly cried. Again.

Shoving the book across the desk, she hung her head in her hands. She was utterly miserable, and the only thing that kept her from breaking into sobs yet again this afternoon was that she'd done almost nothing else since she returned to Islingham four days ago but cry. And think of Sebastian. Then cry some more...until she simply had no tears left.

Not even her work at the orphanage was able to distract her. She'd hoped that catching up with the accounts would provide enough distraction that she might be able to lose herself for a few hours in the sums and columns. But her mind only continued to wander, and she'd messed up the figures...Three hundred pounds for soap? Oh, she should never have come into her office in the first place!

But she would have gone mad if she'd remained at home.

Aunt Rebecca and Uncle Hamish had been surprised at her unexpected return—and concerned, although they were kind enough not to press for the real reason she'd fled the city for home. All she could tell them was that her season had not gone as planned and that she missed Islingham. Which was the truth. For the past four days, she'd mostly stayed at home and paced, cried, then paced some more, until the silence and stillness of the house drove her into the village to the orphanage.

But even here, amid the familiar noise and chaos of the children, her thoughts were not her own.

By now, Sebastian had undoubtedly found a lady to formally court, and she would have eagerly accepted, knowing he planned on marrying her. After all, what woman in her right mind would refuse a man like him? If a handsome, golden-blond duke with a brilliant mind and witty sense of humor, a wonderful family, and oh, so much passion inside him just waiting to burst out had offered for *her*—

But he hadn't.

And never would.

Unable to stop herself from wallowing in misery, she folded her arms across her chest and hugged herself tightly as she wondered if Sebastian ever thought about her.

But of course he didn't. She cursed her foolishness as she wiped at her wet eyes, a few tears apparently left in her after all. Why would he? What they'd shared was precious but fleeting, especially for a man like him who'd left a string of broken hearts fluttering in his wake over the years. By August, he'd most likely have forgotten all about what happened between them.

But *she* would never forget. And so she couldn't remain here.

Islingham was her home, and after having experienced the disappointments of London, she never wanted to leave it again, content to spend the rest of her days here with the orphans and the people she loved. But that was impossible now. She would have to find a position someplace else as a governess or a teacher, perhaps as a manageress for another orphanage. But she had to be gone by August. She *had* to. Having to see Sebastian with his wife, to see the children she would give him and the home they would create together at Blackwood Hall...Miranda squeezed her eyes shut and pressed her hand hard against her chest and the shattered heart inside— *Oh God*, she simply couldn't bear that!

"Miss!" Mr. Grundy ran into her office, hat in hand and visibly agitated. "Miss, come quickly!"

She sat up and swiped at her eyes, hoping he hadn't seen the tears. But of course he'd seen them, although he was too kind to say anything. "What's the matter, Mr. Grundy?"

"You're needed in the rear garden—real quick!"

Panic flashed through her, and dread instantly replaced her own sorrow as her mind immediately feared the worst. The children! They'd been quiet all morning, and even though they'd been squirreled away in their classroom, they'd been *too* quiet. And that was never good. She'd been too distracted by her own selfish problems to notice that something was wrong. If the children had hurt themselves because of her own self-pity, oh, she would *never* be able to forgive herself!

She jumped to her feet and ran through the building, out the kitchen door and into the garden—and stopped.

She stared and blinked in wonder. And utter bewilderment.

The space had been transformed. The small spot of lawn within the garden walls where the housekeeper normally hung the laundry to dry and where the children played their games now resembled a fairy-tale land. Pink satin streamers billowed among white sheets strung up like curtains, and dark red ribbons stirred gently on the warm afternoon breeze. Everywhere, there were roses...dozens and dozens of them in all colors and sizes, spilling out of buckets and vases, pitchers and barrels, and whatever else could hold them, right down to teacups big enough to hold only a single bud. Their sweet scent filled the air and surrounded her like a soft cloud from heaven. And in the center, fashioned of papier-mâché and wood, stood a miniature pagoda, exactly like the one at Vauxhall.

Around the small structure, the children had gathered in a group, all of them holding red roses. When they saw her, their faces lit with excitement and they began to sing.

"What is all this?" Miranda rested a stunned hand on Mr. Grundy's arm as the handyman gently led her forward into the garden, a beaming smile on his weathered face.

She laughed with incredulity; the happiness of the children and Mr. Grundy was infectious, despite the heavy weight that pressed onto her heart. And always would. "What play is this? I thought we were studying *Romeo and Juliet* this—"

"You are."

Her breath strangled at the sound of the deep voice, and her heart stopped.

Sebastian.

Like a ghost from her tortured dreams, he slowly stepped out from behind the rows of children and crossed the garden toward her. He held out his hand.

But Miranda didn't move to go to him. She could only stand there, staring at the apparition of him and pressing her hand against her chest, as if she could physically hold back the stuttering lurch of her heart. Because he couldn't be real. He *couldn't* be. He was in London with his family—

Yet the agonizing torment swirling inside her chest told her that he *was* real, that he wasn't a dream that her fevered mind had conjured up from her desperate longing to see him again. As she stared at him, every pounding beat of her pulse was torture, and each step that brought him closer sliced new agony into her chest. But even now, as the anguished memory of his parting words flooded back to her, she couldn't look away.

When he stopped in front of her, he reached to gently pull her hand away from her heart and folded his fingers over hers.

She flinched at the burn of his touch. She couldn't help it, or the way her fingers trembled in his. Or the soft cry of pain when he raised her hand to his lips to kiss her palm. His handsome face blurred behind the tears that now streamed unbidden down her cheeks. Leaving him in London had been agonizing, but having him return to her here—unbearable!

"Miranda," he whispered, sudden concern darkening his face as he cupped his palm against her cheek and brushed at her tears with his thumb. Behind him, the children continued with their song, and the sheets danced around them on the soft breeze. But inside her chest, the pain was blinding, so terrible that she could barely breathe. "Don't cry, sweet. You know how much I hate it when you cry. This was supposed to make us happy."

Happy? She forced back a sob of desolation. How on earth did he think that tormenting her like this could make them both happy? Unless…unless he was troubled about having to face his guilt every time he saw her in Islingham, unless he thought that making an elaborate enough apology would make them all get along again as if nothing had ever happened between them. Was that why he was here—an *apology*? Certainly, if she were willing to overlook what happened, to never give it another thought and go back to being no more than friends, life would be easier for him and his new bride. Her forgiveness would make *him* happy, even if it cut her into pieces.

Anger swelled inside her, and she stepped back, breaking contact with him, unable to bear it another second. Oh, this was so typical of the Carlisle brothers and the way they'd always handled their mistakes. The bigger their blunder, the bigger the apology they had to give in order to set it to rights. But there weren't enough roses in Lincolnshire to heal the damage Sebastian had done to her heart. And she doubted if she could ever forgive him. She should laugh at him—yes! Make him see that he meant nothing to her. Or slap him for humiliating her once again by putting on this show.

Yet hurting him was the last thing she would ever do, because even now her foolish heart still loved him.

"You don't need to worry about me, Your Grace," she whispered, the admission barely more than a breath. As she turned her face away so he wouldn't see the pain he put there, she caught sight of the cook and housekeeper peering out the window at them. Oh, perfect! Now her humiliation was complete. She choked out, "I—I'm going away. I've decided to leave Islingham so that you won't be bothered by me."

With a somber expression, he closed the distance between them. "I hope not," he told her, caressing her cheek with his thumb. "It would be a shame if you continue to make me chase after you after I've come all this way."

"Chase after..." Blinking hard as confusion trampled at her heart, she tried to clear the hot tears from her stinging eyes, but only caused more to fall. "I don't— I—I don't understand," she stuttered out between sobs. "Why are you really here, Sebastian? Why did you go to all this trouble just to...just to..." *Just to permanently end what we shared?*

Unable to finish the sentence, she pressed her hand against her mouth, squeezed her eyes shut—

"Just to propose," he finished gently.

Her eyes flew open, and she searched frantically for answers in his tear-blurred face. "Propose?" She couldn't dare hope—it would be so utterly foolish and ludicrous...But her heart had a mind of its own when it came to this man. And always would. "To me?"

He laughed gently and reached once more for her hand. "Yes, sweet, to you."

When she tried to wrench her hand away, he held tight, refusing to let her go. She feared he could feel her heart somersaulting furiously in confusion. "But—but you said you could never marry me."

"I was wrong." His broad shoulders sagged with solemn regret, and he kissed her fingers tenderly, as if seeking absolution. "Since my father died, I thought I had to honor him by being the perfect son, which meant being the perfect duke."

"And marrying the perfect duchess," she interjected. She couldn't prevent the stab of jealousy that made her strike out at him even now. He'd hurt her, so inexcusably. "You thought I could never be that for you."

"Yes," he admitted, remorse flitting across his features. "Because I wrongly thought that was what my father expected of me. But I know better now. Yes, the title was important to him, so was making certain its legacy would be respected. But he also knew how hard being a duke could be, that I would need help to oversee the dukedom and take care of my family."

"He didn't mean me," she whispered, lowering her face.

"Maybe not you exactly, but a woman who loves me the way you do, who makes me laugh and smile, who makes me happy, now and for the rest of my days." He cupped his palm against her cheek. "You do all that, and more. Forgive me, Rose, for not believing in you until it was almost too late."

She shook her head, her heart tearing anew. "But I'm…I'm not good enough for you," she breathed out, so softly that her words barely made any sound.

His face darkened with anger. "Don't *ever* say that again, do you hear?" He cupped her face between his hands. "I'm the one who isn't good enough for you. But if you can find it in your heart to forgive me, then I promise to spend the rest of my days proving my worth to you."

He leaned in to place a soft kiss against her lips, and she gasped at the raw emotion she tasted in him.

"Forgive me, sweet," he whispered against her lips.

She shook her head, unable to find her voice beneath the tidal wave of emotions warring inside her. "You were so set on finding a society daughter to be your duchess—"

"*You* are the woman I want to be my duchess," he assured her, his eyes shining with unabashed certainty as he stared down at her. "You're the toast of the London season and the savior of orphans. A woman so believing in love that you were willing to sneak into a man's bedchamber to get it."

A hot blush colored her cheeks, and she turned her face away. Oh, would he never let her live that down?

He took her chin and turned her back to look at him. "When you sing hymns at Sunday service, you dream of being an opera singer, and every time you read or watch a play, you dream of being onstage. You cause mayhem everywhere you go, and there's not a peer in England safe from your spilled wineglass." When she stared at him, her lips parting in incredulous disbelief that he would say *that* as a compliment, he added tenderly, "And you're the woman I love. The only woman I want for my wife."

A sob tore from her. The nightmare had turned into a dream.

"I love you, and I need you to be by my side to guide me, to counsel me and argue with me, to challenge me and love me . . . to save me." His sapphire blue eyes took on a pleading aspect as he took both her hands in his. "Save me, my sweet Rose."

He lowered himself to one knee and withdrew her red slipper from beneath his jacket. The same slipper he'd been holding hostage since January. In all the turmoil and confusion of the past few weeks, she'd forgotten all about it and their pact to help each other find love this season. And how he'd promised that she would get it back only when he'd found a bride and the marriage offer was accepted. She laughed through her tears.

"Will you marry me, Miranda?" He reached for her leg and gently lifted her foot to remove her shoe, then placed the slipper delicately into place. "Say yes so that I can go hat in hand to your uncle Hamish and beg the man to let me have you."

She could barely breathe for the sudden rush of emotion pulsing through her, all the love she held for him surging to the surface and filling her to her soul. Her fingers trembled as she touched his cheek. "Sebastian—"

"Marry him!" the children shouted at her, urged on by Mr. Grundy, who circled around them and waved his arms to encourage them to shout even louder. Unable to contain their curiosity any longer, the housekeeper and cook rushed through the door into the garden and joined in the chorus of chants. "Yes! Yes!"

She glanced around the garden at the people who helped her with the orphanage, at the elaborate trouble they had gone through to make this moment as romantic for her as possible, and at the children she loved—then her eyes landed on Sebastian, and the way he gazed up at her made her heart bounce. He wasn't seeing the troublemaking girl in braids, nor the seductress in masquerade...He had finally come to see the woman she was and the role she could play in his life. And he loved her.

"Yes," she choked between fresh tears, this time of pure joy. Stepping into his arms, she laughed and nuzzled her face against his shoulder. "Yes, I will marry you!"

Wrapping his arms around her, he pulled her down onto

the grass with him. He leaned over her and gave her a scandalous kiss that sent the orphans cheering.

"You knew I'd say yes if you asked," she whispered, cupping his face in her palms. "You know how much I love you."

He flashed her a crooked grin. "Well, I'd hoped."

"Then why all this?" She waved her hand to indicate the transformed garden, the magical pagoda, and all the children who had once again broken into song. "You went to so much trouble."

"Because you are worth it." His arms tightened around her. "And because I know how much the children mean to you. I wanted them to be part of this. Besides," he told her, his eyes gleaming as he leaned in to kiss her again, "*Romeo and Juliet* needed a proposal scene."

EPILOGUE

Chestnut Hill
One Beautiful August Day

$\mathcal{M}$iranda laughed as Sebastian ran with her down the hall, the skirt of her rose-colored gown held up to keep from tripping as they fled from their own wedding breakfast for a moment's privacy.

"Shh," he warned, his mouth coming down to capture hers as he opened his bedroom door and pulled her inside. "They'll find us." His lips trailed down her throat. "And the last thing I want right now is to be found."

Neither did she. But she couldn't tamp down her happiness and laughed again even as he continued to kiss her, even as he walked her backward across the room to the bed. *Their* bed now, and her heart somersaulted with joy.

Through the window, open wide to let in the fresh air of the warm summer day, she heard the noise of the party on the lawn below and tried to summon any feeling of guilt that they'd abandoned their own celebration. But when his hands brushed up her body, caressing over the satin gown and the aching curves beneath, she abandoned any possibility of feeling anything else today but sheer bliss.

He touched his lips to hers. "Close your eyes."

She did as he bade her, trusting him completely with her heart and now with her life and her future. But she felt him move away from her, heard him cross the room to his dresser and pull open a drawer...Curiosity raced through her as she felt him return to her.

"Now, open."

Her eyes fluttered open, and she gasped at the necklace he held up in front of her. A rose-shaped ruby pendant, and the most beautiful piece of jewelry she'd ever seen—second only to her wedding ring. "Oh, Sebastian, it's stunning!"

"I'm glad you like it." He grinned and motioned for her to turn around, then gently placed the gold chain around her neck. "Because it's your wedding gift."

Her fingers trembled as she brushed them over the necklace. Tears of happiness once more threatened at her lashes, as they had all morning from the moment she crawled out of bed at dawn, too excited to sleep another wink. Even as her auntie, Josie, and Elizabeth helped her dress and rode with her in the carriage to the parish church, she felt as if she were floating in a dream. And now she knew she was wrong.

She wasn't in a dream. She was in heaven.

"Thank you," she breathed, unable to speak any louder around the knot in her throat.

"I had it made for you." He placed a kiss at the nape of her neck, and the heat of his lips shivered deliciously through her. "A rose for my Rose."

"It's perfect," she sighed. *Everything* about today was absolute perfection. Because of Sebastian. How was it possible to love anyone this much?

He fastened the clasp. "How did you come up with that name anyway...Rose?"

Then his hands trailed down her back to unfasten the row of tiny pearl buttons keeping the snug-fitting, old-fashioned bodice of her dress in place. So snug-fitting, in fact, that there was no room for a shift or stays beneath the low-cut neckline and the form-fitted waist, and an appreciative groan of pleasure sounded from him when he discovered that for himself. Her lips curled devilishly—the exact reaction she'd hoped for.

His hands peeled the satin down her curves and off, to let it pile at her feet, until she stood in only her stockings and the gold necklace, the ruby pendant dangling in the valley between her bare breasts.

"You don't know?" She rolled her head as he pulled her back against him and stroked his hands over her body, caressing at her breasts before wandering down to her hips, then lower still to the aching heat throbbing between her legs. When his fingers slid into her cleft, she quivered against him, already aching for him there, so eager to make love to him as his wife.

He lowered her onto the bed and followed down on top of her, his mouth never leaving her body as he quickly stripped from his own clothes. The rose pendant lay between her breasts, shining in the sunlight that slanted across the bed, the same sunlight that turned his hair golden as he lowered his head to kiss at her nipples.

When he took one between his lips and sucked, she moaned and arched beneath him, curving her body eagerly into his. Oh, wicked man! And finally all hers, now and for the rest of their lives.

He chuckled at her enthusiasm, the sound tickling at her breast. "I thought the name was just part of the masquerade."

He licked his tongue across her nipple and elicited a plaintive whimper from her, a formless plea for more.

She writhed beneath him, her hands fisting at the sheet as she fought to keep back the rising wave inside her. This was their first joining together as husband and wife, and she wanted to make it last as long as she could.

"Rose," she panted out as he shifted his body into the cradle of her thighs, evidence of his own desire pressing against her lower belly, "is my...middle name."

He leaned up onto his forearm to gaze lovingly down at her, his blue eyes sparkling. "Miranda Rose Carlisle," he murmured and touched his lips to hers to kiss the name onto her. "My Rose." Then another kiss, this one lingering, hot and breathtaking, one that made her shake with arousal and need. "Duchess of Trent." Another kiss, this one teasing her lips open to allow him to plunge deep inside her mouth and claim all of her kiss for him and him alone. "Baroness Althorpe."

She tightened her arms around his neck, her thighs trembling with sweet anticipation, and she whispered, unable in her happiness to speak any louder, "Your wife."

"And the name of our first daughter." He lowered his hips and claimed her.

Tossing back her head as a wave of utter happiness crashed over her, she moaned and wrapped her legs around his waist, locking her ankles at the small of his back. As she welcomed his body as deeply inside hers as possible, never wanting to let him go, the moan transformed into a laugh of utter happiness. "But I'm not with child."

"Soon, love," he murmured against her temple as she shattered in his arms, her love for him refusing to be restrained a heartbeat longer. "Very soon."

Capturing the Carlisles is the goal of many a young lady looking to marry—but it takes a woman like Annabelle Greene, who's unafraid of seizing what she most desires, to tame a reckless young rogue like Quinton Carlisle...

A preview of

When the Scoundrel Sins

follows.

CHAPTER ONE

Cumbria, England, Near the Scottish Border
September 1822

$\mathcal{W}$ell, well—what have we here?"

Spinning around, Annabelle Greene gasped with surprise at the sound of the man's deep voice. Her arms flew up to cover her bare breasts, and she dropped down until the cold water came up to her chin.

She stared at the tall stranger standing at the edge of the pond, right beside the pile of her clothes where she'd undressed, where she placed them most summer evenings when she took a quick dip before dinner. But on all those other evenings, not once had her swim been interrupted. Certainly not by a man.

She swallowed back both her startled fear and her mortification that he'd come upon her like this, naked and vulnerable. And anger took over.

"Who are you?" she demanded in her sternest possible

voice, which dripped with irony given the weakness of her current position. Heavens, she couldn't even run away! "What do you want?"

She didn't recognize him in the shadows as he stood silhouetted against the sunset. But surely, he wasn't one of Sir Harold's men from the neighboring estate, certainly not dressed as he was, like a gentleman out for a ride. And he wasn't one of her own tenants, not in that expensive maroon redingote and tall beaver hat. Yet Castle Glenarvon was isolated enough in the wilderness of the Scottish borderlands that few people wandered onto the estate by mistake, and just as few on purpose. And from the look of him, with his broad shoulders confidently squared beneath his jacket and his head held high, he wasn't making a mistake.

An impish grin blossomed on his face. "Belle," he called out, a laughing lilt to his rich voice, "is that you?"

Oh no. Her shoulders sagged beneath the surface of the pond. Now she *knew*!

God help her, she would know that grin anywhere. That overly smooth, charming smile could persuade the king to surrender his crown.

"Quinton Carlisle," she called out tersely, peeved that he picked here and now of all times to arrive. Typical Quinn. Always showing up at the most inconvenient moments. And incidentally—as if he had some sort of sixth sense for it— where currently stood a naked woman.

Even the last time she'd seen him, when he was just twenty-one and fresh out of Oxford, he was well on his way to becoming a rake. He and his two older brothers had cut a swathe through London's most notorious venues that season, as if in competition to outdo each other with drunken debauchery. The three had been the foremost topic of gossip, as if the quality couldn't quite believe that the

Carlisle brothers actually belonged to their hallowed ranks. But while the ladies scorned them in public, privately they swarmed to them, and especially to Quinton, whose charming smile had them eagerly surrendering their hearts . . . and other body parts.

No wonder he hadn't paid Annabelle much notice that spring. Why would he give any mind to a shy, country gel who felt more at home in bookshops than in ballrooms when he had the sophisticated ladies of the *ton* vying for his attention? Such a foolish cake she'd been! She should have known when he charmed her into surrendering her first kiss in the Earl of St James's garden that it meant nothing to him.

"So it *is* you." With an amused glimmer in his blue eyes, obviously thrilled that he'd caught her in such an embarrassing situation, he lowered himself onto his heels and closer to her level. "Up to your neck in it as ever, I see."

"And you as ever a bother," she muttered, goaded into the same bickering they'd engaged in when they were children, just because he enjoyed tormenting her.

He gave a short laugh. A lock of blond hair fell across his forehead as he removed his hat and ran his fingers through the thick waves, which were just as golden as she remembered. His charmingly crooked grin grew impossibly brighter.

Oh, she knew that look! And she knew the effect it had on women. Even now, having experienced the devilishness that lurked behind that angelic face, that same grin once again swirled through her, curling her toes into the muck at the bottom of the pond.

He pulled off his leather riding gloves and slapped them against his hard thigh as if finding her in such an embarrassing—and increasingly colder—position was a humorous joke. And clearly at her expense. "I wasn't certain if it was you," he taunted, "or if mermaids had come to Scotland."

"We're in England," she shot back. "But if you'd like to travel on to Scotland, it's just ten miles that way." She gave a jerk of her head toward the mountains in the distance. "Safe travels!"

The cut flew out before she could stop herself. And instantly she regretted it. If he were offended—worse, if he left... what on earth would she do? The pest aggravated the daylights out of her—he always had, blast him—but the last thing she needed in her desperate straits over Glenarvon was to make him ride off before she even had the chance to put her plan into motion.

Thankfully, instead of being offended, he laughed, his eyes sparkling brightly. That, too, was typical of him... boundless energy and magnetic personality. "Your loyalty to crown and country is admirable, Belle, but I don't think *Rule Britannia* applies to duck ponds."

Oh, the devil take the man! Pressing her lips together, she glared murderously at him, not trusting herself to respond without saying something else she would regret.

He was just as aggravating as she remembered, despite being six years older, more mature—if only physically, certainly *not* intellectually—and definitely broader and more muscular. A sinking dread fell through her that perhaps she'd made a mistake by inviting him here.

But she'd had no choice. She was quickly running out of options, and her desperation had driven her to it.

Yet she certainly hadn't expected him to arrive like *this*, with her naked in the water and her clothes lying on the bank beside him. But leave it to Quinn to do just that. The man always did have terrible timing.

They'd known each other since they were children. As distant relations to the late Viscount Ainsley and his wife, she and Quinn had met often at estate parties and on the rare occasions when Annabelle accompanied Lord and Lady Ainsley to London. They had raised her since her own parents died when she was just a little girl, and now she remained at Glenarvon as a companion to Lady Ainsley. Quinn's great-aunt Agatha. And a woman Annabelle was beginning to believe was mad as a hatter.

But her primary concern at the moment wasn't his aunt and how on earth she was going to resolve the mess that the late viscount had created in her life—it was getting out of the pond and over to her clothes without Quinn seeing her naked. And judging from the relaxed way he rested back on his boot heels, his forearm lying casually across his thigh, he didn't plan on being a gentleman and leaving.

"Lady Ainsley is up at the house," she informed him, goose bumps forming on her skin. Good Lord, the water was freezing! A few minutes more, and her teeth would chatter.

He crooked a challenging brow, knowing exactly what he was doing in keeping her there. "But it's so much more fun here with you."

Beneath the pond's surface, she clenched her hands into fists.

"The groom said you were out here," he explained, "and I thought I'd say hello before greeting Aunt Agatha and settling in at the house. So…hello." Even in the dim light of the fading sunset his eyes sparkled like the devil's own. "This feels like old times."

Old times she very much wanted to forget. Inviting him here was turning into a terrible mistake.

Her eyes darted longingly to her clothes at his feet.

He followed her glance. "Are you really…?" He gasped

in feigned shock as he reached down to hook a finger in her dress and lift it from the ground. "Goodness, Belle! You all truly do live wild here in the borderlands, don't you?"

Despite the chill of the water, her face flushed hot. Leave it to Quinn to so cavalierly point out that she was naked.

But of course, he couldn't have cared less about her humiliation. And he certainly wasn't flirting with her, most likely thinking nothing more of her uncomfortable situation than of the opportunity it gave him to torment her, just as he'd done when they were children. After all, he would never see her as a woman. He would never see her as anything more than the skinny, stick-with-ears bluestocking she was when they were younger.

She sighed in aggravation. And shivered with cold. "Would you please—"

"My, my, how careless!" With a shake of his head, he clucked his tongue chastisingly. "Some wild animal could stumble upon your clothes and carry them off, or the wind might simply blow them—"

"Quinton James Carlisle, don't you dare!" But her threat lacked all force, since she could do nothing to stop him. And drat him, he knew it, too.

Which only caused his grin to widen. She could see on his face how tempted he was to do just as she feared and walk away with her clothes, leaving her as naked as Eve in the garden. The deceitful snake!

"Same Belle I remember." He laughed good-naturedly, as if he truly were happy to see her. And, of course, to tease her again. "Always too serious for her own good. Tell me, do you still prefer to spend your time with books rather than with people?"

"Certain people, yes," she bit out. *And especially you.*

As if he could read her mind, he nearly doubled over,

hooting with laughter. The rotten scoundrel actually laughed! When he should have had the decency to be remorseful about what he'd done to her all those years ago.

She grimaced with annoyance. Oh, why couldn't he simply do as she'd hoped for once and minimize the discomfort for both of them? But of course not. Quinn never did anything to make her life easier. Not if he could get a good laugh out of it.

That much about him hadn't changed during the past six years, although the rest of him was most definitely different...taller, broader, more solid. And impossibly more masculine. He'd matured from a lanky university student into a full-grown man, right down to the handsome line of his jaw. The tight fit of his buckskin breeches accentuated the hard muscles of his thighs and his narrow waist as much as the redingote stretching tight across his back exemplified the wide breadth of his shoulders. Since she'd last seen him, he'd transformed into a golden mountain of a man, just like his older brothers, yet retained the same charismatic grin he'd possessed since he was a boy.

If he were anyone else, she would have said he was attractive. Perhaps even handsome. Unfortunately, she knew the Carlisle brothers too well, and she knew what lurked beneath their captivating exteriors. Sebastian was the serious one, Robert was the risk-taker, and Quinton...Well, Quinn made his way through the world by his charm.

But his charisma no longer worked on *her*. She'd gained immunity. The hard way.

"A gentleman would say his good-byes and leave me in privacy to get dressed." Her teeth began to chatter, and as she shook from cold, she prayed he couldn't see it. Or anything else she didn't want him to see.

"Then it's a very good thing I'm not a gentleman," he

replied with mock earnestness. He dangled her dress higher, as if taunting a dog with a bone. "If you want your clothes, Belle," he coaxed devilishly, "you can always come out and get them."

For a fleeting moment, she was tempted. Oh, so very tempted! And just to see the startled look on his face, because she was certain he thought her incapable of ever doing anything so daring. Perhaps the girl he knew from before wouldn't, but the woman Annabelle had become might just do something exactly as bold as that.

She trembled at the idea, and despite the cold from the chilling water, an odd yearning of excitement fluttered up from low in her belly. As if she just might possibly be as daring and wild as he suspected she wasn't—

She sneezed.

"God bless you," he offered solemnly, then trailed his hand into the water at the edge. "Brrr! That is rather cold, isn't it?"

Her eyes narrowed to slits, and she distrusted herself to speak, knowing this time she really *would* say something indelicate enough to drive the pest away.

"Better come out now, Belle." He continued to toy with her, using her dress as bait. "You're turning blue."

Her breath caught in her throat. *Blue.* Her eyes stung with sudden tears at his thoughtless words. To be that inconsiderate, that unkind to her even now after all these years as to bring up that horrible prank—but he only smiled at her, oblivious to the cruelty of his offhanded comment.

Of course, Quinn wouldn't think anything of it. *His* reputation hadn't been ruined because of a bucket of blue paint and a sweet old book buyer who had only been trying to help her after it came crashing down on her head that day in the library, leaving all kinds of blue handprints all over her dress. And just in time for the ladies attending Lady Ainsley's garden party to come rushing inside at the commotion and find them together.

His life hadn't been destroyed. But *hers* had. All because of his childish joke.

Although she could hide her body beneath the water, she couldn't hide the dark humiliation gathering on her face like storm clouds or the agonizing mix of anger and utter wretchedness swelling up inside her at the reminder of what he'd done to her all those years ago. The same cruel joke that might yet cost her Glenarvon.

From the puzzled expression in Quinn's eyes, he noted the sudden change in her but didn't yet realize the full implication of what he'd said, and she didn't dare speak past the tight knot in her throat to explain for fear she might cry. Because she would never allow herself to cry in front of him, never allow him to see how much his teasing had hurt her.

"Belle, are you— Oh Christ." He lowered the dress to the grass as the stupidity of what he'd so thoughtlessly said sank over him, and his grin faded. His eyes softened apologetically. "I'm sorry... It was so long ago that I'd forgotten all about it."

But she hadn't, and doubted she ever would.

"Here." He placed the dress back onto its neat pile where she'd left it and rose to his full height, then turned his back to her and walked off a few paces to give her privacy. "Come out whenever you're ready."

* * *

With his back turned and his eyes focused on the darkening shadows painted across the countryside by the fading sunset,

Quinn heard the soft splash of water behind him as Belle moved quickly toward the bank.

He smiled. Annabelle Greene. Quick-tempered, defensive, serious...exactly as he remembered. Easy to excite and irritate. And a helluva lot of fun to torment.

When they were children, he'd loved to spend his time thinking up ways to goad her to frustration. After all, she'd been an easy target. As a bluestocking whose nose was forever pressed into one book or another, she was always painfully proper and prim even as a child, impossibly shy, and never let herself have any real fun. So he'd nicknamed her Bluebell, a combination of her name and bluestocking, just to antagonize her. The name stuck.

"Are you all right?" he called out over his shoulder as he heard her emerge from the water, partially turning his head. Then he added, just to taunt her, "Bluebell." He couldn't say what it was about her that fueled his puckish side, but Quinn enjoyed taunting her, far more than he should.

"I-I'm fine!"

He heard her teeth chatter when she answered, and fleeting guilt stabbed him for keeping her in the cold water just because teasing her amused him. Or perhaps her answer was forced out between clenched teeth in anger at the use of her nickname. *That* would certainly be the Annabelle he knew.

Good Lord, had it really been six years since he'd seen her?

The last time had been in London when she was starting her first season. As a young lady not quite grown into womanhood, she'd been at that age when her curves were just beginning to blossom and soften. The stick-with-ears she'd been all her life had suddenly grown into her long legs and big honey-hazel eyes, her previous gawkiness turning graceful and her shyness mellowing into a natural demureness that other ladies only pretended to possess. The Bluebell had suddenly turned interesting, even to the jaded buck he'd already become.

And then, somehow, without quite knowing how it happened...he'd kissed her.

Even now, after all these years and countless intimate encounters with experienced ladies, he remembered that innocent kiss. All fumbles and eager awkwardness, hidden from sight beneath the rose bower at St James House in the middle of the countess's annual ball. He couldn't remember what possessed him to go into the shadows with her, or what exactly led to having his arms around her, his mouth on hers, her willing body pressed hard against his. But he remembered the sweet tang of honey on her lips, the wild scent of heather that clung to her skin, the pliant softness of her curves...the utter confusion that gripped him afterward.

She was the Bluebell, for God's sake. Aunt Agatha's companion. Innocent and inexperienced. And wholly intriguing for all of it. She'd left him wanting to steal away with her again.

Until his brothers ruined everything, including the rest of his London season.

He'd foolishly confided in Robert, who thought it hilarious that he'd kissed a bluestocking. So hilarious, in fact, that Robert devised a practical joke to drop a bucket of blue paint over his head when he went to meet Annabelle in the library of Ainsley House. But Belle arrived first. By the time Quinn entered, she was already gone, with only a puddle of paint and a very red-faced, blue-handed octogenarian book buyer left behind, surrounded by a gaggle of society ladies all snickering behind their flitting fans as if something more than book buying had been going on.

Of course, it hadn't. Belle would *never*...but it was exactly the kind of incident that the busybody gossips of the *ton* loved to seize on and cruelly spread. Especially to someone like Annabelle, who had never been accepted into their ranks in the first place.

In the aftermath, Annabelle and Aunt Agatha suddenly left London, putting an abrupt end to her season. And Quinn pummeled Robert, which made their parents send both of them immediately back to Chestnut Hill.

Six years had passed, and he hadn't seen her since. Although based upon the barbs they'd just exchanged, she hadn't changed. And oddly enough, he was more relieved than he wanted to admit that she hadn't.

He offered affably, unable to stop himself, "Need any help with your stockings?"

"Just stay right where you are!"

"But I'm very good with ladies' stockings."

"Oh," she muttered beneath her breath, "I'm certain you are."

He chuckled. Same old Annabelle, all right.

It was good to know that some things hadn't changed, especially when everything else in his life was turning on end. Including the unexpected invitation to visit Glenarvon, which had nearly knocked him flat. So did its implications. Because Aunt Agatha had implied in her letter that she had financial matters to settle, which only boded well for him.

To say his prospects as a third son were limited was a grand understatement. Oh, certainly he'd proven himself successful in managing the family's estate, assisting Sebastian after he'd inherited when their father died so unexpectedly. More successful, in fact, than anyone who knew of his wild reputation would ever have imagined. In just two years, he'd increased profits by over fifteen percent.

But it was Sebastian's estate, not his. Proving himself on his own merits meant that he had to find another path for himself, where being the brother of the Duke of Trent meant nothing, where his own capabilities decided his success. He also knew he wasn't the church or military type, neither desiring to end men's lives nor save their souls.

So he'd set his sights on America. Several thousand acres already awaited him with a land broker in Charleston, where he planned to create not only his own American estate but also a trade business. He had ten thousand pounds in savings and a decent allowance that would see him settled into a fine living there for himself. An allowance that Sebastian kept threatening to take away if he didn't start to behave, although Quinn knew the threat was empty, especially since Sebastian was now happily married and…well, *happy*. It was hard to fear a growling dog when the animal had lost its bite.

But he had only twelve weeks to make his way to Charleston before the contract was voided and the land went to another buyer. Given that deadline, this trip to the borderlands wasn't convenient, but he wasn't too proud to pass up any additional blunt he could get his hands on.

Of course, he also knew that the visit to Glenarvon included seeing Annabelle Greene and that they hadn't parted under the best of circumstances. But he'd assumed that they'd been good enough friends once that they could tolerate each other for a few days before he rode on to the coast. Then his new life would begin. And not a moment too soon.

"Quinton! You got dirt in my stockings!"

He rolled his eyes at her angry grumble and grinned. Yep. Exactly the Bluebell he remembered.

Unless…

How much *exactly* had the Bluebell changed during the past six years?

The temptation to satisfy his curiosity about her was too great to ignore. And who could really fault him for taking a quick glance? After all, any man would be curious about a woman he hadn't seen since she was eighteen, since the night she let him kiss her beneath a rose bower and stole his breath away. A now *naked* woman standing right behind him...

"And grass all over my dress."

The last time he'd seen her she'd been on the cusp of womanhood. Would she be the same gangly girl he remembered? Would she still be nothing but skin and bones, sharp angles, and big feet? Fate would undoubtedly make him pay for this, but he couldn't help himself—

He glanced over his shoulder.

His breath hitched in his throat when he caught sight of her in the fading golden-purple sunset, all curvy naked and dripping wet, her body half turned toward him as she hurried into her clothes. *Sweet Lucifer.* Full breasts with dusky-pink nipples drawn taut from the cold water, round hips and long legs that stretched all the way up from her toes to her...Well. She'd certainly grown into her feet, all right, along with the rest of her.

He swallowed. Hard. No, not a single sign left of the stick-with-ears.

The Bluebell had become a woman.

And God help him, he wasn't prepared for that, or for the visceral reaction in his tightening gut. Good Lord, for the *Bluebell*. And when she turned to drop her shift over her head, unknowingly teasing him with another angle of her ripe body, the new view was just as breathtaking.

He was wrong. Fate wasn't making him simply pay for

this stolen glimpse of her. Fate had just punched him in the gut for it.

He turned around before she caught him drooling after her like some green pup. Clenched at his sides, his hands trembled, and he inhaled deep, slow breaths to steady himself.

Well, things had certainly changed in the past six years. In all kinds of new and interesting ways.

Coming to Glenarvon was proving to be a grand idea.

"Just one moment more," she called out. "I can't quite reach..."

More fabric rustled behind him, and Quinn imagined her lissome body twisting to reach to fasten up her dress, her breasts straining tantalizingly against her low-cut bodice as her back arched. One long leg half exposed by a raised skirt revealing the lacy edge of her stocking, which he could slowly roll down her thigh and follow along in its wake with his mouth—

"I'm almost through."

Squeezing his eyes closed, he tried not to think of how round and full her derriere was as she bent over to slip on her half-boots. He blew out a harsh breath of aggravation that she of all women could elicit such a response from him that even now his cock tingled.

"Hurry up, will you?" he prodded irritably. Because he wasn't certain how much longer he could stand there, not looking.

"There," she announced. "I'm dressed."

Thank God. He turned.

And froze beneath the full force of her smile.

Sweet and genuinely enchanting—and far more beguiling than he remembered—Belle gazed up at him through long, lowered lashes. In her sprigged muslin dress, with her damp, caramel-brown hair now pinned into place, she looked perfectly proper, as if she hadn't just been caught swimming naked. She barely came up to his shoulder, yet packed the punch of an Amazon with her quiet allure and natural grace. Gone was her insecurity, replaced by a shining confidence he remembered seeing in her only once before, right as she'd wrapped her arms around his neck to kiss him.

And *that* surprised him nearly as much as seeing her naked.

"It's good to see you again, Quinton," she admitted quietly.

She held her hand out to him, and he caught the scent of heather wafting on the air. The same wild, floral scent he remembered from six years ago.

"Welcome to Castle Glenarvon. I'm so very glad you're here." Her cheeks pinked delicately, and the tingle in his cock turned into an ache that swirled up his spine as she added, "So much more than you know."

ABOUT THE AUTHOR

Anna fell in love with historical romances—and all those dashing Regency heroes—while living in London, where she studied literature and theater. She loves to travel, fly airplanes, and hike, and when she isn't busy writing her next novel, she loves fussing over her roses in her garden.

You can learn more at:
    www.AnnaHarringtonBooks.com
    Twitter at @AHarrington2875
    http://facebook.com/annaharrington.regencywriter

Sign up for Anna's newsletter to get more information on new releases, deleted scenes, and insider information!
    www.annaharringtonbooks.com

Fall in Love with Forever Romance

STARLIGHT BRIDGE
By Debbie Mason

Hidden in Graystone Manor is a book containing *all* the dark little secrets of Harmony Harbor...including Ava DiRossi's. No one—especially her ex-husband, Griffin Gallagher—can ever discover the truth about what tore their life apart years ago. Only now Griffin is back in town. Still handsome. Still hating her for leaving him. And still not aware that Ava never stopped loving him...

Fall in Love with Forever Romance

HOMETOWN COWBOY
By Sara Richardson

In the *New York Times* bestselling tradition of Jennifer Ryan and Maisey Yates comes the first book in Sara Richardson's Rocky Mountain Riders series featuring three bull-riding brothers. What would a big-time rodeo star like Lance Cortez see in Jessa Mae Love, a small-town veterinarian who wears glasses? Turns out, *plenty*.

THE BASTARD BILLIONAIRE
By Jessica Lemmon

Since returning from the war, Eli Crane has shut everybody out. That is, until Isabella Sawyer starts as his personal assistant with her sassy attitude and her curves for days. But will the secret she hides shatter the fragile trust they've built? Fans of Jill Shalvis and Jennifer Probst will love Jessica Lemmon's Billionaire Bad Boys series.

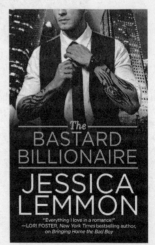

Fall in Love with Forever Romance

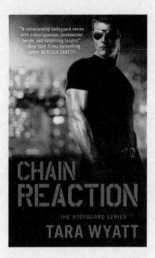

CHAIN REACTION
By Tara Wyatt

Alexa Fairfax is practically Hollywood royalty, but after she discovers a plot more deadly than any movie script, Alexa desperately needs a bodyguard. So she accepts the help of Zack De Luca, a true friend with a protective nature—and chiseled muscles to back it up. Zack is training to be an MMA fighter, but his biggest battle will be to resist his feelings for the woman who is way out of his league...

IF THE DUKE DEMANDS
By Anna Harrington

In the *New York Times* bestselling tradition of Elizabeth Hoyt, Grace Burrowes, and Madeline Hunter comes the first in a sexy new series from Anna Harrington. Sebastian Carlisle, the new Duke of Trent, needs a respectable wife befitting his station. But when he begins to fall for the reckless, flighty Miranda Hodgkins, he must decide between his title and his heart.

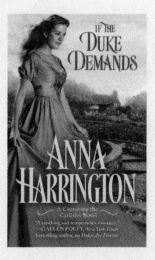